Praise for Gallagher Gray's Hubbert & Lil mysteries

PARTNERS IN CRIME

"Deftly plotted and well-paced . . . Two wonderful sleuths make their debut."
—*San Francisco Chronicle*

"Weaves a wondrous web of work relationships shrouded by ghosts of a long-ago scandal . . . In the classic British cozy tradition right down to the body with the antique dagger in its chest."
—*The Drood Review of Mystery*

A CAST OF KILLERS

"With a fond eye for the eccentric, Gray gives the streets of Hell's Kitchen the air of a gritty English village."
—*Publishers Weekly*

"Gray has the rare talent of being able to combine humor with sensitivity, and high comedy with realistic portrayals of genuine people."
—*The Virginian-Pilot & The Ledger-Star*

Also by Gallagher Gray
Published by Ivy Books:

HUBBERT & LIL: PARTNERS IN CRIME
A CAST OF KILLERS

DEATH OF A
DREAM MAKER

Gallagher Gray

IVY BOOKS • NEW YORK

Ivy Books
Published by Ballantine Books
Copyright © 1995 by Gallagher Gray

All rights reserved under International and Pan-American Copyright Conventions. Published in the United States by Ballantine Books, a division of Random House, Inc., New York, and simultaneously in Canada by Random House of Canada Limited, Toronto.

Library of Congress Catalog Card Number: 95-94080

ISBN 0-8041-1247-9

Manufactured in the United States of America

First Edition: July 1995

10 9 8 7 6 5 4 3 2 1

CHAPTER ONE

1. The phone rang in the middle of his crème brûlée, an inevitability that T.S. had anticipated ever since he'd approached the crucial step in the recipe. There was no way he could answer its shrill summons: Brenda and Eddie stood guard on the counter with the concentration of vultures, tails switching as they greedily eyed the cream and waited for his attention to wander. Besides, T.S. had already scorched his first two attempts. And at this rate, he'd never perfect the dessert in time for next week's dinner with Lilah.

It was Auntie Lil on the phone. The cats jumped as her deep voice, amplified by the answering machine, boomed through the apartment. They scurried to hide behind the sofa, having learned—like many humans—that Auntie Lil had a habit of charging around corners just when you least expected her the most. Her incredibly loud voice was often the only warning of her impending presence.

"Theodore! He's coming over and the apartment is a mess," she was pleading. "You've got to get over here and help!"

Auntie Lil was asking for his help? How odd. Plus, she was begging without a trace of her sometimes imperious manner. And who was "he" anyway? T.S. gently whisked the cream into the yolks while Auntie Lil continued to

1

plead. He had seldom heard her so excited. Who could it be? She had so many gentleman callers . . . even at eighty-four, there seemed no end of suitors flocking to Auntie Lil's door. Her independence was irresistible.

She could not possibly mean Herbert Wong. Herbert had often seen Auntie Lil's apartment in its chaotic glory. There was no point in cleaning for him. In fact, hadn't Herbert said just last week that it reminded him of Times Square after New Year's Eve?

"*Please*, Theodore. I know you're at home. Pick up the phone. I haven't seen him in over twenty years. You don't know how much he'll tease me if he sees it like this."

Now she was positively groveling. It was a first. His curiosity got the best of him. He switched off the burner, checked to make sure that Brenda and Eddie were still behind the couch, and picked up the telephone.

"Why, Aunt Lil," he said pleasantly. "I just walked in the door."

"I know perfectly well you've been standing there listening to me beg. But I don't care. You've got to come over and help me clean up."

"What has inspired you to care what someone else thinks?" he asked, enjoying her rare discomfort.

"It's Max." Her sigh was eloquent. "I never thought I'd see him again."

"Max?" T.S. thought hard, but no face came to mind. "Who's Max?"

"I'll tell you when you get here. But hurry. He's leaving his factory in an hour and a half. We haven't got much time."

"His factory?"

"*Max Rosenbloom*, Theodore. Max Rosenbloom of Max Rose Fashions."

"Oh, *that* Max Rosenbloom," T.S. repeated with exaggerated awe. His sarcasm was wasted. Auntie Lil had hung up.

Max Rosenbloom? T.S. stood staring out the picture window of his Upper East Side apartment, hardly seeing the thin ribbon of York Avenue far below. He'd heard many bizarre stories about Auntie Lil's varied past, all of which he thoroughly believed. But never had he heard a word about a Max. His curiosity was killing him. And it also came close to killing his cats—he woke from his reverie to discover that the crème brûlée had sprouted craters, no doubt where sandpaper tongues had lapped at the custard. But Brenda and Eddie were too quick for his preoccupied reflexes. They'd stolen their tastes and disappeared before he could exact his vengeance.

2. When Auntie Lil flung the door open, he saw at once that she was suffering a paralysis even more severe than that typically produced in her by the thought of cleaning. She was wearing a gray sweat suit and had wrapped a neon-green bandanna around her head Indian-style, causing her white curls to stick up like the frosting swirls on a Betty Crocker–perfect cake. One spiraling lock had escaped and dangled over her left eye, where it met a dusty arc smudged across the ridge of her wide cheekbones. This alone made her look demented. Her eyes confirmed the impression. They were dilated with adrenaline.

"Good grief," he stammered, "you look absolutely panicked." He stepped inside the apartment, crashing into a waist-high stack of cheap detective magazines hastily piled by the front door. She had some serious housecleaning in mind. T.S. eyed Auntie Lil with concern. "You've had far too much coffee," he announced.

"I can't help it!" She wandered aimlessly toward her dining room table and shoved aside a stack of towels and a bag of butterscotch candy. "I'm so nervous that I don't know what to do. I hate being this weak. He'll be here in an hour. Perhaps I should brush my hair. Oh, dear." She collapsed in a chair, not seeming to mind that she had just plopped down on a pair of bedroom slippers shaped like little pink bunnies.

T.S. was astonished: Auntie Lil was babbling. And while she might lecture, digress, or monopolize a conversation, Auntie Lil had never babbled before. Yet here she was, staring at a fruit bowl filled with tubes of oil paint and hastily cleaned brushes, mumbling incoherently to herself. Whoever Max Rosenbloom was, he had a power over Auntie Lil that was unprecedented in family history.

T.S. realized at once that he would get no useful information from her. Furthermore, he saw that he had no time to waste. If this mysterious Max was showing up in an hour, T.S. would need every minute and every fiber of his meticulous being to clean Auntie Lil's apartment in time. He fetched her a glass of milk after she turned down his offer of a drink and left her to sip absently while he waded into the fray.

The apartment was in its usual state—one of confusion. While not dirty, it was supremely cluttered and stuffed to the very seams with mementos and cherished debris accumulated through eight decades of Auntie Lil's colorful life. The walls were hung with crooked rows of photographs, depicting people of all shapes and skin shades posed against backdrops that ranged from exotic Tahitian beaches to Pennsylvania coal mines. Each photo prominently featured a younger version of Auntie Lil, beaming alongside smiling friends. T.S. knew many of their stories, and his own life seemed impossibly dull compared with the vibrant mass of humanity immortalized on her walls.

Though a flicker of stubborn inner fire remained, the outer sparkle faded—shrinking to a flat pinpoint that turned inward across the years. "Could you leave me for a while, Theodore?" she asked in a voice that, oddly enough, suddenly sounded very much younger.

"Do you think you should be alone?" he protested, unwilling to leave.

"I won't really be alone," she said quietly.

Reluctantly, T.S. turned to go. He paused unnoticed at the doorway and watched as she methodically searched for a number of small objects. First she retrieved a tarnished bracelet of silver from a small box on a shelf and placed it on the dining room table beside the leather album she had left there earlier. Returning from the living room, she added a cobalt-blue art deco vase sprinkled with silver stars and, beside it, a tiny watercolor that had long been propped on the mantel. It was a private and unfathomable shrine.

When Auntie Lil wandered back to her bedroom in search of more mementos, T.S. inched closer and peered at the surface of the faded painting. It showed a small waterfall in front of an English Tudor cottage; yellow flowers bloomed at the base of a sturdy wooden door. Then he saw that she had opened the leather album to two pages filled with fading black-and-white photographs. They had thin white ruffled borders and a brownish surface tint, but the images were clear: the same man and woman shown in a dozen different places and times. Here they were marching at the front of a parade, in a setting that was clearly New York City of another era. Then the couple reappeared on a beach dressed in bathing costumes that evoked the Depression, then arms around each other. A small boy stood at the corner of the photograph staring up at them, his eyes wide as he scrutinized the couple for clues to his own romantic future. The background showed a carnival made up of dusty tents bearing painted signs that promised exotic attractions. Other photos showed the pair standing triumphantly at the top of a mountain; posed on bicycles comically old; basking in the sun by the side of a lake; and sprawled across a blanket in a meadow. There were two photos of the couple riding horses in a desert. They wore blue jeans and matching light-colored shirts. In one, half of the sun could be seen setting spectacularly behind a mesa.

The final pose showed the man and the woman in evening dress, their heads pressed together as they beamed out at the photographer. Behind them, T.S. could spot half of a large orchestra and other couples twirling on a dance floor. He examined the photo more closely. What faces they had! Determined and strong, eyes blazing at the camera defiantly as if they had joined together to fight a lost battle and found themselves unexpectedly winning. The man had thick black hair, and a wide square nose that fit his strong chin line well. The woman had startling clear skin with a glow that was visible even in the old photograph. Her cheekbones were wide, her eyes large and oval, and her nose unabashedly masculine.

T.S. scurried back to the door when he heard his aunt approach. He slipped out before she could see him and paused in the hallway to pull his coat around him in response to an imaginary chill. He walked back to his car contemplating the eternal mysteries of time and love.

He had never thought of Auntie Lil as a great beauty. Yet, posed beside Max Rosenbloom, she had radiated a magnificence that had, quite literally, taken his breath away.

CHAPTER TWO

1. The private grief that overtook Auntie Lil remained hidden to the outside world. Within twenty-four hours, however, her indomitable spirit triumphed. When she called T.S. the next evening, he realized that the Auntie Lil he loved so much had returned.

"The two events are connected," she said at once. "Our meeting and his death."

Concern would not let T.S. skip the subject of her sorrow completely. "Are you all right?" he asked.

"Of course I am," she snapped back. Her peevishness reassured him. "It will do no one any good, least of all Max, for me to sit around weeping. Someone killed him and I intend to find out who."

"I thought revenge was a dish best eaten cold," T.S. pointed out feebly, taken aback by the rage that hummed beneath her words.

"Cold does not begin to describe my resolve at this moment," Auntie Lil answered tersely. "I loved Max for nearly fifty years. And I knew him well enough to be certain that he would want me to spend every breath I have left finding out who killed him. A car bomb? What a cowardly way to kill someone. Max did not even have the satisfaction of meeting his murderer face-to-face."

T.S. did not hear this last remark. He was too busy trying

11

to puzzle out her love for Max Rosenbloom. How could she have loved him for fifty years? T.S. had never even heard of him before. Was it possible to deeply love someone and not see them, even when you lived in the same city?

He simply did not know. T.S. did not understand matters of the heart. That was the price he was paying for having buried himself in his career as a personnel manager at a stuffy private bank for the last thirty years. When he had retired recently at the early age of fifty-five, T.S. had been somewhat dismayed to discover that while he knew much about other people, he knew very little about himself.

"Are you going to help me or not?" Auntie Lil demanded, affronted by his preoccupied silence.

"Of course I'll help," T.S. said. "Despite what I find to be a rather imperious tone on your part. And mostly because it would do no good to refuse."

"I'm sorry, Theodore," Auntie Lil apologized. "You have no idea how many years I have sifted through over the past twenty-four hours. If I sound abrupt, it is only because I am afraid that letting go of my anger will leave me with nothing else."

"No offense taken. What do you want me to do?" T.S. asked. They sparred constantly, but he loved her very much. If Auntie Lil needed his help, she had it.

"I got the *Times* this morning, but, as usual, the information is dry as toast. They spent three paragraphs saying nothing. Can you bring me every media report you can find on the murder? I know nothing about his personal life for the past twenty years—only that his business had continued to grow."

In other words, her pride would not allow her to go tabloid shopping where she might be recognized. Well, T.S. had done worse in his life than buy tabloids. Besides, he

knew a good newsstand off Times Square that sold papers from all around the country to thousands of people every day. He could buy the *Daily Ax Murder Chronicles* there and not receive a second glance.

"I'll be over after dinner," T.S. promised, not willing to risk a meal at Auntie Lil's. Whether she cooked in or ordered out, the end result was the same as far as he was concerned: heartburn every time.

2. "If you had known him, you'd understand what a loss his death is," Auntie Lil explained. Papers from all over the state, and a few from Florida, were spread across her dining room table. The old photo album lay open at her elbow. "He was a dream maker, a man who knew what he wanted and very quietly set about to make those dreams come true. I never knew anyone else like him. He believed in many things, in justice and opportunity and all those ideals that America doesn't stand for anymore because everyone is too busy shopping at malls. He despised stupid people and lazy people, and hated cowards, but he loved everyone else. It didn't matter what color you were or what age you were or who your family was. If you could do the job, Max would let you do it. And he'd reward you well."

"You worked for him?" T.S. asked.

"Of course not. I quit working for his father the day I met Max. Can you imagine what a mess that would have been? It was bad enough without that complication."

Auntie Lil did not say anything more, so T.S. had to be content with what he gleaned from the media. The first newspaper account painted the story of a successful businessman: Max Rosenbloom, age seventy-five. Founder of Max Rose Fashions, one of the first successful mass-market manufacturers of reasonably priced quality women's apparel. Had joined his father's modest tailoring business following World War II, then turned it into one of the largest wholesalers on the East Coast within a decade. His influence was easily overlooked by the public since Max Rose fashions were often sold under store brand names—an approach that he had pioneered and profited from handsomely. But he had been more than a marketing whiz in the pre-MBA specialization days. He was also the inventor of several machines now standard in the industry, including a computerized pattern method, an integrated finishing component, and a hidden security tag system.

T.S. read the next paragraph with even greater interest. Max had testified a few years ago as part of a failed federal investigation into Mob influence within the garment industry. "Sure it was there," that was the essence of his testimony; every day someone new approached him for bribes and threatened to block the shipping of his merchandise. And every day he told them the same thing: he hadn't come that far to give in to every two-bit crook that swaggered down Seventh Avenue. But he didn't name anyone and claimed he didn't remember their names. T.S. wondered if this was true.

"You read all that stuff about the Mob?" T.S. asked.

"I read about it when it happened." Auntie Lil looked at him from over her reading glasses. She usually tried to hide this weakness from him. That she wore them was a sign of her preoccupation. "I have absolutely no doubt that what Max said was true. He did not give in to strong-arm tactics. He was an early union organizer, and he'd run into thugs before. He knew how far he could go, how to fight back, and how to bend the rules. He was probably the only manufacturer in New York City they let alone."

"Sounds unlikely," T.S. said as he unfolded another newspaper. "Look at this headline. They're flat out claiming it was a Mob hit. They report that it was a profession-

ally constructed bomb attached to the underside of the car. With a timer." He pointed to another publication. "This one says Mob hit, too. And it reports that Max wasn't even driving his own car. Says it belonged to a relative."

Auntie Lil grabbed at the newspapers, her face flushing a dangerous red as she scanned the lurid headlines. "The one thing I am absolutely certain of is that Max would never become involved in organized crime," she said. "He was scrupulously honest and detested the cowardice of violence." She stared at T.S. "People all over the country are reading this garbage and judging him. It is up to us to clear his name."

"Clearing his name could be harder than finding the killer," T.S. pointed out.

"Then we had better get back to work," she replied.

They read further. Auntie Lil was not pleased to discover that her beloved Max Rosenbloom had a wife.

"She's *forty* years younger than him," T.S. pointed out, surprise overruling his usual tact. "Her name is Sabrina."

"Let me see that," his aunt demanded tersely. She read the paragraph carefully. "This doesn't sound like the Max I knew. He detested younger women. Found them silly. Why, I was nine years older than him and we fell in love anyway. That was one of the things he liked about me. I cannot imagine why he would be married to someone so much younger."

But you're going to find out, T.S. thought to himself.

"No children," he announced, scrutinizing an account from a Florida paper. "But lots of nephews and a niece. One brother and one sister. Looks like he spent part of the year down in Sarasota, where he spread money around like water, if the publicity they gave his death is any indication. Wonder who inherits the business?"

"My money's on the brother," Auntie Lil said. "His

name is Abe. He's a year older than Max, but he had neither the brains nor the drive that Max did."

"The private service was this afternoon, but the graveside is tomorrow morning," T.S. said. He was holding a Garden City newspaper. "Kind of quick."

"He's Jewish," Auntie Lil replied. "It's supposed to be within twenty-four hours." She grabbed the paper from his hands. "It starts at eleven. That's a bit early for me." She rapidly calculated the distance. "It must be near his house in Garden City. We'd have to leave around nine-thirty to be safe. Let's see, I have a black silk pant suit that would do nicely . . . and that hat from Paris would match."

"It's been raining for the past six hours," T.S. protested. "And it's supposed to rain all night. Have you any idea how muddy the cemetery will be? I'll probably have to tote you around like a sack of potatoes while wading through slime."

"You said you would help," she said mildly. "This will give us a look at the family and probably lots of employees."

"You're serious about catching the killer, aren't you?"

She looked at him over her glasses. "Dead serious," she said.

3. The morning ride to the graveside service gave Auntie Lil a chance to sketch in the details that the newspapers lacked. "He was a man of change in a time of change," she explained to T.S. "He had extreme ideas, I suppose, but back then they seemed possible." As she talked, the picture of a fearless, powerful man emerged. Max had rejected his father's business at first, then rejected his religion as well. He had embraced communism in the thirties and helped to found the United Garment Workers.

When the war came, he discarded communism, regained his faith, and led early failed efforts to force the United States to help German Jews. After a year in Europe organizing private rescue efforts, he had enlisted and been sent to Italy. When he returned, he joined the family business after a decade of animosity, recapturing the love of his adoring father and displacing his older brother, Abe.

"It was a sad situation," Auntie Lil explained. "Abe was a hard worker, but he never had Max's vision. Abe didn't go to the war, he had a weak heart. He stayed behind and supervised the women who worked for Max's father back then. They did all right, but the company missed the chance to grow that the wartime economy should have given it. When Max came home a war hero, he made up for lost time. He expanded that company from five full-time tailors into a major manufacturer by the end of the 1950s. His father was so proud of him. Max was all he talked about. It couldn't have been easy for Abe, but Max was Max and no one could blame him for being who he was." She dabbed at her eyes with one of the handkerchiefs jammed into her large pocketbook. "The world just isn't the same without him. We never spoke, but I thought of him often. Especially lately. I thought the time was drawing near to see him again and then . . ." Her voice trailed off and she was quiet for the remainder of their journey, lost in memories. There was nothing T.S. could say to console her, and so, wisely, he chose to remain silent.

When they arrived at the cemetery, it was immediately obvious that they were not the only interlopers there. A trio of haggard and overweight men eyed arriving mourners suspiciously. They wore tattered sport coats and flowered ties that looked as if they had bought them from the same street merchant on the way out of town, for two bucks apiece. A neon sign mounted on the roof flashing WE'RE

NEW YORK CITY COPS would not have been any more obvious.

"They're casing the joint," Auntie Lil whispered tersely. Her crime vocabulary was heavily influenced by old James Cagney movies. T.S. would not have been surprised to see her climb the nearest water tower and shout, "Top of the world, Ma!"

The cemetery was located off the Meadowbrook Parkway. The steady stream of cars whizzing past added a wet background hum to the sound of light rain drumming on car roofs. The daylight had not changed since seven o'clock that morning—it was still a brownish gray topped off by sullen-looking clouds. T.S. felt as if he had to keep moving at all costs; if he stopped, he would begin to mildew. He quickly retrieved Auntie Lil's gargantuan black pocketbook from the car. She produced an umbrella from its depths, and he held it above them both.

They scurried past a long line of gas-guzzling parked automobiles. There seemed to be an endless supply of Cadillacs, Buicks, and other land boats, with an occasional BMW or Mercedes. T.S. was startled when a figure popped out from behind one of the Cadillacs. She was a hard-looking woman in her midthirties, with short, straight hair dyed platinum except for defiantly black roots. She wore a trench coat indifferently over a tight black sheath. She also wore black high-top tennis shoes. Lifting a cigarette to her mouth, she stared intensely at T.S., winked, then dropped the butt and ground it out in the mud. Her eyes swept over Auntie Lil before dismissing them both.

Unnerved, T.S. turned his attention to the next part of their journey. He had correctly predicted the status of the graveyard grounds. Stepping off the asphalt road was like wading into the bayou. All about them, figures floundered in the muck. Fortunately, Auntie Lil detested high heels, so she was spared the task of stopping at every step to pull her shoe out of the saturated grass. Others were not so lucky. Ahead of them, a small flock of women fluttered and balanced on one foot, like sandpipers along the seashore. They were helped by scowling husbands, who glared alternately at the ground and at their wives before roughly yanking the legs of their spouses free from the mire. People limped and staggered toward the grave like survivors of a Civil War battle.

"We must be fashionable or die," Auntie Lil muttered. "Who are these people anyway?"

That was a good question. A crowd of around one hundred mourners was gathering around a grave site near the center of the first cemetery section. A wide expanse of AstroTurf stretched over the swampy ground for several yards around the freshly dug hole, where a small tent protected the luckier attendees. The rain distorted perspective and the burnished coffin seemed tiny, almost toylike, from where T.S. and Auntie Lil stood.

Of course, T.S. reflected, it might be a small coffin. A car bomb didn't leave a whole lot behind to bury.

The crowd shifted and stamped anxiously in the damp cold, like a herd of cattle waiting for the barn door to open. From behind, the early arrivals looked no better than those who had arrived later. The carefully teased hairstyles of the women had caved in under the weight of the rain and now tilted in sunken failure like fallen soufflés. Many of the men had suffered the same fate. Former pompadours squatted on broad foreheads like berets that had been sat upon. Here and there, a soggy skullcap topped off the wet look.

T.S., who was meticulous in his grooming but detested excessive use of personal-care products, patted his own thick mane of graying hair carefully. A hurricane could not conquer its upward vitality. He was proud of it and could be forgiven this small vanity. His hair saved him from being ordinary looking and made him look distinguished in a relaxed kind of way. He was a firmly built man of normal height, with a hint of middle-aged spread. His broad face was a more masculine version of Auntie Lil's, from the wide cheeks that bloomed with good health to the broad nose and generous lips. It would never occur to T.S. knowingly to abuse the sturdy body that fate had given him—such antics were imprudent and disrespectful to oneself. Like Auntie Lil, he carried himself with the conviction and pride of one who is comfortable in his own well-weathered skin.

The crowd shifted impatiently as the long minutes passed, but perked up considerably when a black limousine drove slowly up an empty driveway opposite the waiting grave. A small man with a gleaming pate emerged from the car. He was round and packed into a shiny black suit. Noticing the crowd's attention, he quickly fished a skullcap from his side pocket and plopped it on his head.

"Max is rolling over in his grave right now," a woman by T.S. whispered to her companion.

"He's not in it yet," the companion muttered back.

The appearance of the penguinlike rabbi was followed by the dramatic emergence of what could only be the grieving widow. First, an impossibly long pair of legs slid from the darkness of the backseat and dangled languidly for all to admire. She was wearing spike heels so incredibly high that a murmur of anticipation ran through the crowd. She'd have to take them off to make it to the grave. The knees appeared. T.S. looked for a black skirt to follow and was kept waiting well into the thigh. At last, clothing made its entrance: ebony knit encased a slim set of hips and a tiny waist that was nicely accentuated by the folds of an unbuttoned, purple raincoat. The upper part of her figure was equally well proportioned, as the skintight dress testified.

"She's wearing a sweater, not a dress," someone nearby muttered.

"Why not? Those boobs probably cost her ten grand apiece," came the anonymous answer. "May as well let us get a good look."

Max's widow had glossy black hair carefully wound in an elaborate twist for the occasion. A small black velvet hat perched slightly back on her head and its sweeping black veil hid her face from the crowd. T.S. was disappointed that he could not see her features. He had been looking forward to scrutinizing Auntie Lil's replacement. So far, it had been a most unlikely show.

"He must have gone mad," Auntie Lil said softly, exchanging a glance with T.S. "She can't even wear black properly."

Auntie Lil was enormously forgiving about people's faults, except when it came to fashion. There she was something of a snob, forgetting that—unlike her—not everyone had been born with an innate sense of what colors and fabrics suited them best.

The widow, Sabrina Rosenbloom, delicately picked her way over the wet lawn. The rabbi scurried beside her on tiptoe, attempting to shield her with a large red-and-white golf umbrella emblazoned with the words STERLING & STERLING PRIVATE BANK.

T.S. stiffened. What was the name of his old employer doing intruding into this funeral? He exchanged a glance with Auntie Lil. It was turning into a strange morning. It was like being in a dream that, like so many dreams, was slightly off-kilter.

The widow had chosen most unwisely to wear high heels, but at least she was graceful at extricating herself.

Waving away the offered help of the soggy rabbi, she freed herself from each step with a pretty upward jerk that resembled a young colt prancing on unfamiliar legs. She left a small trail of holes behind her.

Too bad they didn't have someone to follow and throw in grass seed as she went, T.S. thought. That way they could resod at the same time.

The crowd rustled expectantly as T.S. exchanged another glance with his aunt. It was time to go into action. They had to get closer to the family. He knew from experience that the best strategy in thick crowds was simply to stick close to Auntie Lil. She could insinuate herself through the smallest of spaces by flashing a charming old-lady smile, then weaseling her way into the next clearing. T.S. grasped a belt loop of her coat and held on. Soon they had slipped past the first four lines of defense and had penetrated close to the fringes of the inner family circle, leaving rows of resentful mourners behind.

The last two rows gave them a little more trouble. A hulking woman with slumped shoulders thrust out one hip and tried to block Auntie Lil from getting by. When Auntie Lil persisted and the woman countered with a glare, T.S. nearly jumped at the sight of her brooding hatchet face and the bloodred lipstick caked on her wide, angry mouth. She wore heavy blue eye shadow and her hair was dyed an improbable black, given her obvious age. The best he could do was murmur an apology as Auntie Lil squeezed by without a glance, dragging T.S. to the front with her. They reached the first row of mourners and T.S. found himself near a tall, well-built man whose expensive raincoat and razor-cut hair reeked of money and executive power. The man had an excellent tan that set off his twinkling blue eyes. Small tufts in the center of his eyebrows lent him a pixieish air. He was staring at the youngest woman in the family circle, his face placid and carefully composed in professional grief.

"How's this?" Auntie Lil whispered to T.S.

"Not bad," he murmured back. "Any closer and we'd be in the grave."

Auntie Lil had warned T.S. what to expect, explaining that Jewish funerals were customarily simple. There would be no flowers and the coffin would be modest, so as not to flaunt wealth. But having reached the graveside, T.S. saw that both custom and class had been tossed to the winds in this case. A row of seven folding chairs draped with green velvet surrounded the yawning hole that would hold Max Rosenbloom. Most of the chairs were occupied by the family. The enormous casket was made of a highly polished mahogany set off with elaborately carved brass fixtures. It was suspended on a metal frame above the grave and festooned with enough roses to wreathe a dozen Kentucky Derby winners. Petals had fallen from many blooms and been mashed rudely into the mud. The floral scent was overpowering and T.S. was struck with a sickening thought: it was the smell of people spending Max's money to show him how sorry they were that he had died and left them tons more of it.

As the young widow tottered toward her center seat, the others cast her dark glances. She was clearly not a Rosenbloom favorite. Both T.S. and Auntie Lil scrutinized the disgruntled family lineup before them. They seemed to be arranged by age. At one end, a young man in his midtwenties sat carefully erect, his dark gray suit peeking out from beneath a raincoat. He had angular features, almond-shaped green eyes, and a delicately curved mouth. His stylish clothing and feathered haircut of glossy black set him apart from the others as an urbanite. Auntie Lil stared at him, then gripped T.S. by the elbow. "So much like Max," she murmured.

Next to the handsome man was a young woman who also stood out, mostly because she seemed to be truly grief-stricken. Her grayish eyes were narrowed in concentration as she stared at the coffin and her determined chin wavered beneath trembling lips. She had blond hair that, unlike most of the other women's, was cut short in a simple curtain.

T.S. saw that Auntie Lil was staring at the young woman, too. He cocked an eyebrow and his aunt shrugged back. She could not place the younger ones, the gesture said. This was a generation that had come after Auntie Lil in Max Rosenbloom's life.

A stout, balding man of about forty-five sat beside the young blond woman, his bottom overhanging the small chair like a mound of dough that had risen beyond the confines of its bowl.

"That man looks like Max's brother, Abe, except that he's too young," Auntie Lil whispered. "It must be one of Abe's sons."

T.S. nodded and examined their subject. The man's few wisps of hair had been combed over the bald center of his scalp. T.S. noticed with distaste that the man had nearly as much hair sprouting from his bulbous nose as remained on top of his head. He was evidently suffering from a cold: every now and then his companion, an overly ripe woman whose makeup was slowly dissolving in the mist, would thrust a Kleenex his way. He'd take it, blow loudly, and hand it back. The woman stored the used tissues efficiently in her purse while pulling fresh ones from the pocket of her raincoat. Her streaked hair miraculously had escaped drowning and was teased in layers of overhanging spikes lacquered with a heavy sheen of hairspray. It looked as though a pile of Yorkshire terrier puppies had fallen asleep on her head.

The transition from the younger to the older generation in the family lineup was abrupt. Although the youngish widow sat sobbing daintily into an embroidered handkerchief at the center of the circle, she was flanked by a pair of wizened old women who had dealt with age in dramatically different ways. To the right of the widow sat a figure that resembled a cross between a brooding vulture and an ill-tempered nun. She was a tall woman dressed completely in black, from her long dress to her clunky, lace-up shoes. A long piece of black cloth draped over her head, making her look like an Italian extra from a Mafia movie. Her face sagged with features: her mouth trailed down in a thin and uninviting line, her nose seemed to melt toward her chin in a mournful slope, and her large, hooded eyes were cast toward the grave as if she blamed Max Rosenbloom for his own death. As T.S. watched, the old woman looked up and spotted him. He twitched in alarm. He found her gaze indefinably malevolent, even when he realized that she was actually staring at Auntie Lil. Perhaps it was the right eyelid—it drooped permanently halfway over the eye, making her look like the evil queen in *Sleeping Beauty*.

"Rebecca Rosenbloom," Auntie Lil whispered to T.S. "I think she's spotted me."

"I'd say so." T.S. gulped. "Does she bite?"

"Yes," Auntie Lil replied abruptly. "Max's sister. Never married. We were never the best of friends."

"Who's the old girl on the other side of the widow?" T.S. asked.

"I think that's Abby," Auntie Lil whispered back. "She's married to Max's brother, Abe."

Abby was not taking the process of aging very well. She was as stout as a beer barrel, but nonetheless packed into a black chiffon dress that twinkled in those spots that peeked from beneath her raincoat.

"She's wearing sequins," Auntie Lil added grimly. "To a funeral."

The sequins were tacky, but at least they matched her glittering black pumps. They also set off her synthetic complexion nicely. Her face had a curiously flat quality to the skin—it gleamed dully, like rubber that had been stretched too thin. Her hair was an unlikely brown and generously streaked with blond. It swirled in a long continuous tube that met at the apex of her crown in a swirl like the top of a meringue.

"That's a wig," T.S. remarked, ashamed at his pettiness but unable to help it.

"I'm afraid not," Auntie Lil answered tersely.

"Where's her husband?" T.S. asked quietly. "One would think he'd attend his own brother's funeral."

"I don't know," Auntie Lil admitted.

At the other end of the semicircle stood an empty chair. Every few seconds one family member or another would glance at it.

"Davy hasn't shown yet," a voice behind T.S. muttered.

"Are you surprised?" another voice answered back.

The service was momentarily delayed while workmen rearranged the heavy lifting machinery that held the coffin. The mechanism was carefully pulled back from the edge of the grave, lest it trigger a landslide of wet red clay. Unfortunately, this adjustment encouraged comparisons to a diving board, with the grave as the swimming pool. Once this had been accomplished, there was a short, whispered conference between the rabbi and the workmen that ended with a helpless shrug of shoulders all around.

"They better hurry before we all fall in," T.S. muttered.

As if on cue, the rabbi turned to the crowd, raised his arms, and began to speak.

A few seconds later T.S. tuned him out. It was obvious, even to a stranger, that the man had not known Max at all. For one thing, he began by saying, "Though I did not know him personally, I understand that . . ." T.S. found this most distasteful. Secondly, the bored looks that descended on the faces of most of the family members belied the inappropriateness of the rabbi's words. Of course, T.S. thought as he surveyed their hard-set faces, these people were unlikely to perk up at all—until the will was read. He had never taken such an instant dislike to such a large group of strangers, at least not since the year he had stumbled into a convention of real-estate developers while vacationing in Miami.

A sharp poke from Auntie Lil brought him back to reality. "Go on," she hissed.

"Go on what?" he asked, bewildered.

"You're supposed to put a rose on the coffin and shovel a clump of dirt into the grave."

"I'm supposed to *what*?" T.S. looked up and saw the other mourners watching expectantly.

The rabbi cleared his throat and repeated himself, nearly shouting in T.S.'s face. "Those of you mourners who wish to may now step forward and show your respect."

T.S. had been to many funerals before, most often as a representative of his former employer. But he had always hung back respectfully on the fringes of the crowd and, he now realized, had not paid sufficient attention to what was going on in the front. As the nearest non–family member to the coffin, it was up to him to begin the ritual.

"Oh, for heaven's sakes, I'll go first." Auntie Lil elbowed her way past him, using her huge black pocketbook as a shield. As she passed in front of the seated family, her eyes met those of Rebecca Rosenbloom. Rebecca's hooded eye quivered violently, then blinked. There was no other sign of recognition.

Auntie Lil took a rose from a large mound at the foot of the grave, then stood a few feet from its opening. She stared down at the mud dubiously. The rabbi cleared his throat loudly and glanced at a nearby workman, who did not take the hint. T.S. did. He hurried forward and gripped Auntie Lil's elbow. God forbid she should fall in.

Still Auntie Lil did not move. She locked eyes with the rabbi. "Aren't you going to lower him in?" she whispered loudly. The family shifted uneasily behind them.

The rabbi coughed discreetly. "There seems to be a slight problem with the lifting mechanism due to the rain. If you would just consider this *symbolic* rather than integral to the *actual* burial, I'm sure that would be just fine." He handed a small gold shovel to Auntie Lil.

"Just do it," T.S. hissed softly. "There are a lot of people waiting."

Auntie Lil sniffed regally, then tossed the rose on top of the coffin as if she were playing horseshoes. It landed dead center. She turned her attention to the grave. She removed her glasses from her pocketbook, perched them on her nose, and handed her huge purse to T.S. to hold. He looped it over his arm, feeling ridiculous.

Auntie Lil was oblivious to the stares of the other mourners. She was peering anxiously over the lip of the grave.

"Go on," T.S. urged. "I've got hold of you. You're not going to fall in."

"It's not that," she whispered, and took another step forward.

"Be careful," T.S. said urgently. She was only half a foot from the muddy edge of the grave and was leaning forward, trying to get a better look down inside. "What are you doing?" he asked, echoing the thoughts of those around him. Visions of Auntie Lil throwing herself into her beloved's grave flashed alarmingly through his mind.

"There's something odd about the bottom of the grave," she said as loudly as a ballpark announcer.

The rabbi coughed again. "Madam," he said grimly. "Take your turn or step aside."

Auntie Lil looked up at him. "There is something in the bottom of the grave," she insisted.

A buzzing ran through the crowd.

"Aunt Lil," T.S. ordered sharply. Her outer calm had been but a facade, he realized. She was deeply wounded by Max's death. Perhaps she had finally snapped.

Auntie Lil shook off his grip and took a tiny step closer, then looked up at the crowd.

"I am not imagining things," she said loudly. "Look. At the edge of the left side. The water's washed the mud down toward the center and eroded the dirt. I'm telling you, there's something sticking out. Something black."

T.S. exchanged a quick glance with the rabbi and they stepped forward as one. "What?" the rabbi said unwillingly.

"It's a body!" Auntie Lil shouted, with an enthusiasm that inventors save for their greatest discoveries. "There's a body in the bottom of the grave. Look! It's a sleeve. And there's an arm attached to it!"

T.S. tried to move forward, but snagged Auntie Lil's pocketbook on a rope anchoring a crucial tent pole. He pulled and the canvas structure teetered ominously. A wave of collected water showered off one side. The family looked up at the roof nervously. Only Max's widow ignored the commotion as she rose from her seat.

"A body?" she said in a tiny voice. She took a step forward toward the grave, then stopped to look back at the empty chair at one end of the family semicircle.

"Aunt Lil," T.S. repeated hopelessly as he struggled to untangle the pocketbook's straps from the tent roping.

"There's a body down there," Auntie Lil insisted, pointing toward the center of the grave as if she were God casting Lucifer from the heavens.

The widow scurried forward and clutched at Auntie Lil. The rest of the family seemed frozen.

"Right there." Auntie Lil took the widow's arm and they peered together over the edge. "See, it's black fabric. A silk blend, if I'm not mistaken. And a handmade shirt from the look of the cuffs."

"Aunt Lil," T.S. muttered hopelessly, finally freeing himself. He dragged his aunt back from the edge of the grave. "What do you think you're doing?"

"Davy!" The widow suddenly shrieked. "Look at the watch! It's Davy!" She stepped perilously close to the edge of the grave and gazed down below, teetering uncertainly on her spiked heels.

The family began to whisper excitedly, then appealed to the rabbi with confused expressions. Sensing that his control of the ceremony was in danger, the rabbi finally took action and darted toward Max's widow. His legs became tangled in the tent ropes and the canvas began to buckle. A mourner screamed. Alarmed, T.S. whirled around to grab at the supporting metal pole, sending Auntie Lil's pocketbook swinging in a wide arc. The heavy leather purse smacked the rabbi in the center of his back. He stumbled toward the grave and grabbed at the widow's raincoat, locking onto her arms as he knocked her over the edge of the grave. He fell on his face in the mud beside the opening but managed to hold on to the widow. Sabrina Rosenbloom's screams rang though the stunned silence of the graveyard.

"He's going over, too!" someone shouted from the crowd.

It was true. The rabbi was being dragged inches closer to the edge of the grave by the panicked thrashing of the screaming widow.

"Hook your heels into the mud," someone called out hopefully. The widow's screams stopped for an instant, then grew louder.

The crowd looked on frozen with disbelief as the plump rabbi slid toward the open grave. T.S., still valiantly holding up the tent pole, was unable to let go and help. He stared at a nearby workman, whose thumbs were hooked in his grimy blue jeans as he gazed, mouth agape, at the slippery scene.

"Do something!" T.S. shouted. The worker just shrugged, but T.S.'s plea spurred Auntie Lil into action. She darted forward and thrust the small gold shovel at the rabbi as if he were a truculent beaver refusing to return to his cage at the zoo. The rabbi raised his face from the mud and spotted the shovel. He made a useless grab for it with one hand, releasing one of the widow's arms to do so. She shrieked with fresh alarm and, displaying an astonishing show of strength, thrust her body upward, so that her head bobbed up above the grave top. She lost her grip on the rabbi's arm but grabbed successfully at his legs, clutching his trousers with both hands. Her veiled hat had fallen off and her face could finally be seen. Her delicate features were screwed up in anger and panic. She looked like an outraged ferret.

"Let go of my pants!" the rabbi demanded indignantly. He made another grab for the gold shovel with his free hand and missed again, but managed to snag the edge of the AstroTurf carpet. Simultaneously, he let go of the widow with his other hand so that he could grab at his waistband.

"Don't you let go of me, you bastard!" the widow shrieked as she tightened her grip around his pant legs.

They were her final words before, in a flurry of unrabbilike oaths and a flash of scarlet undershorts, the rabbi's tenuous grasp on the AstroTurf gave way. With a sucking sound, the pair slid down the steep embankment as swiftly as a pair of otters at play.

In horrified fascination, the family and crowd pressed forward, endangering the already crumbling edge. One enterprising fellow inched toward the lip of the grave.

"They're still alive!" he screamed, as if the pair had tumbled into a volcano instead of a mushy six-foot-deep grave.

"Looks like they're fighting or something," he added. "No, wait, they're trying to climb back up."

An echo came from the bottom of the grave. The crowd leaned forward.

"What are they saying?" Rebecca Rosenbloom demanded, stamping her booted foot impatiently. She did not look entirely unhappy that the widow had slid into the grave, but she was displeased about not having a better view and had thrown her black shawl on the muddy ground in a fit of pique.

Never short of nerve, Auntie Lil crept closer and stood beside the man at the edge of the grave. They listened together to the shouts from below.

"What are they saying down there?" someone repeated impatiently. The cacophony issuing from the grave sounded like a caldron of wildcats being boiled.

"The old lady was right," the man at the edge yelled back. He looked at Auntie Lil with admiration.

Auntie Lil took her triumph with characteristic modesty. "I told you so," she announced to the assembled mourners. "There's another body at the bottom of the grave. And the widow insists that it's someone named Davy."

CHAPTER THREE

1. Pandemonium erupted following the announcement that there was a bonus body in the grave. Reaction was swift. A third of the crowd headed immediately for their cars, ignoring the distracted protests of the plainclothes detectives there. Clearly, a good number of the mourners had prior experience with law enforcement and were not eager to stick around to chat. These early departers were met at the edge of the grounds by two well-dressed men flashing federal badges, but not even this show of government muscle was enough to stem the tide. The remaining crowd members erupted in a verbal volcano of overlapping exclamations, revealing dozens of opinions on Davy and his relationship with Max.

"He *would* do something like this," one woman shouted, as if Davy had committed suicide using the novel method of suffocating himself in graveyard mud.

"Wait until Abe finds out," someone said. "It'll give him another stroke." Several people murmured their uneasy assent.

"Max spoiled the crap out of the kid. Let him get away with murder. It's fitting that he should steal the spotlight at the old man's funeral." This speaker was shushed into silence by more tactful mourners.

"My God," an overdressed female declared at the top of

33

her lungs from a spot not two feet from the stunned family. "Did you hear her shriek when she saw it was Davy? I told you there was something going on between them." A trio of voices chorused agreement.

T.S. and Auntie Lil joined a small huddle of guests in staring at Abby, Max's sister-in-law. Her rubbery complexion had faded to an alarming beige. She tottered as if faint, and was helped to her chair by the tall executive with the boyish face who had stood close to T.S. Abby sat, staring blankly at the grave as if expecting Davy to rise from the dead. The bald middle-aged man with the cold stood gazing down at the ruddy clay opening, his open mouth forming a small, dark oval against his rigid, deeply flushed face. His hands trembled at his sides. His female companion had slipped her hand into his raincoat pocket and was clutching a Kleenex to her own open mouth. It did not entirely conceal a small, uncertain smile.

The young man and blond woman in their midtwenties stood together at one end of the grave, arms around each other's waist. They stared down at the muddy scene in silence, tears glistening on their cheeks. They seemed to be among the very few mourners genuinely saddened at the declaration that Davy was dead. Everyone else was acting as if they were at a particularly exciting cocktail party. Whoever Davy was, he had few friends among this crowd.

"Who's Davy?" Auntie Lil demanded impatiently, grabbing a plump bald man by the elbow and pulling him toward her. He slipped on a patch of mud and crashed into T.S. but did not apologize.

"You've got a grip like a plumber," the man protested, rubbing his elbow and glaring at Auntie Lil.

"Who's Davy?" Auntie Lil demanded again. "I found the body. I deserve to know."

The man's eyes narrowed suspiciously. "Seems like you

would already know if you were a friend of Max's," he said. "Davy was his favorite nephew. The kid was going to inherit every buck Max had, or so some people said."

One of the detectives had hurried back to his unmarked car and radioed in for help. In the meantime the remaining officers had commandeered lengths of rope from the sullen cemetery workers and gone fishing for the widow and rabbi. The pair was pulled from the open grave with the enthusiastic assistance of several volunteers. They emerged looking like the losers of a particularly sadistic tug-of-war.

Safe at last, the mud-covered widow began to shriek, piercing the air until Rebecca Rosenbloom rose from her chair, marched ceremoniously over, and slapped her full across the face. Stunned, Sabrina Rosenbloom shut her mouth and stepped behind the rabbi for protection. He was too busy digging mud out of his eyes to be of any help to anyone, but if the old lady swung again, at least he'd go down first.

This provided fresh fodder for the gossips trying to make themselves and their theories heard. Auntie Lil was in danger of pulling a neck muscle from overzealous eavesdropping. She hardly knew where to turn next. T.S. could not separate the voices well enough to glean any useful information. He used the time to look around instead. Twenty yards away, leaning against the widow's limousine, stood the young woman T.S. had seen on the way in. Her wrinkled raincoat had fallen open, revealing her tight black sheath and the incongruous high-top tennis shoes. Who was she? Was she simply an interested onlooker? One of those kooks who enjoyed attending funerals? If so, she had hit pay dirt.

T.S. contemplated several other theories about her identity until his thoughts were interrupted by the arrival of a swarm of police cars. Their lights flashed through the fog of the graveyard and sent eerie red-and-blue shadows flickering across the gravestones. It looked like the set for a Michael Jackson music video.

Police officers were suddenly as abundant as mourners and a rigid processing system was established within minutes. A pair of men dressed in orange rubber overalls shimmied down ropes into the grave. They carried a black bag and a lumpy knapsack between them. One had a camera slung over his shoulder. Other officers began quickly taking down names and addresses. There was no shortage of volunteers to describe what had happened. After Auntie Lil had been pointed out by a dozen or so onlookers, she began to take on the air of a beauty pageant winner. She stood at the edge of the AstroTurf, modestly accepting congratulations with queenly aplomb. The only break in her orgy of egoism came when a detective pulled her aside for questioning.

T.S. gave his own statement and, deciding that enough was enough, claimed Auntie Lil and began to firmly escort her back to the car. She became petulant at having to leave the scene. It was the most excitement she'd had in months.

"You aren't going to get any more information right now," T.S. pointed out sensibly. "The place is a zoo and it's starting to rain even harder. It's time to go."

She reluctantly complied. On the way back to the car, they heard the rumor repeated several times: Davy had been shot in the head. No one mentioned Max. In all the excitement, the man had been completely forgotten. He'd probably be buried later, once the lifting mechanism was fixed.

A small line of cars had gathered at the cemetery exit, where the mud-covered rabbi inexplicably stood guard. As each car pulled up to the gate he tapped on the window and leaned inside, mumbling something to the occupants.

"Surely he's not soliciting gratuities," Auntie Lil speculated, horrified.

"Why not? He's going to have a hell of a dry-cleaning bill," T.S. said. Suddenly the rabbi's muddy face loomed against the car window in frightening detail. T.S. rolled it down hurriedly before the rabbi smudged the pristine glass.

"I have been asked by the family to inform you that the mourning will take place at the family home as scheduled," the rabbi said mechanically. He noticed Auntie Lil and his mud-rimmed eyes widened in anger. "You tried to hit me with a shovel!" he said.

T.S. thanked him profusely and pulled away before Auntie Lil could answer.

"Hmmph." Auntie Lil sniffed unapologetically after T.S. had let his disapproving silence speak for itself. "That was a wretched eulogy and that man deserved to fall in."

T.S. refused to comment. Auntie Lil did not even notice. "Oh, Theodore," she said as they reached the highway, "This is all so exciting. Max would have loved it. Did you see those people? How horrible to think that he spent his life surrounded by such ... such *bloodsuckers*. I can't wait to hear what they have to say."

T.S. looked over at her as if she were daft, and nearly sideswiped a bread truck in the process. "No," he said. "Absolutely not. We are not going to the mourning."

She stared at him innocently. "Why ever not? Max was a dear friend of mine."

"Why ever not? Are you insane? You just created a huge scene at the funeral, which ended with the widow and rabbi plopping down on a very dead nephew. I seriously doubt they'll even let you in the front door at the family home."

"*Me?* I did not kill the nephew and you were the one who knocked the rabbi into the grave." She stared straight ahead and primly adjusted her pants over her sturdy ankles.

"It might have been me, but it was your pocketbook."

"I will leave the pocketbook in the car."

"No. No mourning. I don't care if I never see another Rosenbloom again. They can bury me alive with Max and his nephew. The answer is no."

Auntie Lil knew when it was time to give in. A little. "All right, Theodore. We'll compromise."

T.S. glanced sideways in suspicious silence. "How?"

"We will drive to the family home. We will park a few doors away. And we will watch who arrives and who leaves. That's all." She announced her offer as if she were bartering over a bolt of cloth with a street merchant in New Delhi.

"What do I get in return?" T.S. asked.

"I promise not to whine about the mourning for the next three days and"—her brow furrowed as she cast about for a good hook—"I promise not to ask you about Lilah for the next three months."

"Six months," he said evenly. "And you've got a deal."

"Done."

They agreed on their game plan just in time for T.S. to take the Garden City exit. They headed for the Rosenbloom home.

2. "This is real cozy," T.S. grumbled, wrapping his raincoat more tightly around him as he slowly drove down the road. "What happens if one of us has to go to the bathroom?"

"Don't be such a wimp," Auntie Lil replied. She squinted at the windshield, too vain to pull out her glasses for a better look. Fog hampered the view as well. It was, altogether, a rather futile attempt at spying.

"Go ahead and put them on," T.S. said.

"Put what on?" Auntie Lil asked innocently.

"Your glasses. I know they're in there." He nodded at her pocketbook.

"Of course," she said as if suddenly remembering. "I had forgotten all about them. And, please, don't let me stop you from putting on your own. I believe they are in your left-hand pocket, Theodore."

She took an eternity to adjust her glasses properly on her nose, then brightened. "Much better. Quite a turnout, isn't it?"

"I'll say. Funny how the people who fled the graveyard before the cops arrived are now stampeding like lemmings to the free food and booze here."

"I didn't realize lemmings could stampede, dear," Auntie Lil said absently.

T.S. was right. The road was jammed with cars parked bumper to bumper. Max Rosenbloom had lived in an affluent Garden City neighborhood. It was filled with huge wooden houses and small Tudor-style mansions, most built in the thirties or forties when bare land was not such a popular barometer of wealth. Unlike newer homes, these featured small but tidy yards, and what land there was had been given over to the house. Every small patch of lawn was immaculately manicured, and every window in every house sparkled. Max had lived in a large stone house situated on a quiet corner. It was ringed with enthusiastically blooming holly bushes that formed a thick hedge reaching to the bottom of the first-floor windows.

T.S. drove past the house, hoping to snag a parking spot from an early-departing mourner. They could see the shadows of guests moving behind the living room curtains. T.S. knew Auntie Lil was aching to peek through them, but didn't want to push her luck. They were conspicuous enough as it was.

"Just what are we attempting to find out?" T.S. asked. "We can't keep circling the block all day."

"I want to know which family members come to the home and who stays away."

"That's easy. They're all here. Gorging themselves on free food and booze."

"No." Auntie Lil shook her head firmly. "Remember the young man and young woman dressed in a much more restrained manner than the others? Neither of them has arrived."

T.S. nodded and turned the corner. Ahead, a neighbor's house was clearly empty, the windows dark and drapes drawn. He backed into the driveway so that he and Auntie Lil had an excellent view of the Rosenbloom house.

They sat and watched as late arrivals scurried inside. Auntie Lil sighed and pulled out a white handkerchief from the cavernous depths of her purse. She dabbed at her forehead and sighed again. "I do believe today is the *wettest* day I have ever seen."

Suddenly the moistness seemed to press in on T.S. like a sponge. The car felt like a hothouse. Soon he felt a terrible need to go to the bathroom. It reminded him of first grade and the rigid boarding school that he'd attended. He'd been too afraid to raise his hand and request permission from the scowling Jesuit. He had suffered in silence instead.

"I have to go to the bathroom," he announced grimly. "I warned you. All this rain . . ."

"Go in the bushes," Auntie Lil suggested without a glance. It was not an elegant solution, but she did not look in the mood to discuss alternatives. T.S. checked out the roadway. The flow of arrivals had stopped. There were no neighbors in sight. It might be safe. But what if he were caught? Or cornered by a snarling dog? He could be arrested for indecent exposure, his whole life ruined. . . . But if other men did it, so could he.

Though it was a blow to his fastidious standards, T.S. hopped from the car and slipped into a neighboring yard, where he was protected by a thick bower of tree limbs. When he returned, Auntie Lil was gone.

She had tricked him. Muttering an uncharacteristic curse, he crept into the Rosenbloom yard. Keeping close to the edge of the thick holly hedge, he tiptoed under the living room windows and slipped around to the side of the house farthest from the street corner. A row of trees delineating the yard from the neighbor's lot provided a thin hiding space. He spotted her damp footprints in the grass and, feeling like a cross between Sherlock Holmes and a Peeping Tom, soon discovered her crouched behind a particularly thick clump of holly bushes. She was peering into a first-floor window and had chosen her position well. By leaning forward, she could peek around the corner and through a wall of French doors that enclosed a large rear porch. Guests moved about the porch, chatting and holding drinks.

"This was not part of the deal," T.S. hissed softly. The sharp edges of the holly leaves scraped at his face and one branch insinuated itself under his jacket, tickling him just above the waistband of his undershorts. When he tried to scratch it, he bumped another wet limb and was showered with accumulated rain. Auntie Lil, of course, remained perfectly dry and not the least bit bothered by their junglelike surroundings.

She waved for him to be quiet. Despite these demands for discretion, her own whisper had the force of a jet taking off. "Look at that! They call this sitting shiva? They're a disgrace to the proud traditions of their people." She motioned for T.S. to take a look. He cautiously raised his head a few inches until his eyes were just above the level of the windowsill. Through the thin gauze curtains, he saw the widow—cleaned up and encased in what looked like a black cocktail dress. She was sitting on a plain wooden crate, leaning back on one elegant arm. A new veil swept back over her miraculously restored hair and there was not a trace of mud in sight. She was laughing prettily at a male guest while she sipped from a martini held in her free hand. A butler hovered nearby with a silver tray, waiting for the refill request.

"She thinks sitting on a crate excuses her from flirting at her own husband's funeral?" Auntie Lil was so agitated that she pushed T.S. out of the way and stole another look inside. "I can't believe this. Take a look at the hallway."

They peeked together at a short passageway leading off the living room toward the back porch. Someone had tacked a piece of plain cloth over the floor-length mirror in accordance with Jewish tradition. But a small cluster of ladies had pulled up one corner of the cloth and were busy inspecting their lipstick and adjusting their sodden hairdos.

"Disgusting," T.S. was quick to agree, although he was referring to their hairstyles and not their failure to uphold the true spirit of Judaism.

"I agree," a harsh voice answered inches behind T.S.'s ear. "They are all absolutely disgusting."

T.S. and Auntie Lil jumped. They turned to find the hooded eye of Max's older sister fixed coldly upon them.

"I know you," she said to Auntie Lil. "So don't pretend you don't know me."

"Of course I know you. How are you, Rebecca?" Auntie Lil held out a white-gloved hand. The old woman did not take it. Auntie Lil let it drop, then very casually flicked several damp vines from her shoulders. It was probably not a coincidence that they landed on Rebecca's black-booted feet.

"I'm terribly sorry about your brother," Auntie Lil said. Whether she liked Rebecca or not, Auntie Lil knew her manners.

"Of course you're sorry. Never stopped loving him, I suppose."

"No, I never did."

"None of them ever did," Rebecca answered nastily. "He always left them before they stopped loving him."

"Actually, I left him." Auntie Lil's gaze was steady and cool. "What he chose to do with the rest of his life was his business, not mine."

Rebecca's good eye narrowed; the hooded eye jumped. Her mouth curled in what may have been an attempt at a smile as she said, "I want to talk to you. I saw you peeking in the window. You Hubberts have got the biggest heads in town. I presume you have a car, so we can talk in private?" She was ancient and skinny, but she had the no-nonsense rapid-fire delivery of an auctioneer.

"Follow me," Auntie Lil said. She used her unfurled umbrella to hack through the bushes and vines as if she were on an anthropological expedition. T.S. and Rebecca obediently followed.

They made a furtive parade back to the car. As much as T.S. and Auntie Lil wished to avoid being spotted, Rebecca Rosenbloom seemed to want it more. She clung close to the hedge and pulled her shawl closely around her face. She slipped into the backseat without a word and sank down against the upholstery, where she would be hidden by the fogged car windows.

"Some people are saying Max was involved with the Mob. Or that someone in the family killed him," she announced. "The papers all say it. The news stations, too. Even the neighbors. Pah!"

Surely she had not just spit on the floor of his car? T.S. fervently hoped not.

"Of course they are," Auntie Lil replied in a superior tone of voice. "Ninety percent of all mur—"

"I'm not interested in your damn statistics, Lillian." The old woman turned to T.S. "She was always so annoying. Spouting facts and figures. The two of them together. Ach! There was no disagreeing with those two. No such thing as a peaceful family dinner. Could we talk about something simple like weather? Oh no, it was always exploitation of the worker and world peace and other nonsense."

"We were right." Auntie Lil sat stiffly, staring straight ahead.

"Please continue," T.S. said as soothingly as possible. "You wanted to talk to us?"

"Yes. I want you to find out who the murderer is. I don't trust the police. I'll give you plenty of money to do it. But if it was someone in the family, I want to know first." She glared at no one in particular. It seemed to be her favorite expression.

"Why do you think I can or would do it?" Auntie Lil asked primly.

"Why? Because you are the nosiest Parker I ever knew. I watched you sniffing around at the funeral even before you found Davy's body. Besides, I read about those other two incidents. . . ." Her voice trailed off as she realized that she was inadvertently complimenting Auntie Lil. Her wrinkled face furrowed in frustration. How could she get Auntie Lil to help out without having to be nice to her?

She decided to be blunt. "Listen, Lillian," she growled. "I'm not in the mood for your crap. You're the most stubborn person I ever met in my life. Most of the time that's infuriating. Sometimes maybe it's good. You loved Max and I know you'd want to find out the truth. Well, I loved him, too. He was my brother. He was a good man. I want to know who did it, and I know you can find out. This family, they don't trust the police. I've already heard more lies in the past two days than in my eighty years all wrapped together. You do it. Here. I'll give you these. They will help." She held out a large brass ring from which dozens of keys dangled. "Go on, take them. Keys to their houses. I've given you copies for everybody. Except mine, of course. I did not kill my brother or my nephew. I've written down their addresses, too." She pulled a piece of paper from a side pocket and waved it about like a flag.

Auntie Lil and T.S. looked at each other. "Where did you get those?" T.S. asked.

"Max was smart enough not to buy all these deadbeats homes and then let them mortgage them away," she said. "He transferred ownership to me so I'd have a nest egg. I own the houses and I have a right to these keys."

"What do you expect me to do with them?" Auntie Lil asked, her eyes sliding to the key ring as she greedily calculated the contents. It was gratifying to watch Rebecca Rosenbloom beg for her help. She had waited a long time for this.

"Go in and look around. I want to know what you find. There are so many bad apples in this family, I don't even know who to accuse first. They're rotten. All of them. Right to the core."

She tossed the keys over the front seat and they landed between Auntie Lil and T.S. with a jangle. The piece of paper with the family addresses fluttered down on top. Both T.S. and Auntie Lil reached for the objects at the same time, then drew away lest they be spotted in an unseemly tug-of-war.

"I need some information before I agree," Auntie Lil

said. "Who were all those people sitting in the family circle? I recognized very few of them."

"Not even the fat old broad in the sequined dress?" Rebecca asked with scorn. "That's Abby, Abe's wife. Don't you remember her? Abe used to drool all over her, call her his wild Irish rose. Hah! That's fitting. She's cheap wine, all right. Don't you remember that time she dumped a martini on your red silk dress? On purpose, I expect."

"I thought it was Abby," Auntie Lil explained. "She looks different."

"That's because only the foundation is her," Rebecca said. "The top is all plastic surgery."

"Where was Abe? One would think he'd attend his own brother's funeral."

"One would, but he's home in bed with a tube up his nose. Been bedridden for almost a year. Had a stroke. Serves him right. Ate crap and drank like a fish his whole life. Max used to warn him to slow down, but you know the jealousy between those two. They were brothers, all right. Fought their whole lives." The old lady shook her head in disgust. A thin strand of gray escaped from her severe bun, which she tucked back in place with vicious efficiency.

"What about the younger ones?" Auntie Lil asked. "Who are they?"

"They all belong to Abe and Abby. They had more kids than the Kennedys. She used to drop 'em every year, regular as kittens. Thought I'd never have to quit congratulating her. For what? Being too stupid to keep 'em from coming? Used to want me to baby-sit when I was young. Hah! Can you imagine?" She sat back with a cackle.

No, T.S. could not imagine Rebecca Rosenbloom in the same room with small children. At least, not without thinking of the Brothers Grimm.

"The dead one is Abe's, too," the old woman added as an afterthought. "Davy. He was the wildest one of the lot. Drank. Ran around with women. Gambled. Pissed away every dime he had and Max was always willing to give him more." She shook her head. "He was Max's weak spot. He was a rotten one, though. Not surprised at all to see him turn up dead. Though I admit *where* he turned up dead gave me a start."

"I think one nephew and one niece are missing from the mourning," Auntie Lil said. "Why? Max was their uncle. Davy was their brother. I saw them at the funeral. You'd think they'd want to be around family at a time like this."

"You're talking about the good-looking ones," Rebecca said flatly. "They hate the family. Don't ask me why. Me, I've got good reasons to hate everyone. But all those two ever got from the family was being spoiled. That makes them ingrates, both of them. Girl's named Karen, got some fancy-pants job somewhere. Boy's named Seth. Good-looking, but queer as a three-dollar bill. You ought to remind Abby of it someday. Gets her goat every time." She hee-heed mirthlessly.

T.S. longed to throw a pail of water on Rebecca Rosenbloom and see if she melted. "What about the middle-aged bald guy with the cold?" he asked instead.

"That's Jacob, Abe and Abby's oldest. Davy's older brother. Dumber than a dead dog. Bungled more business deals than Donald Trump. Max hated him. Who wouldn't?"

For someone concerned about the family name, Rebecca Rosenbloom was not exactly brimming with the milk of human kindness for her relatives.

"What about the woman who was feeding him tissues?" T.S. asked.

"His wife. Some cheap Italian who was lucky to get him, sorry as he is. Hah! Did you catch her wig? Pure plastic.

There's no love lost between her and that gold digger Max married. Remind themselves of each other, I expect."

T.S. briefly considered that maybe Max Rosenbloom had blown himself up to escape from his sister.

"You going to do it or not?" Rebecca Rosenbloom demanded of them. "If not, give me my keys back."

She leaned over the seat and reached for the brass ring, but Auntie Lil held a white-gloved hand over them to stop her. "Perhaps we will see what we can turn up over the next few days," she promised smoothly. "If it looks promising, we will continue."

Rebecca snickered. "Knew you wouldn't miss being handed a blank check to snoop around. Call me with anything good. Number's on the list." She nodded toward the information she had supplied, then slipped from the car without another word. She scurried across the road with the haste of a hermit crab on its way back to its lair.

"Good God. Has she always been like that?" T.S. stared after her with distaste.

"No. She's mellowed with age." Auntie Lil picked up the keys and examined them, then studied the address list. "She might have marked which keys belonged to who."

T.S. stared at her incredulously. "You've got to be kidding. We just had a gold mine dumped in our laps and you're complaining?"

"Not complaining," Auntie Lil said, her eyes narrowing as she watched Rebecca slip back inside Max's house. "Just kvetching. And wondering what she really wants."

CHAPTER FOUR

1. It was nearly 5 o'clock by the time T.S. convinced Auntie Lil that further surveillance was useless. They headed back to her apartment in Queens. Fortunately, they were traveling west and escaped the traffic jam that clogged the highways leading from Manhattan to Long Island. T.S. took great satisfaction in zipping past the irate eastbound commuters. The older he got, the more he craved the thrill of going against the crowd.

"I'm so hungry I could eat *your* cooking," T.S. declared when they finally reached her apartment. He flopped down on her small white sofa, grateful that the results of his cleaning frenzy of a few days before had not yet been obliterated by a host of new projects. He was too exhausted to move his own body, much less bolts of cloth or easels holding half-finished paintings.

"I suppose you expect me to take that as a compliment?" Auntie Lil sank down beside him and took off her sensible shoes, massaging her feet with technical precision. "That really is the most despicable family I have ever encountered."

"No wonder you didn't marry Max," T.S. observed, hoping to wangle a few details out of her. The attempt failed.

"That wasn't why I didn't marry him, but it would have been a good enough reason," she said. Her eyes lingered on

49

the telephone and she brightened. "Let's invite Herbert over and make him cook!"

It was a tempting idea. T.S. and Auntie Lil had reached a truce about Herbert Wong after a brief period of territorial wrangling over just whose friend he was. First hired by T.S. many years ago as a messenger at Sterling & Sterling, Herbert had figured prominently in their adventures since T.S.'s retirement. In the process, the elderly Asian man had developed a deep and abiding affection for Auntie Lil and the attraction was mutual.

Initially, their amiable companionship had irked T.S. Auntie Lil always seemed to spirit his most interesting friends away. Time had healed this minor wound, however, especially when T.S. realized that the two old people were, in their own way, conducting a restrained romance. Herbert was full of bows and smiles and extreme flattery. Auntie Lil returned his affection by exempting Herbert from her typically brusque assessments of human behavior and by frequently affixing her astonishingly intense attention on him. When she wanted, Auntie Lil could make her target seem as if he were the only person alive on earth. With Herbert, it was what she wanted.

T.S. had no idea what they did on the two or three evenings they spent together each week. For all he knew, they were out taking tango classes. In fact, given what he did know about them, they probably were. Lately, Herbert had taken up cooking with a vengeance, and T.S. had to admit he was very good. His cooking reflected his personality. His dishes were usually perfectly balanced and hinting of some surprising and indefinable ingredient.

"We can't just order him over like some houseboy," T.S. protested.

"Of course we can," Auntie Lil insisted, and turned out

to be quite right. Herbert was delighted to come over and cook.

He arrived in less than an hour, bearing a bag bursting with fresh ingredients for a stir-fry dish he remembered from his youth. He entered the living room briskly, his posture typically erect. He was a small but perfectly proportioned man. His sturdy shoulders tapered down to a trim waist that showed but a hint of thickening around the middle. He wore a shiny black suit over a purple T-shirt, an outfit that would have looked ridiculous on a man one third his age but somehow made Herbert seem exquisitely in fashion. His hair was thinning above a round, bemused face and his slightly mottled scalp and forehead gleamed with a burnished glow reminiscent of ripe pears. Herbert's face was finely lined and always deeply tanned. T.S. had never thought to ask why. Perhaps he spent his mornings on a pier that jutted out into Long Island Sound, merging with the elements and achieving harmony with the world. That would be Herbert Wong.

Herbert was a perfect match for Auntie Lil: strong, determined, and quite at ease with who he was and what he had achieved in life. His calm presence was also a blessing after the tumultuous events of the day. T.S. was able to sip a Dewar's and soda while the two friends clattered pots and pans and chatted in the kitchen.

Halfway through dinner T.S. realized that he should have been eavesdropping all along. Auntie Lil had lured Herbert over for reasons that had nothing to do with his culinary talent.

"So we begin tonight?" Herbert asked politely as he offered T.S. more homemade spring rolls.

"Yes. I've got a strategy all worked out." Auntie Lil ignored T.S.'s surprise. "We'll start with the widow, and if she's home, we can nip over to Abe's house instead."

"Aunt Lil," T.S. warned. "You've got to be kidding. I'm exhausted. I can't go ransacking people's houses tonight. And may I point out that we could be arrested?"

"You needn't come, Theodore. Herbert and I can manage quite well."

"Herbert doesn't drive," T.S. protested.

"I do." She stuffed a spring roll in her mouth and chewed with gusto. Auntie Lil approached eating the same way she approached life: dive in, plow through, and bring on the second course.

"You are not driving at night," T.S. replied firmly. "You are dangerous enough in the daylight when the rest of us can spot you coming."

"Then you will simply have to come along as wheel-man." She smiled and pushed the dish of duck sauce his way.

After so many years of being subject to her tricks, T.S. could not understand how she continued to outflank him at every turn. She would have made an incredible general or, better still, a dictator.

"Wheelman, huh?" He shook his head. "I hope you don't expect me to burn rubber."

2. Auntie Lil loved to milk maximum drama out of an event and she was squeezing every drop out of this one. She was dressed entirely in black, from her sweatsuit to her tennis shoes and socks. An ebony beret perched on her head at a jaunty angle, making her look like a very elderly French cat burglar.

"What a subtle disguise," T.S. said. "You really blend in. And that hat will look great in a lineup."

"You're just mad because you couldn't change clothes, too."

It was true. He'd been too tired to drive into Manhattan and was still trapped in the suit he had worn to the funeral. There had been a time in T.S.'s life when suits fit him like second skins and he had felt naked without a coat and tie. But each passing month since retirement had taken him farther and farther from such a mind-set. He had come to loathe the confinement of formal clothes and longed for a sweater and his comfortable Hush Puppies.

It was just before midnight and traffic was light. They reached Max Rosenbloom's house without incident and cruised slowly past. The street was bare in front of the dark and silent home. The mourning was over, the freeloaders having cleared out for greener pastures. Herbert volunteered to check the garage and was back in a flash, reporting that no cars were inside. Perhaps the young widow was out being consoled by friends. Probably a very special friend, T.S. silently concluded, one quite skilled at making her forget her sorrows.

Auntie Lil wanted to be the one to go inside. She was not about to hand the most exciting portion of their assignment over to someone else. Herbert volunteered to accompany her, so T.S. let them off at the corner with bemused irritation. Let them sneak around in the bushes until they tired of this gumshoe nonsense. He'd take a nap someplace quiet. He parked a block away under a large tree on the edge of a park, as agreed, and settled back for a nap.

Auntie Lil held the flashlight while Herbert tried each of the keys on the ring in succession, coming up with the right ones halfway through. "Double-locked," he muttered. "Better keep a lookout for a burglar alarm."

But there was no security system. At least, not that they could tell. No flashing lights, piercing sirens, or snarling Dobermans to welcome them inside. There was, however, a small cream-colored creature shaped like an elongated mop that may have been a dog. It made small yipping noises as it raced in a frenzied circle around them. Auntie Lil could not tell which end was the front. That mystery was cleared up when it wet the rug in excitement, leaving a small puddled stain that shone in the gleam of Herbert's flashlight.

"Max would never have had a dog like that," Auntie Lil whispered. "If indeed that thing is a dog."

"I will search the upstairs," Herbert told her. "Can you handle down here?"

"Certainly."

Herbert crept up the heavily carpeted steps, followed by the friendly dog, who left little droplets on each step in its ecstasy.

It was a strange feeling rummaging through someone else's life, especially when that someone was Max and he had married such an unlikely woman. Auntie Lil examined the photographs displayed throughout the house. She sighed. His face was large and squared off, topped by abundant white hair that swept back in a white mane. He had a habit of staring into the camera with the unapologetic intensity she had remembered from their time together. In contrast, the photos of his wife showed an overly made-up but pretty woman, whose expressions ranged in vacuousness from attempted coquetry to vapid boredom. Why had he married her? What had made him compromise so late in life?

Auntie Lil was not doing a very good job of searching the downstairs. She found one interesting item: an empty, velvet-lined pouch that might have held a gun at one time. It was hidden in the back of a foyer-table drawer. But other than that, she couldn't seem to get past the photos of Max. In fact, she was still standing in the hallway with her flashlight examining a professional portrait when she heard the crunch of a car pulling into the driveway. Someone was home.

She whirled in alarm and raced to the front door, peering out of the stained-glass side inserts. Max's widow, Sabrina, hopped from the front seat of a low-slung red Porsche. She wore a thick fur coat and was holding a small remote-control device toward the garage door, angrily clicking buttons while she moved it about in the air, hoping to trigger the radio sensor. The little dog came yipping down the inside steps to greet its mistress at the door. Herbert was hot on its heels.

"We've got to get out of here," he said firmly, grasping Auntie Lil by the elbow and leading her through the darkness toward the rear French doors. Their exit was blocked when a figure stepped out of the kitchen into their path.

"No," a voice said quietly. "The neighbors are sitting in their back room overlooking the French doors. You can't go out that way. Follow me. We can get out through the basement."

Too frightened to be surprised, they followed the mysterious figure down a steep set of stairs into a damp basement area. Their feet pattered across the concrete floor. Auntie Lil pointed her flashlight at their leader, briefly illuminating wavy blond hair with very black roots. At the rear of the basement they spotted a large window that opened up at ground level above a washer and dryer. Herbert helped Auntie Lil climb up on top of the dryer. She unlocked the window and pushed it open with a screeching sound that made her heart stop. She and her partners climbed out the window, scurried through holly bushes, and dashed across the yard. The lights flicked on in the living room behind them as they fled down the block and cut over toward the small park, searching for T.S. and the car. Herbert led the way while the young woman hustled Auntie Lil with a firm grip on her elbow. No one bothered to stop and introduce themselves.

T.S. was startled awake by the frantic tapping of Herbert's flashlight on his car window. He quickly unlocked the car doors. It seemed as if the entire rear seat filled with people within seconds. He groggily flipped on the overhead light.

"Turn that damn thing off," Auntie Lil hissed. "And get us out of here. *Fast.*"

T.S. cut the light and started the ignition, pulling out into the street with a very puzzled expression. Hadn't he seen *three* people in the backseat? A few blocks away, he pulled over into the poorly lit parking lot of a private high school and turned around for a better look. He peered at a strange tableau: Herbert Wong was jammed in the middle of the backseat and flanked by Auntie Lil and the blond woman T.S. had noticed at the cemetery. She looked up at T.S. and winked.

"Who are you?" T.S. demanded.

"My name is Casey Jones." She held out a hand to T.S., and feeling foolish, he shook it. Herbert repeated the gesture solemnly. Auntie Lil took a more direct approach.

"My word, you saved our butts," she said. "Who are you and what were you doing in Max's house? Don't tell me you were burglarizing the place, too?"

"I'm a private investigator," Casey told them in a voice that held a tinge of Southern drawl. "Max hired me a couple of weeks ago to follow his wife. I saw enough to want to know if she had anything to do with his murder. If she did, I'm going to nail her. Max was a good guy. And it kind of pisses me off when people blow up my clients. Besides, he has about three months left on his retainer." She smiled brightly at them as if this explained everything.

"What do you mean you've been following Max's wife?

What did you find out about her?" Auntie Lil demanded.
"Tell me everything you know."

Casey pulled her tattered raincoat more closely around
her and shivered. She still wore the tight black sheath underneath. "Not so fast," she said. "First of all, who the hell
are you? I saw you at the funeral and, I think, in some old
photographs that Max kept stashed in a locked trunk upstairs. And I watched you checking out his photographs
downstairs just now—but how do I know I can trust you?
And who are these guys?"

They had a stare-off, each of them taking turns examining one another in the dim light of the car as if they were
four complete strangers. No one seemed to know how to
begin.

"Let us adjourn to a coffee shop," Herbert finally suggested. "Perhaps a little caffeine and better lighting will il-
luminate the subject. It seems we are in danger of having
the soup spoiled by too many cooks, don't you think?"

3. "The worst thing is that she had birth-control pills
hidden from him. Underwear drawer, third from the top.
Concealed inside a small pocket sewn into a tacky-looking
lingerie set." Casey Jones had thoroughly searched the
house before Herbert and Auntie Lil had arrived.

"What's so terrible about that?" T.S. asked. "Max was
old but he wasn't dead. At least not yet."

"Kids was one of the main reasons why he married her
in the first place," Casey explained. "He wanted to start a
family. He said he realized he had made a mistake putting
it off until so late in life, but that if Strom Thurmond could
do it, so could he."

"Do what?" T.S. asked, mystified. For once, Auntie Lil
had been shocked into silence.

"Have children in his seventies. Max was determined. He wanted to have an heir."

"That explains the unsuitable marriage," Herbert said solemnly.

"Unsuitable is a very nice way to put it," Casey mumbled with a mouthful of toast. She had downed three fountain Cokes, a double helping of corned beef hash, and fried eggs as she spoke.

"You okay?" T.S. asked his aunt. Perhaps they were being insensitive, discussing Max so lightheartedly.

"Sorry," Casey told Auntie Lil. "Didn't mean to offend you. Max was a blunt kind of guy. It's just natural to be blunt when you're talking about him."

Auntie Lil managed a smile. "I'm perfectly all right. It's just so sad to think that Max never got the family he wanted and that . . . well." She stopped speaking and looked down at her cup of coffee. The others looked tactfully away.

"May we hear more of the contents of his home?" Herbert inquired to break the uncomfortable silence. "I was unable to conduct a thorough search due to the untimely interruption."

Casey launched into an enthusiastic description of the contents of Max Rosenbloom's house. She had, it seemed, ferreted out every secret.

"The wife is a pill freak," she told them. "All kinds of prescription drugs. Ones to get her going, ones to slow her down. I think she was hiding them from Max. They weren't exactly out in the open in the medicine chest, if you know what I mean. A couple bottles were on top of the dresser. I guess with him gone, there's no point. But she kept a regular pharmacy in the closet in a shoe box beneath a pair of purple pumps."

"Purple pumps?" Auntie Lil asked.

"Listen, that lady's got more shoes than Imelda Marcos. Purple pumps were just the start. She was spending his money as fast as she could pull credit cards from her wallet. She's going to be pretty damn surprised when they read the will."

"You know about the will?"

Casey smiled at them and carefully slathered jam on her fourth piece of toast. "Sort of," she said. "There will be some unhappy family members, I can guarantee it."

"You've read it?" T.S. asked.

She shook her head. "No. I just know that Max had a new one drawn up a couple of months ago. Signed it last month. He said his mind was made up and that the family was going to be very surprised. That's all I know. Said he'd finally come to his senses and was leaving his money to someone who would know what to do with it. I don't know who. There's not a copy of the will in the house, or I would have found it. It's probably with his lawyer or the executor. I remember he said something about having set up some trusts with the help of a company that had a fancy Old World kind of name like Gold, Silver and Crumpets, Inc."

"Sterling and Sterling?" T.S. interrupted.

She munched thoughtfully. "That's it."

Auntie Lil and T.S. exchanged a glance. "There's no way I could get a copy of it," T.S. said quickly. "It would be illegal. We'll just have to wait until probate."

"Surely a man cannot disinherit his wife," Herbert protested. "Even if she is a bit . . . high-spirited."

"Prenup," Casey explained happily. "He had her sign the tightest prenuptial agreement I've ever seen. With a chastity clause. Darryl Zanuck would have approved."

"A what?" T.S. asked incredulously. "And how did you happen to see the prenuptial agreement?"

"Max showed it to me. It was the whole point of his hiring me. He came to see my boss about a month ago and wanted his wife followed. Since my boss is too lazy to do anything but eat, he turned the case over to me. Are you going to finish those?" She stared at Herbert's untouched fried potatoes, and he hastily pushed his plate her way. She dove in happily with her well-used fork and ate as she explained. "It seems that Max was not kidding about having a child. He wanted one, and if Sabrina was going to be his wife, she had to give it the old college try. But he wanted to be sure it was his kid. Didn't want her running around and procreating with someone else, if you catch my drift."

"We catch your drift," T.S. said grimly.

"Fidelity figures as prominently in the prenup as in a stereo ad. Sabrina would have gotten a nice piece of change even if they did divorce—but not if they had divorced because of her being unfaithful. But there's more." She swept her hair off her face wearily, the black roots gleaming in the fluorescent glare of the diner lights. "Sabrina didn't have a snowman's chance in hell of having a baby for one very good reason and never mind the pills. She lied about her age. Max said she was thirty-five. Hah! If she's thirty-five, I'm the ghost of Marlene Dietrich. I've seen Sabrina's high-school yearbook. The lady is forty-six and, I might add, has no intention of ruining her fabulous figure with a baby this late in life. Hence the insurance of birth-control pills. I figure she also didn't want a kid because then she'd have to share the old man's bucks with a little Max. Or a little Maxine."

"Why did she think she was going to get his money?" Auntie Lil asked.

"She *was* getting his money in the version of the will before this last one," Casey explained. "Or at least a big chunk of it."

"But Max caught on that she was not exactly Mother Teresa," T.S. said.

"You got it. Believe me, this lady will never be proposed for sainthood. I've watched her in action for almost a month now. She gets off on seducing males. Some sort of power thing. But once she's had them, the thrill is gone. She needs another fix."

"Was Max happy?" Auntie Lil asked. Her face was kept carefully still, but it was obvious that the answer was important to her.

Casey took her time. "He wasn't unhappy," she finally said. "He seemed like the kind of guy who understood that life comes with the good and the bad, you know? By the time he asked me for help, he knew his wife had a fidelity problem and he was dealing with it. What he wanted from me was proof enough to get her out of his life with a minimum of fuss."

"Who do you think killed him?" T.S. asked the private detective.

Casey shrugged and spread out her hands. "I don't know. But I think the family knows. What I wouldn't give for a peek inside their houses. I'd say there's plenty of secrets hidden behind those expensive walls."

An unspoken signal was sent and received. T.S. nodded and Auntie Lil turned to Casey. "We have keys to all their houses, not just Max's," Auntie Lil announced, describing Rebecca Rosenbloom's request. Casey did not react as they expected.

"And you *trust* her?" the private investigator asked incredulously. "If I were you, I would stay away," she added. "The woman is setting you up. She's probably mad as hell over her brother's death and looking to start trouble. And don't look at me to help. One breaking and entering a week is plenty for me." She mounted an assault on a chocolate soda that had arrived shortly after she'd polished off her second breakfast.

"Good advice," T.S. agreed firmly. "I've been a fool. Our searching days are over. Look what happened tonight. You could have been caught. In fact, maybe you'd better give me those keys." He held out a hand, but Auntie Lil ignored him.

"I am perfectly capable of showing some restraint," she informed T.S. "I will put the searching of family homes on hold until I think about it a little more. You may be right. Rebecca Rosenbloom is not to be trusted." She stared wistfully out the picture window. "Still ... I'd like to get a peek at Abe and Abby's home before I give up."

T.S. shook his head firmly. "No. Your burglarizing days are over. You'll just have to save the beret for your next trip to Paris."

4. By the time T.S. had driven Casey Jones back to her car and returned Auntie Lil to her apartment, it was nearly 3 o'clock in the morning. Herbert lived a few blocks from Auntie Lil and was dropped off in front of his building. T.S. walked his aunt to her door and wearily said his good-byes, promising to call the next day. Auntie Lil thanked him for being a good sport and watched from the window as his car disappeared down the street.

As soon as he was out of sight, she walked straight to a small table next to the sofa and rummaged through its top drawer. After extracting a container of dental floss, dozens of rubber bands, and a hair comb she'd been seeking for weeks, she found what she wanted and pocketed the car keys in her coat. The ride down to the basement garage was quick—at this time of night, there was little call for the elevator. Her Plymouth was parked far in the back because she took it out so seldom, and the walk to it was a long and lonely one. Auntie Lil did not mind. She moved quickly, hands in her coat pockets. Behind her, a figure slowly approached. She was inserting the key into the door lock when a small, burnished hand reached out to stop her.

"Lillian," Herbert Wong said quietly. "You must not attempt these excursions on your own."

"Herbert! How did you know I'd be here?"

"I know you very well."

"Yes, it's infuriating," she admitted.

"If you insist on driving out to Long Island again tonight, then I insist on accompanying you as a safety measure."

Auntie Lil was staring down at the floor. "Aren't you tired?"

"Aren't you?" he asked in reply.

The two old friends eyed one another, then climbed inside the Plymouth. Herbert wisely belted himself with all available safety devices. He had ridden with Auntie Lil before. They emerged slowly from the garage exit and turned onto the deserted side street. All around them stood the dark and silent buildings of Queens, but when they pulled onto the highway, they could see New York City behind them, blazing in electric glory despite the late hour. Its glow illuminated the sky and shrank slowly to darkness as they turned eastward and drove.

5. Auntie Lil was not surprised to see that Abe had a bigger house than Max. "He always went for the trappings," she explained to Herbert as they stared up at the enormous cement-and-steel home. It loomed in odd contrast to the lawn, which was inexplicably decorated with dozens of ceramic figurines that stood out like uninvited country cousins in the otherwise elegant neighborhood. "Max was interested in the work," she added. "Abe was interested in the rewards."

She glanced up and down the smoothly paved street. It was empty. They scurried up the long flagstone walk. Herbert scratched lightly at the window, anticipating a possible round of excited barking. There was nothing but silence. "No pets," he whispered.

The lock opened with a well-oiled click. They slipped inside and waited beside the front hall closet, listening for noise. It was one thing to search an empty house; it was another when the occupants were asleep upstairs.

Fortunately, the occupants were most assuredly asleep: deafening snores drifted down the main staircase at regular intervals, deep and ratcheting. It sounded like a shoe with a loose sole had gotten stuck in the bell of a bullhorn. They crept to the base of the steps and stared upstairs in horrified wonder.

"It can't be Abe," Auntie Lil whispered cautiously. "He can hardly breathe."

"Either it's the wife or a three-hundred-and-fifty-pound male nurse," Herbert agreed. They stared at each other in sudden alarm. "Wait here," he decided, firmly guiding Auntie Lil back down the steps. "I'll check the upstairs. You search down here."

They went swiftly to work, Herbert creeping upstairs as silently as a shadow and reappearing less than ten minutes later. Auntie Lil was caught, quite literally, with her hand in the cookie jar. Her guilty figure was illuminated by a circle of light that shone in through the kitchen window from behind the backyard pool.

"What are you doing?" Herbert whispered sharply.

"These are Pepperidge Farm," she explained.

"No excuse. Come on. The wife is a restless sleeper."

"The dead son did not live here," Herbert announced once they had safely reached Auntie Lil's Plymouth. "Three bedrooms do not look as if anyone has lived in them for years. There are two others that are occupied. The wife was snoring loudly in one. Abe was in the other. He's lying in a hospital bed and there's a respirator against one wall. It is like a hospital in there. Except, no nurse. And something even more interesting."

"What?"

"He keeps a gun in a drawer by his bed. Loaded."

"You went that close?" Auntie Lil stared at him disapprovingly.

"He didn't notice me," Herbert assured her. "I was like the wind slipping past, nothing more." He coughed modestly.

Auntie Lil pondered the significance of the gun. "Their son was shot in the face. Or, at least, that was the rumor going around the cemetery."

Herbert nodded. "Maybe so. But not by this man. He is totally bedridden. And I do not think that a father would shoot his own son in the face. Nor a mother. Besides, there was genuine sorrow in that house. I could feel it. There was a large portrait of a young man propped against one wall in the hallway. Someone had leaned it there in their grief."

Even Abby, Auntie Lil decided grudgingly, probably had maternal feelings. "I found nothing downstairs," she admitted to Herbert. "Photographs of some of their children, but none of the younger two I saw at the cemetery. They've been expunged from the family, it's obvious. Other than that, it was just a lot of plastic-covered furniture." She shivered.

"Shall we try the home of Jake Rosenbloom?" Herbert suggested. "We still have an hour until sunrise." He consulted the list of addresses that Rebecca Rosenbloom had provided. "I believe it is only a mile or two from here."

But when they arrived at the considerably more modest home of Abe and Abby's oldest son, a snarling rottweiler threw its heavy body against the front door the instant Herbert inserted the key. An upstairs light went on immediately. They scurried into the bushes with only seconds to spare before the front door opened. The huge dog had been restrained by its unseen owner, a sign of its probable viciousness. It slobbered as it pulled frantically at its leash, straining to leap free and charge into the front yard. The beast's body was silhouetted perfectly against the glare from the streetlight, down to the two rows of jagged incisors and a thin string of drool that dangled from its snapping jaws.

Auntie Lil and Herbert decided right then and there that their housebreaking days were over. They would find another way to solve the mystery.

CHAPTER FIVE

1. Sleeping late was never a problem for Auntie Lil. No one ever dared phone before noon. The next day was an exception. T.S. rang up just past ten o'clock and kept her on the line so long that she finally demanded to know what he wanted.

"I was just checking to see how awake you were," he confessed. "I kept having this feeling that you had gone back out last night."

"Nonsense, Theodore." She yawned elaborately. "I was so exhausted that I could hardly move. I went right to bed and would still be sleeping—if you had not called."

T.S. mumbled a sheepish apology. "It's just that I think we should both take it easy," he told her. "This is too big for us. There's more in the papers today. It was a professionally made car bomb, that much is certain. And the nephew they found in the bottom of the grave had definite connections to organized crime. They say he was into the loan sharks. I think this is a good one to sit out, don't you?"

Auntie Lil was quiet. "You may be right, Theodore," she finally agreed. "At least long enough to let the professionals have a chance at solving it first."

"That's a relief. I thought you'd argue. We must be getting more reasonable in our old age. I'll phone you in a couple hours to see how you're doing."

67

"No need," she assured him sweetly. "I'll be out at the hairdressers. I'll give you a call in early evening."

She hung up her phone and stared out the window, seeing not the pristinely blue day that had followed yesterday's downpours but, instead, a similar day over forty years ago. It was Italy, she was young, and Max was alive. They stood together, hand in hand, staring out the tiny window of a whitewashed hotel, gazing at the blue of a sky that met the blue of the sea in one great unbroken line. All of their lives stretched before them.

The raucous forced laughter of teenagers beneath her window brought her back to the present. She watched their rude flirting absently, then shook her head with conviction. No, she decided, she was *not* getting more reasonable in her old age. Age could claim her body piece by piece. But, by God, her spirit belonged to her. Let T.S. sit at home inside his safe apartment. She would do what she could.

Three miles away T.S. frantically scanned his neat racks of shoes for his finest black leathers. He thought that he had thrown Auntie Lil off the trail rather neatly. Now he could act without worrying about her safety.

Having deluded themselves into thinking that the other had been safely dissuaded from taking further action, Auntie Lil and T.S. busied themselves with new ways to unravel the murders of Max and Davy Rosenbloom.

2. Although Auntie Lil sometimes filled in at other companies during the heavy production seasons, she had not returned to Max Rose Fashions in over twenty years. She knew, however, that over these years the facilities had expanded steadily, taking over neighboring offices until the company occupied nearly all of a huge brick building that

dominated Thirty-first Street between Sixth and Seventh Avenues.

She stood outside the giant structure, staring up at its small windows. As always, she was assaulted with one overriding impression of the garment district: *noise*. Behind her, engines roared as trucks jockeyed for good unloading positions. Young men yelled for clearance as they wove racks of clothing and rolling platforms of boxes in and out of the noisy crowd. It was lunchtime and the streets were thronged with workers on their breaks. Laughter and shouts rang out against a steady stream of impatient honking from stalled traffic. As she passed a deli a wave of sound rolled out through the open door into the street with a life force of its own. The human voices blended in a cacophony as loud and reliable as that of the machines whirring endlessly on the floors above.

No one ever just spoke in the garment industry: every word was shouted, every gesture exaggerated. Auntie Lil's naturally booming voice had served her well on the job, but it was no wonder that outsiders felt she must be partially deaf.

In abrupt contrast, Max Rose Fashions was eerily quiet. The elevator opened onto a spacious floor divided into reception, sales, and office areas. Directly behind the reception section, twin rows of cubicles flanked a hanging rack of next season's offerings. A long row of bagged dresses and pantsuits dangled silently beneath dark spotlights. Normally, the area would be bustling with prospective buyers and sales representatives as they examined garments and then returned to the cubicles to negotiate orders and prices. Today, the area was empty and forlorn looking. There was not even anyone behind the front desk to greet Auntie Lil. She took a right and headed down a long hallway toward the accounting and executive offices that occupied one side of the building. Workers and machinery were relegated to the inner darkness of the lower cavernous warehouse floors.

The offices were empty as well. Odd, she thought, even though Max had died. She paused in front of one and read the doorplate: DAVID ROSENBLOOM. So the dead nephew had worked with Max at the factory. At least in theory: his desk was bare and the surrounding room equally sterile. Perhaps someone had cleaned it since his murder. A few doors down, she discovered an office for the second nephew, Jacob. Auntie Lil stuck her head in his door and saw a room crammed with folders, file cabinets, and empty coffee cups. At least it looked like he actually did some work. The names on the other doorplates were unfamiliar—she had been gone a very long time. She saw that Max had appointed someone named Thomas Brody chief executive officer. At the far end of the hall, she heard a slightly familiar female voice, obviously speaking on the telephone. She slowed before she reached the door and listened, unseen in the hall.

"Relax. I'm the only one here," the voice said. "Half didn't come in and the other half are downstairs being questioned now. . . . Yes, by the police. Who the hell else did you think? The police, the FBI, the feds, the CIA . . . Hell, for all I know there are a couple of Canadian Mounties in there. . . . No, they did not even come close to asking. . . . Of course not, do I seem stupid to you?" Her voice was silent for a moment. "That's very unlikely. There's no way they could get a tap in two days. . . . I'm trying to find out now. . . . Yes, I am sure he had something to do with it. . . . Well, whoever took care of it did a very messy job. Half his face was blown off. So much for professionalism. . . . Right . . . right . . . keep telling me that. I'm sure you were lunching with the pope when it happened. . . . Okay. Twenty minutes." The phone slammed down abruptly.

Auntie Lil waited a minute and used the time to creep back up the hall. She then retraced her steps noisily, calling out "Halloo! Halloo! Is anyone here?" in her very best little-old-lady voice. When she reached the occupied office again, she stole a look at the nameplate: JOYCE CARRUTH-ERS. Of course. Auntie Lil remembered her as a young bookkeeper who, she suspected, had harbored a crush on Max for years—to no avail. She was hardly Max's type. In addition to being suspicious, resentful, and narrow-minded, Joyce Carruthers had been incredibly tall with stooped shoulders and a face that unfortunately resembled Abraham Lincoln in drag. She had always worn far too much makeup and grossly mismatched clothes for someone in the garment industry. The too tight sweaters and hip-hugging skirts that Auntie Lil remembered from the fifties had given way to a too tight turtleneck, knit miniskirt, stockings appliquéd with sequined roses, and stiletto heels that increased the bookkeeper's already impressive height by at least eight inches. Her hair was elaborately coiffed in a pseudo-messy explosion currently in vogue. Heavy gold earrings shaped like fans dangled from her ears and pulled her lobes down with their weight. Given that Joyce Carruthers was now nearly sixty years old, her costume was atrocious bordering on frightening.

Twenty-five years had not improved the bookkeeper's disposition any more than her sense of style. She glared at Auntie Lil, making it obvious that she resented the intrusion. Her fingers were poised above the keyboard of her computer as if she were impatient to get back to work. Oddly, beneath the garish makeup, her hatchet face had gone white. And did her fingers tremble? Perhaps Auntie Lil's sudden appearance had frightened her.

"Can I help you?" she asked Auntie Lil in a cold voice.

Pretending to be flustered, Auntie Lil took a moment to study her. Something about her face had changed. Auntie Lil felt as if she were staring at a figure in a wax museum that did not quite match its subject. The skin was pulled back too tightly on either side of the nose; it had flattened her unwrinkled and slightly distorted features unattractively. Her eyes were elongated and the brows were plucked to within a hair of disappearing entirely. Flat, sheenless expanses of skin occupied the spots where Auntie Lil had been expecting wrinkles. "Joyce?" she asked in a deliberately tentative voice.

"Yes. Can I help you?" the woman replied tersely, as if she did not recognize Auntie Lil. Yet Auntie Lil was sure that she had.

"I'm Lillian Hubbert. Do you remember me?"

The woman stared for several seconds, her feelings hidden behind the smooth mask of her face. "I should have known it was you that caused all that fuss when I saw you at the funeral. You trampled me worming your way to the front."

So, thought Auntie Lil. I was right. Here is a woman who was in love with Max for many years. "Where is everyone else?" she asked.

"They're busy being questioned. This mess has managed to bring us to a standstill just when we have spring orders to fill." She glared at Auntie Lil as if this were her fault.

"Questioned? By the police?" Auntie Lil inched in the door.

"What's it to you?"

Auntie Lil was at a loss for an excuse, so she offered the truth. "I came down to see what might have happened to Max. He was on his way to see me when he died."

"Indeed? I was not aware that the two of you had kept

in touch." Joyce stared at her, eyes narrowed. "Curious that he never mentioned you to me. As his comptroller, we were very close."

Auntie Lil merely shrugged and inched farther in the door.

This territorial encroachment did not go unnoticed. "I'd love to stay and chat," the comptroller announced sarcastically. "But I have a date for lunch and do not wish to be late." She stood up abruptly, smoothing her skirt down over her stomach.

She had starved herself into birdlike form, Auntie Lil noticed with disapproval. What in heaven's name was wrong with a healthy figure these days?

She was also rude, brushing past without an apology and waiting in the hall until Auntie Lil followed. She shut the door to her office with a bang and gestured for Auntie Lil to exit through the reception area.

How dare she? Auntie Lil thought. Who had died and appointed this scrawny little bookkeeper the queen of Max Rose Fashions? "Thank you, but I'll wait here for some of the others to return," Auntie Lil said firmly. "You go on ahead." She stared the woman straight in the eye and willed her determination to show.

It worked. Joyce Carruthers shrugged and tottered down the hall on her high heels.

The second she heard the old elevator doors creak shut, Auntie Lil scurried back down to the crabby bookkeeper's office and tried the door. It was locked. But Joyce had not stopped to double-lock it. That meant it could be slipped with a credit card. Auntie Lil checked the hallway. It was empty. She pulled out her Macy's charge and went to work, sliding the plastic between the door and the jamb and expertly applying pressure to the left. The lock clicked open easily and she scurried inside, closing the door behind her.

She heard a door open at the far end of the hallway and held her breath. Had Joyce forgotten something in her office?

Within seconds, a pair of voices passed by. "What was that all about?" an unseen male was asking. "Did they make you feel guilty or what? I felt like dropping to my knees and confessing when I haven't done a damn thing."

"If you ask me, the one they ought to have questioned is Davy," another male replied.

"Yeah. Except he's dead," the first man pointed out.

"Which is unfortunate for the cops. But lucky for Max Rose Fashions. He'd have run us into the ground within a year."

"True," the other voice agreed. "But my hands are clean. And my head is clear. I'm looking for a new job starting tomorrow."

"Shhh . . ." his companion warned him. "Here comes Brody."

"So what? He'll be the first one out the door."

Auntie Lil heard a door slam and the nonsensical murmur of executives greeting one another for the tenth time that day. Soon, their voices faded down the hall and Auntie Lil went to work searching the comptroller's office. She didn't get far. When she tried to access the computer, a password request popped up and she was forced to return to the main menu. The files and desk were just as unproductive: Joyce kept every drawer and credenza compartment carefully locked.

How irritating, thought Auntie Lil, how utterly suspicious of the woman. What was she supposed to do now?

The phone on the desk rang, sending a jolt of adrenaline pumping through Auntie Lil's heart. She picked up the receiver slowly, adjusting her voice to a higher octave.

"What?" she asked crabbily, knowing that Joyce was not the kind of woman to waste time on pleasantries.

"I'm going to be a few minutes late," a male voice announced gruffly. "Listen, I need to know right now if the cops asked about V.J. Productions."

"What?" she snarled back, coughing to disguise her voice.

"Don't get cute," the voice warned. "Did they ask about V.J. or not?"

"No!" Auntie Lil barked, slamming down the phone. She would not push her luck.

Her heart was pounding. When the phone rang again, she did not dare touch it. If it was the same man, that meant she had aroused his suspicions. Let it be. His confusion would buy her time.

She scurried to the elevator, looking over her shoulder but not quite sure whom she was looking for. The man on the phone had sounded so . . . *mean*. So cold and efficiently cruel. What was Joyce Carruthers doing talking about the investigation into Max's death to someone like that? She pondered this question as the old elevator creaked down toward the lobby. It stopped on a lower floor to pick up a janitor dragging a damp mop and wheeling a bucket of soapy water. As he loaded his equipment on she caught a glimpse of the sample-cutting-room floor. It was as empty as a stage waiting for the actors to take their places. The sewing machines and cutting tables and hanging racks of clothes brought back memories of Max surrounded by the chaos of designers shouting, seamstresses laughing, and cutting machines humming behind it all. She could almost see his face and sturdy figure in the center of the enormous floor as he effortlessly choreographed the chaos, his energy radiating out like the sun, commanding all to whirl around his power. God, how his people loved him.

Tears sprang to her eyes at the memory. She dabbed at them furtively with the tip of one white-gloved finger. The janitor stared straight ahead, stony-faced, his mop held at rigid attention by his side.

"Have a nice evening, ma'am," he called out kindly as Auntie Lil hurried out into the afternoon crowds.

3. It felt odd to be wearing a suit and riding the subway down to Sterling & Sterling once again. If T.S. closed his eyes and listened to the hum of the train, it felt as if the last few years had never happened, that it had all been but a dream and he was now waking to find that he had never retired from the bank at all. Having tortured himself with this thought, he shook himself back to reality with profound relief. Sterling & Sterling's formality and old-fashioned ways were fine if you didn't know any better. But once you experienced freedom, it was difficult to return to the stuffiness without feeling suffocated.

He was worried about his welcome. His departure, planned as a normal retirement, had turned out to be a rather spectacularly devastating mess for the firm. No matter. Today he had legitimate business, and so far as he knew, no dead bodies preceded his visit this time around. As he neared the Wall Street corner where the venerable and still very private bank stood in polished granite-and-brass glory, T.S. squared his shoulders and did something he had never dared to do: he used the clients' entrance.

He did not recognize the guard on duty but received a respectful nod nonetheless. If you came in the clients' entrance, you were given the benefit of the doubt. This was a safe gamble on Sterling & Sterling's part because Effie, the receptionist, could sniff out impostors no matter how well cut their clothing. Or, displaying an aptitude even more valuable in these modern times, she could discern an heiress or computer company president no matter how tattered and worn the blue jeans.

She recognized T.S. at once. "By gum!" she cried, snapping to attention and rising from her chair smartly, despite a plump physique. Her headset wires crisscrossed her chest as if she were a matronly jungle guerrilla equipped for telecommunications warfare. "This is a red-letter day indeed. A five-star event!" She held out a pink, rounded hand and nearly wrung T.S.'s arm from his shoulder. Despite her grandmotherly bearing, Effie was a fervent war-movie buff. Her hobby had permeated every aspect of her existence, from her jargon-peppered vocabulary to her ramrod posture and her marinelike approach to greetings and farewells. The one thing she did not do was salute, and for this T.S. was profoundly grateful.

"Effie, how lovely to see you. I can rest easy tonight knowing that the citadels of Sterling and Sterling are so competently guarded." He was teasing her and she loved it. Many people took Effie for granted. She basked in whatever attention she could get.

"Thank you, sir." She sat down smartly to dispatch an incoming call, then looked up at him with bright eyes. "Things are going very well here, sir. Very well indeed. That young Mr. Freeman knows just what he's doing. My bonus was up ten percent last year. Just imagine! Perhaps they should have cleaned out the old partners a long time ago."

T.S. agreed silently. "It's actually Preston Freeman that I've come to see. Without an appointment, I'm afraid." He gave her his best smile. Even as an old friend, he was pushing his luck to ask to see the managing partner of America's oldest and largest private bank without an appointment.

The smile worked. "I'll just call Helen and see what we

can do." Effie set to work briskly, and within a few minutes
T.S. was being ushered back by an elegantly groomed partner's secretary to the sanctum sanctorum itself: the Partners' Room of Sterling & Sterling. Stepping inside was like
entering a past century. Rolltop desks were lined up in
homage before a huge marble fireplace topped by an enormous oil painting of the firm's founder and his four myopic
sons. The silence was profound. Not even the soft clatter of
fingers on computer keyboards broke the hush—the only
modern accoutrements allowed were telephones.

Not that it mattered. The rolltop desks were empty. They
always were these days. Modern finance had intervened and
the partners were always *gone*: gone to Geneva, Tokyo,
Luxembourg, São Paulo, or beyond. Barring a trip, they
were usually upstairs in a department where they had access to computers and could get some damn work done.
Thus with a thin veneer of pretense had Sterling & Sterling
dealt with the march of time.

"Mr. Freeman has converted conference room three into
his office," the secretary explained briskly. T.S. recognized
her but could not recall her last name. How profoundly life
could change in a matter of months.

No wonder the new managing partner had needed more
room. The trim middle-aged man sat behind an enormous
desk, engrossed in paperwork. The desk was a huge,
leather-topped affair given to the firm by an Indian prince
one hundred and fifty years earlier. Its stuffed elephant-feet
legs had finally been replaced in the late seventies, when
client outrage at the endangerment of species had reached
its peak (and Sterling & Sterling had landed the Save Our
Animals account). Surrounding this traditional seat of
power were computer terminals, so numerous that T.S. felt
as if he were part of a multimedia display. Each computer
scrolled constant information on one of the world's major

financial markets, interspersed with local news for whatever country was being tracked. Preston Freeman literally did not have to lift a finger. All he had to do was raise an eyebrow to check events in any potentially profitable corner of the world.

T.S. stood before the preoccupied man and gently cleared his throat. The partner looked up in surprise. He was perpetually trying to figure out a way to make a job bigger, a transaction greater, a deal more luminous than it at first appeared. He was the king of cross-selling financial services and a genius at it, too. Even more rare, he was an honest genius. In fact, everything at Sterling & Sterling—always— was aboveboard. The bank's reputation was its single greatest asset.

"T.S." Preston Freeman rose from his chair and extended a hand. His smile was genuine, as it should have been— T.S. had once saved his bacon and was largely responsible for his being head of the firm today. "What can I do for you? It has been a while, hasn't it?"

T.S. agreed and settled down in the visitor's chair, a lush green-leather contraption with brass studs peppering its surface and carved horn armrests. Everything at Sterling & Sterling reeked of animal sacrifice, he realized suddenly. Didn't anyone ever just give the firm a nice set of silver?

"I need some information," T.S. explained without preamble. Preston Freeman was too busy and too astute to appreciate being bushwhacked from behind. "It's about a friend of my aunt's." He explained the situation, including Max's death. Freeman nodded—he'd read about it in the news section of his computer information network. "I think there was a representative from Sterling and Sterling at the funeral," T.S. continued, acutely aware that he had suddenly snagged the managing partner's undivided attention. He was also uncomfortably reminded that he was perilously close to asking Freeman to commit the ultimate indiscretion: betrayal of a client's confidence.

"It's a personal matter," T.S. hurried on. "Hard to explain. My aunt is obsessed." He spread his hands and shrugged, hoping that Freeman remembered Auntie Lil. That would make further explanation unnecessary.

"I've met your aunt," Freeman agreed amiably, and nodded for T.S. to continue.

"I'm wondering if Max Rosenbloom or Max Rose Fashions was a client here," T.S. finished. "No details, of course, I could never ask you to"—he coughed nervously—"betray any . . . confidences. . . ." Oh hell, he was out of practice when it came to discreet conversation, a side effect from hanging out with Auntie Lil. He let his words trail off and waited uncomfortably to be rescued by Freeman.

"I'm certain he was a client," the partner admitted. "I see no reason why that should not be public knowledge. We handled a number of transactions for his firm in our corporate finance area when I was there full-time." Freeman swiveled in his chair to a nearby terminal and moved his fingers rapidly over the keys. Screens faded, new ones appeared, instructions were rapidly typed, and lists of names began to scroll with a greenish glow. "We did work for his firm several years ago, two years before that, and—" Suddenly he stopped and sat up straighter. "Oh, I see." He briskly shut off the computer and turned back to T.S., his friendly manner a shade cooler. "I have erred. There may be a confidential matter involving Max Rose Fashions currently in play here at the firm. I must ask you to respect the confidentiality of that information. However . . ." Freeman's eyes shifted to the telephone and he hesitated, curiosity battling with discretion. But even financial geniuses are human. Curiosity won.

"Just a moment, please," he said to T.S., and punched

out a four-digit extension. T.S. knew that meant he was calling another department at Sterling & Sterling. "Regina?" he asked pleasantly. "This is Mr. Freeman. Bob around?" Of course Bob was around. Everyone was around when the managing partner called. In fact, Bob was on the line within ten seconds. "Bob, are you handling something for Max Rosenbloom right now? Of Max Rose Fashions?" There was a short silence. "Indeed? What are the particulars?" More silence. "I see. Have you consulted Legal on this one? What is our exposure?" Another silence—and another twinge in T.S.'s gut. "When do you think? All right. I'll handle it. But I need to know more. Be down here this afternoon with the file."

Preston Freeman hung up the phone and regarded T.S. without expression. It was more than unnerving. It was downright ominous. Abruptly, the partner jumped to his feet and T.S. followed, a sense of dread inescapably closing in on him. "I regret that I cannot tell you any more at this time," Freeman said, his hand extended in farewell. He avoided T.S.'s eyes. "Our firm's lawyers will be in touch with you within a few days, I'm sure." His manner, T.S. noted, had grown cold. He could not understand the change.

"Nothing more?" T.S. asked. "Is there some sort of problem?"

"Problem?" The managing partner's laugh was a mirthless bark. "Isn't it always a problem when lawyers get involved?"

CHAPTER SIX

1. "Something's up," Casey Jones reported to Auntie Lil later that afternoon. She was crammed in a phone booth in the parking lot of a diner just off Long Island's Sunrise Highway. Worse, she was fighting an intense urge for a double cheeseburger and triple order of fries. Surveillance always made her hungry.

"Something's up?" Auntie Lil repeated. She'd spent the last hour back at home puzzling over the phone call she'd overheard at Max Rose Fashions. It was getting her nowhere.

"Definitely. I'm standing right across a service road from Sam Ascher's office now. He was one of Max's lawyers. I recognize the name from the prenup. I followed the wife here an hour ago. Imagine my surprise when her visit turned into a family reunion. They're all here—the scary sister, most of the nephews, his brother's wife, Abby, and a handful of assorted unidentified suckers-on."

"The reading of the will?" Auntie Lil suggested.

"Maybe. If so, they didn't waste much time. But then, they probably wouldn't. After all, they've got airfare to Palm Beach coming up and some of their cars must be at least six months old. Listen, I'm starving but I'm going to stick it out a few more—wait ..." Casey was silent and Auntie Lil could hear the steady whiz of cars streaming past in the background. "Hold the phone," Casey muttered briefly, and the silence returned. This was maddening to Auntie Lil: to think that something big was going down and she was stuck in her apartment miles away. Oh, to be fifty years younger.

"Oh, my God . . ." Casey muttered.

Auntie Lil couldn't take it anymore. "What!" she cried. "Tell me!"

"They're hot. *Steaming*," Casey reported. "Whatever went on in there has really teed them off. Two of the nephews just roared out of the parking lot in their cars, spraying gravel. The old-crone sister looks like she's hyperventilating right now, and good old Abby is staring off at the traffic like she's ready to throw herself under a van. And . . . heeeere she comes—the widow. Oooh, black widow, I should say. She's in a venomous mood. She just said something nasty to Abby." Brief silence. "Now, *that* was an interesting hand signal. Make that twin hand signals. Must be some sort of code." She laughed. "So much for family harmony. Yes, no doubt about it. Max has just shafted his family royally."

Auntie Lil was not a vindictive person, but the thought cheered her immensely. It was bad enough to think that Max had carried so many people during his life without complaint. At least he had broken free in death.

"How can we find out the particulars?" Auntie Lil asked.

"Well, as soon as it goes to probate . . ." Casey's voice trailed off. "I could try a couple of sources, but I can't promise anything."

Auntie Lil let her go after extracting a promise to call back the second she had any news. She was deep in thought when the phone rang a minute or two later. She hesitated—all afternoon, someone had been calling and hanging up. It was annoying, but not necessarily alarming.

Still, it could be Casey calling back with more news. And if it was her harasser, she'd just tell him off once and for all.

"Yes," she demanded sternly. No pervert was going to push her around.

"Is this Miss Lillian Hubbert?"

"Yes it is," she replied crisply. "Who is this?"

"This is Sam Ascher. I represent the estate of Max Rosenbloom."

"Yes?" Her voice grew fainter. The coincidence was a bit . . . alarming.

"I realize that you are probably still deeply upset about Max's death."

"Yes, I am," Auntie Lil agreed. "I loved him very much."

"I also realize that this may seem a bit . . . unseemly." He paused. "The haste and all . . . But I'm being pushed somewhat by the family. They seem very, uh, anxious to settle the estate."

"I've no doubt that they are."

"They've asked for an official reading of the will tomorrow. We . . ." He coughed nervously. "We had a preliminary meeting today, and I tried to let them know that there were still some legal issues that had to be explored, that it was complicated, that it was premature—" His legal disclaimers sputtered to a halt and he took a deep breath. "Well, let's just say that maybe it is best that we get this over with as soon as possible."

"Get *what* over with?" Auntie Lil demanded.

"If you could just be here tomorrow at two o'clock, it will all become clear." He gave his address.

"I assume I may bring representation with me?" she asked.

"Of course, of course. Although this is all very friendly

and ... Oh, bring whoever you want," he conceded irritably. "This whole thing has become one big pain in the ass. Never in my life have I had to contend with an entire ... *pack* of people clamoring for my license. I don't know what possessed Max. You must be some kind of a woman."

"I beg your pardon?" Auntie Lil said stiffly.

"He's always been so levelheaded. With the exception of his wife, of course." He coughed again. "You did, uh, know he was married, did you not? That could create problems here."

"What difference does that make?" Perhaps this was a prank call after all.

"Because if any *promises* were made ... Verbal promises, I mean. They would have to be taken in the context of his current ..." He hesitated and fumbled on: "I mean, sometimes we say things in the privacy of our bedrooms. .... People do get carried away. You have to realize that he may have been captivated by your youth and that a compromise may be in your best interests in this situation—"

She cut him off swiftly. "Young man, I do not know what you are babbling about and I do not care to listen any longer. I will see you tomorrow at two o'clock. Perhaps you will be coherent by then." She hung up the phone and stared down at the receiver. What had that crack about her youth meant? Good Lord, what youth? She was the oldest person she knew.

2.   Auntie Lil was a practical woman and would have preferred real representation. Unfortunately, her lawyer was unable to attend as he had recently divorced his wife and was entertaining a young woman in Aspen. Given these circumstances, Auntie Lil settled for quantity over quality.

T.S., Casey Jones, and Herbert Wong all accompanied her to Sam Ascher's office. Casey masqueraded as her niece and wore an iridescent bottle-green dress for the occasion. Herbert Wong wore an impeccably conservative suit, as he planned to give the impression—but not actually claim—that he was Auntie Lil's lawyer.

Given the hostility that greeted her when she arrived, Auntie Lil was grateful for the support. A gray-haired secretary led them down a nondescript hall to a back conference room. They had arrived intentionally late and found the Rosenblooms assembled in a glum circle around a large mahogany table. Though there were a few strangers—obviously lawyers—interspersed among the family, no one seemed to be leading the group. A burly man in a navy sport jacket sat apart from the others and huddled in a too small chair that had been pulled into a far corner. He checked the new arrivals out with professional thoroughness, then returned to scowling at his shoes.

Although it had not been her intention, one of the few remaining seats happened to be at one end of the long table. Herbert held her chair out and Auntie Lil sat down with quiet dignity. She'd faced a lot worse than the Rosenbloom bunch in her day. T.S. and Herbert flanked her while Casey went in search of an extra chair. The cop in the corner had parked his feet up on one, and she glared at him until he got the hint. When he was slow to remove his feet, Casey simply pulled the chair out from under them and dragged it across the carpet until she was sitting behind Auntie Lil. She plopped down with little ceremony and began studying each member of Max's family. For the first time she had a view of them unimpeded by darkness, distance, or discretion. She planned to make the most of her opportunity. Auntie Lil joined her in staring.

Nearly the entire Rosenbloom clan was there. Abby,

Max's sister-in-law, sat near one end of the table, her face haggard underneath the harsh office light. She had neglected to take enough time with her makeup and had hastily daubed on powder that was a shade too light. It only accentuated her wrinkles. Bright spots of rouge stood out clownlike on her cheeks, and her eyes were red and weary looking. She stared down at the tabletop, oblivious of her surroundings. She had lost a son, Auntie Lil reminded herself. It was something a mother should never have to go through.

The widow, if grieving, was concealing her sorrow very successfully. She sat beside her lawyer, her slender frame elegant and resplendent in a bright red knit suit. Her hair tumbled to her shoulders in glossy waves. A small black veil the size of a lily pad was Sabrina's only concession to traditional mourning garb. She was idly inhaling from a long cigarette and blowing tiny smoke rings, rolling her heavily lined eyes lazily as she watched the hoops float toward the ceiling.

Max's oldest nephew, Jake, sat to her right. He stared down at his folded hands, his face a careful mask of concern. His wife sat stonelike next to him, moving only long enough to lean over now and then for a quick glare at the widow.

Rebecca Rosenbloom sat near the far end of the table, flanked by two lawyers but thoroughly ignoring them both. She wore a navy-blue dress and a curved pearl comb anchored her upswept hair. The look was centuries removed from her graveyard persona. Her eyes swept over Auntie Lil as if she did not recognize her. Only a slight quiver of the hooded eye betrayed any emotion at all.

Max's youngest niece and nephew were conspicuously absent, but a lone lawyer pointedly ignoring the others may have been representing Seth and Karen.

The click of the door opening interrupted the uncomfortable silence. A small man, as plump and sprightly as a puffin, scurried into the room. He winced apologetically and bobbed a small bow. Shutting the door carefully behind him, he looked about the room with a desperate smile, perhaps hoping that a little goodwill—no matter how artificial—would soothe the raging waters. He had a thick manila folder tucked up under one arm and a pair of glasses dangled from a cord around his neck. Perching his spectacles on the end of his nose, he approached the conference table like a dog sniffing out a bone. Each Rosenbloom received a nod, each lawyer a quick handshake. When he reached Auntie Lil's end of the table, he slowed and took the time to stare at each of them in turn. A brief frown crossed his doughy face before the smile returned.

"Miss Hubbert," he gushed. "It's certainly a pleasure. Max spoke most highly of you." He thrust a plump hand at Casey Jones, determinedly ignoring her skintight dress. Casey stared down at his hand as if she'd just discovered half a worm in her apple.

"Surely there's no need to be hostile," the lawyer pleaded. "We are all bound by a common friend here." A sad frown crossed his face at the rebuff, then he thrust his hand at Casey again.

Auntie Lil stared at Sam Ascher. Suddenly their previous conversation made sense. "*I* am Lillian Hubbert," she announced, gripping the perplexed lawyer's hand. "And just to put the record straight, young man, Max and I were very old friends. We have not seen each other in more than twenty years. The 'pillow talk' you referred to yesterday is a figment of your imagination and this young lady is not Max's paramour. Are there any other vital facts you may require?"

His mistake was devastating to the lawyer's dignity. He

turned purple, clutched at his folder, bowed an apology, and slunk to the other end of the table. There, another lawyer took pity on him and offered Sam Ascher his chair.

"Let's get started," Sam Ascher mumbled. "This is all very strange." He looked up at the assembled crowd and found courage in outrage. "Frankly, I do not like this at all," he declared. "I do not understand the rush. All of you were well taken care of while Max was alive. He was very generous with his gifts. If you've invested properly, then . . ." His voice trailed off as he realized that this was not the best time for an impromptu lecture on fiscal responsibility. He contented himself with a final salvo: "Frankly, I am not through exploring all of the legal ramifications of Max's actions, but here goes." He paused to glare at no one in particular, then proceeded to read the contents of the file in front of him.

No one spoke as he read and there were no outbursts, except for an occasional gasp and a harrumph or two from the lawyers representing members of Max's family. When Sam Ascher was done, he reassembled the file neatly and placed it in front of him, precisely aligning it with the edge of the table. He folded his plump pink hands and stared at the crowd. The silence was profound.

"So you see," he said pleasantly, "Max was quite clear about his intentions."

The widow's self-control gave way. "What the hell did all that mean?" she shrieked as half the attendees jumped at the sound. "What the *hell* did all that mumbo jumbo mean? How much money do I get?"

The reading of endless legalese had restored a sense of superiority in Sam Ascher. He eyed Max's widow calmly. "It means, Mrs. Rosenbloom, that you are entitled to the three hundred thousand dollars stipulated in the prenuptial agreement you signed three years ago. That's one hundred thousand for each year you were married, assuming that you upheld the conditions of the agreement, such as the faithfulness clause. I mention that purely at random, of course."

"What about the rest of his money?" she demanded. "He was worth millions."

"Yes, he was. However, you only receive three hundred thousand," the lawyer repeated.

"He can't leave it to that old bag," Sabrina screamed, jabbing a taloned finger Auntie Lil's way.

Auntie Lil rose and faced her. "I will thank you not to speak to me in that manner," she said coolly. "Your behavior is despicable."

Jake leaped to his feet. "How dare you call her despicable," he shouted, glancing at Sabrina Rosenbloom. His wife's face went white as she stared at her infuriated husband.

"Sit down!" Sam Ascher roared. They sat. He addressed his next comment to Max's widow. "Mrs. Rosenbloom, you receive three hundred thousand dollars and one-fifth ownership in Max Rose Fashions. I would suggest to you that it's not a bad return considering what you contributed to the marriage."

Sabrina Rosenbloom rose again and drew herself up to her full height as she ripped the black veil from her head. She threw it in the middle of the table, where it landed on a flower arrangement. Pushing her lawyer out of the way, she leaned over three groveling family members until her face was only inches from Sam Ascher's. "You listen to me, you useless piece of legal debris," she spat out in a voice that could have curdled custard. "This is New York State. I get half. Period. End of discussion. I know my legal rights."

The lawyer paused, then rose to his feet and drew himself

up to *his* full height. "Perhaps your lawyer will explain it to you very, very slowly once you have *left* my offices. Mr. Rosenbloom had no assets to split with you during your marriage. They were placed in trust three years and three months ago. In fact, just a month before your wedding. And control of that trust was to go to Lillian Hubbert upon your husband's death, as well as to his nephew, Davy Rosenbloom. If Davy did not survive Max by at least forty-eight hours, his half of the trust was to pass to the alternate beneficiary. Who happens to be Mr. Theodore Stanford Hubbert. I think it seems quite clear to me."

"Just how much is this trust worth?" Rebecca Rosenbloom asked. Her face was a deathly chalk white.

Sam Ascher coughed nervously. "Sixty-six million," he mumbled. "Give or take a few hundred thousand."

"Sixty-six million dollars and he left none of it to his own family?" Jake demanded.

"I wouldn't say that," the lawyer protested. "Your brother and sister received five hundred thousand dollars apiece. Your aunt Rebecca received a similar sum."

"But Seth and Karen aren't even here," Jake's wife protested.

"They don't have to be," Sam Ascher said. "This is not Off Track Betting. Besides, Max was quite generous with your husband. Jake has been left one-fifth of Max Rose Fashions. That equals a healthy sum."

"So what?" Jake demanded. "I can't control the company. I have to share it with four other people." He pointed to Auntie Lil. "She owns one fifth, too, if I understand you right," he whined.

"That is correct," Sam Ascher answered evenly. "Miss Hubbert now owns one fifth of Max Rose Fashions."

Jake glared at Auntie Lil and continued: "Then there's Karen and Seth. They don't know the first thing about running a business and they each get a fifth? That's not fair. I've spent my life working there for him."

"You can control my fifth," the widow offered sourly. "So long as you keep the profits coming."

"God forbid you be left without your customary cash flow," Jake's wife spat out.

"My, aren't we talking like we know one end of a balance sheet from the other?" Sabrina retorted.

"Ladies, please," a lawyer interrupted. He held up a hand for silence, but it had no effect. This time it was Abby who spoke.

"What about the other will?" she asked plaintively, her voice high and hesitant. "He left money to Davy in that will. And to Jacob. And . . . and to all of us."

"The content of any prior will is immaterial," Sam Ascher explained. "Max was quite clear about changing his mind. After the bequests to Seth, Karen, and his sister, Miss Hubbert was to receive the remaining cash in addition to her half of the trust assets."

"What about our houses?" Jake demanded. "Who gets those? He owned my house and Mom and Dad's. And what about his own house? Does she get it or not?" He jerked his thumb at a suddenly even-more-alarmed widow.

"Yeah," Sabrina Rosenbloom demanded, "what about my house?"

Sam Ascher coughed nervously. "Max was not, in fact, the legal owner of your homes. Ownership was transferred to a third party several years ago, whose identity I am not at liberty to reveal."

Most of the Rosenblooms turned to the group huddled at the far end of the table and a low and angry murmuring erupted. As one, Auntie Lil, T.S., Herbert, and Casey shrank from the hostility radiating their way.

"Don't look at us!" T.S. protested. "I'm not your land-lord." His companions murmured similar disclaimers.

"That trust is illegal!" Rebecca Rosenbloom suddenly cried. During the arguments, her face had changed color from pale white to vivid red. It was now as mottled as a strawberry. She pointed a bony finger at Auntie Lil. "You did this," she accused in a slow and angry voice. She stood and banged her fists on the table, hissing at Auntie Lil in her fury. "You planned this all. I know you had something to do with it. Admit it now, Lillian Hubbert! Max would have told me about the trust. Why didn't he tell me? I'll have my lawyers comb over that will every day and every night until we find a way to invalidate it."

A discreet cough from a nondescript man leaning against the wall drew their attention. The speaker's voice was soft but absolutely self-assured. "You may review the paper-work all you wish, Miss Rosenbloom," said the lawyer who had offered Sam Ascher his seat. "But as legal counsel to Sterling and Sterling—trustees to the late Max Rosen-bloom—I can assure you that his actions are perfectly and completely legal. You will not overturn this will, and you will not be able to negate the trust. I will stake my profes-sional reputation on that fact. We do not make mistakes at Sterling and Sterling, particularly when sixty-six million dollars is involved." He blinked once and crossed his arms as if the matter had been settled, at least for him.

Rebecca Rosenbloom was not through. Her elongated features trembled with rage and the droopy eye quivered as if it were about to explode. She turned to the policeman sitting—no longer bored—in one corner of the room.

"She did it!" the old woman screamed, finger pointing at Auntie Lil. "She killed my brother. She's been after his money from the start. I can lead you to the proof!"

CHAPTER SEVEN

1. Auntie Lil was not one to hesitate when she smelled trouble on the way. Once she realized that her fingerprints would be found throughout two Rosenbloom homes, she spent the better part of the evening on the telephone discussing the situation with her lawyer, Hamilton Prescott. He was every bit as old-line and respectable as his name—if one was able to ignore the fact that he had recently dumped the youngest daughter of a railroad magnate and was currently holed up in America's trendiest ski spot with his very own snow bunny. Auntie Lil was of the opinion that this single indiscreet escapade on his part was simply a manifestation of the temporary insanity that sometimes gripped men once they passed the age of sixty.

Hamilton Prescott was competent, sympathetic, and apologetic: if they arrived with a warrant, Auntie Lil had no choice. She would have to let the police in. But if they also wanted to question her, it meant they were taking the Rosenbloom family's charges very seriously. She was to cooperate but to say nothing except that her lawyer was on the way. As for him, he was bored with his companion, could not understand what had possessed him to come to Aspen in the first place, and was taking the first plane back to New York. She would not have to go through it alone, he assured her.

Auntie Lil knew it was not her newfound wealth that was causing Hamilton Prescott to fly to her side. He was family lawyer to many billionaires, never mind millionaires, and sixty-six million would not even make him blink. It was his desire to protect her.

Apparently, this was a desire shared by everyone else in her life. She had vigorously fought to keep T.S., Casey, and Herbert from spending the night at her apartment. They were of the mind that she might be dragged from her bed at the witching hour. None of them doubted that the Rosenblooms would be calling for her blood.

She had only wanted to be alone. Alone with her memories of Max and time to puzzle out what it was that he wanted his legacy to mean.

She had discouraged Herbert Wong even more than the others, warning him not to phone unless she made contact first. She had also thoroughly scrubbed any surfaces he might have touched in her apartment. She did not want him connected with their searches of the Rosenbloom homes. Let the police wonder who her mysterious accomplice had been. There was no reason why Herbert should be damaged in the resumption of a feud that had simmered for decades without him. Besides, the police would suspect that the extra fingerprints belonged to T.S., and he, of course, would not come up as a match since he had remained in the car (or behind in bed).

They came early the next afternoon. The police officers were visibly skeptical once they realized that their target was an eighty-four-year-old woman. The female detective eyed Auntie Lil with something akin to amazement as she produced rubber gloves and different-size pouches to hold potential evidence. The two older detectives contented themselves with dubious glances before they thrust the proper paperwork at her and went to work. The younger man produced a fingerprint kit and dusted several surfaces, in pursuit, perhaps, of evidence that Max had been there. Finding no prints at all, he gave Auntie Lil an odd glance and abandoned his task to aid the others in searching.

While they roamed through her apartment Auntie Lil read the warrant carefully. It was five pages long and authorized the potential uncovering of virtually any scrap of contact between her and Max Rosenbloom.

She had never felt so violated in all the eighty-four years of her life. The invasion of her apartment hurt much more than the Rosenblooms' suspicions that she might have killed Max. Max was the most secret part of her heart. He represented those years of her life that had meant so much more than all the years before and all the years since. To have the sacredness of her memories exposed to the probings of three bored strangers hurt her beyond measure. She sat at the dining room table holding the photo album tightly to her chest. She would give it up last and protect it until that time came.

She derived some comfort from the chaos confronting the search team. T.S. had used the stash-and-hide method of housecleaning during his whirlwind visit several days before. His haste was becoming increasingly obvious as the detectives opened crammed closets and overflowing drawers. The woman officer flung open the hall closet and discovered a mannequin draped in purple satin wearing an Elizabethan crushed-velvet hat. The hat's feather popped free and smacked the detective in one eye, triggering an involuntary scream. One of the officers was forced to crawl beneath Auntie Lil's bed and pull out bolt after bolt of wedged-in cloth, covered with dust and trailing various pieces of jewelry caught in the fabric.

If the fact that the bathroom cabinet was filled with art supplies surprised the third detective, he did not show it. He merely poked through the brushes and squeezed tubes with a careful eye, then turned to examining the books piled high in the hallway. He did not hurry. They were probably on overtime and racking up thirty dollars an hour.

T.S. arrived just as the detectives were speculating that the face in the portrait of the mutant Othello might be Max Rosenbloom's. He took one look at the surrounding chaos and thanked his maker that he had dragged the detective magazines down to the basement earlier that week. Lurid headlines of lovers run amok would have gone over big with this crowd, he was sure.

"How long have they been here?" he asked Auntie Lil, joining her at the dining room table. He moved her pink bunny slippers off the chair so he could sit down.

"I called you right away," she said woodenly, the album clutched tightly to her heart.

He saw at once how much the search was costing her. "I'm sorry." He patted her hand gently. "I'll be right beside you. I won't let them take your things."

"We can't stop them," she said quietly, and, to her horror, found herself perilously close to tears. Auntie Lil never cried, not unless her life was in danger. But then, it felt quite suddenly as if it were.

"They won't stop," she added. "Not until they win one way or the other. None of them have ever liked me. I was always an outsider. Someone who might take Max away from them and then what would they do? They could not make a move or earn a dollar without him." She stared down at the small mementos of their life together, at the watercolor and the blue vase. "I never wanted anything from Max except to be with him. That's why he's left it all to me."

"Almost all," T.S. reminded her gently. "I don't understand why he left the rest to *me*. I never met the man."

She looked at him quietly. "There are things about it that I don't understand myself." She sighed as a series of thumps behind her signaled the opening of yet another closet. This time a plaster bust collection of great composers purchased years ago in Vienna tumbled from the top shelf of the hallway closet onto the balding head of the older officer. She saw without caring that Wagner's face had cracked. Oh well, she'd always thought him a bit overwrought.

Flustered, the detective attempted to replace the remaining busts on the closet's top shelf. In doing so, he pulled the wooden slat from its bracket, sending the entire upper half of Auntie Lil's closet crashing to the floor. Stacks of concealed detective magazines rained down on the poor man's head. He landed on his rump and was buried up to his waist in cheap newsprint.

"I took those to the basement," T.S. whispered. He eyed his aunt sternly.

She lowered her eyelashes, but did not actually attempt to bat them. "I saved them just in time," she whispered back. "That could be a valuable collection one day," she added indignantly. "I've got all of the 1960 issues."

T.S. groaned and helped the detective up from the floor, hastily stacking the magazines title down in an effort to preserve Auntie Lil's reputation. The man was too dazed to notice and spent a quarter of an hour on the couch, recuperating from the blow.

An hour later the search was over. The officers had selected various objects and letters to bring with them—but none with any significance to Max that Auntie Lil could see. "I'm afraid I'm going to have to ask you to come into Manhattan, ma'am," the oldest officer informed her. "The officer in charge of the case would like to question you." He glanced at T.S. "I suggest you bring your lawyer with you."

"My lawyer is on his way back from Aspen. My nephew

here will inform him of your actions. I'll go with you now, however. I wish to speak to the officer in charge."

The cop shrugged and reached for the photo album. "I need to look at that."

She would not hand it over.

"Ma'am, page three of the warrant lists any photographs of you and the deceased together—"

"For God sakes, these photographs are forty years old!" T.S. broke in angrily. "What possible relevance could they have?"

"Sir, page three of the warrant lists—" the detective repeated.

"I'll bring the album myself," Auntie Lil interrupted. She stared the man in the eye.

No one argued.

The officers were not uniformed, but that did not mean that they were unobtrusive. The moment Auntie Lil emerged onto the sidewalk in front of her home flanked by this trio, the entire neighborhood knew that the long arm of the law had reached out to tap Auntie Lil on the shoulder. The teenagers hanging out on her street inched closer and watched as she marched to the unmarked car.

"Whoa, Granny," one called out. "Looks like you been pinched." His companions giggled uneasily—little old ladies were the last bastion of respectability in their world. This was not a sight that they really felt was funny.

Auntie Lil gave the youths a brave smile, modeling it after Ingrid Bergman in *Casablanca*. Her spirit was returning. The victory of the photo album had revived her. She would not let them take Max and their memories away.

2. T.S. was dispatched to the airport to pick up Auntie Lil's lawyer. By the time he arrived at the precinct with

Hamilton Prescott, Auntie Lil had been fingerprinted and installed in an empty interrogation room. No one had even asked her name yet.

"Where is everyone?" T.S. asked his aunt. She was paging through the photo album, running her fingers over photographs of Max.

"They gave up as soon as I got here," she said simply. "I did just what you told me. I said I would say nothing until my lawyer got here." She smiled bravely at T.S.'s companion, who bowed briefly in homage to her good sense.

Hamilton Prescott looked every inch the part of the expensive lawyer. He stood out against the grimy surroundings of Midtown South like a debutante at a convention of shoe salesmen. He was a small man, no more than five and a half feet tall, but extraordinarily dignified. His snow-white hair was abundant and carefully cut to give the impression of order and power. Between Aspen and the station house, he had managed to change into an expensive dark blue suit energized by subtle gray pinstripes. His handkerchief matched his tie.

"Who's in charge of the investigation?" he asked Auntie Lil, placing an ostrich-skin briefcase on the scarred metal table.

"I am," a loud voice interrupted from the door.

"You?" Auntie Lil asked faintly, her heart beating rapidly in her chest.

"Me." A man entered the room with a smile that would have sent small children running for cover. He wore a good suit, but it hung on him badly. He was stout and his belly sagged over his belt as evidence of sedate middle age. He had a large, rounded head and doughy features. Thinning strands of greasy black hair were combed ineffectually over his balding pate in a transparent attempt to hide a receding hairline.

"Lieutenant Abromowitz," T.S. said faintly. He held out a hand. It was gripped in the lieutenant's hammy fist, mechanically pumped and returned slightly mangled.

Lieutenant Abromowitz pulled out a chair. The angry screech of metal legs on linoleum sent a collective wince through the room. "We meet again." He smiled nastily and plopped down across the table from Auntie Lil.

"I should have known," she said. "Midtown South. The White Collar Crime Task Force."

The detective's smile grew thinner. "That was last month. This month I'm back on homicide. Thanks to you."

"To me?"

"Maybe it's more accurate to thank your good friend, the recently deceased Max Rosenbloom. I've been keeping an eye on him through the task force. They consider me something of an expert on Max Rosenbloom. Which is why I'm back on homicide. Specifically—his. Being an expert on Max, I'm a little surprised that your name has never come up in connection with him before. Yet I understand he left you quite a pile. Care to explain who, what, when, and how?"

Hamilton Prescott coughed and produced a business card, presenting it to the lieutenant with a discreet flourish. "We've met, sir," he reminded the detective. "I am, of course, Miss Hubbert's lawyer."

"Of course." Lieutenant Abromowitz flipped the card slowly in his hands without looking at it. He was staring quietly at Auntie Lil, and she did not like it one bit. He looked much too smug for her comfort. He had not even bothered to goad her, and this was most disturbing. He looked like a man who held all the aces on the first draw.

"Are you a criminal defense specialist?" Lieutenant Abromowitz asked Prescott in a cheerful voice.

"No, sir, I am not," the lawyer replied in his faintly Boston accent.

The detective stood up with an elaborately staged yawn. The chair screeched again beneath him. "Then I suggest you find *Miss Hubbert* here someone who is. She's going to need one." He smiled happily at Auntie Lil.

"May I speak to you outside in the hallway?" the lawyer responded firmly. He did not approve of sarcasm.

"Certainly." Lieutenant Abromowitz nodded to Auntie Lil and led Hamilton Prescott out of earshot, down the hallway.

"I don't like this," Auntie Lil whispered to T.S.

"No wonder," T.S. said loudly back.

The next few minutes passed in agonizing slowness. Auntie Lil sat without speaking, the photo album pressed like a talisman against her chest. She could feel her heart beating steadily against the smooth leather. She concentrated on the sensation and it calmed her. Closing her eyes, she imagined Max on his horse, galloping across the desert at sunset. Courage. He had always said that she had more courage than any other human being he had ever known. She would need all of it now.

When her lawyer returned, he was alone. Abromowitz had been persuaded to wait a day, Prescott explained. "They want you to come back tomorrow for questioning."

"You'll be here with me?" Auntie Lil asked.

The lawyer shook his head. "I'm afraid the lieutenant is right, Lillian. You need a criminal defense specialist. I have someone in mind. I'll give her a call this afternoon. I'm sure she'll agree to take on your case once I explain the situation."

"It's a woman?" Auntie Lil said. She felt a little bit better. She'd never had a woman lawyer before and she liked the idea. But then, she'd never been under suspicion of murder, either.

"What have they got?" T.S. asked Hamilton Prescott. "They can't be serious about suspecting Aunt Lil."

"Unfortunately, they can. At least enough to justify questioning her. As the older sister insisted, her fingerprints were indeed found throughout Max Rosenbloom's residence and also in the home belonging to his brother." Prescott stopped and eyed Auntie Lil steadily. "I'm sure there's an explanation for this phenomenon. You'll want to let your new lawyer know."

T.S. was staring steadily at Auntie Lil. "Let me get this straight. Her fingerprints were found in Max's house, and in *Abe* Rosenbloom's?"

"That is correct." Prescott coughed nervously as Auntie Lil turned away from her nephew's furious glare.

"You lied to me," T.S. pointed out indignantly. "See where it's gotten you?"

"Oh, Theodore," she began.

"Don't you 'Oh, Theodore' me. Never again." He lifted a finger, then could not decide what to do with it. He wagged it foolishly in the air. "Never again lie to me, Aunt Lil. I mean it. Don't even think about it. You've really gotten yourself into trouble this time. My God, fingerprinting and everything."

The lawyer cleared his throat nervously. "Actually, they want to fingerprint you as well," he informed T.S. "I would recommend, perhaps, that you not—"

"No need," T.S. interrupted with exaggerated dignity. "They may fingerprint *me* all they want. I am not the sort of person who breaks into other people's homes." He held up his palms. "Ink away."

3.   Herbert Wong could not stand being unable to help Auntie Lil. At the same time he was not given to rash action. This dichotomy translated into a decision to wait for T.S. in the lobby of his Upper East Side apartment. He'd wait all day, if need be, to see if he could be of behind-the-scenes assistance. He was a patient man and had been there for two hours already when T.S. returned from the precinct.

Mahmoud the doorman let T.S. know he had a visitor before he was even out of the cab. "More trouble, Mr. Hubbert?" he asked, raising his eyebrows and wiggling them furiously. It was his idea of discretion. He nodded in the direction of the lobby and T.S. spotted Herbert sitting solemnly on the edge of a small settee.

"Mr. Wong is my friend," T.S. said calmly. "His presence does not necessarily indicate trouble."

Mahmoud shrugged skeptically. "He is also your aunt's friend. And *she* always means trouble. Not that she isn't a most lovely and generous lady." Translation: she was a notorious overtipper and Mahmoud was caught between loyalty to his pocket and allegiance to an actual resident of his beloved building.

T.S. sighed and went to rescue Herbert. If an overly familiar doorman was the price he paid for a rent-controlled apartment that overlooked York Avenue, so be it.

Herbert was resplendent in a shiny black suit and a black T-shirt. No tie. He looked like a guest star on *Miami Vice*. However, as always, his innate dignity transcended his sartorial excess. "T.S." He rose politely and nodded, his head gleaming beneath the lobby lights.

"Herbert." T.S. put an arm around the elderly man's shoulders and led him into the elevator, away from Mahmoud's prying eyes. "We need to talk. Aunt Lil is at this very moment sitting in the offices of a criminal defense specialist. And let's hope that her lawyer is a good one."

Herbert's guilt was overwhelming. Within a few minutes he had confessed his role in the break-in of Abe and Abby

Rosenbloom's home. He was properly repentant and exceedingly angry at himself for having participated in a scheme that ultimately landed Auntie Lil in the soup.

"She is impossible to stop once she gets it in her head to do something," he finished with resignation. "Nonetheless, I must atone for my capriciousness. There must be something I can do to help. If we do not find who really killed Max Rosenbloom, then Lillian may be in grave danger. It is not that I believe the police really suspect her of the murder. It is their desire to quickly wrap up the case that I fear. She might become a scapegoat. All it would take is some common criminal out to get a reduced sentence for his crime by turning into a fake informer. He could say that Lillian hired him to plant the bomb, and who would be able to dispute it?" As his imagination sketched in the scenario he grew increasingly agitated.

T.S. was trying to calm him down when the telephone rang. Herbert glanced at his watch. "She is a very punctual woman," he announced.

"Who is?" T.S. asked.

"Miss Jones. I asked her to contact me here every hour on the hour until we connected."

T.S. groaned. He could tell that his home was going to become Crime Central Station. His perfect order, his harmonious efforts, would be disturbed by frantic doings and chaotic plans.

"I have an idea," Casey told him before T.S. could even say hello. "Can you get to my office within half an hour?"

T.S. looked at his guest. "Herbert and I can get a cab."

"Good. Meet me here." She gave an address in the West Village and hung up before T.S. could protest.

Twenty minutes later T.S. was peering at dingy storefronts in a part of Greenwich Village barely a block from the busy West Side Highway. "This is it," he finally announced, and the cabdriver screeched to a halt in front of a low building.

The Acme Detective Agency had a corner location. Any discretion achieved by the venetian blinds masking the front windows was negated by twelve-foot-high red letters proclaiming ACME INVESTIGATIONS, INC. followed by LICENSED & AFFORDABLE in six-foot blue cursive. A giant gold badge of undetermined origin completed the display.

They were buzzed in the front door by the fattest man that T.S. and Herbert had ever seen. He was perched on a listing wooden office chair, busily jamming a submarine sandwich into his mouth. "She's in the back," he muttered through a thick mouthful of meat and cheese.

They stepped around a trash can filled with ice and cans of beer and explored a small hallway until they found Casey's office cubicle. She was on the telephone and nodded for them to sit and wait. "Look," she yelled into the receiver, "I just take the pictures. If you want to take it out on someone, take it out on your wife." She slammed the phone down and tossed an enlarged color photograph across the desk.

T.S. and Herbert examined it carefully. It showed the extended Rosenbloom family assembled in front of a large stone fireplace. Max Rosenbloom sat in a chair in the center of the front row. His various relatives were gathered around him. Sabrina Rosenbloom was perched on one arm of her husband's chair, but the emotional distance between them was apparent even in a staged photograph.

"What's this?" T.S. asked.

"That's stolen," Casey replied. She grabbed a backpack from a hook on the back of her door. "I knew it would come in handy. Let's go. We'll take my car. My money's on the wife and I intend to nail her."

"Where are we going?" Herbert asked politely as they

raced after a rushing Casey. They passed the enormously fat man in the front office. He did not even look up from his dessert of a small mountain of cheesecake.

"We're going to the Hide-Away Tide-Away Motel in Long Beach," Casey explained. "I followed Sabrina Rosenbloom there a couple of times, once with the dead nephew, Davy. If she was having an affair with Davy, I need more proof. Maybe we'll find a witness or two that we can use to weasel information out of her. I need T.S. for my cover and you can come along for the ride."

4. Herbert waited in the car, while, reluctantly, T.S. agreed to act as if he and Casey were seeking a room for the afternoon.

"I feel so guilty," he admitted. They stepped into a dingy lobby decorated with the pale aqua and anemic orange seen throughout south Florida. The tired nautical theme was continued in a couple of sagging life preservers and a torn net draped over the walls.

"Feeling guilty is part of the appeal," Casey explained. "Try to look really aroused while you're at it." She grinned at him, her cheerfulness dispelling his embarrassment.

"Got a room?" she asked the desk clerk in a businesslike tone. The clerk was a cadaverous youth with pale red hair and very bad skin. His ghostly complexion did little to bolster the seafaring theme.

"Maybe," the kid said in a bored tone. "Got thirty bucks?"

"Thirty bucks?" Casey looked incredulous.

"We're famous," the clerk explained. He gave an unctuous smile.

Suddenly T.S. remembered where he had heard of the Hide-Away Tide-Away Motel before. It had figured promi-

nently in a recent tabloid case involving a sixteen-year-old
girl, a thirty-six-year-old mechanic, and his unsuspecting
wife. The wife had been shot in the face by the teenager
and now mumbled out of the side of her mouth like a gangster in a bad forties movie. The sixteen-year-old had been
installed in an upstate jail, where she endured endless abuse
from other inmates jealous of her media appeal. The mechanic, meanwhile, was tooling around town, proclaiming
his innocence long after anyone ceased to care. The Hide-
Away Tide-Away had been named by the teenager as the
site of their alleged amorous encounters.

"Of course, room nine goes for a little bit more on account of its historic value," the clerk informed T.S., as if he
could read his thoughts.

"I am not paying thirty bucks for a night in this dump,"
Casey told him. "I don't care who's been playing hootchie-
kootchie between your sheets."

"That's thirty bucks for an *hour* in this dump," the clerk
corrected her importantly. He smiled thinly, revealing teeth
that were the color of cardboard.

"An *hour*?" Casey repeated slowly. She pulled a gold
badge from her pocket and flashed it at the suddenly nervous clerk, stashing it back out of sight as quickly as she
had produced it. "I can tell this is a really upscale joint.
You charge extra for clean sheets?"

"I don't want any trouble," the youth said immediately,
his posture correcting to a respectful stance. He held up his
hands in the universal gesture for "It's not my job."

"Good. Then tell me if you've seen any of these people
before." Casey tossed the color photograph on the counter.
"Take your time."

The clerk sucked on his teeth and stared at the photograph thoughtfully, lingering over first one face and then

another. He began to nod his head halfway through the process, as if he had just discovered a great truth about life.

"What?" Casey demanded. "Why are you nodding?"

He touched Sabrina Rosenbloom's face with a tobacco-stained finger. "She's a regular. Comes here a lot. Nice lady."

"Unless you're married to her," Casey pointed out. "Who with?"

"The good-looking guy on the end there." The clerk placed his finger on Davy Rosenbloom's face. "Kinda young for her, not that she's not a babe for an old dame. Of course, you know what they say about men reaching their sexual peak in their twen—"

"Thanks," Casey interrupted before he could get started. "How often did she come here with him?"

The clerk looked perplexed. "Can't say. I only know of one time for sure."

"Are you positive about that?" Casey asked. "Just once?"

"I'm not a video camera," he said defensively.

"Did you ever see her here with anyone else?"

"Well, sure. I said she was a regular."

"What did they look like?" Casey stared at the kid expectantly.

He looked slightly panicked. "I don't know. They looked like *guys*. Lots of guys. Tall, short, fat, thin."

"Any shifty-looking guys?" T.S. asked, ignoring Casey's rolled eyes.

"They were all shifty looking," the clerk explained. "Nervous, like you."

Casey laughed and gave T.S. a meaningful glance that he failed to interpret properly. "Give him forty bucks," she instructed T.S. when he did not move fast enough.

"What?" T.S. asked, placing a hand protectively over his wallet pocket.

"Give him forty bucks," Casey repeated. She slipped the clerk her card as T.S. reluctantly handed over two twenties. "The first twenty is for helping us out today. The second is to keep your mouth shut about this if anyone else comes around asking."

The clerk whisked the money away and examined Casey's card. "I thought you were a cop," he whined.

"Maybe I am," Casey said with a shrug. She flashed him a smile and pulled T.S. from the lobby. "We won't be needing a room after all," she called back. "We kind of lost the mood, know what I mean?" She playfully slipped her arm around T.S.'s waist as they walked back to the car. It was all T.S. could do to keep from blushing.

Herbert was eager for details and T.S. filled him in. T.S. thought they had pulled it off rather nicely, but Casey was dissatisfied. She sulked in the backseat, muttering, as T.S. drove them back toward Manhattan.

"What's the matter?" T.S. asked. "It confirmed what you thought about the widow and Davy."

"Big deal. I already knew they met there once. I need more." She glanced out the window. "I really hate women like that. I'm going to make her pay."

T.S. was silent. He was not a professional like Casey, but even he knew better than to let his personal feelings interfere with his objectivity.

CHAPTER EIGHT

1. The next morning, Auntie Lil could not dissuade Herbert Wong from accompanying her to the police station. "I don't want to involve you," she said.

"You should not be alone," he insisted. "And as T.S. is unable to accompany you, I am going with you."

"I'll be fine. My lawyer is meeting me there." Auntie Lil selected a hat with an enormous cabbage rose on it and fastened it on her head.

"But you should not be alone on the journey there," Herbert explained. "And I am not afraid of the police. They cannot seize me. This is America."

Auntie Lil chose not to enlighten him. It was her opinion that the last flames of U.S. patriotism were fueled by immigrants. She would not be the one to douse the fire.

They were not so insane as to drive into midtown Manhattan on a weekday. Instead, they hailed a cab. As the meter ticked away mercilessly Auntie Lil reminded herself firmly that she could afford it.

Streets with police precincts were the only places in New York where head-in parking was allowed. Patrolmen and detectives could take advantage of this special perk so long as they displayed the proper sticker on the windshields of their private cars. This made the remaining thoroughfare extremely narrow. A single car could block traffic, especially on a workday, when trucks from the nearby garment district clogged the street as well. It was no wonder that a line of cars and trucks began to honk the second that Auntie Lil and Herbert disembarked in front of the entrance to Midtown South on West Thirty-fifth Street. Several motorists revved their engines in vague warning. A large truck made matters—and tempers—worse by cutting into the line behind them.

"Hold your horses," Auntie Lil yelled at the traffic, triggering a fresh round of beeps.

Herbert waited to the side as Auntie Lil paid the driver. The cabbie was afraid she had made a mistake with her generous tip and sped away the instant she told him to keep the change. A gust of wind blew by and Auntie Lil hesitated in the middle of the street, clamping her hat firmly onto her head. Without warning, the truck behind her leaped toward her, bearing down with gear-grinding speed. She froze, transfixed by its size.

"Lillian!" Herbert screamed, springing forward with the quickness of a man a third his age. He knocked her across the lane of traffic and pinned her to the hood of a parked car seconds before the truck roared by. Herbert locked eyes with the driver and then the truck was past. Its sliding back door had jostled open and the bottom half of a rack of swinging clothing could be seen amid a cloud of black exhaust as the vehicle roared down the street and turned a corner.

"Ouch!" Auntie Lil pushed Herbert off and rubbed at her spine. Her hat drooped over one side of her face, hiding her frightened expression.

"That was deliberate," she said. "Someone just tried to kill me."

Herbert looked skeptical. "We must not be too hasty to

reach that conclusion. The driver looked frightened. Perhaps his gas pedal jammed."

"It was deliberate and the driver looked determined, not frightened," Auntie Lil said firmly. "He was a Pakistani, I think. About five-foot-seven, midtwenties, weighed one hundred and fifty pounds, slight mustache, thinning hairline with a long dark ponytail. Dressed in a plaid shirt. Big ears. Couldn't see his pants. Wish I'd gotten a better look."

"What color were his eyes?" Herbert asked in a rare burst of teasing. He was relieved that the incident had not squelched Auntie Lil's spirit.

"I couldn't tell. Probably brown." She stared hard at Herbert. "You don't believe me, do you?"

Herbert bowed slightly. "I am sure you felt it was deliberate," he said enthusiastically, hoping his tone would make up for his lack of conviction. It didn't and he tried again. "I noted the appearance of the truck, should the police require it. It had unusual graffiti—there was a blue moon painted near the cab with the words *Kid Blue and Poppy* near it."

Auntie Lil was not mollified. "If you don't believe me, who will?" she asked, leading the way into the police station.

"About time." Lieutenant Abromowitz was waiting for them at the front desk and led them upstairs into a large interrogation room. One side of the wall was covered with a dusky mirror. Anyone who had ever seen a cop show on television knew that the wall was actually a one-way viewing panel. In fact, the biggest problem that most detectives had was convincing suspects to knock off the grimaces and winks—no one was watching them from the other side. The NYPD had neither the manpower nor the desire to do so.

"Someone tried to run me down," Auntie Lil explained breathlessly. She made a beeline for the one chair that was not cracked. "Right outside your front door."

"Convenient for us," the lieutenant said. "In case we have to investigate, I mean."

"I'm serious." Auntie Lil adjusted her hat and glared at the detective. "Someone just tried to rub me out."

"I can understand the impulse," Lieutenant Abromowitz admitted, smoothing his hair over his growing bald spot. He did not believe a word she said.

"This is not a joking matter," Herbert broke in indignantly.

"Who are you?" Lieutenant Abromowitz fixed him with a bloodshot eye. "Why do you look so familiar?"

He never got his answer. In order to distract the lieutenant, Auntie Lil made a huge fuss over the arrival of her new lawyer. "Sadie!" She rushed to the plump woman's side and escorted her to a chair. "Someone tried to run me down out front."

"What?" Sadie Schwartz automatically pulled a yellow legal pad and pen from her briefcase. As an experienced criminal defense lawyer, she took notes about anything that happened or was said in front of the police. Auntie Lil repeated her information, describing the incident and the truck as best she could. Her lawyer diligently copied it all down.

"Well?" Sadie asked Lieutenant Abromowitz when Auntie Lil was through.

"Well, *what*?" The detective glanced pointedly at the clock. "Do you mind if we get started? You are down here because *I* have a couple of questions."

"My client was attacked," Sadie Schwartz declared indignantly.

Lieutenant Abromowitz sighed. "Listen, I've known this sweet little old lady here for a couple of years now, while you've only known her a couple of hours. So I'm going to give you a break and humor you about the whole thing and tell you that you are free to file a report *after* we are done with questioning today. But I think you should know right now that this particular little old lady sees murder, mayhem, mystery, and conspiracies in everything. Trouble follows her around like a cloud."

Sadie looked at Auntie Lil for confirmation.

"I follow *it*," Auntie Lil corrected him with as much dignity as she could muster. "It does not follow me."

Sadie capped her pen and sighed, then began to pull various stacks of paper from her briefcase. "I just want to remind you of a few things before we begin," she informed Lieutenant Abromowitz. What followed was a lengthy reading of statutes and court decisions concerning the expanded rights of suspects under questioning versus the rights of witnesses being interviewed. She was astutely attempting to force a decision from the lieutenant: was Auntie Lil considered a witness with information valuable to the investigation of Max Rosenbloom's death, or was she actually under suspicion of murder herself? It was a clever move on her part and a devil's bargain for Lieutenant Abromowitz. He'd have to show his cards or there would be legal hell to pay.

Auntie Lil grasped this within seconds and beamed at her lawyer. Sadie Schwartz was not a tall woman, but she carried a lot of weight nimbly on a slight frame. It did not slow her down. She was a human cannonball. Her head was small and rounded, and her hair was a neat cap of sleek black. Her features were small and sharp, particularly her penetrating eyes. She wore a pair of small gold-rim glasses on a cord around her neck but never seemed to use them. They dangled over her ample bosom and expensive dress in lieu of jewelry. As a defense lawyer, there were few better choices than Sadie Schwartz: she was tough enough to handle the most truculent defendant, but capable of looking like everyone's mom when the need arose.

"Okay, okay." Lieutenant Abromowitz finally held up his hands in defeat, stemming the flow of court decisions. "Miss

Hubbert is not actually a suspect at this time. She is a material witness that we believe may be concealing information crucial to the motive behind Max Rosenbloom's death."

Satisfied, Sadie nodded for the detective to continue. "Don't say a word until I give the okay," she instructed Auntie Lil.

Auntie Lil nodded obediently and waited for the onslaught to begin.

"Why did Max Rosenbloom call you the morning of his death?"

"I don't know," Auntie Lil admitted. "He didn't say." She paused. "It was very personal. He said he needed to talk to me. He never arrived, of course."

"You haven't seen him in twenty years, and he just calls up and says he's coming over?" Lieutenant Abromowitz asked skeptically.

"That is correct," Auntie Lil said softly. "That was Max."

"But if you had not seen him in so long, why are your fingerprints all over his house? Not to mention his brother's house?" The detective smiled thinly.

Herbert Wong shifted ever so slightly in his chair, a small wave of discomfort rippling the surface of his usual calm.

"You're not going to believe this, but . . ." Auntie Lil began, falling back on the most pitiful of clichés. She went on to describe her encounter with Rebecca Rosenbloom and the offering of the keys. "I have them right here," she announced dramatically in response to the detective's lack of enthusiasm for her tale. She hauled her enormous pocketbook onto the table and began to search. Unfortunately, the keys had fallen into the considerable depths of her purse and she was forced to stack a variety of objects in front of her as Lieutenant Abromowitz watched: a box of colored pencils, numerous memo pads, a trio of fountain pens, a true-crime paperback she'd been meaning to read, a clear plastic box containing a molar pulled during her last dentist's visit, an extra pair of sweat socks in case her feet got wet, four half-eaten rolls of chocolate candies (each with a different flavor center), long-forgotten reminder notes hastily scribbled on scraps of scratch paper, a pair of reading glasses, an electronic Rolodex that she did not know how to use, an electronic video game that she did know how to use, a napkin she had accidently stolen several weeks before while dining out at a restaurant, her black beret, two packs of tissues, five sets of unidentified keys, a bottle of aspirin, a small photograph of Max she had taken to carrying over the last three days, an unused portable cosmetic kit given to her by a niece last Christmas, a checkbook plus three books of checks with starting numbers hundreds of digits apart, six credit cards, a tattered driver's license, and—at long last— the set of keys belonging to Rebecca Rosenbloom.

Lieutenant Abromowitz waited calmly while the pile mounted. He had viewed the internal madness of her pocketbook on prior occasions. But Sadie Schwartz could not hide her astonishment or resist the temptation to peek inside her own comparatively barren briefcase during the ceremony.

Lieutenant Abromowitz took the keys and examined them carefully. "We'll have to check the story out."

"She's going to deny it," Auntie Lil protested. "She hates me. Max left me all of his money."

"I know," the detective said. "Which brings me to the next question. *Why?*"

Thus began a series of probing questions about Auntie Lil's life and Max Rosenbloom. Some of the questions were extremely personal in nature, but Auntie Lil answered them all. The detective made it easier for her. Either Lieutenant Abromowitz had been attending sensitivity seminars or Sadie Schwartz was having an impact. He remained respectful, did not push, and confined his facial expressions to an occasional raising of an eyebrow. All went well until about an hour into the inquest.

"How long have you been associated with V.J. Productions?" he said.

"What?" Auntie Lil asked. The sudden change of subject confused her.

"V.J. Productions, Inc.," Abromowitz repeated impatiently. "We know that you're an officer of the company. How long have you been one?"

"An officer?"

Sadie gently nudged her with a foot, but this did not slow Auntie Lil down. "I have absolutely no idea what you are talking about," she said. "I am not the officer of any corporation, and I am not involved in production anymore. I retired twenty years ago, young man."

"Oh?" He pulled several photostats of tax forms from a pile.

"I work during the busy seasons now and then," she conceded. "But not for a company called V.J. Productions."

The lieutenant raised an eyebrow and stared, his upper lip quivering with the scent of his prey. "We have the evidence, Miss Hubbert," he said evenly. "We've traced an entire series of holding companies backward. Your name is all over the corporate resolutions."

Auntie Lil locked eyes with her lawyer. "I have never heard of this company in my life," she insisted, although a nagging voice inside her head said otherwise.

"You've made a mistake," Sadie told Lieutenant Abromowitz firmly.

"I don't think so." He shuffled his sheaf of papers and extracted several computer printouts. "Our investigation shows that Max Rose Fashions made regular payments to a vendor named V.J. Productions, Inc., over the past year for a total sum in excess of one point one million dollars. But we can't seem to find any evidence of a service or product provided in payment for that money, nor has the company filed corporate taxes during that time. Since Miss Hubbert here is company president, I thought perhaps she could explain."

"*President?* I most certainly am not. I have no idea what you are talking about."

Lieutenant Abromowitz banged his fist on the table in sudden fury and raised his voice to an angry growl. "I'm talking about blackmail, Miss Hubbert. Systematic extortion of money from the man that you claim to have loved."

"I am not a black—"

"You said my client was a potential witness, not a suspect," Sadie interrupted.

"She is. She's a potential witness in the murder of Max Rosenbloom. And our number-one suspect in the extortion of him prior to his death."

"She's neither," a confident voice interrupted from the doorway. A small man stood framed by the steel door; his thick brown hair and abundant beard gave off red highlights under the glow of the overhead bulb. He looked to be in his midthirties. His hair was lightly touched with gray and combed back from an oval face softened by a trace of laugh wrinkles around a pair of watery blue eyes. He was dressed neatly in a gray suit and wore a regulation blue necktie.

The fact that all eyes were upon him did nothing to ruffle his innate composure. He stepped briskly into the room and handed Lieutenant Abromowitz a business card. A gold-stamped embossing of an official seal in one corner glinted under the overhead lights. Lieutenant Abromowitz stared at the card and said nothing.

"I've been explaining the situation to your commander," the newcomer told Abromowitz in an apologetic tone.

When the detective still did not speak, the man nodded politely to Auntie Lil's entourage and produced another card for Sadie Schwartz's benefit.

"Special Agent Frank O'Conner," he explained. He bowed his head slightly toward Auntie Lil. "Miss Hubbert, I am an assistant U.S. attorney with the Federal Task Force on Organized Crime. We'll be taking over control of the investigation into the death of Mr. Rosenbloom as it overlaps with an ongoing investigation currently being conducted by my office. I'd like to apologize for your treatment here today. I'd also like to ask you a few questions myself. You are under no suspicion whatsoever in the death of Max Rosenbloom."

"Certainly," Auntie Lil replied, relief flooding through her. Here was order, here was calm. Better yet—here was the power of the entire federal government bowing to her.

"You say that an attempt was made on your life an hour ago? In front of this precinct?"

Auntie Lil hesitated. So someone had been watching her from behind the one-way mirrored wall after all. "That is correct," she finally said.

"Can you tell me what the truck and driver looked like?" O'Conner asked.

Lieutenant Abromowitz marched from the room.

2. T.S. was both disgruntled and disappointed. He was disgruntled because he had been forced to skip Auntie Lil's interrogation session due to a prior legal appointment. He had spent the last three hours with a mealymouthed lawyer being advised of options, given Max Rosenbloom's surprising will. He was tired of lawyers and longed to converse with a human being who did not end every statement with multiple-clause qualifiers. And so he had called Lilah at her vacation home in Maine.

Only now he was disappointed because, after his weeks of waiting for Lilah to return to New York, she was not coming. And it was all his fault. His mention of organized crime was keeping her firmly in the North Woods.

"Theodore?" Her husky voice hesitated. "This time Auntie Lil has gone too far."

"We're not really involved. The police have it under control."

"Organized crime? I don't think so." There was a silence. "Do you think they know who you are?" she asked.

"I don't know. I don't even know if organized crime has anything to do with Max's death. It's just a rumor."

"Oh, Theodore. Don't be naive. Of course organized crime is involved. If you *think* they're involved, they are involved. It's the first law of New York City. I know. I own six service businesses myself. It's a constant battle to keep their influence at bay. I'm very worried. About you. About your safety."

It was gratifying to hear her worry about him, but less gratifying that she was staying in Maine for another few weeks. "Come up here," she urged him. "We could spend a few weeks alone. Let this whole thing blow over."

It was tempting. He had been so emotionally isolated from others during the first fifty-five years of his life that everything he did with Lilah had an intoxicating newness. Two weeks together would be a tonic for the sadness that overwhelmed the Rosenbloom mess. He could use Lilah's calm support, especially after the strain of watching Aunt Lil struggle over Max's death.

Aunt Lil. He could not leave her to face the police or the Rosenblooms alone.

"I can't," he told Lilah reluctantly. "Aunt Lil needs me.

In fact, she's downtown being questioned now. With her lawyer. Prescott recommended a criminal defense specialist. I'm supposed to meet her in an hour."

"Oh, Theodore. Please promise me that you'll be careful."

"I promise."

"I don't trust you. I'm sending Grady to keep an eye on you." Grady was her chauffeur, a huge Irishman of indeterminate criminal background. He had reformed after a tumultuous youth on Manhattan's West Side and a cooling-off stint in Ireland. He was now zealously loyal to Lilah. T.S. wasn't so sure that this loyalty extended to him.

"I don't need a chauffeur to look after me," he protested.

"You need Grady," she overruled him. "He can be there in an hour. He's at the Connecticut house right now."

T.S. did not argue. Lilah was right about one thing: he and Auntie Lil were in over their heads. They could use all the help they could get.

3. "Why would someone go to the trouble of putting your name on a dummy corporation?" Agent Frank O'Conner asked Auntie Lil. "We've traced the filings. Someone was in a hurry. It was all done over the past week. It started right after Max's death. There were payoffs to backdate the documents. Who would want to hurt you?"

"I don't know," Auntie Lil admitted.

"It had to be someone at Max Rose who was setting you up to take the fall for them. What did you have to do with Max Rose Fashions?" O'Conner asked.

"Nothing," Auntie Lil said. "Nothing at all."

Agent O'Conner extracted a black-and-white photograph from his briefcase and slid it across the table to her.

"That's me," Auntie Lil exclaimed, examining the glossy image. It showed her leaving Max Rose Fashions several days before. She was clutching her hat to her head and peering up at the sky.

"It certainly is you. We've been watching his offices off and on for about six months now. We picked you up as you were leaving it on Tuesday. Know that guy?" O'Conner pointed out a stocky guy in a windbreaker leaning against the front window of the deli two doors down.

"No."

"You should. He's been tailing you since the day after the funeral. Him or a buddy."

"What?" Sadie Schwartz glared at the special agent. "My client's life has been in danger and you've been letting it happen?"

Irritation flickered across the special agent's face, then disappeared, banished under a supremely trained degree of self-control. "How would I know he was following her, unless we were following *him*?" O'Conner tapped the man's face methodically and Auntie Lil pulled it toward her for a closer look. He had a broad face with thick features and a nose that had clearly been broken. His thick head of hair stuck out in a halo of frizzy curls.

"Bad perm," Auntie Lil observed.

"Bad guy," the agent answered.

"What else do you know about my client?" Sadie demanded. "I will advise her to withhold all cooperation until you tell us what's going on."

"This man works for Joseph Galvano," Frank O'Conner said, running a thumb over the frizzy-haired image in the photograph. "Ever heard of him?"

Auntie Lil shook her head. Sadie frowned.

Herbert looked stricken. "Joey 'the Snake' Galvano," he muttered quietly.

"Correct. The Romeo of organized crime. Can't keep his hands off the ladies, especially when they're married to someone else. But that is not your problem here." O'Conner watched Auntie Lil carefully. "I don't want to alarm you, Miss Hubbert, but we've had taps on Galvano's phone lines for some time now. That's all I can tell you. Someone who works for him has been calling you over the past few days at your apartment. Maybe to see if you're home. Maybe just to scare you. Who knows? The point is—if they have your phone number and have been following you, they know where you live."

"They're going to harm me?" Auntie Lil asked.

The agent shrugged. "I certainly think that they will try to make contact with you."

"Why?" Sadie asked.

"Why?" Agent O'Conner stared hard at Auntie Lil. "Ask Miss Hubbert here."

"I have absolutely no idea," Auntie Lil protested.

Agent O'Conner was quiet for a moment, then spoke directly to Auntie Lil. "Maybe you really don't know anything about Max Rosenbloom and his business. Frankly, neither do we. At least not much—and we've been watching him on and off for a long time now. Ever since he testified two years ago. He may be clean. But someone at that company isn't. We've followed Galvano's men to the factory many times. That's how we picked up you. The point is that it sure *seems* to us, and probably to Galvano, as if you do know something. And that could be very dangerous."

"Why would they think that Lillian knows anything?" Herbert asked.

The agent shrugged. "Why did the lieutenant who was here earlier suspect you?" he asked reasonably.

"Because I discovered the body at the bottom of the grave, I suppose," Auntie Lil answered. "When no one else would have noticed. Because Max was on his way to see me when he died. So it looked as if he had something very important to tell me. Because Max left me his money, making it seem as if we had been much closer in recent years than we had." She hesitated, then continued: "And maybe because I . . . visited his house and that of his brother. Under the cover of darkness, shall we say."

"As if you were looking for something," Agent O'Conner pointed out.

"But I didn't know what I was looking for," she protested.

"You know that. I know that, if I give you the benefit of the doubt. But Galvano doesn't know that. All he knows is that Max may have told you something you shouldn't have heard. And that you've been snooping around Max's office and home ever since."

"How could he know I was snooping in Max's offices? All he knows is I went inside the building," Auntie Lil pointed out. "I could have been expressing my condolences to the staff."

The agent pulled a small tape recorder from his briefcase and placed it in the center of the table. "Remember this?" He pressed a button and the tinny sounds of a recorded telephone conversation filled the room.

"What?" a crabby voice asked after picking up the telephone. Auntie Lil recognized the voice as her own.

"I'm going to be a few minutes late," a male voice answered gruffly.

"That's Joey Galvano," the agent interjected. "*That's* how he knows you were snooping."

"Listen, I need to know right now if they asked about V.J. Productions," Galvano continued on the tape.

"What?" Auntie Lil snarled back on the tape, following it with a cough to disguise her voice.

"Don't get cute," Galvano warned. "Did they ask about V.J. or not?"

"No!" Auntie Lil yelled back. The sound of the phone being slammed down ended the recorded conversation.

"I had no idea who was calling or why. I was just fishing," she explained.

The agent nodded toward the tape. "Unfortunately, you forgot to tell Mr. Galvano that you were just fishing. The truck incident this morning may have been an accident. Or it may have been a misguided attempt by one of his men to take care of the problem for him. I tend to think it was the latter."

"What are you saying?" Sadie Schwartz demanded.

"I'm saying that whether or not Miss Hubbert here is suspected by the cops isn't important. What's important is that she's suspected by Galvano and his men. And that's what you should be worried about."

4.   Casey followed T.S. into the bedroom and threw herself across his bed. She had grown increasingly agitated since their trip to the motel the day before. Now she seemed positively possessed by the Rosenbloom case. "We're missing something," she said, picking at the textured surface of his hand-loomed Irish bedspread.

"Casey—please. I'm trying to concentrate." T.S. scrutinized his tie rack, his annoyance mounting. He hated Lilah not coming. He hated the thought of being responsible for all of Max's money. Most of all, he hated having his routine interrupted. Already he was late meeting Aunt Lil, then Casey had barged in after flirting her way past Mahmoud. And where the hell was Grady anyway? He'd never meet up with Aunt Lil if this kept up. He might as well face the truth. He was under siege, his orderly life turned upside down by a useless doorman, a criminally inclined chauffeur, and an overexcited private detective.

"Don't you see the significance of it?" Casey insisted. She hopped up from the bed and modestly smoothed her dress down over her generous thighs.

Good Lord. T.S. took a minute to examine her outfit. How could he have missed it before? She was wearing a tight green dress accented along the bottom hem with fake leopard fur. She wore a leopard-skin pillbox hat that matched the trim.

"Like it?" Casey asked, whirling around to give him the full effect. "Belonged to a neighbor who died a couple weeks ago. I had to clean up the place. Yuk. But there was some cool stuff in the closet. It's the real thing, you know. Not a reproduction. From about 1962, I'd say."

"Just don't let Auntie Lil see it," T.S. warned wearily. "She dresses strangely enough as it is." He selected a conservative tie to complement his conservative suit, which matched his conservative shoes. The perfect outfit for crossing your fingers and hoping your aunt doesn't get indicted.

"Just listen to me," Casey insisted again, back to business. "We have to take a closer look at the family. Let the cops take a look at the Mob."

"Why's that?" He'd had enough of looking at Rosenblooms.

"I don't know why yet. That's why I'm here. I thought you could help."

"Can't help. You'll have to get in line. Auntie Lil has dibs on me. She's at the police station right now."

"Great. I'll go with you."

He suppressed a groan. His apartment had been invaded by this sleazily exotic woman and there was nothing he could do about it. Worst of all, his cats loved her. Brenda and Eddie crept out from beneath the bed to sashay about Casey's ankles. They stood on their hind legs and sniffed anxiously at the fur trim of her dress.

"Ugh," Casey said. "I hate cats."

"That explains it," T.S. replied. He picked up both pets and marched them into the living room.

5. "He's going to try to set up a meeting to talk to you," Agent O'Conner explained.

"How do you know?" Sadie demanded.

The special agent shrugged wearily. "Because we have him bugged out the wazoo, okay? Enough said. I personally heard his voice saying not two hours ago that his men should hold off on 'any action' until he has a chance to talk to you."

"Any action?" Herbert asked faintly. "That sounds ominous."

"I'm glad at least one of you grasps the seriousness of the situation." Agent O'Conner snapped his briefcase shut grumpily. He had expected the old lady to cooperate at once, but she was turning into a handful at a time when he already had his hands full.

"My client is not wearing a wire," Sadie said firmly. "Too dangerous."

"I'm not asking your client to wear a wire," O'Conner said. "We're not in the habit of forcing little old ladies to entrap criminals, okay?"

"There's no need to get excited, young man," Auntie Lil pointed out. "Or to call me a little old lady."

"My apologies." The agent paused. "I want this man very badly, Miss Hubbert. Everyone in this city seems to think he's some sort of benevolent godfather, a colorful character who pays for great fireworks on the Fourth of July. The truth is that Joseph Galvano is an amoral, selfish, dangerous sociopath. He floods the city with drugs and could care less if grammar-school children buy them, so long as they're not his children. He kills whenever the whim strikes him, extorts money from hardworking businessmen, and makes fun of his supporters behind their backs. I am taking this creep down if it is the last thing I do on this earth. And, believe me, that's a very real possibility."

Auntie Lil decided she liked Special Agent O'Conner very much indeed. "What exactly do you want me to do?" she asked.

"I want you to meet with him if he asks. In his car in a public place. We have his car bugged. We'll be just a few feet away from you at all times. You won't be in any danger, I can promise you that. We've covered every contingency."

"Then why even bother to tell me?" Auntie Lil asked. "It might have been better if I hadn't even known."

The special agent stared at Auntie Lil. "I'm telling you so that you'll agree to meet with him. Are you telling *me* that you would have agreed to meet Joey Galvano without police protection or knowing what it was that he wanted?"

"Maybe," Auntie Lil admitted.

"You'll do it, then?" Agent O'Conner asked. "We expect him to try to set something up within a day or two."

"Of course," Auntie Lil answered, but even her loud voice was drowned out by her lawyer's.

"*Maybe* she'll do it," Sadie said. "But I don't like this car idea."

"It has to be his car," O'Conner explained. "That or his club. Those are the only two scenarios that we have wired. And the club is out. Too dangerous. Too many exits and entrances and inside hallways. In the car, we can surround and follow, if need be."

This last sentence was met by silence as Auntie Lil contemplated the implications.

"What exactly do you expect her to accomplish?" Sadie finally asked.

"Just talk to him," Agent O'Conner explained. "About Max and his murder. You can be very upset, if you want. Cry even. He's a sucker for tears."

"That shouldn't be hard," Auntie Lil interrupted in steely tones.

The agent nodded an apology and continued. "The point is, he's usually very, very careful about who he talks to and what he talks about. This is one of the first times he's decided to take care of something himself. It's probably your age, Miss Hubbert. No offense. Galvano has a soft spot for his mother and older ladies, at least when he's not putting the moves on them. He'll be very respectful. I think he just wants to know if Max ever mentioned him to you or mentioned him in connection with his nephew Davy. That nephew's name has been coming up a lot. The point is: You listen, he talks. You talk, he listens. We'll see what we can get."

"We'll expect full immunity in return," Sadie said crisply, pulling her legal pad toward her. "Federal and state. You can do it, so don't tell me you can't. My secretary will send you a preliminary agreement tomorrow morning. Nothing goes down until that's been settled."

"Agreed." As the agent shook hands with Auntie Lil a commotion in the hall interrupted them.

"Seeing as how you're taking over the case, I brought you some new suspects," Lieutenant Abromowitz announced from the doorway. "The more the merrier." He gestured for Casey Jones and T.S. to enter, taking great pleasure in his petty revenge. "Not interrupting, am I?"

"Aunt Lil." T.S. stared at Frank O'Conner. "What's going on?"

No one answered.

Casey was lingering in the doorway, watching a trio of officers walk down the hall. "I love men in uniform," she announced with enthusiasm, breaking the silence.

"Oh, yeah?" Lieutenant Abromowitz puffed up his chest.

She stared him up and down. "You're not in uniform." She stepped around him as if he were a tree in her way and plopped down in a chair across from Special Agent O'Conner. "What's going on?" Casey demanded. "Why did this goon drag us up here?" She pointed a thumb at Abromowitz, who was lurking in the doorway still trying to think of a snappy comeback.

"Thank you, Lieutenant," Agent O'Conner said pleasantly. "I'll take it from here."

Casey flashed O'Conner an interested grin and the agent squirmed uncomfortably. When he realized she was checking his bare hands for evidence of a wedding ring, he hid his hands in his lap and turned his full attention to T.S.

"Mr. Hubbert," he said, offering T.S. his business card.

"How did you know who I am?" T.S. demanded, ignoring the card.

"As I was telling your aunt . . ." Agent O'Conner began, but his voice trailed off as he finally broke down under the pressure of Casey's unceasing scrutiny. "I don't believe I know you," he said faintly, staring uneasily at her.

"You're *federal*, aren't you?" Casey cried, leaning forward and cupping her face in her hands. She gazed at him with adoration. "I just *love* the feds."

Special Agent Frank O'Conner flushed a deep pink.

Herbert Wong began to laugh ever so quietly. It sounded like coffee percolating over a distant campfire.

CHAPTER NINE

1. T.S. was adamant. If Auntie Lil was meeting with Galvano in his car, the rendezvous had to take place in as safe a spot as possible. And Herbert Wong had to be nearby. Frank O'Conner thought this last request absurd: what could one elderly Asian man do that six trained agents could not?

"You'd be surprised," T.S. said, and stuck to his demands.

O'Conner came up with a counterdemand: Casey had to butt out. He would not discuss the plan in front of her. Whether this stemmed from personal discomfort or professional caution was impossible to tell. But Casey took the news cheerfully and announced that she thought they were all wasting their time anyway. She would head out to Long Island and spend a few days tailing various Rosenblooms.

After much debate, it was decided that Auntie Lil would ask to meet in Galvano's car in front of the Federal Courthouse in lower Manhattan. It was also agreed that Agent O'Conner would look the other way should Herbert Wong happen to be standing nearby disguised as a Sabrett hotdog man. But, O'Conner warned them, Herbert was not to attempt to take any action under any circumstances. And he was on his own so far as a costume and props were concerned. Herbert agreed and set off in search of a cart.

"Will Galvano meet me in front of the courthouse?" Auntie Lil asked.

"He'll agree," O'Conner said. "It's not like he keeps out of sight. He knows he's got nothing to worry about, and he wants information from you. He owns more lawyers than your average midtown firm."

The special agent was correct. Two days later, just before eleven o'clock in the morning, Auntie Lil received a phone call from a man identifying himself as an associate of Joseph Galvano. Would she care to meet with Mr. Galvano and discuss the late Max Rosenbloom? "Mr. Galvano has details about his death that he thinks you might want to hear," the caller said. "He doesn't trust the police. Thinks you ought to hear it from him."

"In that case, he can call me himself," Auntie Lil said, hanging up. She was only halfway through her third cup of coffee and hence a little grumpy.

Two more cups of coffee later he called. "Miss Hubbert?" a deep voice asked. Yes, she decided, it had been Galvano calling Joyce Carruthers several days before. Only then he had been rude and demanding. Today he was oily and far too nice.

"Is this Miss Lillian Hubbert?" Galvano asked when she hesitated.

He'd been listening to too many Tony Bennett records, she decided. His voice was a bad imitation of the singer's. Only completely without warmth. "Yes, it is. Who is this?"

"This is Joseph Galvano. Do I need to say more?"

"Yes, young man, you do. Who are you and what do you want?" Auntie Lil knew that the conversation was being monitored and that Agent O'Conner would not be happy with her attitude. But she didn't care. Auntie Lil had assured him that a little-old-lady pose would not fly. Galvano was no fool, she pointed out. He already knew she wasn't the type. More important, she felt safer being herself.

"Who am I?" Galvano asked hesitantly.

"Yes. Who are you?"

"I'm a businessman." He recovered smoothly. "I did business with Max Rosenbloom."

"He never mentioned you," she said.

"You talked to him about business a lot?"

"Not at all. But I'm not unfamiliar with the industry and I don't recall your name. Do you own a company I might recognize?"

Galvano attempted a low chuckle. The effect was ominous. It sounded like dice rattling in his throat. "Perhaps I did not make myself clear. I am not in the same business as Mr. Rosenbloom. I am more of an . . . entrepreneur, shall we say." When this comment was met by silence, he pressed on. "I'm sure you've heard of me, Miss Hubbert. Joseph Galvano?" More silence. "Joey Galvano? Joey 'the Snake' Galvano?"

"Oh." Auntie Lil let him sweat for another second. "*That* Joseph Galvano."

"Yes," he said, relieved. "That Joseph Galvano."

"Well, Mr. Snake, what is it that you want from me?"

He let it pass. "I thought we should meet. Swap memories of Max. Discuss some points of mutual interest. Perhaps I could even shed some light on his unfortunate passing. I understand you'll be taking over his business."

"Possibly. I have inherited control of his estate and one-fifth of his company. Whether or not I'll be taking over the business is a different matter entirely."

"All the more reason to talk. You could use an ally at this time."

And you could use a good electric chair, she thought to herself.

"Where and when?" she asked politely. "There's no harm in talking."

He chuckled. "No harm at all."

"Just the same, since you are *that* Joseph Galvano, I'd feel much safer if we kept it informal and in a very public place."

"I own a club and you want to meet in a public place?" he said in mock dismay.

"Very public," she answered crisply.

"There's public and there's public, Miss Hubbert," Galvano protested. "I can't be standing around in the middle of wide-open spaces. It's bad for my personal safety, if you understand me."

"I understand you. Your car, then. I assume you have a car and driver."

"I do. Shall I pick you up at your apartment?" he offered.

"I don't think so. I'll meet you somewhere where I would feel safe."

"Please, Miss Hubbert." His feelings were hurt. "I am not in the habit of harming old ladies. You have nothing to fear from me."

"Nor you from me. Therefore, let's make it in front of the Federal Courthouse on Chambers Street. Tomorrow afternoon? We can sit there and chat for a few minutes."

He was silent for a moment. She was afraid that she'd been too bold. "Okay," he finally conceded. "That's very clever of you. If you feel that you need half of the world to see you get into my car, have it your way. As I say, you have nothing to fear. I am a legitimate businessman. I'll pull up in front of the courthouse at one o'clock. I've got tinted windows, so keep an eye out. All right?"

He was polite, she noticed. But he also had to be the one

giving orders in the end. "Certainly, Mr. Snake," she agreed. "I look forward to our meeting."

Ten minutes later the phone rang again. " *'Mr. Snake'?* " a sputtering voice asked.

"Agent O'Conner. Lovely to hear from you. I thought everything went according to plan, didn't you?"

" 'Mr. Snake'? Miss Hubbert—don't play around with this guy. Just listen to him, get him to talk as much as possible. And then get out. I'm having second thoughts as it is."

"Don't you worry, Agent O'Conner. I'm going to be fine." Auntie Lil hung up, hoping it was true. She had decided that the scariest thing about Joseph Galvano was how much like the rest of the world he seemed.

2. By noon, Herbert was parked outside the Federal Courthouse, mustard bottle in one hand and hotdog fork in the other. He'd had a little trouble with the regular vendor, who had refused to move from the corner until Herbert slipped him fifty dollars. "Just go down one block," Herbert urged him. "Just for today. You'll make more money there anyway. It's criminal court. They eat more hot dogs."

The stout man accepted this logic and wheeled down the block. Like most New Yorkers, he was happy to have his extra fifty and vamoose.

Business was brisk and a line soon formed. Herbert was so busy juggling hot sausages with all-beef frankfurters that he started to worry about missing Auntie Lil. He needn't have. She was in line demanding a hot dog with all the trimmings half an hour before the appointed meeting time.

"He may have men watching," Herbert muttered as he piled sauerkraut on her hot dog.

"A little more of that please, Herbert. Don't worry. Everything is under control."

"No doubt." He bowed slightly as she walked away, munching on her hot dog. Now, *that* was a woman, he thought to himself for at least the hundredth time.

Just before one o'clock, Herbert noticed an alarming increase in his business. It seemed as if scores of men and women were waiting in line, demanding knishes, more mustard, less fried onions, extra napkins, and more. "What in the world is going on?" he wondered as he hurried to meet their demands.

What was going on was that Agent O'Conner had called in a few favors. Half of the federal workforce in lower Manhattan had conspired to keep Herbert too busy to get into any trouble. O'Conner had bribed several offices full of allies to a free lunch at Herbert's cart. Their only task was to keep Herbert busy. A free lunch was a free lunch and they happily complied—some of them twice.

T.S. knew this because he was sitting in a sound truck next to Agent O'Conner. It was disguised as a Con Ed vehicle and pulled up next to another van parked by a gaping hole in the street nearby. "This is a little obvious," he muttered, staring anxiously out the tinted back windows of the truck. Joey Galvano had not yet arrived. He could barely see the tip of the feather that festooned Auntie Lil's enormous hat as it poked above the portal window of the courthouse door.

"Relax," O'Conner assured him. "We're parked above a legitimate electrical problem and those are real electricians working below us. Con Ed has been trying to fix this junction for over a week. It's our best bet for picking up what they say."

The inside of the van was lined with digital recording equipment. Any wall or floor space remaining was well carpeted. T.S. and Agent O'Conner sat with their backs against the rear doors, watching two technicians adjust dials and check sound levels.

"Put it on the speaker, okay?" O'Conner told his men. "But give me the extra headphones."

"If we can get anything, I will," the bigger of the two technicians growled. He had worn a perpetual scowl ever since T.S. had been introduced. Listening to crooks enjoy the high life probably irritated him, and T.S. could not blame him for it.

"I thought you said this was going to be easy," T.S. said, eyeing the technician anxiously.

"It will be. Bobby's just a pessimist. Right, Bob?" Agent O'Conner said.

"Yeah, I'm a pessimist," Bobby agreed sourly. "And I'm also a realist. The mike in his car should have been replaced two weeks ago. I'm telling you, it's ready to go." He held up a hand for silence. "I'm starting to pick something up. I think they're getting close. But we're going to need a new bug in the limo soon. Better tell Hank."

"How did you bug his car?" T.S. whispered. Excitement and fear gripped his stomach like a vise. The wait was excruciating.

Agent O'Conner smiled thinly. "We have our ways," he tersely replied.

3. Herbert was really annoyed now. He saw the limousine approach slowly and the tinted windows confirmed his suspicion that this was Galvano. But his attention was being diverted by a tall man in a shabby blue suit who was demanding more sauerkraut. What was the big deal about sauerkraut anyway? Good heavens, people were picky.

He'd always just asked for the works and been happy with whatever he got.

Auntie Lil saw the limousine as well. She stood in the rotunda of the courthouse and carefully adjusted the brim of her hat. It was lilac, with an abundant arrangement of silk spring flowers blooming about the brim. Brightly colored feathers cascaded down over her left ear, including one long blue plume that rested on her shoulder. It matched her flowered shawl very nicely. More to the point, it concealed a small voice-activated tape recorder taped to the inside of the brim. She didn't care what Agent O'Conner said. She was making her own record of the meeting. She had lined the inside of the hat with matching silk. Even if she had to take it off, she'd be fine. He'd have to probe it with his fingers to find the device.

She took a deep breath and moved slowly down the courthouse stairs. The driver hopped out of the car and waited for her approach. He nodded as he opened the back door for her. She could feel the driver's tightly coiled biceps as she brushed past: no amount of grooming could conceal his animal power.

"Miss Hubbert. A pleasure to meet you indeed." Joseph Galvano's smile belonged in a toothpaste ad. For morticians. He was a handsome man, tall and slender with abundant black hair that was brushed loosely off his face. Touches of gray at the temples lent respectability. There was not a drop of hair oil in sight. He had delicate angular features, with a long narrow nose and thin lips. His cheekbones were slightly higher than normal, lending his face a hint of the Far East. His deep tan added to this impression.

What we have here, Auntie Lil decided, is a modern Genghis Khan.

"Mr. Snake," she said, shaking his hand. She was glad she had worn gloves.

"Please," he said smoothly. "Call me Joey." His suggestion had more than a bit of steel in it. Auntie Lil took the hint.

"How about Joseph," she suggested. "It becomes you, I think."

He smiled thinly in reply, and she got the impression that the Grim Reaper probably grinned a whole lot like that. "Fine," he said. "I'm glad you agreed to this little meeting. I've been curious to meet you ever since I heard that Max left his fortune to you."

"I didn't realize that was public knowledge," she answered evenly.

"I have lots of friends," Galvano explained. "I usually hear things first."

"Is that so?" Auntie Lil adjusted her hat on her head so that it drooped over the back of the seat. "Don't want to crush the flowers," she explained.

"Feel free to take it off," he told her, reaching for the brim.

"Oh, no." She held up a white-gloved hand and smiled. "I wear big hats to distract people from my hair. It's always a mess. I feel naked without my hat."

"I see you believe in big pocketbooks, too." He smiled at her again, revealing two rows of tiny white teeth. Was it her imagination or were they all incisors? He reached for her handbag.

"Oh, this." She managed another smile and gave it to him. "My nephew teases me about it. Says I carry my whole apartment in it."

"It sounds convenient to me," Galvano said, unsnapping the clasp and peeking inside. "It seems unfair that men only get to take what they can cram in their pockets. I had an elderly aunt like you, Miss Hubbert. Carried half of Little Italy in her leather purse. What's this? Oh, one of those electronic Rolodex contraptions." He was methodically searching the contents of her bag as he spoke, poking long fingers into every crevice and feeling the lining carefully.

"Are you in the leather apparel business?" she asked. "You're taking such an interest in my purse."

He handed it back to her and his smile faded. "No. Just curious. It's so hard to find good workmanship these days. It was one of Max's biggest concerns."

"Indeed? You knew him well, I take it?" She settled back against the soft leather of her seat and willed her heart to slow in her chest.

"Well enough. How well did you know him, Miss Hubbert? Your importance to him is a surprise to me, I must confess."

"Funny. You sound just like the police. I'm a suspect in his death. They've questioned me twice already. Can you imagine?"

"You? They can't be serious. How unpleasant for you. Being questioned by the police is always a bother." He patted her knee. Even through the fabric of her light wool pantsuit, she could sense the iciness of his fingers. What in the world did women see in him? He was a Halloween skeleton dressed in a nice suit.

"Yes." She sighed deeply. "It's quite a pain, really. Here I am trying to grieve over his death and they keep bringing up old memories. I just wish they'd let me be."

"I know how you feel. Still, his death was sort of curious. Don't you think?"

"Made all the more curious by the fact that his nephew was found shot to death in the bottom of his grave," she conceded in a master understatement.

"Yeah. There are some people who are even saying that it looked like organized crime," Galvano said. He shook his head at the injustice of it all. "It's very hard for my people to get away from such accusations. It's not fair, I tell you, to work hard to find a better life for your family. And then to be accused of all sorts of criminal activity simply because of what country your grandfather came from. Your family came from where, Miss Hubbert?"

"Germany," she said stiffly. They were running out of small talk.

"Germany." He thought it over. "Italy and Germany were on the same side during World War Two, weren't they?" He looked to Auntie Lil for confirmation.

"Yes. They were." What was he getting to?

"Well, then, perhaps we should discuss being allies as well." He seemed pleased to have come up with such a complex concept.

"Perhaps. I'm still not quite sure what it is you want from me," Auntie Lil admitted.

"Let's just discuss the situation. Swap information. You can tell me what you know about Max's death and I'll tell you what I know. Tit for tat. No cops involved. We're on the same side in this thing."

She pretended to think it over.

"I know you've been poking around," he said easily. "I've got friends. You've been to his office, you've been asking questions."

"Why are you so curious to know what happened to Max?" she asked.

"Let's just say that I want to make sure that no one I know was involved." He stared at Auntie Lil. His eyes were small for his face. Like a lizard's. "You say you worked in the business for a while? If so, you'll understand that sometimes people who work for you do things because they think that's what you want them to do. Even if maybe you didn't come right out and ask them to. Only sometimes they're wrong. *Capiche?*"

"Capiche," Auntie Lil agreed.

"Good. We'll talk about it over lunch." He held up a hand when she started to object. "I want to take you to a restaurant where my old auntie used to eat. This is real Italian. You're going to love it." He tapped on the divider between the backseat and the driver. "In fact, I won't take no for an answer." The car began to move.

4.   "He's leaving with her!" T.S. yelled, craning to get a better view from the tiny back window. "Do something."

"Relax," Agent O'Conner reassured him. "This is not unexpected."

"It is to me!" T.S. said furiously. How could he have agreed to this? Had he been insane? Aunt Lil was being borne away by the oiliest mobster alive and he was trapped in a van letting it happen?

"He's taking her to Puglio's," Agent O'Conner said. "Look, sit down and shut up, will you? I'm having trouble hearing." He held the headphones tighter to his ears. "Can you pick them up, Bobby?" he asked the technician.

Bobby scowled harder. "Yeah. He's jabbering about Little Italy, so they're heading that way."

Agent O'Conner spoke rapidly into a small black box pinned to the inside of his lapel. "It's yours, Hank," he said. "They're headed for lunch." He sat back with a sigh.

"That's *it*?" T. S. demanded, grabbing the agent's coat and crushing the black box with his thumb. "Tell the driver to move this van."

Agent O'Conner calmly pried T.S.'s grip from his jacket and smoothed out his suit. "We can't," he explained patiently. "The van is too obvious. We have another team following them. Besides, we have his restaurant bugged, too. He always goes to the same place. We're fine."

Bobby the technician pulled one headphone away from his ear and scowled at Agent O'Conner. "It's not Puglio's," he announced. "I can't quite pick it up. Jeez, Frank. Don't recognize the name. It's Saint something or another . . . damn. It's fading out. There's a lot of cellular traffic in this area."

T.S. felt faint with panic and remorse. In his confusion, he attempted to open the van's back doors. They were locked. "Let me out of here," he demanded. *"Now."*

"Relax. We'll pick them up." Agent O'Conner did not feel as calm as he sounded. "Give them a few minutes' head start and then we'll move. We'll find them. His limo sticks out like a sore thumb. Those streets in Little Italy are narrow. We'll pick them up."

5. Herbert Wong was blessed with a complete lack of indecision. His compass had been set true at birth. He never had to hesitate about anything—he knew where he wanted to go, always. Rarer still, he knew why.

When the limo pulled away from the curb in front of the courthouse, he did not hesitate. Untying his white apron, he tossed it on top of the cart and took off running across the fields of City Hall Park, leaving behind a long line of customers. He did not care. Traffic was heavy as always in lower Manhattan at noontime and that meant he had a chance. He didn't know where the car was headed or how long he could keep up. Maybe the feds were following and maybe not. None of these factors mattered. All that mattered was that he had promised Lillian that he would protect her. Nothing could stop him from doing just that.

Herbert was a fit man who watched his diet and exercised scrupulously. He had his own brand of religion, one based on harmony of body and spirit. He believed in his abilities—both physical and mental—and this put him light-years ahead of most human beings. Keeping the limousine in sight at all times, he cut across the lawns of the public park and easily beat the car to Broadway. He followed it another block, where it turned up Church Street. He suspected the probable destination was Little Italy. If so, he had the stamina. But traffic on Church flowed more quickly. He was having trouble keeping up when a motorcade heading toward City Hall saved him. Traffic stopped to allow a procession of sleek limousines to pass. Thank God for a pomp-loving mayor. Herbert took the opportunity to grab a two-block head start, pushing through the heavy lunchtime crowd, banging shoulders and muttering a constant stream of apologies.

It was a good thing he had worn sneakers. He nearly lost Galvano's car when the avenue turned into West Broadway. He caught up with it at Canal, where heavy traffic from the Holland Tunnel once again slowed the limo's progress to a crawl. He kept easy pace through the outskirts of Chinatown. He even darted across Canal directly in front of the car in hopes that Lillian would see him and be reassured. He could not bear to think of her feeling trapped and alone.

Herbert waited calmly next to a street vendor hawking illegal fireworks until he was sure that the limo was heading up Elizabeth Street. Pulling his jacket collar up over his face, he determinedly dogged Galvano, breathing evenly to conserve his power. The Feast of Saint Gennaro—universally hated by all neighborhood residents—had recently taken place in Little Italy. The gaudy tinsel decorations sagged tiredly from overhead wires and the gutters were piled high with the debris produced by ten days of greasy food and illegal games of chance. Several streets were closed to traffic as cleanup crews toiled, aiding Herbert's cause. He sent a small prayer of thanks to every god he could name. He liked to cover all bases.

At last the limousine slowed to a halt in front of a small restaurant at the corner of Carmine and Mott. An intricate portrait of Saint Teresa decorated the front window, but there was no restaurant name in sight. Herbert stepped under the awning of a small electronics store and watched as a lovely young woman hurried out of the restaurant to help Auntie Lil from the car. The girl's olive complexion, dark eyes, and glowing hair gave her an eerie resemblance to the saint in the window. She escorted Auntie Lil politely inside. Joseph Galvano followed.

Herbert waited for a moment, then willed himself to project as much dignity as he could muster. He was a Chinese businessman taking time out for lunch, he decided. Until he remembered that he was wearing a windbreaker, not a suit jacket. Another subterfuge was called for. He hurried inside the electronics store and purchased a small 35mm camera without even bothering to haggle over the price. Pushing his credit card at the delighted clerk, he asked for a roll of high-speed film as well. You could not be too careful. For all he knew, he'd be pushed against the wall and searched. An empty camera would be far too suspicious.

Bells tinkled as he entered the restaurant, camera dangling around his neck like a proper Asian tourist. The interior was dimly lit and smelled of garlic, olive oil, and simmering tomatoes. The inside of the restaurant was much larger than it appeared from the sidewalk. Saint Teresa's had long since taken over its next-door neighbor's space. A waist-high stucco wall ran down the center of the restaurant, and small tables were arranged on either side of this partition. Most of the handful of patrons ate silently, hunched over platters heaped high with food. Clatter and faint music emerged from a small kitchen in the rear, visible through the small round window of a swinging door. Herbert spotted billows of steam through the glass. But where was Lillian?

A loud cough alerted him. Auntie Lil was seated on the other side of the stucco wall. Joey Galvano sat across from her, busily studying a wine list.

Auntie Lil's enormous hat drooped over the dividing stucco, making it seem as if a vase of flowers had been placed on top of the wall for decoration. The arrangement was quivering: she had turned his way. Herbert relaxed. His presence had been noted. He eased his finger to his camera and casually recorded the tableau on film.

"Can I help you?" the lovely hostess asked, appearing from the kitchen. She seemed agitated and twisted a wet washcloth in her hands.

Herbert bowed deeply and affected a heavy accent. "I wish to dine," he told her. "I have come all the way from Singapore. My colleagues tell me I must not miss your cooking when I come here to New York."

The young woman was nervous but polite. She had been told to keep the dining room as clear as possible. But she could not turn the stranger away, not if he had come all the way from Singapore to sample her cuisine.

"This way," she said, leading him to a table in a far corner against one wall.

"If you please, madam," Herbert insisted with another bow. "I wish to dine along this low wall where I can view your charming street. I find it most pleasurable to watch the people walking past." He raised his camera as if offering proof that he was a voyeur, then headed determinedly for a table behind Auntie Lil. He sat down before the hostess could protest. Now he was separated from Auntie Lil only by the low wall and one other unoccupied table.

The girl cast an anxious glance at Galvano, but he was

too engrossed in the wine list to notice one small Asian man slipping into place. Once seated, Herbert was blocked from Galvano's view by Auntie Lil's hat.

He did draw the attention of a table of beefy men sitting near the front door cramming chunks of garlic bread and strings of dripping spaghetti into their mouths. They looked like a quartet of bulls slurping mash from a trough. Herbert grinned at them in the overly friendly fashion of the village idiot. It worked. The goons satisfied themselves with a round of suspicious glares, then returned to their lunches. Herbert set his camera down on the table and carefully clicked off a few photographs of the bunch. They were not for his Christmas card.

6. T.S. was beside himself. He was trapped in a stuffy van around the corner from the restaurant arguing with Agent O'Conner. "What do you mean, you can't pick them up?" he demanded. "What's the use of all this?" He waved his hand at the equipment lining the truck walls.

"That's receiving equipment," the agent explained miserably. "We can't receive anything unless it's being sent. Get it? It's not all that complicated."

"Don't get snippy with me," T.S. said, sinking against the carpeted back doors. He put his head in his hands. "You're the one who claimed that you had that cheap crook 'bugged out the wazoo,' I believe you told my aunt. You're not the one whose favorite relative is stuck inside some restaurant where they probably blow gangsters away as the blueplate special. Good God, I hadn't thought of that." He stared anxiously at O'Conner. "Suppose she gets stuck in the middle of gang warfare?"

Agent O'Conner stared back, unblinking. "Mr. Hubbert, frankly speaking, I believe your aunt can take care of herself. I'm more concerned about not having a record of their conversation. Even if Galvano says something incriminating, I have no proof. She's eighty-four years old, and you and I both know she's a little bit deaf or she wouldn't shout all the time. And you can call her eccentric, but a jury might find her pretty damn strange." He sighed miserably. "The defense would make mincemeat out of her on the stand. I'd be laughed out of the courtroom. This whole operation is a wash." He kicked a carpeted wall in frustration and sank next to T.S. to commiserate.

7. Auntie Lil was calculating how long she had before her microcassette recorder ran out of tape. Since it was voice-activated, it could accommodate ninety minutes of conversation, not including silences. If only Galvano had not chatted his head off on the way here. He'd said absolutely nothing of use, just offered a half hour of memories involving every old female relative he'd ever had. She had resisted the urge to reciprocate with a rundown on every crook she'd ever known. Still, there should be a good forty-five minutes left, if she was careful to . . .

"I'm picking up the tab if that's what you're worried about," Galvano told her, interrupting her thoughts. "I mean, you look like you're adding and subtracting in your head or something. You're my guest. Lunch is on me. Order what you like."

She smiled despite her dismay at having her mind read by a gangster. "I was just having trouble deciding between the shrimp or the calamari," she lied.

"We'll have both," Galvano told her. He waved the hostess over and ordered. Auntie Lil did not argue.

Once they were alone again, Galvano lectured her on the proper technique for making marinara sauce. She listened politely, wondering how a man who liked to talk so much could survive in this bug-happy world.

"Let's get down to business," Galvano said suddenly. He cast a practiced look around the restaurant. So far as he could see, they had privacy.

"All right," Auntie Lil agreed. "You said tit for tat. Did your men kill Max?"

"Whoa!" He held up a tapered palm and smiled unctuously. "You go right for the jugular, Miss Hubbert. But since you asked, no—they did not. And if they had, I would not be sitting here with you. I'm here because I want to know the truth as badly as you."

"Did you have his nephew killed?"

"No. In fact, his death is costing me a lot of money."

Their food arrived before she could ask why. When you were Joseph Galvano, you seldom had to wait for anything. The hostess brought in a tray of platters piled high with bowls of fried shrimp, calamari, side orders of spaghetti, and stewed green beans. Rich marinara sauce had been ladled over the seafood and a small mountain of garlic bread completed the order. Auntie Lil took a deep whiff and sighed. This was an unexpected benefit. The food smelled heavenly.

"Mangia," Galvano said, serving Auntie Lil a generous portion of each dish.

"Thank you," she replied, ladling even more of the food on her plate. She attacked her lunch with gusto. Galvano watched with astonishment. Auntie Lil ate the way she lived: with gusto and without apology.

"Got a good appetite for someone your age," Galvano remarked as he picked at a forkful of fried shrimp and sauce. He would have liked to bury his face in the food but had long ago determined that he had to choose between wine and roses or fat and beefy. There were enough obese gangsters running around town.

"I like good food," Auntie Lil admitted, dipping her garlic bread into a pool of sauce and munching happily. She was starting to relax but knew enough not to be lulled into stupidity. "Why would Davy's death cost you money?" she asked.

Galvano pretended to think over his answer, but Auntie Lil knew that whatever he chose to reveal today had been planned in advance. She'd listen but reserve her right to remain skeptical.

"I tell you this in confidence," he said at last.

"Of course." She hoped Herbert could hear and shifted her hat slightly so it did not entirely block the way.

"You're right about Max not being the type to do business with me. He didn't like me. I can't understand it, but that's the breaks." His feelings were wounded at the recollection. "I guess he had a misconception about me. A lot of people do."

Auntie Lil murmured something unintelligible.

"I tried to get him to see things my way. We'd have had a very profitable relationship. He'd have none of it. The man was a control freak. I've seen the type."

Oh Lord, thought Auntie Lil. There are too many talk shows in this world. Today, even gangsters fancy themselves amateur psychologists.

"His nephew was a different story," Galvano said. "Davy knew a profit opportunity when he saw one."

Of course. She should have thought of that before. Davy had been a womanizer, a gambler, a shirker, and, by all accounts, a man of weak moral character. In short, the perfect soul mate for Joseph Galvano.

"He approached me," Galvano explained defensively, although she had not uttered a word. "I had washed my hands clean of Max Rose Fashions, understand. If a person doesn't want to cooperate with me, fine. I walk away. No problem."

Right. It was who cleaned up after you that was the problem. "I understand," Auntie Lil said.

Galvano tore a tiny piece of garlic bread and nibbled at it fastidiously, his small white teeth dainty in their precision. Like a weasel might eat a mouse.

"He had an idea," Galvano said. "It was a good one. If Max would agree to take his company public, the whole family stood to profit. A lot."

"Not to mention you?" she suggested.

He ignored her tone and continued: "Of course. I'm a businessman. Davy offered me a partnership of sorts. For my expertise, you might say. IPOs are hot right now. Initial public offerings. Taking a private company public. Max Rose Fashions could have cleared an astronomical amount of money. Maybe a hundred fifty million or more. You know the apparel business, Miss Hubbert. It's a whole new ball game every ninety days. You can be up on top one season and down the next. But Max always stayed in the middle and the middle is starting to look pretty good to a lot of investors. Shares in his company would have sold out in an hour."

"But Max didn't want to give up control," she stated matter-of-factly.

"That's right. He told you?"

"No. I would have expected it. That's Max."

"When Max wouldn't go for it, Davy asked me for a loan. It was all aboveboard. He wanted to hire an investment bank to look into some corporate options. He thought that maybe if he took the numbers to Max, he'd see that it made sense to at least consider going public. I loaned him the money. He had some fancy bank working on it. The projections were supposed to be ready next week."

"I hadn't realized you were such a serious businessman," she remarked.

"It's the greatest racket in town. The markets, I mean." He shrugged. "And it's completely legitimate." His skeletal smile unnerved her. She busied herself with lunch.

"Why would Davy come to you?" she asked Galvano. "There are banks. There's his own father."

"The kid's credit was . . . poor, shall we say. With banks. With his family. Hell, with everyone. And he knew me. From . . . prior business ventures. He knew I was good for the bucks. It wasn't peanuts. We're talking a hundred grand here. Just for the bank's retainer. I stood to lose everything, you know, if the plan didn't fly. I was doing him a big favor."

Auntie Lil knew only too well that Joseph Galvano would never lend Davy Rosenbloom money unless he had absolute assurance that he would get it back—along with a nice fat profit. "What was in it for you?" she asked sweetly.

"I won't lie. I stood to profit." He dabbed the corners of his mouth with his white cloth napkin and peeked at his reflection in the window. He had a habit of glancing in mirrors and preening when he thought no one was looking.

"Profit how?" she asked.

"If the company went public, I was going to get a cut of it. Consultant fee. Plus first dibs on a nice chunk of stock. I'd have ended up as a major shareholder."

"How major?" Auntie Lil was no slouch when it came to voting rights. She'd seen too many fine garment houses go down the tubes because management hadn't been equally aware.

"A modest share. Around fifteen percent is all."

Right. No doubt, Galvano would have ended up as the

largest single shareholder, with control over a majority of the remaining shareholders. Translation: Davy Rosenbloom and Joseph Galvano had been conspiring to push Max right out of the business he'd taken decades to build.

"What does V.J. Productions have to do with it?" she asked. She thought he must have had something to do with her name being placed on the phony corporate papers. How many other people had known she was inheriting Max's money in time to have them altered so quickly?

Galvano was not surprised that Auntie Lil knew about V.J. Productions. He had already figured out that she had been on the phone in the bookkeeper's office when he had mentioned V.J. the other day. Just the same, he looked about as innocent as an altar boy heaving a rock through a stained-glass window in the middle of Communion. "V.J.? That's nothing," he assured her. "Just a little problem we're trying to untangle."

"We?" she asked, eyebrows raised. "It seems I've been dragged into your little problem somehow."

"Look, I had nothing to do with your name being on the papers," he said smoothly.

Then how had he heard about it at all? she wondered.

"Look, I was only interested in the company's financial health," he said. "It had to be in tip-top shape. Max Rose Fashions would be an attractive takeover candidate if it went public. If the finances were in order."

"Why wouldn't they be in order?" she asked.

He sighed. "You make this very difficult for me," he pointed out. "This was to be a friendly lunch, I thought."

"What's unfriendly about wanting to know why you were poking around in Max's books?" Auntie Lil asked. "He was my friend. You're not a company owner. Why were you going through his books?"

"Joyce said there was a problem."

"Joyce Carruthers, the bookkeeper?"

"That's right. She and I have been friends for several years now."

I bet, Auntie Lil thought wryly. The two of you are perfect for each other. Like two iguanas in a tub of frogs.

"She keeps an eye on things for me," he explained.

"And in return, you keep an eye on her?" Auntie Lil asked. She couldn't help it. She should have known twenty-five years ago that Joyce Carruthers would turn out to be a traitor. Selling Max out to this cheap bum after all those years. It made her sick.

"She's a lonely lady." Galvano shrugged. "But a good comptroller. She'd noticed this extra account during her internal audit this year. V.J. Productions, Inc. She couldn't figure out who it was, said the accounts receivable fellow was signing the checks on the authorization of Davy. I am just as interested as you in finding out who V.J. Productions is. And where the money paid to them goes. And who tried to drag you into this."

She didn't believe that one either. But she'd let it pass. What she really wanted to know was *why* Joseph Galvano had Joyce keeping tabs in the first place. Did he not trust Davy? Was there some other situation she was not aware of?

"Do you know Max's widow, Sabrina?" she asked. Auntie Lil was nearing the end of her capacity to eat, a feat that was seldom achieved. She pushed her plates to one side and the hostess scurried to clear their table.

"I know of her," Galvano said casually. "Never met the lady."

Apparently not, Auntie Lil thought. Or he would not have referred to her as a lady. She sighed. "I guess it's my turn, then. Tit for tat." Galvano nodded and she plunged in, telling him some of what she knew about Max's family situation and the rumored circumstances surrounding Davy's death. Everything she said had been cleared by Agent O'Conner and she did her best to pad the meager facts with conjecture and useless details.

"Bunch of moochers," Galvano said when she was finished. "I could tell whenever I met a new one of them. Max made all the money and they always had their hands out. Believe me, I know what that's like." He patted his pockets and smiled. "And now, Miss Hubbert, I have a personal favor to ask of you."

Uh-oh. Here it came. She smelled trouble. "What kind of favor?" she asked.

"It's not safe for you to continue poking around," he told her pleasantly. "I worry for your health. And safety. I got a soft spot for old ladies. I admit it. I don't want to see you get hurt."

"You worry for my health?" she asked skeptically.

"Look, Miss Hubbert. No disrespect intended. But you are kinda old. You're vulnerable. You should be home knitting. Whoever did kill Max and his nephew, they weren't kidding. I think it's best you stay out of it. Concentrate on Max's business. You're a wealthy woman now. You and I, we could make a lot of money together. Going public's not a bad idea, you know."

"You want me to do business with you?" she asked incredulously.

He held up a palm. "No. That's not what I'm asking. It's too soon. I understand you need time to grieve. I'm respecting your need for personal space."

She wanted to throw up the two pounds of Italian food she'd just eaten. How could this man talk about respecting personal space when his specialty was killing people?

"We'll talk later," Galvano decided. "Today, I want you

to butt out. That's all. I'm going to find out who did this and I'll let you know. But, for now, butt out."

That did it. No one told Auntie Lil what to do. "Don't you tell me to butt out, young man," she said. His condescending tone was as irritating as his words. "Max was the finest man I ever knew. He had dreams and he made those dreams come true. And he never hurt a single person along the way. He was a good man and an honest man. And he would want me to find out the truth. Which, I assure you, I am going to do. And pardon me if I say that I can hardly believe in my heart that you are the proper person to carry the banner of truth forward from this mess."

"Nice talk from an old lady," he said grimly. He took a tiny sip from his wine, his small eyes hardening into glittering beads. "Come to think of it, I never did like my old auntie. She was too damn bossy for her own good."

"Just because you've met me doesn't give you the right to order me around, Mr. Galvano," she said indignantly. His phony politeness, his presumptuousness, his silky voice and smooth style of dressing—she'd had enough.

"I've never been afraid of anyone or anything in my life," she told him. "At least, not for long. And I won't be intimidated by you." She threw her napkin on the floor. "This is not Max's legacy. You understand? He doesn't deserve murder, he doesn't deserve the rumors swirling around his greedy family. He doesn't deserve to be buried with the taint of . . . of organized crime all around him. And most of all, he doesn't deserve having his name uttered in the same breath as yours. Understand, *Mr. Snake*?"

His face flushed with anger. The skeletal smile faded as his face became a deathly mask. "You misunderstand me," he told her coldly. "I'm not *asking* for your cooperation. I'm *telling* you to drop it. Walk away with your millions and don't look back, Miss Hubbert. You don't belong in this. Get out while you can."

"While I can?" she asked, deeply enraged. "Are you threatening me, Mr. Snake?"

"I am not the type to threaten anyone," Galvano said quietly. "I don't need to waste the energy. But I don't like people getting in the way of my business, understand?"

She was too far gone to be prudent. "Yes, I understand. You'll bury me beside Mr. Hoffa if I don't butt out."

His skeletal smile was back. "You flatter me, Miss Hubbert. But Jimmy Hoffa was a little before my time. Besides, I don't bury people. I crush them." He placed a small round of garlic toast on the table and ground it into crumbs with the heel of his hand. "I crush them like the junk they are. Now you see them. Now you don't." He brushed the crumbs onto the floor and scattered them with a well-shined shoe. "Easy come. Easy go."

Before she could retort, one of his thugs approached with a portable telephone in hand. Galvano tried to wave it away, but the goon persisted. "Fat Eddie," he explained with an apologetic shrug. "Got a problem down at the yard. You better talk to him."

"Speak of the devil," Galvano told Auntie Lil with an appropriately satanic smile. "What?" he growled into the phone, his temper aroused by his uncooperative lunch companion. He listened intently and his scowl deepened. "I'll be there in an hour. Hold off until then." He jammed the antenna of the phone savagely back in place and handed it to his bodyguard. "Bring the car around. You guys follow. I need someone to drop this lady off and pick up Little Tony. We're going to have to deal with this in person."

"I am perfectly capable of hailing a taxicab," Auntie Lil said firmly. There was no way on God's green earth that she was getting into a car with that crowd of thugs. They looked like refugees from the World Wrestling Association.

Galvano sighed heavily. "Miss Hubbert, Miss Hubbert, Miss Hubbert." He shook his head sadly. "I fear that we may meet again. And it may not be pleasant."

"I hope you have told me the truth today," Auntie Lil answered. "If not, I intend to find out."

The hostess was approaching slowly, wringing her hands. Perhaps the lunch had displeased him. Galvano dismissed her with an arrogant wave, then rose abruptly. He bowed his head in farewell, running his fingers through his hair to restore the meticulous cut. "It's been a pleasure," he lied as he hurried out the front door, carefully brushing his suit free from crumbs. The herd of beefy bodyguards stampeded dutifully after him.

Auntie Lil wanted to run out the door herself. She knew the lunch bill would be no problem. Galvano probably owned the joint and no payment was needed. She just wanted to make contact with Herbert immediately. It was the same urge she felt when she got dirt on her hands. She wanted to wash them clean as soon as possible.

She waited until Galvano's limousine had passed from view and the hostess had scurried back into the kitchen. "Did you hear all that?" she muttered out of the side of her mouth as she stared out the front windows of the restaurant.

"I did," Herbert replied. "You were foolish. But brave."

"Do you think he killed Max?" she asked Herbert.

"No, Lillian," he answered, shaking his head firmly. "He did not."

CHAPTER TEN

1. Herbert and Auntie Lil left the restaurant separately and took different routes eastward through Little Italy and Chinatown. Wary of a tail, Auntie Lil cut through three fish markets and a handful of souvenir shops on the way. Herbert simply disappeared in the crowd. Twenty minutes later they remet on Pearl Street.

"There's something I need to say," Auntie Lil told him. "Before we meet the others again. I could not have done it without knowing you were there. I have had many fine friends in my life. But never one as wonderful as you."

Herbert colored. "It is the great pleasure of my life to be your friend, Lillian," he said with a bow. "You have my undying loyalty."

Embarrassed by their display of affection, they busied themselves looking for a cab. Before they could hail one, a Con Ed van roared up to the curb. The back door opened and T.S. gestured frantically for them to climb inside.

"Hold on to your shorts, Theodore," Auntie Lil assured him. "If anyone was tailing me, I lost him in the fish market." She hiked up her pantsuit and executed a ladylike scoot on board.

"We had an awful time following you," T.S. said. "You took ten years off my life."

"It was positively too exciting," Auntie Lil declared. She

noticed Agent O'Conner. "Don't you look green around the gills."

"It was a little too exciting," Agent O'Conner mumbled. "The only good news is that Bobby picked Galvano up in his car after lunch. He's called his men off you for the time being. That was clever of you to say that you were under suspicion and being followed by the cops. It will keep him away from you. At least for a while."

O'Conner looked miserable. His plan had failed. He'd stuck his neck out getting the task force to agree to the scheme in the first place. Now the day was a waste of time. They had nothing.

Auntie Lil crawled into the cramped quarters and the blue feather on her gigantic hat smacked Bobby the technician in the face. He pushed it aside with a scowl. Civilians irritated him. He busied himself moving a pile of equipment to the far end of the truck.

"AKG. Why, that's German equipment! The best in the world for precision," Auntie Lil exclaimed. She squinted at the digital recording devices against the wall. "And of course, those must be Sony. Mine is just plain old American." She unpinned her hat and extracted the microcassette from the lining, using a long hat pin to pick the stitches free. "Still, it may have recorded something."

Agent O'Conner stared at her, speechless.

"Won't be as good as yours, of course," Auntie Lil admitted modestly.

"We didn't get anything," O'Conner stammered.

"You didn't get anything? You mean you didn't hear him threaten me?" Auntie Lil was indignant. She looked at her tape recorder and punched a button. It worked fine. "Wait until you hear what he said."

"You taped it?" Agent O'Conner interrupted. His voice was as high-pitched as a ten-year-old girl's. Hope flickered in his eyes. No, it was too much to expect. But . . . had she really? Why that wonderful old broad . . .

"Of course I taped it." She colored slightly. "Not that I didn't trust you, of course, but I wanted to have my own record in case you refused to—"

Agent O'Conner snatched the tape recorder from her hand. He rewound it quickly, sending tiny squeals through the van.

Bobby scrutinized the recorder with a professional's eyes. "If the quality is poor, it could be enhanced," he said, locking eyes with O'Conner.

"That was dangerous," T.S. admonished his aunt. "Not to mention foolish."

"I had Herbert to protect me," she replied sharply, with an accusatory glance at O'Conner.

Agent O'Conner was too enraptured to notice the rebuke. He pushed a button almost fearfully and held the small device up to his ear. He broke out in a smile as he heard, "Don't you threaten me," in a muffled but audible voice that was clearly Auntie Lil's. Galvano's voice followed: the volume was faint, but he was on the tape.

O'Conner's eyes widened. "It's here," he said in an awe-struck whisper. He handed the recorder to Bobby. "See what you can do with it. I need it by tonight." He motioned for the driver to start moving. "We can drop you off wherever you want," he offered. "I'll get back to you in a couple of days."

"You'll what?" T.S. asked.

"Get back to you." O'Conner was absently stroking his beard, calculating the legal ramifications of Auntie Lil's hidden tape recorder in his mind.

"No, you won't," T.S. declared firmly. The van bumped over a pothole, sending them jostling violently in the air. The recorder flew from Bobby's hands and landed near

Auntie Lil's left foot. She snatched it up and exchanged a glance with her nephew.

"You are not going to place my aunt's life in danger and then simply discard her," T.S. told the agent.

"That is correct," Herbert added. Everyone turned to stare. He had been so silent that his presence had been forgotten. "If you do not discuss the implications of what has just happened with us immediately, I will not testify."

"Testify?" O'Conner asked slowly.

"Yes. Testify. I heard every word that was said," Herbert announced. "Unlike you, I was present at the proper restaurant. And I have total recall, let me assure you." He coughed modestly. "I even have a few photographs." He held the camera out of reach of the eager agent. "Not so fast, Mr. Agent O'Conner. I agree with my friends. It is unseemly for you to dismiss us abruptly. After all, we did do your work for you today."

The agent looked at them one by one, then sighed in defeat as he noted their determined expressions. "What's the deal?" he asked.

"Information. Right now," Auntie Lil demanded.

"Information about what?" he asked. "I can't reveal anything that could compromise the investigation."

"We won't ask you to," Auntie Lil promised. When Agent O'Conner reluctantly agreed, she began to repeat parts of her conversation with Galvano with occasional assistance from Herbert. "Do you believe Galvano when he says he had nothing to do with the murders?" she asked the agent when she had finished.

O'Conner thought about it. "It's possible he's telling the truth. If you want to take him literally. It's out of character for him to blow up someone in such a public place and the murder of the nephew was amateurish. But I would guess that he knows more than he's saying about who's responsible."

Auntie Lil then explained about the arrangement Galvano claimed to have struck with Davy Rosenbloom. "Could this be tied in with V.J. Productions?" she asked the agent.

"Possibly," he admitted. "Galvano would never advance money unless he knew he was getting it back. V.J. could be that mechanism. Davy could have been siphoning funds out of Max Rose Fashions through a dummy vendor, with the proceeds going to pay back Galvano. Though the one point one million dollars in payments to V.J. is a hell of a lot more than the hundred thousand he claims to have lent. My conclusion: We're missing a piece of the puzzle. Probably a big one. Max Rose Fashions was not in good financial shape at the time of the deaths. There's a motive for murder there somewhere."

"Galvano claimed not to know Max's widow," Herbert pointed out. "Have you any evidence to suggest otherwise?"

The agent looked away. "I can't discuss evidence with you. But it is possible that he did not know the widow personally."

T.S. blew a gust of breath from his mouth in disgust. More legal gobbledygook.

"Okay," O'Conner said defensively. "We don't have any photographs or phone calls linking the two." He eyed the tape recorder hungrily. Auntie Lil tucked it out of sight in her pocketbook.

She returned to the scheme about possibly taking Max Rose Fashions public. "Did you know about that?" she asked.

The agent shook his head. "No. But I'd like to hear more if Galvano is involved. I'll get him any way I can, including securities fraud."

She explained about Davy's plan to engage an investment bank to run actual numbers as an enticement to convince Max.

"It's got to be Sterling and Sterling," T.S. interrupted. "I got the distinct impression that there was something going on in the corporate finance area involving Max Rose Fashions when I was there." He shook his head in warning. "Davy went to Sterling because he knew that Max trusted their opinion. He probably came to them as a representative of Max Rose Fashions. They never thought to question his authority."

"We'll check on it for you this week," the agent promised in a much too friendly voice. "Could I have that tape recorder now?"

"Not until I know what you're going to do about Joyce Carruthers," Auntie Lil said. "She's been ratting to Galvano about Max's business for who knows how long."

Agent O'Conner sighed. "We have no reason to arrest her. Yet. Besides, if we moved in on her right away, who do you think Galvano would suspect of telling us?" He stared at Auntie Lil. "For your own protection, I suggest you just sit tight on the bookkeeper, okay? In fact, sit tight on the whole thing and leave it to us." He held out a hand and tried the firm approach. "Give me that recorder," he demanded. His plea was blithely ignored by Auntie Lil.

"Oh, give him the damn thing, Aunt Lil," T.S. muttered. "My head hurts from worrying about you. I want to go home."

"But what about Galvano threatening me?" Auntie Lil demanded indignantly. "Can't you arrest him for that? Isn't that a criminal act? You can't just go around saying you're going to kill people, can you? He mashed a piece of toast to bits right in front of me. He was clearly letting me know my life was in danger."

"It would depend on what he actually said," Agent O'Conner explained. "Word for word. And it would be up to a jury to decide if he was really threatening you with murder or just mouthing off. It would help if he had said specifically why he might want to get rid of you."

"I don't think he did," she admitted. "There's one way to find out." She retrieved the recorder from the depths of her purse and pressed the fast forward button. "It was just before he left," she said. "I was worried about running out of tape." When she pressed the play button, the monumentally obtrusive noise of munching could be heard. It sounded like giant termites were invading the van.

"What's *that*?" O'Conner asked.

Auntie Lil blushed. "The fried calamari was delicious," she explained. "Very crispy. And the garlic bread was quite crunchy as well."

"We can drop that out," Bobby assured them. He was changing his mind about this bunch of civilians, especially the broad. There weren't many people who could sit across the table from Joseph Galvano and keep their appetites. The old lady had spunk.

"It's a little further along than I thought," Auntie Lil apologized, playing with the buttons. "I hope I got it on tape."

"If you didn't, I heard every word," Herbert assured her. He mimicked Galvano's voice: " 'I don't bury people. I crush them. I crush them like the junk they are. Now you see them. Now you don't.' " Herbert looked solemnly at the others. "There was a short silence at that point," he explained precisely. "Then Galvano says, 'Easy come. Easy go.' Right after that, one of his men came up with the telephone and told him that a Mr. Fat Eddie was on the line."

"That's right," Auntie Lil agreed eagerly. "And Galvano said, 'Speak of the devil.' "

"He what?" Agent O'Conner asked. He stared at Bobby. The two of them looked as if they had just been given a particularly hard question on a quiz and knew the answer but could not quite bring it to mind.

"Fat Eddie?" O'Conner repeated. "That's from . . ." His voice trailed off.

"Yeah. The September tapes," Bobby agreed. "You remember. He was talking to . . . you know, the one who . . ." He stopped and swallowed, searching for suitably discreet words. "There was that guy that *disappeared*? About the time of . . ."

"Yeah. And Fat Eddie is . . ." Agent O'Conner stopped and gazed at the tape recorder as if it were the Holy Grail. "Crushes people like . . ." he repeated thoughtfully. Suddenly he locked eyes with Bobby and broke into an enormous grin, then pumped a fist in the air. "That's *it*," he shouted. "I can smell it. It's there, it's got to be there." He planted a huge kiss right on Auntie Lil's nose, then whooped and thrust both hands in the air. He looked as if he had just scored the winning touchdown in the Super Bowl. "The man is going down," he crowed. "Way, way downtown."

2. "Did you understand a single word that Agent O'Conner said?" T.S. asked Auntie Lil and Herbert. They sat in T.S.'s living room, cups of coffee before them.

Auntie Lil shook her head. "No. And frankly, I thought he'd gone lulu on us. He pounced on that tape recording like Galvano had confessed to some horrible crime. But it seemed sort of vague to me when I heard it again." She looked to Herbert for his opinion.

"The significance escaped me," Herbert admitted. "But I do not think it has anything to do with Max's death. The September tapes, they said. That's before the murder. But I do know that we will get nothing more from Agent O'Conner. Unless he needs us again."

Auntie Lil nodded. "We were just a tiny part of something much bigger. He has no use for us anymore."

T.S. sighed. "Let's hope Joseph Galvano feels the same way. That lie about you being followed by the cops can't last forever. Once Galvano thinks he can get at you unseen, he may be back."

A vigorous pounding at the door interrupted the silence that greeted this ominous remark.

"Casey," T.S. murmured. "Right on time. I wonder what her objection is to being announced."

Casey was toting a bag of White Castle hamburgers. "The one good thing about Long Island," she explained, popping an entire sandwich into her mouth and chewing lustily. She offered the bag around but her generosity was unanimously declined. She was wearing yet another early-sixties-style sheath and it clung to her ample figure like Saran Wrap. The dress was bright orange and had small yellow balls of yarn dangling from the hem like the trim on an overstuffed sofa.

"Did you find out anything important?" she asked them. "Like if Agent O'Conner has a girlfriend?" She plopped down on the sofa and put her feet on T.S.'s glass coffee table. He winced but held his tongue.

"We neglected to ascertain Agent O'Conner's romantic status," Herbert admitted. "Though we found out plenty else."

"He's kind of cute, don't you think? In a shy way?"

T.S. had to disagree. Agent O'Conner had fled the room

after three minutes in Casey's presence. But it wasn't shyness motivating him. It was self-preservation.

"He seems involved in his work to the exclusion of all else," Auntie Lil pointed out. "Men who are fixated on their work sometimes find they have little time for the other things in life. Max was that way at times."

They were silent, his name serving as a reminder of why they had gathered.

Casey broke the mood by wadding up an oily hamburger wrapper and tossing it across the room into a trash can. "You're right. Let's get down to it. I found out some things that may be useful."

"Such as?" T.S. asked.

"Such as you're a millionaire." She smiled broadly.

"Maybe," he corrected her. "The terms of the trust state that I only inherit if Davy died within forty-eight hours of Max."

"Then you're a certain millionaire," Casey said. "The coroner estimates Davy's time of death at approximately four to ten hours after Max was killed by the bomb. You inherit. Congratulations."

T.S. ran a finger under his collar. It suddenly felt very tight.

Auntie Lil was silent, staring out the window.

"What is it, Lillian?" Herbert asked.

She shook her head and smiled bravely. "It's nothing, Herbert. Casey—does Max's family know?"

"Oh, yeah. If I were T.S., I'd be looking over my shoulder right now."

"What else did the medical report say?" Auntie Lil asked.

"Plenty," she said proudly. "Want to know how I got the info?"

In truth, none of them did. She offered an explanation

anyway: "The investigation of Davy's death has turned into a jurisdictional nightmare. The Babylon cops say it's theirs because that's where the body was found. Manhattan South says no way, it's connected to Max. And, of course, the feds are poking around, too. This gives *moi* an idea. In the middle of all this squabbling, I waltz in and bat my eyes at the clerk who's being kicked around by everyone in the state who has a badge, except maybe the school crossing guard. He's a lonely guy, never married, a little overweight, likes steak and—"

"Spare us the gruesome details," T.S. suggested, his mind still whirling at the thought of thirty-three million dollars. His half of the trust's assets. That meant he was as rich as Lilah. Maybe richer. The thought of instant entrée into her monied world was an appealing aspect of his new wealth that he had not considered before.

"It's nothing sordid," Casey promised, interrupting his thoughts. "Just a couple of margaritas and a dinner at Ralph's Steakhouse. He let me see the report. Hell, I saw the entire file. And there's nothing in it of any use at all. They have zippo. The only real information comes from the coroner's report. What's most important is the time of death. Even if the coroner is way off, he's got a lot of room for mistakes before you go over the forty-eight-hour threshold. Important point number two: Davy was shot in the back of the head by *three* bullets. Exact make of gun unknown, but similar to a Smith and Wesson .44 Magnum. One bullet would have been enough, but whoever shot him was pretty serious. He died within seconds." She bit into another silver-dollar-sized burger and chewed thoughtfully.

"You also learned other facts?" Herbert prompted. He was starting to get hungry watching her wolf down all those White Castles.

Casey nodded. "He was killed elsewhere, not at the

grave site, and presumably stashed somewhere for a night and a day. He was dumped into Max's grave the night before the funeral, after rigor mortis had set in and gone."

"Someone killed him and *kept* him?" Auntie Lil said. "That's keeping your cool."

"Unless the killer freaked and it took a day and a half to calm down." Casey checked her bag for another hamburger and looked disappointed when she found it empty. "The cops looked at the family right away, since they still thought at the time that Davy was inheriting all the bucks. But everyone has a pretty good story for the period of time he was missing."

"No doubt they were with each other, mourning Max's death," Auntie Lil guessed.

Casey nodded. "You got it. Jake claims he went straight to his parents' house after Max was killed to break the news. Says he never saw Davy that night or since, and spent the latter part of that evening with Max's widow. Jake's wife corroborates his story and says she was with him the whole time. The younger brother and sister didn't hear the news about Max until the next day. They were both out with friends the first night—there's plenty of witnesses—and were at their jobs the next day when they heard. Rebecca's got about the best alibi of all. She seems like a pretty tough old bird, but she collapsed at the news that Max had been killed and was under sedation and a doctor's care for a good twenty-four hours before she rallied to do her Morticia Addams imitation at the funeral. She didn't kill Davy."

"Did they question any employees?" T.S. asked. He knew they'd be eager to talk.

"Plenty. But no one seems to know anything except that Max was a saint and Davy was a bum. Although a lot of people claim that Davy shot out of the factory like a bullet when he heard the news that Max had been blown up. No pun intended." Casey shrugged. "They've found no forensic evidence indicating where Davy was killed or stashed. There's just not much to go on. All the rain didn't help. I get the feeling that the cops are pretty sure Davy was into the loan sharks and got blown away when he couldn't pay back on time. They're holding the body and not releasing it for burial. The family is screaming bloody murder, though not bloody murder by any of them, I might add."

"Then surely the police believe that Max was killed by accident when he borrowed Davy's car?" Herbert said.

Casey shook her head. "They seem pretty convinced that Max was involved with the Mob somehow and the primary target of the bomb. Or maybe that Davy planted the bomb to try to get the money to pay back his markers, knowing he'd inherit."

"But did Davy know that his inheritance would be doled out by a trustee?" T.S. asked. "That he'd never be able to get his hands on a lump sum?"

"That's the big question," Casey said. "And we'll never know the answer."

"The timing of Davy's death must be important," Auntie Lil said. "It was so soon after Max's death. Was it someone in the family seeking retribution?"

T.S. shook his head. "It sounds awful, but no one I've met so far in that family seems upset enough over Max's death to want to blow his murderer away."

Casey shrugged. "Which brings me to another point that you should know. Since it concerns your pocketbooks." She cleared her throat apologetically. "Jake and the widow are going to try to block Max's final will. Jake's been visiting every member of the family methodically. This leads me to believe that they're contesting. That and clever detective work on my part which involved a two-hundred-dollar bribe given to the secretary at an otherwise reputable law firm patronized by the Rosenblooms. And for what it's worth, Widow Rosenbloom has found chastity. Though it seems a bit late to me. She hasn't gone out in days. Stays at home and sometimes Jake comes to see her. I'd make a snide remark, but he doesn't stay long enough for hanky-panky. Not even considering it's Jake. Plus, he's had his wife with him most of the time. In fact, it's odd. A lot of the Rosenblooms are staying put. Not moving from their homes."

"Who else isn't moving?" Auntie Lil asked.

"Rebecca," Casey said. "She was pretty hot about you getting the money at the reading of the will. But now all she does is stay inside, curtains drawn. A delayed case of grief or something."

"Or something," Auntie Lil said. "Maybe she knows who's really responsible."

"If so, she's ahead of me," T.S. grumbled.

"It's convenient that the Rosenblooms are just sitting around at home. It's almost as if they were asking you to visit, don't you think?" Casey asked Auntie Lil. "I vote we take a look at each family member. If you need to, lie to get in the door. It works for me. Say that you want to discuss a possible settlement of the will or something."

"I have no intention of giving that family any money," Auntie Lil said firmly. "If Max had wanted them to have more, he would have given them more."

"Like I said, *lie*. It's easy," Casey insisted, unaware that Auntie Lil was capable of telling some real whoppers if she had to.

"I would like to get a better look at some of them," Auntie Lil admitted. "Especially the youngest niece and nephew. As outcasts, they might be more likely to talk."

"Karen and Seth," Casey reminded them. "Only she's

been married and divorced, so her last name is Friedman. And you're right about them being outcasts. I've never seen them at any other family function. Max didn't even mention them to me when he hired me. But I do know where they live."

"How?" Auntie Lil demanded uneasily. Casey's methods, while barely legal, always tended to emit a faint air of criminality about them at first glance.

"Jake has been to see both of them in the last few days," she explained. "No doubt to get them to join in the lawsuit. But I don't think he's having much luck, on account of the fact that he stomps back to his car each time like he's got gastritis. Which, if there's any justice in this world, he does."

"You two can go talk to Rosenblooms," T.S. interrupted. "I'm going down to Sterling and Sterling. If what you say is true about the medical report, then I now have a legal right to find out what's going on. After all, half that money is mine." He said this glumly because he had decided that he felt awful, parity with Lilah be damned. He'd done nothing to deserve the money and had inherited it by default thanks to a gruesome murder. Enthusiasm for his newfound wealth escaped him. T.S. had not worried about money since the early years of his career, and his tastes had remained simple despite his growing salary. Now that he had access to millions, his imagination failed him. There wasn't a thing he wanted to buy or a place he wanted to see. Besides, he was an orderly man who depended on routine to get his bearings each day. This much money was definitely not routine and he resented it.

"I will accompany you," Herbert offered, as if knowing T.S. needed support.

No one in the room, with the exception of Auntie Lil, was willing to turn Auntie Lil loose alone. It was decided that Casey would cover Auntie Lil while she questioned the Rosenbloom clan. This would give Herbert and T.S. time to visit Sterling & Sterling. Reluctantly, T.S. also agreed to visit Seth Rosenbloom.

"Why me?" he complained. "I'm no good at that kind of thing. And I'm sick of Rosenblooms."

"Nonsense, Theodore. You've been interviewing people your whole life." Auntie Lil patted his knee. "Just pretend you're interviewing him for a job."

"I will accompany you there as well," Herbert offered. "I welcome the opportunity to meet people of all types. Besides, I suspect he's where the action is."

"Speaking of action," Auntie Lil began as she outlined her escapades of the day for Casey. Certain details were enhanced for dramatic effect: she finished up with a retelling of Agent O'Conner's strange reaction to Galvano's final taped words.

"I know a little bit about Galvano's history," Casey said. "But I don't see what the excitement is about. But if O'Conner's happy, I'm happy. Especially since it looks like Galvano is out as a murder suspect in Max's death. I don't want to mess with him."

"Just because he didn't confess on his knees to Aunt Lil doesn't mean he didn't do it," T.S. pointed out.

"True. But I've said all along: Galvano's more efficient that that," Casey said. "I've got my favorite suspects. How about you?"

"Maybe Abe is faking it," T.S. suggested, hoping to head off a guessing session. "Suppose he's not really sick. He's been faking that stroke for a year, and every night he creeps from his bed and roams the family homes with a gun looking for more victims."

"*Abe.*" Auntie Lil stared at T.S. while she thought it over.

"I'm kidding, Aunt Lil," T.S. said. "Just kidding."

"Maybe," she said. "But it is a good idea to at least talk to Abe. Think about it—here's a man lying in bed, everyone thinks he's asleep most of the time. They would discuss things in front of him. Ignore him. He may well know more than he's saying."

"That wouldn't be hard. He's not saying anything," T.S. pointed out.

Auntie Lil crossed her arms. "He will be by the time I'm through with him."

CHAPTER ELEVEN

1. Only Casey's assurance that Abby was more likely to be absent in the morning kept Auntie Lil from rushing off to visit Abe that night. "She leaves every morning for an hour," Casey promised. "Usually to do a little shopping. Would you rather talk to him with or without her?"

Considering that Auntie Lil's fingerprints had been found all over the downstairs of Abby's home—and that Auntie Lil was not eager to discuss why—Auntie Lil opted for a visit when Abe was alone.

They arrived at the Rosenbloom home just before eleven o'clock the next morning. It had a deserted look despite the late-model Cadillac parked in the driveway. The curtains were drawn against the sun and two days' worth of newspapers littered the driveway. Even the ceramic figurines crowding the lawn looked lonely.

"That is not a happy house," Casey said. They parked two doors down and scrunched low in their seats to wait. "Don't worry about being spotted. No one's home around here but maids. As soon as Abby leaves, you go in. He'll talk more if it's just you." Casey did not add that she wanted to keep a close eye on anyone who might be following Auntie Lil.

Fifteen minutes later Abby emerged from the doorway of her home. She wore a pink coat with a matching wool hat.

It did nothing to brighten her appearance. Her makeup had been haphazardly applied: one cheek was much redder than the other and a small river of mascara trickled from her left eye. Her hair was untidily tucked up under her cap and deep worry lines creased her forehead. She strode directly to her car without pausing to lock the front door behind her.

"Does it lock on its own?" Auntie Lil asked.

"It's not locked," Casey assured her. "She's left it open each of the two days I've checked this week."

"Then she's not too afraid of getting killed," Auntie Lil remarked.

"Unless she's careless. Or distraught with grief." Casey stared hard at the scurrying figure. "Is she wearing bedroom slippers?"

She was indeed. Despite the fact that she wore expensively tailored silk trousers, Abby had pink fuzzy bedroom slippers on her feet.

"Not a good sign," Auntie Lil observed as they watched her drive away. "What about nurses? Will there be anyone else inside?"

"No nurse right now. Abe's off the respirator and doing okay, I hear. I suspect they only hire a nurse when the old guy's going through a particularly bad time and hooked to the machine. Sometimes Rebecca stops by to check on him, but she hasn't lately. He'll be alone."

Auntie Lil nodded and slipped from the car. She pulled her coat tightly around her and looked about nervously, unable to shake a slightly guilty feeling. Yet there was little likelihood that she would run into a neighbor in this deserted wealthy subdivision. And even if she did, what was wrong with visiting an old friend? It wasn't like she was slipping in under the cover of darkness to ransack the house. She'd already done that.

The door opened easily. It was odd to be returning to the

house during the daytime. It seemed so *ordinary*. Not frightening at all. She resisted the urge to check the kitchen for more Pepperidge Farm cookies and instead crept directly upstairs to the bedrooms. A slightly antiseptic smell identified Abe's bedroom as the one at the far end of the hall. She checked the other rooms carefully as she passed by—she was not in the mood to be surprised by anyone. The bedrooms were decorated with coordinated drapes and bedspreads and filled to the brim with ornate furniture. Abby's bedroom was a mini-museum to overstuffed pink objects and was dominated by an enormous dressing table covered with enough cosmetics to supply three modeling schools. Yet these rooms and, indeed, the entire house, were as sad and lifeless as a mausoleum.

Abe Rosenbloom lay sleeping in his bed. It was an ugly metal affair that stood out grotesquely against the rest of the normal furniture in the bedroom. His breathing was raspy but even. A silent respirator stood against one wall.

Auntie Lil crept closer for a better look. Abe had started to lose his hair and the remaining wispy strands were brushed back from a broad brow that was clammy and pale from illness. His nose was round and flattened. He had broken it once in a fight. In sleep, his face was calm and quiet. Too calm. Auntie Lil shivered—he looked dead.

But Abe was not dead. "Who's there?" he asked in a creaky voice. He ended his sentence with a soft cough.

"It's Lillian Hubbert," she said. Auntie Lil stood by the side of the bed and touched one of his hands. It was cold. She rubbed the skin to restore circulation.

"Lil?" he asked. He opened his eyes with effort. "So it is. I heard you were at the funeral. It's sad about Max, isn't it? They won't tell me much more. Only that Max and my Davy are dead."

"Yes, they are dead." Without warning, she was overcome

by the urge to weep. For days she had been surrounded by people who had not known Max. She had carried the weight of his memory alone. But here was his brother, someone who knew and understood the power that had been Max. She held back sniffles and could not speak.

"Ahhh," Abe said. "Go ahead and cry, Lil. You always were too stubborn to cry about anything. I'd cry myself. If I could."

She forced herself to regain her composure. She had less than an hour and had no time for tears. "I'm sorry," she told him. "Seeing you reminded me of him."

Abe slowly moved his free arm across his body, holding it carefully in the air as if it were in a sling. He patted her hand. "You really loved him, didn't you? I envied him that. I've been thinking of Max a lot. Nothing else to do lying here in bed. I wasted so much time hating him. What did it get us? Nothing. It didn't make me happy. It didn't make me smarter. It didn't do anything but create this mess of a family, torn apart by greed." He stopped as a small spasm of coughs overtook him. It subsided as quickly as it came. "It cost me Davy," he ended. "My hatred cost me my son. It's the price God wants me to pay."

"God didn't kill Davy," Auntie Lil said gently.

Abe did not hear her. "It's never going to end. This family's hatred has a life of its own. I look forward to dying. It's the truth. I do."

"Don't say that," Auntie Lil said. "You've got other children. You have your wife."

"My wife." His smile was sad. "Abby and I had everything we could ever want. Clothes, homes, cars, money. But we never had a tenth as much as you and Max. And I'm not talking about the things that money can buy. Why did you do it, Lil? Why did you leave him? It was the worst I ever saw him. I thought I'd be happy to see him suffer, but

I wasn't. I felt like I had lost something, too. He came out of it stronger, of course. Always did. Went on to make more money, more machines, have more success." He closed his eyes and rested for a few moments. Auntie Lil patted his hand and did not hurry him.

"Abby would throw a fit if she knew you were here," he finally said. "But I've been expecting you."

"You have?"

"I knew you'd come. The day Max died, I could hear them talking below. The boys were shouting, Abby was wailing like she had a knife stuck in her gut. I knew Max had died when I heard her. I always thought his death would set me free. It didn't. It left me alone. But the second I heard he died, I thought of you. And I knew you would come. You want to know a sad thing about the world?" he asked suddenly.

"What?" She shrank from the question.

"It's changed. That's what." His breath was overtaken by a racheting cough. He waited a moment and continued. "It should have been me that died. I've been useless for a year. Useless to Max. Useless to my family."

"It shouldn't have been anyone who died," Auntie Lil said.

"Max should never have married that woman," Abe said. "He got soft in his old age. He was old enough to be a grandfather, but he wanted kids. I liked her at first. Thought she was a classy lady. But she's not. She's not worth the dirt you walk on, Lil. Max knew it, too. It was funny. It's as if he knew he was making a mistake even before he did it. Didn't invite anyone to the wedding at all. You know what I think? I think he had decided that everyone was entitled to one big mistake and he was going to have his." They were silent. A cuckoo clock chimed downstairs. Neither one of them heard it. They were thinking of Max.

"He left me his money," Auntie Lil said. "He left half to me and half to my nephew. Your family is very angry."

"Let them be angry. Max gave away the store while he was alive. Bailed me out every time I tried to go out on my own and failed. I wasn't always ungrateful, Lil. I stopped hating Max a long time ago. I stopped when I saw that it was contagious. Brothers should never hate brothers." He closed his eyes as if a spasm of pain had hit. She waited in the long, quiet moments.

"I knew he wasn't leaving me anything," Abe said at last. "I didn't tell Abby. She would have had kittens."

"You knew?"

"He came to see me and told me everything a month ago. About the trust and the cash bequests. Of course, the estate was going half to you and half to Davy then. But Max didn't want to leave Davy cash. He knew it would be gone in a week and thought it would last longer if there was a trustee to rein him in. I didn't think that Davy would . . ." His voice trailed off.

"I'm sorry. You're ill. I shouldn't be bothering you." Auntie Lil smoothed the covers around his shoulders. He had grown even paler from the effort of speaking. It was time for her to go, no matter how many more minutes they might have before Abby returned.

"I'm afraid," he said suddenly, the words splitting the silence with unexpected strength. "I'm afraid and I don't know of what."

"You're afraid?" she repeated softly.

He did not answer for a minute. "I don't mean afraid for my life. That's nearly gone. Besides, I keep a gun in the drawer by the bed. Silly, isn't it? It's older than I am and I can hardly hold it, much less use it. But I feel better with it there."

"Do you know who killed Max? Is that why you're afraid?"

He shook his head slowly. "I don't know who killed Max. Or who killed Davy. It could be anyone. Because hatred grows. It's everywhere. It will never stop. I think anyone could have killed them. My wife. My sister. Any one of our hundred and twenty employees. Even me. Anyone can kill anyone these days. And they do."

"Is that what you're afraid of?" she asked.

"No." He was quiet, trying to put his thoughts into words. "I'm afraid of my wife's anger," he finally said. "Afraid of what it may do to her. She's angry at me for being sick. I'm no help to her right now. She's angry at me that Davy died. She's angry at everyone. *I miss my son.*" He swept an arm in the air and it flailed wildly. She hurried to coax it back to his side, stroking his arm to calm him.

"Don't talk about it anymore," she said. "I should never have come."

"No. You were supposed to come," he whispered. "I've been lying here praying for you to come. I need you. I want you to do something for me."

"What?" she asked.

"Davy is dead," he said. "But Seth is still alive. He's my youngest. He has a good heart. He loves me and I love him. But Abby won't let him in the house. I know that's why he hasn't been to see me. My daughter, Karen, sneaks in when Abby isn't home. I tell Abby to leave the door open in case I have to call the paramedics while she's gone, but really it's so that Karen can get inside. So I do see her. And of course I see Jake. He comes by all the time. But I want to see my son Seth before I die. Will you find him and tell him to come? Tell him I'm sorry. Tell him that now I understand that all the things we used to get angry about really don't matter at all."

"I will," Auntie Lil promised. "I'll find him and tell him."

"And be careful," Abe warned. His voice grew faint. He coughed, then apologized. "I'm not used to so much—"

"I know," she said. "Don't talk. I have a few minutes. I'll just sit here awhile."

Auntie Lil sat in the silence of the sterile bedroom, holding Abe's hand and watching him fall back to sleep. As he relaxed, his features spread and she could see more clearly his resemblance to Max. They had been so different at one time, the two brothers, both in looks and in temperament. Age and death had evened the score. For the first time she wondered what it must have been like for Abe—never quite able to catch up to Max, no matter what he did. Always chasing Max the war hero, Max the inventor, Max the business whiz, Max the prodigal son come home.

It was a sad world, Auntie Lil thought when she finally slipped from the lonely house. It was a sad world and Abe was right about one thing: things had surely changed. There would never be another Max.

2.　T.S. and Herbert sat silently in the backseat of Lilah's limousine, each lost in thought. Grady, the chauffeur, whistled an Irish folk song as he drove. He seemed happy to be helping out and T.S. was comforted by his support.

Herbert could barely contain his excitement. In the deepest recesses of his mind, he had long harbored the wish that was about to be fulfilled. He was to accompany T.S. to Sterling & Sterling—not as a messenger but as the honored associate of a client.

For fifteen years he had worked as an in-house courier for the bank, delivering securities within the Wall Street district. Yet despite his dignity, intelligence, and ability to do a fine job, Herbert had remained a mere messenger in his coworkers' eyes. This status had subjected him to a wide variety of indignities he had tried hard to overlook: being ignored by younger men in more expensive suits who felt it beneath their dignity to comment on his existence because he wore a windbreaker; secretaries ordering him to bring them back cups of coffee as a way to assure themselves that they, at least, were not on the bottom of the feeding chain; and, worst of all, complete invisibility so far as Sterling & Sterling partners were concerned. To be ignored by the very men upon whom Herbert bestowed his undying loyalty was the worst indignity of all.

Given the strict pecking order of the firm, Herbert could be forgiven his euphoria. He had selected his finest suit and most conservative accessories for the groundbreaking trip through the client door.

T.S. was equally resplendent. He sat in the limousine, looking and feeling like a takeover king, his confidence fortified by the alacrity with which his request for an appointment with Preston Freeman had been granted. Yes, the managing partner could work him in that afternoon, his secretary had assured T.S. In fact, he had been about to call T.S. to set up a meeting himself.

When they reached Sterling & Sterling's corner, Grady was magnificent. He stopped the limousine at the client entrance, cheerfully blocking a long line of traffic behind them. Before either T.S. or Herbert could climb out, Grady was there to open the door with a deep bow. Only T.S. was close enough to spot the twinkle in his eye.

A guard tipped his hat to them as they entered the marble rotunda that greeted all monied visitors. Both Herbert and T.S. unconsciously straightened their ties before they pushed through the inner entrance doors.

"Feels a little different, doesn't it?" T.S. asked Herbert quietly. They were marching down the long marble hallway of the banking platform, approaching the Partners' Hall. The slick stone floor gleamed beneath the glow of brass chandeliers and their footsteps echoed importantly through the cavernous room. The air seemed richer, the lights more golden. Herbert breathed slowly, conscious that many pairs of eyes were watching their approach. Word had leaked that the rarest of surprises had happened: an employee was returning to Sterling & Sterling *as a client*. Since every client of the firm was a multimillionaire or more, this was no small accomplishment.

"Mr. Freeman is expecting you in conference room two," the uniformed valet informed them. He nodded politely as he escorted them through the swinging doors, and Herbert felt ashamed of the swelling in his heart. One must not be filled with pride about such unimportant measures of character as money, he reminded himself firmly. Nor must one break into a jig of exultation at an inappropriate time.

The conference room was small and filled from top to bottom with memorabilia gathered during two hundred years of international banking and commerce. Photographs, prints, maps, and framed souvenirs crowded every surface, rendering the wallpaper nearly invisible. An ebony-topped table graced the center of the room. All but two of the chairs grouped around it were occupied. The occupants were all males of various ages and physical types, but all wore the same somber expression. No one seemed to recognize Herbert as the messenger who had toiled so diligently on their behalf a few years before. And no one acknowledged that they already knew T.S. Perhaps they felt it impolite to refer, however obliquely, to their stint as members of the working class.

Managing partners were allowed to be different. "Hubbert," Prescott Freeman said cheerfully, doing his best to wring T.S.'s arm from his socket. "Welcome to the rarefied air of a client meeting." The assembled bankers chuckled obediently.

"This is my associate, Herbert Wong," T.S. said, clearing the way for Herbert to have his arm wrung from its socket.

T.S. and Herbert took their seats at the table, huddling close together with the same instinct that inspired settlers to circle their wagons against attacking Indians. T.S. surveyed the men at the table. He recognized Sterling & Sterling's lawyer from the meeting with the Rosenblooms. He also identified the head of the tax area and Sterling's trust company subsidiary. The other faces were less familiar. "Quite a crowd," he said nervously, trying a smile. To his horror, the bankers produced another round of obedient chuckles, as if he had said something witty. Thirty-three million was more effective than Pavlov's shocks when it came to behavior modification, T.S. decided.

"Yes, well, we have quite a relationship with . . ." Freeman announced brightly, but ran out of words and began to drum on the table with his fingertips. He was searching for a way to begin a delicate task and none of the gathered minions dared interrupt. He finally opted for the direct approach. "This is just the damnedest thing, T.S.," he said. "I hardly know where to begin. But Herman here tells me that the firm is protected from a legal standpoint and, indeed, that we have a fiduciary responsibility to discuss the situation with you as soon as possible. Based on the medical report fixing David Rosenbloom's time of death, you are clearly the inheritor of one half of Max Rosenbloom's trust. And, of course, your aunt receives the rest. I have to say that this is surprising to me and to my associates. Our representative handling the drawing up of the wills and the trust joined us after your time here and did not recognize your name. Not, of course, that we pass around information about our clients between departments." He smiled bleakly. "We had no idea you knew Max Rosenbloom. It's been a shock."

"But I *didn't* know him," T.S. said. "And if you think you're surprised, imagine how I feel."

A profound sigh escaped the lips of a younger executive. He colored slightly, caught in a daydream. If only *he* could have inherited that much money out of the blue. Why, he knew an up-and-coming company that would return his investment fourfold. . . .

"At any rate," Freeman continued with a sharp glance at the offender, "Herman tells me that we are free to discuss the status of Mr. Rosenbloom's estate and holdings with you. I assume that is why you are here."

"And that takes all of these people?" T.S. looked around the table. The faces no longer seemed so friendly. The gap between client and banker now yawned between them. He felt a sense of unexpected loss.

"It's a very large estate," Freeman explained. "And it involves ongoing participation by the firm. There are contracts in place. . . ." His voice trailed off and he nodded at a slender young man who sat hunched at one end of the table. "Robert, if you could summarize. This is Robert Smalls, head of Corporate Finance. I believe you may know him from, um, before?"

T.S. shook his head. Good Lord. There were babies running this place. "No, I don't know you yet. But I have very important information to tell you," T.S. told the startled executive. "That's why I requested this meeting. It has come to my attention that you may be involved in a project for Max Rose Fashions that was commissioned fraudulently. I refer specifically to your work investigating the profitability of taking the company public. I have learned that this assignment was awarded without Max Rosenbloom's knowledge. Not, of course, that you would have any reason to have suspected it, since it was his nephew who approached you."

Most of the table turned to stare at Robert Smalls, but the head of Corporate Finance did not notice. He was too busy staring at T.S. as if he were daft.

"Oh, dear," Prescott Freeman said, and fell silent.

"What are you talking about?" Smalls asked T.S. "It's true that we are exploring the marketplace for a possible fit with Max Rose Fashions. And that going public is one option. But it is not true that Max Rosenbloom was unaware of our work. That is simply impossible. He approached me personally to begin the assignment, I met with him barely a week before his death to discuss our progress, and we've sent him weekly updates on our work for his firm for the past ten months."

Oh hell, T.S. thought. So much for his dignified facade as a well-informed wealthy client. "Are you sure?" he squeaked.

"Of course I'm sure. I knew Max well."

T.S. and Herbert exchanged a glance. Joseph Galvano had clearly told Auntie Lil that he had lent Davy money to hire Sterling & Sterling without Max's knowledge. Which meant one of two things: either Galvano had been lying to Auntie Lil, or Davy had been lying to Galvano. And if Davy had been lying to Galvano—and Galvano found out—maybe Galvano had had Davy killed in retaliation.

"Perhaps you would like me to summarize the situation," Smalls offered delicately. "It might clear up any confusion." He perched a pair of small metal-rim glasses on the end of his nose and opened a thick folder. "Max Rose Fashions first approached us about a year ago," he said. "Max himself was the emissary. His company was in trouble. It was overextended, and because it had committed heavily to the production of synthetic sportswear, it was caught with an outdated inventory when natural fabrics staged a comeback. Cash flow was at an all-time low. Max wanted a loan. We wanted to give him a loan—we've had a long and fruitful relationship with his firm. But we could not agree to a loan outright." Smalls coughed apologetically and shrugged his shoulders as if such a distasteful decision had been personally abhorrent to him. "We could not agree to an outright loan for several reasons. Number one, Max's age. There was a distinct possibility that he would retire or, uh, otherwise be removed from active management of the firm abruptly due to his age. This was an unacceptable risk because, frankly, no one else in top management at that company knew what they were doing. Particularly after his brother suffered a stroke and retired. The second obstacle to a loan was that Max had not developed sufficiently clear plans of management succession to cover the first contingency. Do I make myself clear?" He looked up and waited.

"Yes," T.S. answered. "His brother was useless. His nephews were idiots. And there was no one else to mind the store."

"Precisely." Smalls missed a beat but recovered. "What we did was bring in an outside financial officer as a condition of the loan. It was a good move all around. We did not force the choice on Max. He chose from a long list of approved candidates and settled on a Thomas Brody. Have you met him?"

"No," T.S. admitted, but the image of a tall man with pixieish eyebrows and wavy black hair came to mind. He had stood near T.S. at Max's funeral and exuded an unmistakable confidence that comes with power. T.S. suspected the man was Brody.

"Brody's a good man. A genius with balance sheets.

Nearly as good as our managing partner here, if I may say so myself," Smalls continued. Obedient chuckles rose and subsided. "However, as sometimes happens in family concerns, there was some resentment, shall we say, of this outsider. Nonetheless, Brody made real progress over the past year, obtaining payment deferrals from some suppliers, unloading a large chunk of inventory overseas, and otherwise tightening the belt."

"Quite so," Preston Freeman added, just to remind everyone that he was in charge.

"So Max was out of trouble?" T.S. asked hopefully.

"Not exactly," Smalls admitted. "Hiring Brody was just the first step in a long campaign to restore financial health to Max Rose Fashions. As you now know, Max had placed most of his liquid assets in an irrevocable trust at that point. The trust now controlled by you and your aunt. One reason for this drastic action, beyond tax advantages and personal wishes, was that Max wanted to limit his personal losses should the company go under. We were faced with a dilemma: Max wanted to keep control of the company he had built, but he was unable to justify this control with financial backing. We worked with him in developing an action plan to make Max Rose more attractive to potential buyers and hoped to negotiate Max's continued involvement as part of any deal. We were doing well. In fact, we had already started preliminary talks with a number of possible merger candidates. Going public was to be a last resort—which is information that, of course, should not leave this room, since we may have to do just that given the current state of company ownership." He snapped the folder shut efficiently and glared across the table at a small round man whose face was nearly lost behind thick glasses. "Not that the current ownership structure was *my* idea of course. It throws quite a wrench in our flexibility."

"I could not convince him otherwise," the small round man bleated back in a high voice. "Don't blame me. We can only advise clients, we can't rope them into taking our advice."

"*Gentlemen,*" Freeman commanded. The room fell silent. "We will discuss internal matters internally. I am sure that T.S. is much more interested in hearing about the particulars of the Rosenbloom fortune."

Actually, T.S. was more interested in Sterling's internal squabbles. But what he got was a dizzying hour of impossibly complex summaries covering investment holdings, tax consequences, trust law, market outlooks, foreign currency implications, management strategies, and countless recommendations that needed his and Auntie Lil's approval. They were advised by various executives to invest overseas, donate a certain amount to charity, roll the money right back into new trusts, wait until next year to receive the funds, and even change their state of domicile to cut the tax bite. Before ten minutes of this barrage had passed, the advice had transmuted into babble that tugged at his ears like the distant drone of a faraway cocktail party. Thirty-three million was looking worse and worse. Doubled, it was a disaster.

"What do you say?" Sterling & Sterling's managing partner asked eagerly once the onslaught had ceased.

The blessed silence that greeted this remark gave T.S. a chance to think. He realized that Freeman's purpose had been to show T.S. that his money was in capable hands no matter what he decided to do. Well, T.S. would not argue with that. There wasn't a bank in the world better than Sterling & Sterling, nor men or women more honest than these. But surely Freeman did not expect him to reach any decisions right then and there. He'd need a good dictionary and a staff of economics professors to make any sense out of their recommendations.

"Well?" Freeman asked hesitantly. "What do you think?"

T.S. stood decisively. Herbert followed. "What I think is that my money is in very good hands," T.S. announced, triggering a release of held breaths all around the table. "I have no intention of moving it and will certainly name Sterling and Sterling to implement any action we elect. Of course, I cannot possibly let you know our intentions today. I must discuss this with my adviser, Mr. Wong, and with my aunt, of course." He was starting to sweat profusely beneath his tight collar and hoped that this pretty little speech would be enough to set him free.

Herbert coughed purposefully. Heads swiveled to appraise him. "As Mr. Hubbert's adviser," Herbert said solemnly, "I would like to see all of your recommendations outlined in writing. So that we may review them more thoroughly." He beamed at the executives and deep inside his heart a profound force leaped to life: power.

"Of course," Freeman agreed instantly. "We'll have it for you by next week. And in the meantime?"

"In the meantime," T.S. said, "carry on, my good men."

He and Herbert strode from the conference room, maintaining a careful silence until they had exited the bank and were surrounded by the comforting chaos of Wall Street in midafternoon.

"What did you think?" T.S. asked Herbert. "How did we do? I've always wanted to say 'Carry on, my good men.' How did it sound?"

"Not bad. It's a good thing you read Mr. Dickens."

CHAPTER TWELVE

1. "It's a terrible idea," Casey mumbled. She stuffed the remainder of her submarine sandwich into her mouth and silently offered Auntie Lil barbecued potato chips from the one-pound bag at her side. Auntie Lil declined out of necessity. She'd already polished off her own hero, a large order of french fries, and a pint of chocolate milk. There was no room at the inn.

"What's so terrible about it?" Auntie Lil demanded. "What can she do? Kill me?"

"Yes. Exactly."

"Not with you right there," Auntie Lil pointed out.

"Don't be so sure. Widow Rosenbloom seems pretty resourceful to me." Casey carefully folded the top of the potato-chip bag and secured it with a clothespin stashed in the glove compartment. There was nothing worse than reaching under the front seat for a snack and encountering soggy chips.

"I must *insist* that we go." Auntie Lil folded her arms firmly and stared out the front window. Her prominent chin protruded more stubbornly than ever.

Casey knew she was licked. "All right. But I'm going in with you, and let's start it off by saying we want to compromise on the estate. That will set the right tone."

"In other words, lie."

"Exactly."

It was midafternoon and they had spent several fruitless hours trying to track down Jake Rosenbloom. Casey was ready to call it a day. Subjects that altered their routines in the middle of being tailed irritated her. To make matters worse, Auntie Lil argued with every suggestion she made. Which was why Casey preferred operating alone.

They parked several doors down from Sabrina Rosenbloom's house to avoid giving warning. A red Porsche was parked in the driveway, but no one answered the doorbell—unless you counted the small dog that was having kittens on the other side of the door.

"She's home," Casey said grimly, leaning on the buzzer again. "I saw her peeking out the window." She raised her voice to stadium level and yelled, "We're not going away, lady. Open up or we'll start spreading your business up and down the street!"

"Nicely done," Auntie Lil whispered as the sullen widow opened the front door.

"What do you want?" Sabrina Rosenbloom demanded. Her heavily made-up eyes bored into Auntie Lil, ignoring Casey.

"I want to talk," Auntie Lil said. She stepped inside before Sabrina could block her way. "Perhaps about a compromise regarding Max's estate."

"I'm not talking without my lawyer here," the widow announced.

"Always a wise policy for someone like you," Casey agreed. She brushed past her to the living room and flopped down on the couch, glaring at the dog when it sniffed about her ankles. "Interesting pet," she remarked. "What species is it anyway?"

"Make yourself at home." Sabrina's sarcasm did not disturb either of her visitors. Auntie Lil perched on the edge of a chair and smiled brightly at the widow, pretending that all was nice and cozy. This forced Sabrina to grab the dog and sit down where she could see them both. Her pet nestled in her lap.

Casey prayed for a repeat of the dog's earlier incontinence while Auntie Lil did her best to get the widow to talk. "I suppose you know who I am?" she began. "Or, rather, what I was to Max at one time."

"Yeah, I know who you are." Sabrina's fall from grace had included a drop-off in elocution. She spoke in nasal tones and made no effort to conceal her defiant accent. Auntie Lil would not have been surprised had she popped gum in her mouth and begun to loudly smack. "You're the lady who cadged all of Max's money from him."

"Cadged?" Auntie Lil asked. "I had not seen him in over twenty years."

"Hah. That's what *you* say." Sabrina rolled her eyes, glanced at her wristwatch, then used a three-inch-long talon to flick a speck of dust from her dog's coat. She wore long spike heels and dangled one shoe impatiently from a toe as she spoke.

"Are you implying Max was unfaithful to you?" Casey asked. "Because I hadn't realized that marital fidelity was one of your strong points."

"Who the hell are you?" the widow demanded, her eyes narrowing in suspicion.

"My niece," Auntie Lil lied. "Surely you remember her from the reading of the will?"

"All I remember is that I got shafted and you walked away with the bucks. Five years of my life I put into that man. Five years and what do I get?"

"About sixty thousand a year," Casey said. "Plus room and board."

The widow stood suddenly, sending the small dog plopping onto the rug with a clunk. Her shoulders trembled. "I don't think I like your attitude," she said to Casey.

"*Please.*" Auntie Lil held up a gloved hand. "This is difficult for us all. I simply came to see if you were willing to reach a compromise instead of pursuing a lawsuit. And to ask some questions about our mutual business interests."

"What kind of questions? And I'm not discussing the lawsuit at all." Sabrina sat back down, establishing beyond doubt that she was not a rocket scientist.

"Were you involved with the management of Max Rose Fashions?" Auntie Lil asked.

"What kind of question is that?" Sabrina examined her nails and spotted an imperfection in the right-hand pinkie. She gnawed delicately at its surface. "I was the wife of the owner, remember? I didn't have to work. What's it to you?"

"We have this issue of shared ownership to deal with," Auntie Lil explained. "I am just trying to get a feel of who wants to be involved in daily management and who wants to remain a silent partner."

"Silent?" Sabrina snorted, and the sound that her slender frame emitted would have made a water buffalo proud. "I'm not remaining silent about anything. I want my share of profits, if that's what you mean. J.T. can take care of business for me."

"J.T.?" Casey asked. "Who's that?"

"Jacob Thomas Rosenbloom," Sabrina repeated very slowly, as if to a dim-witted child. She glared at Casey from under false eyelashes. "Max's most loyal nephew. Remember him? He got shafted by Max, too."

"Oh, yes. Davy's brother. You were quite close to Davy, weren't you?" Auntie Lil asked. "You knew him very well, people say."

"Yeah, I knew Davy. Why? Is that a crime?" She sat

back in her chair and crossed her legs, hitching her already short skirt up past well-toned thighs.

"I was just inquiring." Auntie Lil kept her temper. "If so, I was going to remark that this must be a very trying time for you."

"I'll say. Very trying." She yawned and did not bother to cover her mouth. Casey thought she looked like a vampire bat getting ready to pounce.

"Must be a hassle dealing with all the bereavement calls," Casey said.

"Are you being smart with me?" Sabrina glared at Casey, then spoke to Auntie Lil. "You better spend some of your money sending your niece here to charm school."

"Yeah. And maybe to a good plastic surgeon, too," Casey said. "Then I can be just like you."

"Casey dear, shut up," Auntie Lil requested firmly. The widow fumed in speechless rage. "You were saying you knew Davy well?" she prompted.

"Look, I know what you're getting at and it's not true. People are just nasty and jealous." Sabrina dangled one foot so violently that her high-heel shoe flew across the living room and hit the fireplace screen. Her dog scampered over for a sniff.

"What are people saying?" Auntie Lil asked sweetly.

"Cut that innocent crap," Sabrina said. "About me and Davy having an affair. That's bullshit. We were friends, and so what? We were the same age. We had a lot in common. He was fun."

If Sabrina was the same age as Davy, then Casey and Auntie Lil were Lewis and Clark. But neither of the other women felt it politic to mention it at that particular moment. Especially when they were interrupted by the doorbell.

Before Sabrina could answer, the door opened and Jake

Rosenbloom stepped into the hallway. He immediately peered upstairs and yelled, "Hey, I'm here! Make it quick, will ya? I got to be back at the office in an hour."

"We're in here," Casey called out. "Join the party."

"Who the hell are you?" Jake Rosenbloom demanded, not recognizing Casey. His voice softened. "Hurry up, Sabrina. The lawyer's not going to wait all day. We have an appointment at three." He noticed Auntie Lil sitting by the fireplace and his face changed. His doughy features scrunched together toward the middle like a bun baking inward. His face grew red and his fists clenched unconsciously at his sides. "What do you mean by bothering my parents?" he demanded.

That hadn't taken him long, Casey noted.

"I beg your pardon?" Auntie Lil asked.

"You heard me. My mother called me to say that you came by to see my father today. She says you were sneaking around while she was out grocery shopping. What business do you have at any of our homes? You stole our money."

"I was good friends with your father at one time and I have a right to see him if I wish," Auntie Lil stated firmly. "Besides, it is not your money and it has never been your money. You just acted like it was."

"Get out of this house," Jake demanded. He marched to the front door and opened it.

"Yeah," Sabrina belatedly chimed in. "You get out of my house this instant. Or else."

"Or else what? You'll have your dog pee on my foot?" Casey grabbed Auntie Lil's elbow to escort her out the door. This did not sit well with Auntie Lil, who was perfectly capable of marching out on her own. Casey, however, was determined to make their exit look as pitiful as possible.

Sabrina and Jake glared at them from the doorway as they took their time negotiating the flagstone walk. What little self-control the widow possessed snapped when they were halfway to the sidewalk. "You think you're so great," she screamed at Auntie Lil. "I'm sick of you, you hear me? Five years of my life wasted listening to him yap about you. You don't look so great to me. You're old and you're ordinary."

"My dear," Auntie Lil said, "age is a state of mind. You'd know that if you bothered to use yours."

The widow slammed the door in reply, but the effect was spoiled when she locked the dog outside and had to reopen it to rescue her pet.

"What was Max thinking of?" Auntie Lil asked. She shivered. "I'd have sooner brought a tiger cub home than that woman."

2. "Seems a shame to waste these good suits," T.S. said to Herbert. "Took me an hour to get dressed."

"We are most presentable in our current attire," Herbert agreed. "Perhaps we should call on Mr. Thomas Brody."

"You make an excellent adviser," T.S. told him. "You've read my mind. Of course, Aunt Lil is likely to throw a fit that we made a move without her."

"I will placate Lillian," Herbert promised. "Besides, she is busy elsewhere."

They reached Max Rose Fashions in style. Grady opened the door with another bow. It was after four and the chaos of the garment district was winding down. They side-stepped a rack of hanging suits and dodged a pack of buyers in the building entranceway. The downstairs lobby was nearly deserted, and T.S. doubted if the company was up and running at full speed yet. They took the huge eleva-

tor up to the seventh floor, sharing it with a heavyset man
toting what smelled like a bag of garlic-and-onion sausages.
When the elevator car stopped at the fifth floor to let the
stranger off, T.S. and Herbert were assaulted by a huge
wave of sound from the cutting floor where samples were
prepared for inspection by buyers. The steady din of sewing
machinery mingled with the chatter of clerks and the shouts
of supervisors. How anyone could navigate through the
racks of hanging clothes, bolts of cloth, and rolling tables
of supplies was beyond T.S.

"Now you know why Aunt Lil talks so loud," he told
Herbert when the closing doors had restored calm.

"At least Max Rose Fashions is back to work," Herbert
observed.

The executives were back to work as well. Or back to
not working, depending on your perspective. Several
strolled through the halls behind the receptionist and three
were clustered on a couch in the waiting area conferring
over a book of fabric samples.

Behind the anteroom, the showroom was bustling with
activity. Potential buyers roamed the long rack dominating
the middle of the area, inspecting the upcoming season's
line. Max Rose Fashions specialized in dresses and ladies'
sportswear. Obviously, florals were in. Bright splashes of
color marked the section of the line reserved for dresses;
the back half of the rack displayed a variety of comfortable
pant and top combinations in different pastel shades. Cubicles on either side of the line were occupied by salespeople
and potential customers. The concentration was almost palpable as pairs of buyers examined fabrics, fastenings, and
the quality of hems—all against a backdrop of constant pat-
ter by eager Max Rose representatives.

"Back to business," T.S. repeated. It occurred to him that
all these people were now toiling, at least in part, on his be-

half. The thought was overwhelming and he pushed it from his mind.

"Can I help you?" the receptionist asked. She was slender, with smooth black hair. Her accent was British.

"Mr. Thomas Brody, please," T.S. said in his most executive voice.

"Do you have an appointment?"

Ah. The universal question wielded by the guardians of corporate citadels everywhere.

Herbert intervened. He bowed and produced a charming smile. "I am sure he will wish to see us," he told the woman politely, with just the right touch of self-deprecation. "This man is Theodore Hubbert, who is now part owner of the company and thus Mr. Brody's boss. I am his adviser. We wish to speak to Mr. Brody about his continued employment here and a possible infusion of cash."

"You catch on quickly," T.S. said in admiration as the receptionist scurried down the hall. This was too important a mission to entrust to the office intercom.

"It is often best to let others speak for you," Herbert intoned wisely. "Particularly if you are attempting to project the air of a very big cheese."

Thomas Brody came out to greet them. T.S. recognized him from the cemetery. He was a tall man in his midfifties with military bearing, trim, with a powerful torso. His face was unexpectedly welcoming: rounded, with a near-button nose and twinkling eyes set beneath the pixie eyebrows. He had a thin mouth and was not smiling, but this did not spoil his deceptively harmless look. He wore no jacket, but his custom-tailored shirt fit perfectly. The sleeves were rolled up to his elbows, and his tie was slung over one shoulder.

"Come in, come in," he insisted, ushering them down the hall. "Preston Freeman phoned not ten minutes ago to say that your meeting with him went well. I assume you want to look over the financials, discuss recent events. I may be able to help, though there are matters unknown to me, of course. Let's talk in here." He spoke at rapid-fire speed, but his tone was beguiling. The effect was to sweep along listeners, guiding them to the course of action that Brody preferred before his audience realized what was up.

It worked with T.S. and Herbert. They sat down in visitor chairs and waited as Brody made himself comfortable in a leather captain's chair. The tie slung over his shoulder was explained by several slices of pizza leaking grease onto a paper plate on one corner of his desk.

"Late lunch," he explained with a shrug. "I've been working round the clock trying to keep the place going. I know you've been briefed. Here's an update: everything is under control, but with Max's death, the suppliers and client base have naturally lost some confidence. I've been running around most of the eastern seaboard this week, trying to plug holes. Meanwhile, the production floors are madhouses trying to catch up, we're stumbling over the cops every time we turn around, my accounting staff is threatening to quit en masse, there's no one here to back me up because neither one of Max's nephews was ever worth a damn, and to top it off, I'm exhausted and this pizza stinks. I asked for sausage. They brought me pepperoni."

No wonder he was exhausted. T.S. needed a nap just listening to him. Brody vibrated like a piano wire.

"I'm sorry about Max," Brody said suddenly. "He was a good man. I understand you knew him well."

"Me?" T.S. asked. "Actually, I never met him."

"Never met him? But I heard you got—"

"Quite so. It's a mystery to me as well." T.S. leaned back and scrutinized the executive. He hoped the man could be trusted. "One day I'll want to take a look at the financials, but to be frank—my head is still swimming from my meeting at Sterling."

Brody grunted sympathetically. "I know. They never use one word when five of them will do."

"I really just wanted to ask you some questions today. About the Rosenbloom family. And operations here."

"Worried about the new ownership structure, huh? Well, I can tell you right now it's going to be a mess."

T.S. debated whether to tell him that they were really investigating Max's death. He decided in favor of discretion. "I don't expect you to compromise your own standing here by revealing your opinion on some of the other owners," he said.

Brody surprised him. "I don't give a tinker's damn about hiding my opinions of the other owners. They already know how I feel. In fact, I suspect I'll be shown the other side of the door any day now. Which is fine with me." He shrugged. "I'm a one-man rescue operation. They bring me in when a company is on its last legs. I breathe life into it, prop it up, give it a second chance. Usually, the only thanks I get includes a nice fat bonus and a pink slip. That's the way it works. That's the way I like it. Anything else would be boring."

"In that case," T.S. said, "what can you tell me about the Rosenbloom nephews?"

"The nephews? They're worthless. Were. Are. The niece is something else."

"The niece?" Herbert asked. "Karen?"

"Yes. She's a lovely lady and no slouch. She worked in marketing for a couple years, I understand. We only overlapped for five months. She left here about six months ago. Don't know why. Some kind of family dispute. But she knew her stuff. Has an MBA from Wharton. If anybody was going to take over the family business, it would have been her. I think Max agreed. He was upset when she left, but said to let her go. He said he couldn't blame her."

"But you don't know why she left?" T.S. asked.

"I can guess. She probably got tired of fighting her pig-headed brothers when it came to running the company in a prudent manner. Not that Davy gave a damn about how it was run. He was never here, always down in Atlantic City gambling or taking a vacation or wrecking another sports car or taking some babe to Acapulco. His only contribution to the firm was to spend expense money like we were the Federal Reserve. Max let him get away with it. He had a blind spot about Davy. I can understand that. He saw him as a surrogate son, and I've got kids myself."

For the first time T.S. noticed the photograph on Brody's desk. It showed the executive in casual dress, sitting on a log with a young woman in her late teens who was dressed in a floral-print smock. She smiled prettily at the camera. The outdoor setting was obviously a stage set from a photographer's studio. A young man a few years older than the girl sat on the ground in front of the log. He was hugging his legs to his chest as if he were cold. The boy had an odd look in his eyes. He stared at the photographer suspiciously and his posture was rigid.

"My son and daughter," Brody explained. "Notice the absence of a wife. She cleaned me out a long time ago. Lives in California."

"Did you like Davy?" T.S. asked.

"Sure, I liked him. Everyone did. You couldn't help it. He was a piece of work. Funny. Quick. Totally worthless. Used to crawl around the production floor shooting the girls in the backside with rubber bands for fun. Had absolutely no sense of responsibility, so he could afford to devote his energies to making people laugh. The women especially loved him. He could charm the warts off a frog. I knew he'd burn fast and burn out quick. Still, I'm sorry he was killed. Besides, he wasn't always that way. I understand he started out promising, brought in a lot of new accounts. Being charming is the mark of a good salesman. It's just that he went wrong somewhere. Hard to say why because I wasn't here. By the time I met him, he was well on the way to being worthless. Waste of a good mind, I say."

"What about his brother, Jake?"

"Jake?" Brody's mouth became a thin line. He pushed the plate of pizza away and sat back. "Jake worked hard. I'll give him that. With Karen gone and his father out of action because of the stroke, he was going to inherit the business. In practice, if not on paper. At least that's what he thought. He would never have succeeded, of course."

"Why not?" Herbert wanted to know. "Diligence is the first step toward success."

"He always has to have things his way," Brody explained. "He is incapable of acknowledging that someone else may have a good—or maybe even better—idea. He seems unable to admit when he does not know about a subject. In short, his entire ego is tied up in even the smallest of decisions here. He is also often rude with the staff. I don't think he could ever command the loyalty that Max got from them. And he'd need it to keep the firm together. I understand that Jake is a lot like his father. Angry at not getting his due. Or, at least, what he perceives to be his due."

"Do you know Jake's father at all?" T.S. asked.

Brody shook his head. "No. Abe's stroke was one reason I was brought in. But he'd been a fixture here as long as Max."

"None of this sounds very promising for Max Rose Fashions," T.S. pointed out.

Brody shrugged. "The insurance is going to help. There

was a pretty hefty key-man policy on Max. Taken out decades ago, before his age was a factor."

"How much is hefty?" Herbert wanted to know.

Brody calculated rapidly. "Close to three million, if you count the violent-death clause that doubled the original amount. The insurance company just approved the claim not fifteen minutes ago."

"Max Rose Fashions will get three million dollars because Max was murdered?"

"Sure. It will at least ease the cash-flow problem somewhat. Help replace some of the, ah, missing funds."

"Missing funds?" T.S. said. "You're talking about the V.J. Productions incident?"

Brody nodded. "Of course. There is just that one incident, to the best of my knowledge. I instituted some pretty tight controls when I came on board. That helped flag the situation. Of course, I wish I could have prevented it entirely."

"Do you know anything more about it?" T.S. asked.

Brody shook his head. "So far, we can tie only Davy to it. Plus the clerk in receiving who signed for dummy goods never received. If you want to talk to him, you'll find him at his local unemployment office. He's lucky he's not in jail. But Davy coerced him by threatening to fire him, so I didn't have the heart to prosecute. Davy authorized the payments to a phony vendor. It caught up with him when the payments exceeded a one-million ceiling and the vendor came to my attention. We're still looking into it. It's taken a month to get this far."

"What did he do with the money?" T.S. asked.

"Gambled it away, I guess. We can't find it anywhere. Neither can the cops."

"Was the deception discovered before or after Davy's death?" Herbert asked.

"We suspected something a couple of weeks before but didn't confront Davy until last week. In fact, he and Max had a terrific argument about it the day that Max died."

"Do the police know this?" T.S. asked.

"Certainly. It's a difficult lead to pursue, I would imagine, since Davy is dead." Brody hesitated. He was reconsidering his candor. After all, T.S. Hubbert represented only one of the new owners. Maybe he should be more circumspect.

"What do you know about Sabrina Rosenbloom?" T.S. asked quickly, sensing Brody's hesitation.

"Very little. She rarely came around. I don't know much about her other than that she's a lousy driver. Wrecked her cars right and left. And that she's a fairly attractive woman." He coughed discreetly. "Or, at least she thinks so."

Translation: Sabrina Rosenbloom had come on to Thomas Brody. But had he responded?

"You don't find her attractive?" T.S. asked. "I thought she was extremely pretty," he added to deflect Brody's suspicion.

"No. I do not find her attractive at all."

"Why's that?" Herbert asked.

"She reminds me of my ex-wife." Brody folded his hands over his stomach. His face became a placid mask.

"I know this is really out of bounds. . . ." T.S. began.

"The answer is no," Brody said.

"No? But I haven't even asked my—"

"You were about to ask me if I thought that Sabrina Rosenbloom was having an affair with Davy, weren't you?"

"Well, yes. I was," T.S. admitted. So much for finesse. "You don't think so?"

"I doubt it very seriously. Not because of any caution on Sabrina's part. She's unstoppable. But because of Davy. As irresponsible as he was, and despite the trouble that he caused for Max—not to mention the money he cost him—Davy loved his uncle. I don't think he would have betrayed Max in that particular manner. And don't forget that Davy had his pick of any eligible young woman in the entire metropolitan New York area. He was handsome, charming, persuasive, and rich. The bastard."

"And now dead," Herbert pointed out. "Those qualities didn't get him very far."

"No." Brody sighed. "I suppose not. But while he lived he had a hell of a lot more fun than I ever did." He sat up straight and tightened his tie. He was ready to get back to work. "Sure you don't want to go over the financials?" he asked hopefully. "They're looking pretty good despite everything. I have a perfect record, you know. In thirty years of rescue operations, I have never lost a company to Chapter Eleven. Bankruptcy is not in my vocabulary."

"No. Thank you anyway," T.S. told him. The men shook hands. Before Herbert and T.S. were out the door, Thomas Brody was back to work.

"Sweet on the niece, Karen," T.S. remarked as they made their way back to the lobby.

"Agreed. And he feels the same way about Jake as everyone else," Herbert added.

"He didn't say much else that helps us," T.S. said ruefully.

"Indeed?" Herbert raised an eyebrow. "I felt an enormous sense of pride in that man. Thirty years and he has maintained a spotless record in a cutthroat profession. Perhaps he wished to maintain it a little while longer."

T.S. thought it over, nodding. "Three million in cash does a lot to restore a company's short-term prospects."

"It does indeed. And perhaps this time around, he was hoping to stay. Ascend to the top of the company, start his own family dynasty. With so many owners, and only one of them interested in hands-on management, it's a possibility."

"A new family dynasty?" T.S. asked. "As in the son in the photo on his desk?"

Herbert nodded. "You know, this case makes me glad I have so few relatives," he said. "All this talk about sons, nephews, nieces, wives, in-laws. I believe it's what the Jewish people call the whole *mishpucha*."

"Not bad, Herbert." T.S. was impressed. "Where'd you pick that one up?"

"Lillian, of course."

Of course.

CHAPTER THIRTEEN

1. "I never thought I'd say this, but I'm too tired to eat." Casey was lounging on Auntie Lil's sofa, idly probing the cracks between the cushions for lost items. She discovered a hidden pair of reading glasses, which Auntie Lil retrieved with silent dignity, a stick of wrapped chewing gum, thirty-six cents in change, and the latest issue of *True Crimes*. "How can you read this junk?" she asked, settling in to scan the pages eagerly. Her feet hung off one end of the couch, dangling like miniature pontoons.

"Make yourself at home, dear," Auntie Lil said with only a halfhearted attempt at sarcasm. She knew she had met her match. "Can I make you a Bloody Mary? You really haven't lived until you've had one of *my* Bloody Marys."

Auntie Lil wasn't kidding. It was spicy enough to make Casey's overbleached hair curl. "Not bad," Casey said, risking another sip. "It's a little like drinking fire."

Two Bloody Marys later both women drifted off into pleasant naps. They were awakened by the ringing of the telephone just past nine o'clock.

"Theodore," Auntie Lil mumbled, fumbling for the receiver.

"Lillian?" a muted female voice asked.

"Yes? Who is this?" Auntie Lil was instantly awake.

"It's me," the voice answered. "Rosalie Benpensata. I

211

work in accounting at Max Rose Fashions. We used to have coffee together sometimes."

Rosalie Benpensata? Auntie Lil thought back. She did remember a young girl, thin and frightened. But that was a long time ago. . . .

Oh, yes. Thirty years ago Rosalie Benpensata had been a young girl just out of high school, one who'd had the misfortune to attract the attention of Abe Rosenbloom. He had been flirting with her for months, making increasingly bold suggestions that they go out to lunch or meet for dinner. The girl had been frightened, not just of Abe but also of his wife, Abby, and what she might do if she found out. Rosalie had come to Auntie Lil for advice. Auntie Lil had told her to just keep doing her job; she would take care of the rest. A word to Max was all it took. He'd spoken to his brother. Abe had hardly looked at the girl after that.

"I remember you, Rosalie," Auntie Lil said. "Don't tell me you still work for Max Rose Fashions?"

"Oh, yes. Max always treated me well. I had no reason to leave. Thanks to you. But I need to talk to you again."

"To me? Why on earth to me?"

"I have some information. About Max's death. I know something very important."

"Then you must go to the police at once," Auntie Lil said. "I'll call them for you."

"No!" the woman shouted. There was a silence while she regained her composure. "No police. I could lose my job. It's about my boss. Joyce Carruthers."

"I know about the missing money," Auntie Lil said. "Is that it?"

"No. It's something much worse. But if I go to the police, I'll lose my job. I want to tell you. I know that you'd keep it a secret. About where you got the information."

Auntie Lil was silent. The girl would surely not lose her

job for reporting the truth, but if she thought she might, it was enough to keep her mum forever. "Can't you tell me over the phone? I've had a very long day."

"No. I want to show you some papers. There are some important files. I've got the keys to the cabinet. But only for tonight. By tomorrow she'll know they're missing." Her breath came in rapid gusts.

"You sound very excited," Auntie Lil said. "Are you in any danger?"

"No. But I've been drinking coffee for hours. Trying to decide what to do. Can you meet me at the factory? It's very important."

"Tonight?" Auntie Lil looked over at a sleepy Casey. Casey stared back with a quizzical expression.

"Yes. It must be tonight. You see, I'm ... I'm going away. Just for a few weeks. I have a lot of vacation time. I think it will be safer that way."

Good heavens, the woman was terrified. What information did she have?

"Very well," Auntie Lil decided. "What shall I tell the guard?"

"Nothing. No one must see us or connect us. It's too dangerous. Meet me at the back entrance on Thirty-first Street. I'll make sure it's unlocked. It's a brown metal door."

"I know it," Auntie Lil said. "Where will you be?"

"I'll wait for you inside. Hurry."

"I'll be there in an hour." Auntie Lil heard the abrupt click as the woman hung up. She stared down at the receiver. So it was not Max's family after all. His murder had something to do with the business.

"What's up?" Casey asked curiously.

"Put on your shoes," Auntie Lil told her. "We're about to learn something new."

2. Casey questioned Auntie Lil all the way to the factory: Who was Rosalie Benpensata? What kind of employee had she been? How long since Auntie Lil had seen her? Casey did not want to walk into a trap.

"I wouldn't worry," Auntie Lil said. "She was a tiny thing. She might have put on weight, but she can't have grown any taller and she was never more than five feet tall."

Casey was not mollified. She parked in front of the back entrance, grateful that spaces were plentiful on the now deserted street. "Pretty dead this time of night," she remarked.

"They start early," Auntie Lil said. "You don't usually find too many people working late. Especially on this block. It's mostly service and delivery entrances."

The back door opened easily, the metal slab giving way to a short hallway painted a dirty beige. The well-worn linoleum beneath their feet gleamed dully under the light of the single bare overhead bulb.

"I don't like the looks of this," Casey said. "Where's your friend?"

"I don't know," Auntie Lil said. "Perhaps she's upstairs. What time do you have?"

"Quarter to ten."

"We're early."

"Let's wait."

"Nonsense. It's cold. We'll meet her upstairs."

Casey had no choice but to follow Auntie Lil through a maze of back hallways. They wound around piles of flattened cardboard boxes and bags of garbage awaiting pickup. "Nice," she muttered.

Auntie Lil tried a door, but found it locked. "That leads to the front lobby," she explained.

"We're trapped?" Casey asked.

"No. I know there's a freight elevator somewhere."

Auntie Lil shut her eyes and thought. "Follow me." She led Casey down a short hallway that forked to the left and ended in front of an enormous delivery lift.

"It looks like Dr. Frankenstein's," Casey said. "Are you sure it's safe?"

"It holds thousands of pounds of deliveries every day." Auntie Lil pressed the call button confidently and the elevator descended toward them with a series of noisy creaks.

"I don't like this," Casey announced for the fifth time. What she really didn't like was the fact that she was unarmed. She loathed guns and kept hers locked in the bottom drawer of her desk most of the time. Tonight, she felt naked without it.

"We don't have a choice," Auntie Lil said. "Rosalie only trusts me, and the information could be vital."

The elevator was large enough to hold a small parade of elephants. Appropriately, it smelled like a circus. "Wouldn't hurt to clean it once in a while," Casey pointed out.

Auntie Lil ignored her. "Most of the floors are locked," she said, examining the call buttons. Only the sample-production-room floor was lit. Auntie Lil pressed the button and the contraption began to creak upward. "Going up?" she asked Casey cheerfully.

"This whole thing stinks," Casey warned. "And I'm not talking about the elevator."

Auntie Lil sighed. "You're supposed to protect me, not annoy me," she said.

"Sorry for being so cautious," Casey groused back. The elevator groaned to a halt and the doors opened ponderously onto the floor of the sample-production area. The harsh overhead lighting outlined the machines and tables in stark relief. They were the only ones there. "Oh, this is very reassuring," Casey announced, peering around. She gestured for Auntie

Lil to get behind her. "Why don't we just bonk each other over the head right now and get it over with?"

"Very funny," Auntie Lil answered grimly.

Casey led the way forward. They had to squeeze between two long racks of hanging dresses parked in front of the elevator, waiting to go out in the morning. Ahead of them, an enormous stack of filled boxes teetered to one side against a wall. Auntie Lil called out "Rosalie? Rosalie?" at intervals. No one answered.

When they reached the end of the rack, Casey made her decision. "Okay. That's it," she said. "We're going back. This is stupid. Turn around now." Before Auntie Lil could protest, Casey was hustling her toward the freight elevator. "No Rosalie. No reply. No can do."

"Casey, I don't know how in the world you get anything done as a private investigator when you're so cautious about—" Auntie Lil did not get the chance to finish. The lights went off. Only the fire-exit lights remained on, sending eerie red shadows spilling across the gloomy floor at the far side of the room.

"Get to the elevator *now*," Casey commanded. "I can't see a damn thing."

Auntie Lil did not have a chance to move. Her world went black. A thick cloth enveloped her head, and she was thrown to the ground. Behind her, she heard the muffled sounds of a thump and a groan as Casey crashed into a rack of clothing. Auntie Lil crawled back upright and swung out into the darkness, kicking and punching. Her fists met only the soft folds of clothing. Behind her, a tremendous unseen struggle erupted. Hangers screeched, clothing swayed, and one of the racks toppled over with a crash. A hand grabbed Auntie Lil's wrist. She pulled sharply and aimed a kick upward. It connected with flesh. There was a grunt as she was released. She fell immediately to her knees and began to crawl through the clothing that impeded her way, fear lending her joints long-lost flexibility. She tugged frantically at the cloth wrapped around her face, struggling to untangle it as she scrambled away. Cursing and scuffling sounds behind her told her that Casey had not yet given up her fight. But just as Auntie Lil reached the end of the racks and freed herself from her hood, two alarming events happened: the fire lights on the floor went out and there was another heavy thump behind her. In the ominous silence and darkness that descended, Auntie Lil knew that she would have to escape on her own. Casey was down.

She stood in the darkness and thought: Whoever you are, you've made a mistake. I've been on this floor. I know the layout. It was decades ago, but I've seen it since. She forced herself to assemble the room in her mind. The center was dominated by large flat tables and several pattern-cutting machines. The machines were seldom used, as the floor was devoted almost exclusively to fashioning samples. Instead, the center tables held giant shears, each scissor point a good three feet long. One of them would serve as a formidable weapon. She had to find her way there. But between her and the center tables lay an outer ring of sewing machines and rolling supply tables. Finding her way through the maze quietly would be difficult. She paused, straining to hear her assailant.

Behind her, she heard the faint rustle of plastic bags. Someone was moving through the racks of hanging clothes, disturbing the more expensive bagged garments. She tiptoed to the left, finding an open path. It was easier to move when she closed her eyes and could concentrate on the map taking shape in her mind. There was an outer ring of walkway that completely circled the room. She followed it just long enough to confirm that she had discovered a clear path. Then she stepped toward the middle and felt through the darkness for evidence of the sewing area. Her hand brushed up against a jar of pins and it started to topple. She grabbed at the darkness, managing to catch the jar before it fell. She held her breath and listened. There was no return sound. Where was her attacker hiding?

Attacker? The fire-exit lights had gone out while the attacker was struggling with Casey. Someone else must have turned out the lights. There had to be at least two people hiding in the darkness. Then it hit her—the lights had gone off to give her attackers an advantage when overpowering Casey, not her. They had not expected Casey to be along. That was why the lights had been blazing when they arrived: they had seen no need for surprise when they thought they would be dealing only with Auntie Lil. That meant they were confident they could overpower her. And probably kill her. If she was dead, what would it matter that she had seen their faces?

It also meant that they would be turning the lights back on once Casey had been subdued. And when they did, Auntie Lil would have no chance of escape.

She had to find the fuse box. She needed the darkness to survive.

Remembering was hard. It was such an insignificant object. It would be near the freight elevator, she thought. Search through your memories. Picture the wall. Was the box there? Go slowly. Be sure of it. Reconstruct the wall, section by section.

Yes. The fuse box was near the freight elevator. She was sure. She inched forward, brushing one hand against the perimeter of the sewing machine circle as a guide. Slowly she moved between the tables, returning toward the outside wall. She broke free to the outer walkway and held her breath, listening. Heavy breathing came from the other side of the room. They were still with Casey. She could not afford to think why.

Auntie Lil crept forward, step-by-step, the effort hurting her now bruised knees. She had to move toward the heavy breathing to find the fuse box, she realized, back toward her attackers, before she could retreat. She breathed silently through her mouth in carefully controlled rhythm, willing herself not to panic. She counted each step silently and dragged a hand along the concrete-block wall for support, imagining her progress in her mind. The heavy breathing grew louder. Where was the fuse box?

There. Her hand touched the cold metal and she carefully located the opening ring. She tugged softly and the lid opened with a metallic creak. She hesitated, listening for sound. Had anyone heard?

There was a grunt and a muffled crash ahead of her as one of her attackers bumped into a sewing-machine table. She held her breath again. Someone was moving through the darkened interior, carelessly, in a hurry, not bothering to conceal their whereabouts. Auntie Lil drew herself up against the wall, desperately wishing she had a table or other barrier to hide behind. Footsteps and heavy breathing drew closer. The shadowy figure discovered the pathway that rimmed the floor and broke free from the jumble of racks and tables impeding his or her progress. The footsteps were heavy, but two curious noises interested Auntie Lil more. Someone was moaning softly just behind the unseen attacker, and there was a slithery sound moving closer and closer.

Auntie Lil strained through the darkness in horrified fascination as the procession passed directly in front of her. But because the windows of the cutting floor were dirty and the moon was hidden behind clouds, she could see virtually nothing but the outline of a bulky figure dragging a body across the polished wood floor. Pressed against the wall, she had a chance of going unnoticed. Another figure emerged from several feet ahead and hurried to help the first one. Auntie Lil was pretty sure they were dragging Casey toward the storage closets that lined one of the walls. They were going to lock her inside. And there was only one reason to lock Casey inside: to keep her from coming to Auntie Lil's aid. It was time to remove the fuses.

Keeping one ear tuned to the sounds of Casey's body being dragged away, Auntie Lil delicately unscrewed the fuses nestled inside the box. They yielded easily and she placed them carefully on the floor. There were nearly twenty.

Her task completed, Auntie Lil was damned if she was going to cower in fear and let them find her hiding in the dark. She weighed the risks of running back toward the elevators. She didn't think she could make it in time. Almost surely, her assailants were younger and quicker. When you were eighty-four years old, that was a given. She couldn't tell if she was being pursued by men or women—or both— but they were certainly strong and determined. She would do better to make her way to the inner circle of the room and obtain a weapon before she attempted to escape or hide. If she could fend them off long enough, maybe help would arrive.

As soon as the figures had dragged Casey's body farther away, Auntie Lil left the wall and silently slipped through the crowded production floor, making her way around the sewing-machine tables and rolling racks of supplies. She tried hard to control her body and breathing, but the effort of restricting her movements so tightly proved exhausting. She was panting heavily by the time she reached the small circular aisle that marked the beginning of the room's center ring.

She forced herself to stop panting. The floor was completely quiet. They had finished their task with Casey. Was she even still alive? Auntie Lil didn't want to think of the alternative. She rested, still listening, then began to search with her hands, hoping to find the pattern tables. At last she touched the smooth plastic of a cutting surface. She inched closer and methodically palmed the table again and again, searching for the oversized shears. She had found the cutting table adjacent to one of the large pattern machines. She avoided the cold steel of its sides, shunning the cruelly sharp edges of its metal cutting blades. It was the most dangerous piece of machinery in the shop, functioning as a combination giant vise and cookie cutter. It was capable of slicing through more than a foot of stacked cloth. Human flesh would be no obstacle at all. She had to get away from it quickly.

Auntie Lil swung around and caught her shoe against the cutting-machine leg, making a soft clunk in the darkness. She groped frantically behind her for the giant scissors, no longer concerned with silence. She felt boxes of pins, pieces of chalk, and the crisp edges of tracing tissue. Where were the shears?

A crash echoed through the silence, followed by a muttered oath and a cascade of smaller crashes. Her attackers had knocked over a rolling table of supplies, allowing Auntie Lil to pinpoint their location. They were on the edge of the outer circle, moving steadily toward her, not more than ten yards away.

She inched to her right, feeling behind her for guidance, probing frantically for the oversized shears. There was no way she could defend herself against two of them without a weapon. Not even stabbing at them could hold them off for long.

They were moving right toward her. She could feel it. And then she heard them reach the inner walkway. They didn't bother to conceal their footsteps. They had tried the lights without success and now they were angry. The heavy thuds of their tread moved briskly toward her, oddly in beat with the pounding of her heart. She began to run, banging into pattern tables as she scrambled away. She swept a whole arm across the tabletop, sending metal objects and spools of thread crashing to the floor. She dashed forward again and heard the scrambling thuds of bodies slipping. At least she was making it hard for them to reach her. She swept another cutting table clean, the contents tumbling noisily to the floor. But it only partially obscured the narrow walkway and the effort was ultimately useless. She would soon complete the circle. If her attackers had any brains, they would split up, change directions, and trap her in the middle. She had to come up with a better plan.

Her hands closed on a pair of the giant shears. She gripped the weapon and waved it in front of her like a sword. If they came after her, she'd at least leave her mark.

The footsteps stopped. Her heart was pounding so loudly it seemed as if it echoed in the cavernous room.

But no, it was not her heart at all. It was a rhythmic thumping from the far wall, backed by the outraged yells of Casey trapped inside a closet. She was throwing herself against the metal door, bellowing and enraged, hoping to force her way out.

The footsteps began again, then hesitated. Auntie Lil could feel them turn back, perhaps wondering if Casey really could escape.

She had to act now.

Darting forward, Auntie Lil thrust the giant scissors into the darkness, throwing all of her weight behind the initial jab. The point caught one of the assailants, and Auntie Lil forced herself to push forward. The shock of absorbing flesh vibrated down the shears and shot straight into the core of her heart. She felt sick, but knew that she couldn't stop. They were going to kill her. She must try to kill them first.

The room exploded in sound. The stabbed attacker screamed hideously, the piercing sound rising and reverberating like the screech of a wounded animal. The cohort began to scream as well. Auntie Lil withdrew the shears and jabbed again at the awful sounds. The pair panicked. One fell. The figure scrambled up and began to hurry backward.

Behind them, the metal closet door flew open, banging against the wall with a clang. Casey shot out of the closet, roaring at the top of her lungs, screaming louder and louder as she drew near. Auntie Lil couldn't see her, but could hear the force of Casey's anger in the strange cries that rent the air. Her terrifying howls struck fear even in Auntie Lil's heart.

"You're dead! Both of you!" Casey screamed, crashing through the room, pushing tables aside, sending racks flying over in her fury. She bored through the darkness like an avenging angel, her terrible war cry splitting the air.

"I've stabbed one!" Auntie Lil shouted, mostly to let Casey know where she was. She hadn't survived two attackers only to be hurt by Casey in the darkness. "I think one of them is bleeding," she warned Casey. "The floor may be slippery."

"Both of them are going to be bleeding soon," Casey screeched. In the brief silence that followed, a faint whistling could be heard. Casey was whirling something over her head.

Neither attacker stuck around to find out what. They rushed past Auntie Lil, shoving her to the floor as they sprinted toward the fire door.

"They're getting away," Auntie Lil shouted. "Don't step on me."

Her warning was superfluous: Casey had already dashed

past. Like a maddened pack of hounds on the trail of a fox, Casey had sensed that the battle had turned in her favor. She was pursuing her prey unto the death.

"Stop!" Auntie Lil screamed into the darkness. She regained her footing and scrambled after Casey. "Stop, Casey! Stop! You've scared them away. That's enough. There are two of them. Let them go."

A tremendous banging erupted from the far wall. Casey had reached the fire door only to find that the attackers had locked it from the stairwell. She beat furiously on the metal surface with the makeshift club she held in her hand. The brutal sounds echoed madly through the room.

By the time Auntie Lil reached her, Casey's breathing was as tortured as if she had just run a marathon.

"Are you all right?" Auntie Lil asked. "Did they hurt you?"

"I'm fine," Casey answered between clenched teeth. "I'm just very, very mad."

3. The two pieces of greasy pizza leaking on Thomas Brody's desk had made T.S. and Herbert hungry. Ignoring his cholesterol count, T.S. suggested an early dinner, then recklessly ordered extra pepperoni. It was worth the risk at *Tony's*, a take-out joint hidden on the outskirts of Chinatown. Auntie Lil had discovered it several years before. Tony was disappointed to see only T.S. and Herbert for dinner—had Auntie Lil been along, the bill would have doubled. The two men ate carefully, mindful of the fact that they were wearing their most expensive suits.

"Feel like tackling the youngest nephew?" T.S. asked Herbert when they had polished off a large pie. Herbert did not answer at first. He was staring out the window with a blissful expression, his neatly manicured hands folded contentedly over his modestly rounded stomach.

"Herbert?" T.S. asked more loudly. "Are you with me?"

"Sorry. That was a most delicious meal. I was just thinking of how I never dreamed of such treats as a young man in Singapore." He smiled happily. Herbert's very best quality—and he had many fine ones—was that he never took anything for granted. Not a pizza, not a single sunset, and, certainly, never a friend.

"Shall we swing by Greenwich Village and try to question Seth Rosenbloom?" T.S. asked. "Max's youngest nephew? You don't have to go with me. I'm not sure what the situation will be."

Herbert nodded. "I would be pleased to accompany you."

"Let me just try to reach Aunt Lil first," T.S. said.

Auntie Lil had not yet succumbed to the lure of an answering machine. T.S. waited patiently through nine rings before he gave up. "They're still out nosing around," he reported to Herbert.

"Then we shall do the same."

Seth Rosenbloom was not home. According to Casey, he lived on the third floor of a small brownstone nestled back from a quiet corner in the West Village. T.S. rang the bell twice without success and was about to turn away when a window opened far above him with a bang. A slender young man with a shock of curly blond hair leaned out and yelled, "Intercom's broken. You rang?"

"I'm looking for Seth Rosenbloom," T.S. shouted back, glancing around to see if anyone had stopped to listen. No one cared. There were far more interesting things going on in the Village than this.

"Are you guys lawyers?" the young man bellowed hopefully.

"Heavens, no," T.S. called back. It was a Charles Dickens day, no doubt about it. First, the rolltop desks and marble floors of Sterling & Sterling, and now, here he was, shouting up from a cobblestoned street at a young man hanging out of a third-floor brownstone window. "We're friends of his uncle Max," he added. He'd be damned if he'd go into details at the top of his lungs.

"You're here about the money, then?" the young man crowed happily. "I heard he left old Seth a bundle."

That was enough for T.S. "Yes, I'm here about the money," he said. In a way it was the truth. "Where is he? When will he be back?"

"We had a fight. He's around the corner sulking at the Swan Dive." The young man pointed west and Herbert and T.S. dutifully followed his direction. Grady drove by slowly, searching for a street wide enough to park the limo. The Swan Dive was on a lovely—and expensive—side street. Ivy grew in thick cascades down the sides of stone buildings hosting charming first-floor shops that offered well-heeled customers antiques, jewelry, and curios. At seven o'clock, the street was already crowded with well-groomed men and women chatting happily among themselves as they headed off to the many restaurants, pubs, and movie theaters in the lively area. The West Village was one section of Manhattan that had managed to stave off the office growth that had plagued New York City in the eighties. It had remained determinedly residential and was populated by writers, artists, heirs, and leftover Bohemians of all sexual preferences. Out-of-towners visited to gawk at the men who walked happily hand in hand down its streets. But T.S. had been a New Yorker long enough to understand that the West Village had nothing at all to do with being gay—it had to do with having money. Lots and lots of money.

"For a kid just out of law school, he's doing okay to live around here," T.S. observed. The Swan Dive was a corner pub at the end of the block, marked by a swinging wooden sign that featured a swan in full flight. Despite its name, it was no dive. It was a small but cheerful piano bar, heavy on the wood paneling and easy on the lights. An enormous baby grand dominated the far end of a rectangular space. There was just enough room beside it for a tiny stage and standing microphone. A small sign propped on an easel atop the piano read OPEN MIKE NIGHT.

T.S. clamped a determined smile on his face. Open mike night meant that while he was questioning Seth, a steady parade of would-be singers would take to the stage, bellowing out tired show tunes with varying degrees of talent. As T.S. revered show tunes, it was going to be an excruciating experience.

"After you," Herbert announced, waving T.S. inside. They were older than the other customers, but were welcomed and escorted to a booth along the large front window.

With his luck, T.S. thought, someone from Sterling & Sterling was bound to stroll past and see him nestled in a cozy gay bar with Herbert Wong. The bank would practically explode with such a juicy rumor. But who cared anyway? T.S. decided, with a rare flash of defiance at his own tedious conventionality. He was a millionaire now. He'd do what he pleased.

"That must be him," Herbert guessed. He nodded toward a handsome young man at one end of the bar. T.S. recognized him from the funeral. Seth Rosenbloom had almond-shaped eyes set far apart and a long angular nose that would have done Michelangelo proud. His hair was sleekly cut and so black that it gave off blue highlights under the overhead lamp. His mouth was wide and generous, though not particularly inviting at the moment. He was staring down at his drink grimly, his slender shoulders hunched in unhappiness.

"He is very sad," Herbert noted.

"Yes. Maybe I can find out why." Leaving Herbert to anchor their booth, T.S. approached the bar. In the instant before he reached the boy, he became acutely aware that he was in a gay bar and about to tap a strange man on the shoulder. What could he say to instantly ward off any misunderstanding? His own panic paralyzed and angered T.S. He was a confident executive, used to dealing with all sorts of situations. It was nonsense that this unfamiliar milieu should stymie him.

"Seth Rosenbloom?" T.S. asked, nervously wondering if other patrons were listening.

"Yes, that's me." The young man had green eyes framed by long black lashes. His eyes were reddened.

"Your roommate said I might find you here."

Seth scrutinized T.S. carefully. "Are you a lawyer?"

"No."

"Good. I'm sick of lawyers. Which is pretty funny, considering that I am one."

"My name is T. S. Hubbert. My aunt is Lillian Hubbert."

Seth looked up with renewed interest. "Well. You are one lucky man right now, I'd say. My brother Jake tells me that you're getting millions."

T.S. shrugged. "Could my friend Herbert and I talk to you about it? We have a booth over there by the window."

"Talk about what?" he asked. "I'm sick of talking about money. All my family wants to do is talk about money. No one wants to talk about Uncle Max. No one gives a crap that he's dead."

"I do," T.S. said with surprising ferocity. "I do, and I can tell you right now that my aunt is absolutely heartbroken."

Seth raised his eyebrows and collected his drink silently, following T.S. to the booth. At the far end of the bar, the piano player took his seat. Music filled the air.

Herbert greeted Seth with a solemn nod of his head. "My condolences on the death of your esteemed uncle," he said. "I am a friend of Mr. Hubbert here. He tells me your uncle was a very great man. I'm sorry he is gone."

"Thank you." The young man slid in beside T.S. "I miss him a lot. We used to talk at least once a week. He put me through law school, you know. Bought me my apartment here. Behind my parents' backs. After they disowned me. I think he was trying to make up for their lack of . . . understanding. And he did. I loved him for it."

An uncomfortable silence followed. Herbert broke it. "Perhaps it is a blessing to be disowned by a family such as yours. I mean no disrespect to those you love, of course."

Seth smiled grimly. "You have a point. It's funny. There were only three people in my whole family I ever felt close to. Uncle Max. He's dead. My brother Davy. He's dead, too. And my sister, Karen. She's not dead, but she's not part of the family either. Anymore. She's joined me in exile."

"Why is that?" T.S. asked. "What did she do?"

"Nothing so horrible as being a crime against nature, as my own mother describes me." Curiously, this admission seemed to cheer him. He swallowed a gulp of his drink and grinned. "Good old Uncle Max. He's made sure she'll never get her hands on any more of his bucks. Good old Uncle Max." He raised his glass in a toast.

"He left you a considerable sum," T.S. pointed out.

"I could say the same to you."

T.S. acknowledged this reply with a nod. An older man had taken the stage at the opposite end of the bar and was cradling the microphone like a torch singer from the forties. T.S. did not recognize the tune, but was immediately enchanted by the haunting melody. "What show is that song from?" he asked curiously.

"That's from *his* show," Seth explained. "He sings it every chance he can get, hoping that one day someone will kick in enough money to get it produced." He looked at T.S. "What are you going to do with Uncle Max's money anyway?"

T.S. had the uncomfortable feeling that this was not going to be as easy as he had thought. For one thing, the kid was a lawyer and managed to get in three questions for every one of his own. For another, T.S. was acutely aware that his discomfort was showing. Until he relaxed, he'd never get anywhere.

"I'm going to start by buying you a drink," T.S. decided. Alcohol, the great equalizer. He waved the waiter over and ordered a double Dewar's and soda for himself and a fresh vodka gimlet for Seth. Despite his better judgment, he even agreed when Herbert insisted on trying a gimlet as well. Herbert seldom drank and T.S. wondered if he could take it.

"Ever had one before?" Seth asked him. "You have to be careful. They're like martinis. Only they taste good."

Herbert waved away his concern. "I am a cautious man. I will be fine." He stared back at the stage in interest. A new performer stood in the spotlight, a tremendously fat man with a sweet tenor voice. He began an Irish ballad, and its lingering opening notes transformed the bar into an Irish pub.

"About your sister," T.S. reminded Seth. Their drinks arrived. Herbert's face lit up after one sip, declaring plainly that vodka gimlets were yet another delicious treat undreamed of during his days as a young lad in Singapore.

"Karen?" Seth sipped at his drink. "Look, I'm not in the mood to talk about my family. Can we talk about something else?"

T.S. was silent. How could he win Seth's trust? "I'm pretty surprised about being left so much money," he finally said. He'd work his way back to the Rosenblooms. "I don't feel as if I deserve it."

"Don't you?" Seth shrugged. "I wouldn't worry about it. I'd take the money and run. Sometimes life hands you a bad surprise, sometimes a good surprise. Don't argue. It will all even up in the end."

"But why didn't he leave it to you?" T.S. asked. "Or to your sister?" He was keeping a careful eye on Herbert as he spoke. Herbert had drained his gimlet and signaled for another. He seemed transfixed by the stage nestled in the far corner of the room and was gazing intently at the newest performer with a rapt expression on his face.

"That's easy." Seth grinned. "He knew it would ruin us. Too much money leads to not enough initiative. That's a direct quote. Uncle Max believed it, and how."

"But he was willing to leave it to Davy."

"He'd given up on Davy years ago and only wanted to protect him," Seth said. "It was the gambling that brought Davy down, you know. Not women. Not drinking. The gambling. It's a terrible thing to see—someone hooked like that, begging to borrow money, eyes bright and hands trembling like some junkie looking for a fast score. Uncle Max loved Davy but knew he couldn't change him. Only Davy could change Davy. But Uncle Max wanted to make sure that if he ever did reform, there would be money to support him. Setting up the trust would have accomplished that."

"You knew he had set up the trust?" T.S. asked.

"You could say that," Seth said. "He asked my advice. I told him to do it before he married Sabrina. She's never fooled me." He paused and smiled at T.S. "Not bad. You've got me talking about the family again."

T.S. was too distracted by Herbert's behavior to reply. Herbert had slipped from his seat and inched to a stool near the stage. A fresh vodka gimlet stood on the bar in front of him, compliments of the bartender. Herbert's eyes gleamed strangely in the glow from the spotlight emanating from the stage. He was listening to the singer with his mouth half-open, silently mouthing the words to a familiar Broadway tune. T.S. had seen that expression before. Herbert had the New York City bug: he was stagestruck. Big time.

"I can't blame your family for being angry about the will," T.S. said, focusing his attention on Seth once again. Maybe if he talked long enough, Seth would come around.

"I can blame them and I do," Seth replied. "Look, Uncle Max gave us plenty while he was alive. No one in the family is hurting for money and no one should complain. They should be grateful for what they have and get on with their lives. It was Uncle Max's money, and if he wanted to leave it to you and your aunt, he had that right."

"I'm impressed that you can say that," T.S. admitted.

"Uncle Max's influence," Seth said cheerfully. He paused. "It's nice to talk about him to someone who isn't busy licking their wounds over being jilted in the will. Wish I could meet your aunt. She must have been some kind of woman."

"She is some kind of woman," T.S. said.

"I wonder why Uncle Max didn't marry her?" Seth said. "He loved her enough."

"I wonder why she didn't marry him," T.S. replied.

"You've asked?"

"I've asked. And she's not telling." T.S. checked on Herbert one more time and willed himself to relax. So what if Herbert wanted to hang out at the bar and drink? No harm in that. If only he had Herbert's sense of adventure. Then he'd be able to establish a better rapport with Seth. T.S. was sure that his own discomfort showed.

"Who knows why any of us end up with who we end up with?" Seth asked suddenly. "I sure can't figure out why

I'm stuck with Bobby. All he cares about is money." He sighed. "I hate money. I'm a lawyer who hates money. Is that a contradiction?" He laughed mirthlessly and gulped at his drink.

"In that case, what are you planning to do with the money Max left you?" T.S. asked. He finished his double scotch and, finally, began to relax. He realized with a sense of surprise that he truly liked Seth Rosenbloom. The young man was without pretense, had a sense of humor, and was remarkably devoid of bitterness.

"I don't want to talk about my life," Seth said abruptly. "I promise you would not understand."

T.S. did not answer. It was true. He did not understand what forces had taken this young man so far from his family, what had made him so different from the rest of the Rosenblooms. But he wanted to try and he needed to extract more information from him. Seth was an observer, T.S. could tell, and he had spent many years watching his family. He would know the secrets. But he was used to keeping secrets. T.S. had to find a way to gain his confidence and get more information from him.

"You don't trust me," T.S. said. Maybe the blunt approach would work.

"Hey, you're okay." Seth flashed him a wide grin and T.S. was amazed at the transformation. He suddenly understood why so many men had glanced down as they passed by their booth. If any of the Rosenblooms came close to possessing Max's legendary magnetism, it was Seth. Had Max been this beautiful, sure, sad, and strong—all at the same time? No wonder Auntie Lil had fallen hard.

"Who do you think killed your uncle?" T.S. asked persistently.

Seth's eyes filled abruptly with tears. He didn't speak for

a moment as he struggled to regain his composure. "I don't know," he finally said in a low voice.

Without warning, the piano player struck a series of deep chords that resonated through the bar. T.S. jumped, nearly knocking over his drink.

"Hey, look who's up next." Seth pointed to the stage.

Herbert was bowing to the pianist. He drained the remainder of a gimlet as the musician finished his thundering introduction. Herbert stepped up on the low stage and faced the suddenly quiet audience. Beneath the spotlight, his pear-tinged skin glowed as if it were gold. He hunched his shoulders forward and clasped his hands together as he stepped to the microphone. Then—to T.S.'s utter astonishment—Herbert *growled*.

Oh, God. How many gimlets had he drained anyway?

But the audience recognized something that T.S. had missed. Herbert growled again and a cheer erupted, inspiring Herbert to growl even louder. Suddenly the piano player jumped full force into "If I Were King of the Forest." Herbert became the Cowardly Lion, his small body seeming to grow as he transformed himself into the bashful beast. He pranced about the microphone, batting at it with imaginary paws as he sang. He shivered and shook and twitched an imaginary tail, strutting and purring in a near-perfect imitation of Bert Lahr in *The Wizard of Oz*. The bar patrons went wild with delight, their whistles and cheers nearly drowning out Herbert's performance. Even the bartender stopped working to watch.

"He's great," Seth said, marveling. "Where'd you find him?"

T.S. was too dumbstruck to reply. Herbert had just pounced—yes, actually *pounced*—halfway across the stage at the piano player and was pretending to scratch the top of the baby grand with lion claws.

As Herbert approached the final stanza the crowd joined in, roaring and singing with him. He finished to wild acclaim, his hands straight over his head as he bowed theatrically to the applauding patrons. Declining the shouts for an encore, Herbert stepped from the stage and moved like a king through the crowd, stopping to shake hands or bow modestly before he sailed regally past.

He slid back into the booth with quiet dignity and smiled at T.S. "Another round?" he inquired politely.

T.S. nodded numbly and for an instant wondered if he had imagined it all.

Apparently not. Before they could order, the bartender arrived with doubles all around and let them know that more waited in the wings. Herbert had been a huge hit. His new fans were fighting to buy them drinks. T.S. stared at the cluttered table and realized that he would never understand a single human being, much less the entire world.

"You were fantastic," Seth told Herbert. "How did you do that?"

Herbert smiled modestly. "It is my favorite movie," he explained. Without another word about his amazing performance, Herbert looked Seth Rosenbloom straight in the eye. "You interest me greatly, Mr. Rosenbloom," he said. "I see in you traces of your uncle. I can tell you are much like him. My dear friend Lillian spoke of him to me quite often. Did you know that we are investigating his death, my friend here and I?"

"Well . . ." Seth looked back at T.S. "No. I didn't. Not really." He sat back in the booth. "What kind of lawyer am I? I've been sitting here answering questions and never thought to ask why you wanted to know."

"My friend Lillian will not rest until she knows who killed Max," Herbert explained. "You must help us. She does this out of love. It is a love that has withstood decades of time and dozens of disapproving people. Now their love has even withstood death." Herbert shook his head with certainty. "She will not stop until she finds out the truth."

Seth looked at Herbert and then at T.S. "What do you want to know?" he asked.

"Everything," Herbert said firmly.

And so, with a single well-chosen song, Herbert won Seth Rosenbloom over. The young man spoke for over an hour. He began by answering their questions about his sister, Karen.

"Karen is the smartest one of us all," he said. "And that really pisses my mother off. She wanted Jake or Davy to take over the business and thought that Karen ought to stay home and have grandchildren for her." He smiled bitterly. "Karen compounded the problem by filing for divorce from this schmuck she never should have married in the first place. They'd only been married a couple of years and Mommie dearest was embarrassed, having invited all of New York to the nuptials."

"Why did your sister file for divorce so soon?" T.S. asked.

"She was married to a creep," Seth answered promptly.

"Who did Karen marry?" T.S. persisted. There had been no mention of an ex-husband in any of the family gossip so far.

"This jerk named Howard Friedman. Grew up down the block. His mother was best friends with my mother. Karen dated him in junior high, hated him in senior high, and remet him a couple years into college. He'd gone from being an ugly creep into being a handsome creep." Seth shrugged. "At least Karen thought so. She had been butting heads with our mother for twenty years by that point. For one shining moment they were finally in agreement. Before Karen came to her senses, she had married him. Turned out Howard didn't really want to work. Thought he ought to be given a cushy job at Uncle Max's factory. He'd married Karen for the money he thought she'd inherit one day. He didn't like it when she went on to business school. There were a lot of other things, too. . . ." Seth's voice faded.

"Those are all problems. But to end a marriage over them. So quickly?" T.S. asked.

"Look, Howard Friedman is not just a creep, he is a *creep*." Seth swallowed the remainder of his gimlet and joined Herbert in ordering another round. "He came on to me, okay? I kept in touch with Karen after I got kicked out of the family. Two years ago we went out one night to have dinner and drank too much. Karen got sick and went home early. Stupid me. I stayed to have a couple more drinks with Howard. He was very insistent and I thought I ought to make nice to my sister's husband. A couple drinks later he made a pass at me. Grabbed me under the table. I slugged him and threw a drink in his face and left him with the check. The next day I started asking around. And I found out that he was a very active member of our street community, shall I say?"

T.S. was perplexed. "What's that mean?" he asked.

"He liked to pick up men along the riverfront and in the rough bars, that's what it means," Seth explained. "To which, normally, I might say, who cares? But he was married to my sister and my sister didn't know and his behavior was putting her in danger. Do I need to explain?"

"I understand," T.S. said.

"And besides that, if some woman wants to be married to a gay man, who am I to judge?" Seth added. "But Karen is my sister and I love her and she deserves better than that. She deserved to be completely loved. So I told her. And she dumped him within a week. So far she's healthy. And Howard Friedman is still a creep."

"Surely your parents would understand," T.S. said.

Seth sighed. "Karen wouldn't tell them the truth. She struck a deal with the creep. She got the apartment, and Howard gave her the divorce. In return, she kept quiet. He didn't want his parents to know, and Karen didn't want our parents to know. Which is why, according to my mom, Karen is a selfish, career-hungry, power-mad feminist out to destroy her brothers' futures and the role of men in the world in general."

"That's a tall order for one woman," T.S. said.

"You know what I think?" Seth said. "My mother is jealous of Karen. Karen can do anything she sets her mind to. And while my mother is hateful, she's also smart. She's smarter than my father, but she always had to take a backseat to him. Mom could have run Max Rose Fashions herself. And part of her may have wanted to." He shrugged. "So does she blame the world for her lack of chances? No, she blames her own daughter for not suffering along quietly like she did. I frankly do not understand women." He looked up and grinned. "Fortunately, I don't have to."

"Why did she quit her job at Max Rose Fashions?" Herbert asked.

Seth explained that Karen had quit abruptly after discovering that Davy was most likely stealing from the firm. "She couldn't bear to turn him in," Seth said. "And she knew it would come out soon enough anyway. She just wanted to get away from the whole mess." He hesitated for a moment. "Another reason was that Karen thought someone was trying to set her up. She said that financial irregularities kept popping up in *her* accounts. She wanted out before she took the fall."

"Who was it?" T.S. asked. "Who would do that to her?"

Seth looked miserable. "Maybe Davy. He was never mean like that, but if he had been gambling, he might have done it."

"Can we talk to her about it?" T.S. pressed on. "Find out more about what she thinks?"

Seth shook his head. "Maybe in a couple of weeks. She's gone right now."

"Gone?" Herbert asked.

Seth nodded. "She couldn't take it anymore. The pressure from the family, the phone calls from the media, the mess about the new ownership structure. On top of it all, her ex called wanting part of the money she inherited from Max. So she took off this morning for a vacation. No one knows where."

"No one?" Herbert asked.

Seth looked up defiantly. "No one but me. And I'm not telling."

They switched the subject and asked Seth about the rivalry between his brothers. Davy and Jake had hated each other bitterly, perhaps for good reason, Seth confirmed. "Jake did everything right on the surface and Davy always did everything wrong," he explained. "But everyone always liked Davy better anyway, especially Uncle Max. He couldn't help it. Jake is such a pompous jerk. He wouldn't know a real human emotion if it fell on him from the Empire State Building."

Sabrina Rosenbloom was a sleaze, but harmless, Seth offered under questioning. "I'm nothing to her, so I rarely saw her in action. She knows her tricks don't affect me in the least. And Uncle Max never mentioned her to me again once they got married. Not once in the past three years."

His last disclosure was also interesting. He had been visited twice in the last three days by his brother Jake, Seth confirmed. Karen had been approached as well. "They want us to join in a lawsuit against the estate," he explained. "The rest of the family wants to have Max's latest will declared invalid and the trusts he set up declared illegal. Supposedly because your aunt exercised undue influence over him when he was in failing mental health. Hah! Good luck proving that one. But if the family won the lawsuit—or forced your aunt to reach a settlement—his estate would be divided between most of the family. It's a lot of money. It's worth a lawsuit to them, believe me." But Seth was not joining, he added. And neither was Karen. They were both ready to move on. Move on away from the Rosenblooms forever.

By the time Seth called a halt to the questioning, they were all weary and slightly tipsy from too much good cheer. Herbert and T.S. said their good-byes and stumbled out into the night, elated at their success. Grady had waited patiently for them and made no comment as they staggered into the backseat. He was no stranger to serious tippling.

"An unusual young man," Herbert remarked during the long ride uptown. The backseat of the limousine was comfortable and he fought to stay awake. He would drop T.S. off, then ask Grady to drive him to his apartment in Queens. "I wonder what kind of lawyer he'll be."

"A very good one, I should think," T.S. replied. He coughed in embarrassment. "I must thank you, Herbert," he said. "You saved me in there. I could not seem to relax. Or connect with the young man. It was too much for me, I suppose. Too different from what I am used to. I'm just too ... I don't know. I'm just too something."

Herbert patted T.S.'s arm. "Don't worry. It was nothing. I knew I must take action or the young man would not be responsive. It seemed to me that you had a branch—no, I believe it is a stick—up your ..." He hesitated, thinking hard. "What is that expression?"

"Never mind," T.S. interrupted grimly. "I know the one you mean."

CHAPTER FOURTEEN

1. Detectives, departing paramedics, and an anxious security guard swarmed over the cutting-room floor. Casey sat glumly on a chair next to Auntie Lil, silent and seething. Her head was swathed in a spectacular bandage that obscured most of her brow. Auntie Lil was unharmed but equally unhappy—Lieutenant Abromowitz was on the scene.

"Let me get this straight," the lieutenant began. "A person you haven't laid eyes on in thirty years calls you up and asks you to meet her on the darkened floor of a closed factory in the middle of a series of murders. And you say, 'Sure, let me get my hat. I'll be right over.' " He stared down at Auntie Lil and waited for her answer.

She nodded miserably, ashamed of her stupidity and embarrassed that the lieutenant had been the one to catch her at it. "I thought the feds had taken over the case," she said in a small voice. "Why isn't that nice Frank O'Conner questioning me?"

"Because that nice Frank O'Conner has moved on to more important things. He doesn't care about these murders. He has bigger—much bigger—fish to fry. So the feds have thoughtfully dumped the Rosenblooms back in my lap." Abromowitz hooked his thumbs in his belt loops and rocked back on his heels. A toothpick dangling from his mouth bobbed up and down as he spoke. "Look, Miss Hubbert, no hard feelings, okay? I have come to accept the fact that you were sent into my life to plague me. You interfere with my investigations, you *confuse* the issues, you bring political power crashing down on my head. You seem to be more difficult to get rid of than a bad case of athlete's foot. But I have never wished to see you harmed. On the contrary, I am not happy that someone attempted to murder you tonight. Particularly in my precinct and in the middle of my case." He sighed. "Can we agree that maybe I really do have your best interests at heart? After all, I am the police and it is my job to find the killers."

"You thought I killed Max," she said in a wounded voice.

"Miss Hubbert, I never thought you killed him," Abromowitz protested. "And I never really thought you were blackmailing him, either. I just needed some leverage to be absolutely sure that you were telling me everything you knew. Put yourself in my shoes. I'm pulled off all of my cases and handed this homicide for one reason and one reason only. I'm Jewish. And the powers-that-be have decreed that when a prominent Jew gets murdered in New York City, a not-so-prominent Jew has to solve it. It plays better in our communities, understand?"

Auntie Lil nodded.

"So here I am, under pressure from the press and my own people to get some progress made quick. This means that when even a small amount of physical evidence shows that you might be involved, I am under an obligation to pursue it. If I came on strong, it's just because my nerves are stretched thin and I have no margin for error here. But I do have your best interests at heart."

"I concede that you have my best interests at heart," Auntie Lil admitted stiffly.

"Good. Now, let's start from the top," Abromowitz said. "I think someone wanted to kill you tonight and make it look like you had a little accident while snooping around the factory. And I want to find out who."

Auntie Lil went over the phone call from Rosalie Benpensata and described their journey to Max Rose Fashions. No, she could not identify her attackers. At least she didn't think so. She wasn't even sure if they had been men, women, or a combination of both. Perhaps if she saw their outlines again, she might know them. She couldn't be sure.

"Did you actually recognize the voice as Rosalie Benpensata's?" Abromowitz wanted to know. "After that many years, you remembered her voice?"

"I didn't recognize her voice exactly," Auntie Lil admitted. "But who else would know about her? She referred to a favor I had done for her thirty years ago. It had to have been Rosalie. No one else knew about it."

"No one else?" Abromowitz asked.

"No one else who could call and impersonate Rosalie. Max is dead. Maybe Abe knew she had come to me about his advances, but he has difficulty speaking without losing his breath. He couldn't possibly have called. Besides, it was a woman's voice."

Abromowitz yelled over his shoulder to a detective hovering nearby. "Is Dave through with the personnel files yet? And where the hell are the owners?"

The man shrugged. "Some guy named Brody is on the way," he told the lieutenant. "We couldn't get an answer at any of the Rosenbloom numbers. We tried them all."

"And does Dave have this Benpensata woman's address yet?" Abromowitz asked impatiently.

The detective looked bored. "How should I know? He's on another floor."

"Well, go find him!" Abromowitz roared, losing his temper at the only person nearby that he was allowed to lose his temper at. The detective scurried off and the lieutenant turned back to Auntie Lil. "This is a mess," he pointed out. He stared intently at Auntie Lil. "You are telling me everything you know, aren't you?"

"Yes," Auntie Lil said.

Simultaneously, Casey rang in with a resounding, "No!"

"Which is it?" He looked back and forth between the two women, but neither spoke.

The building's security guard interrupted, approaching Abromowitz nervously. He was an old man and his hands shook. If the attackers had escaped out the front lobby, he would have keeled over from a heart attack. But according to him, no one had either entered or left that way.

"Sir?" the old guard asked fearfully, his hat bobbing in his trembling hands.

"What?" Abromowitz barked in irritation. "Can't you see I'm interrogating?"

"Have you contacted Mr. Rosenbloom yet?" the old man asked with a gulp.

"Which Mr. Rosenbloom? This place stinks with them."

Point of fact, there was only one Mr. Rosenbloom left who was involved with the family business. The guard wisely chose not to point this out to Abromowitz. "Jake Rosenbloom," he explained, his face starting to crumple. "He'll fire me. I know he will. He'll say it's my fault and then I'll have no health insurance and we'll lose the house and . . ." His voice weakened. "He's been trying to fire me ever since his uncle died," he finished miserably. "I don't know what I'll do if he does."

"Look, I'll put in a good word for you, okay?" Abromowitz promised. "If we can ever get in touch with the bastard, I'll let him know it couldn't possibly be your fault."

The man nodded gratefully and shuffled away.

"Jesus," Abromowitz said. "Is this the twentieth century or what? The guy acts like an indentured servant. Where was I?" Neither Auntie Lil nor Casey professed to remember, Auntie Lil because she knew she was in enough trouble and Casey because she had been kicked sharply on the shin by Auntie Lil.

"You know," Abromowitz said to Casey, "this escapade tonight is something that I've come to expect from Miss Hubbert. But you're a professional. Or say you are. And you led her right into this trap."

Casey was indignant. "*You* try controlling her," she spat back at the lieutenant, with a healthy glare toward Auntie Lil.

2. T.S. was horrified at the message awaiting him on his answering machine. He played it twice to make sure that Auntie Lil was not seriously injured, then fled right back out the door for his second trip of the day to Max Rose Fashions. He arrived in time to share an elevator with Thomas Brody. The chief financial officer was dressed elegantly, his tuxedo immaculately fitted to his powerful frame. He had obviously been at an important function and had just as obviously been imbibing there. He reeked of alcohol and his eyes were preternaturally bright.

"Looks like this interrupted your evening," T.S. said politely. He smelled no better than Brody after all the Scotches he'd downed at the Swan Dive. Together, they raised the temperature in the elevator a good ten degrees.

"It was boring anyway," Brody said. "Your aunt's okay, I hear. That's good news."

"Yes. It's the reaction of the police I'm worried about." They rode the rest of the way up in grim silence.

"Who are you?" a uniformed cop demanded when they reached the sample-room floor. Brody identified himself and introduced T.S. The cop nodded glumly and returned to his doughnut, sniffing suspiciously at the air as they passed.

"No wonder this company's in trouble," Abromowitz said after Brody introduced himself. "You can't get in touch with anyone who knows what's going on."

"Well, I am the chief financial officer," Brody explained stiffly. "And these two people are part owners. In case you've forgotten." He gestured to Auntie Lil and T.S.

"Who's Rosalie Benpensata?" Abromowitz demanded.

Brody spread his arms wide. "I give up. Who *is* Rosalie Benpensata?"

"Don't get smart with me." Abromowitz glowered at Brody. "She works for you."

"I assure you she does not."

"She's an accountant," Auntie Lil explained. "You must know who she is."

Brody shook his head. "We have over a hundred employees and I don't know them all, but I do know the financial professionals. There's no Rosalie Benpensata on staff." He turned to Auntie Lil. "What were you doing here in the middle of the night anyway?"

Abromowitz interrupted. "I suppose you can account for your whereabouts for every minute of tonight," he said.

Brody paused and his face grew red. He waited until he had returned to his normal color before he spoke. "I suppose I can," he said calmly. "I was on the dais at a dinner honoring the new mayor. As a matter of fact, I was seated next to the new chief of police."

Abromowitz nodded slowly. "Just doing my job," he muttered.

A beefy detective barreled through the fire-exit doors, breathing heavily.

"God, Spencer. Take the elevator, will ya?" Abromowitz commanded when the man arrived at their circle, huffing for breath. "I can't afford to have anyone else kick off right now, know what I mean?"

"Rosalie Benpensata's dead," the beefy detective told him. "She died twelve years ago. Of cancer. It's all in her file." He thrust a thin brown folder at the lieutenant.

Abromowitz ignored it. He was staring at Auntie Lil. "What was it you were saying about no one else in the world knowing that you'd done a favor for Rosalie?" he asked.

3. "Forget what you think," Abromowitz commanded. "Just tell me what you know."

They were gathered in T.S.'s living room and made a truly motley crew. Casey and Auntie Lil had refused to be taken to the emergency room for checkups, both declaring that they would rather die than be subjected to the waiting and abuse that a visit to a New York City hospital in the middle of the night typically entailed. Casey had blood on the front of her yellow dress, and a large purple bruise was creeping like a stain from beneath her head bandage. Auntie Lil had a long scratch on one cheek where a metal hanger had caught her, and her hair stood up in unruly curls. T.S. was rumpled and reeked of alcohol. Only Thomas Brody looked composed in his tuxedo.

Abromowitz was the most irritable and disheveled of them all. He had just been through a very long day and then been called back to the scene when the precinct got the call from Max Rose Fashions. But despite his exhaustion, he had insisted on accompanying them home to T.S.'s apartment. They had all agreed that it was safer for Auntie Lil to stay with T.S. for the time being. After being informed of the attack, Herbert had been persuaded to stay home and was assigned the task of bringing Auntie Lil fresh clothes and supplies in the morning.

Once upstairs, Abromowitz had informed them that he was not leaving until they told him everything—and he meant absolutely everything—that they knew about the Rosenbloom case.

"How do I know you'll use the information well?" Auntie Lil demanded. "After all, you thought I killed Max. Which anyone knows is completely ridiculous."

"Look, for the last time—I never really thought you killed him," Abromowitz said. "But I thought you had information I needed. And I had to satisfy the family. They were calling for your blood. With good reason. You did have a motive: lots of money. And physical evidence supported their claims that you'd been snooping. What was I supposed to do? At the very least I had to bring you in for questioning."

T.S. could not tolerate another battle of wills between Abromowitz and Auntie Lil. He was too tired. He forestalled a war by dropping to his knees at Auntie Lil's feet. "Aunt Lil," he said in as patient a voice as he could muster, "someone tried to kill you tonight." He held up a hand to stifle her protests. "No, don't argue. They weren't trying to scare you. They wanted to kill you. And if Casey hadn't been there, they would have succeeded."

"We should never have gone there in the first place," Casey muttered.

T.S. nodded. "But it's over. And now I want you to tell Lieutenant Abromowitz everything you've learned about the Rosenblooms to date. I know I am going to tell him everything. And so is Casey." He shot a glance at Casey, who nodded glumly. "That's the way it's going to be. This has gotten too dangerous. Do what the man says."

Abromowitz had folded his arms over his ample chest and was nodding sagely throughout T.S.'s speech. This was intensely aggravating to Auntie Lil, but she agreed to cooperate anyway.

"Good," the lieutenant said. "Who wants to go first?"

Casey did. She intended to get it over with, she announced, then go take a shower and change into something more comfortable. This was the first that T.S. had heard about her plans to stay over at his apartment, but he could not in good conscience protest. She had sustained a hard blow on the head. It was not prudent for her to be alone.

Casey told Abromowitz what she could: that Sabrina had definitely been cheating on Max Rosenbloom; that she had visited her favorite motel at least once with Davy, along with most of the male half of Long Island; that her infidelity could cause her to lose what little money she'd stood to gain by Max's death; that Sabrina had lied to her husband both about her age and her willingness to have children; and that the family had not known that they had been cut out of Max's will.

"And you don't have a clue as to who attacked you tonight?" Abromowitz asked when she was through.

Casey touched her forehead and flinched. "I know they were strong. At least one of them was bigger than me. But they were kind of slow and indecisive, I guess. Out of shape, too. I'd be surprised if they were professionals."

Abromowitz nodded. "Your turn," he told Auntie Lil.

Being asked to describe what she knew, but not what she thought, was torture for Auntie Lil. She outlined what she felt were the most important facts about the case so far: Abby had banished Seth and Karen from the family, but Abe wanted to see his son again, and did see Karen regularly; Joyce Carruthers, the bookkeeper, was feeding information regularly to Joseph Galvano, but the mobster had

not yet succeeded in infiltrating Max Rose Fashions; and
Joyce had been in love with Max years ago and resented
Auntie Lil. Abromowitz interrupted and told her to stick to
the facts, and Auntie Lil retaliated stiffly by saying that it
was a *fact* that someone had tried to run her down with a
truck, no matter what Abromowitz and everyone else tried
to say; that it was a *fact* Abe kept a gun in his bedside table, but she didn't know what kind; that it was a *fact* Abe
knew the contents of Max's final will but had told no one
else; and that it was a *fact* Jake had found out very quickly
when Auntie Lil visited Abe and had been very angry about
it. When it became embarrassingly obvious from his questions that Abromowitz had not been given a rundown by
the feds on Auntie Lil's conversation with Galvano, Auntie
Lil also let him know that Davy's death was costing Galvano a lot of money, so she doubted he'd had anything to
do with it.

"Not bad," the lieutenant admitted when she was
through. "Nearly all of that was *fact*." He paused. "There
was no mention of that long-ago incident in Rosalie
Benpensata's employee file. Are you sure you never told
anyone what you did for her? Whoever called knew about
it."

Auntie Lil nodded emphatically. She was sure she had
never told anyone.

"Would Max have told anyone?" the lieutenant insisted.

Auntie Lil shook her head. "No. He believed in keeping
things like that very private. Besides, it would have been
embarrassing if it had gotten out. People would think he
couldn't control his company if he couldn't control his own
brother."

"Would Abe have told anyone?" Abromowitz asked.

Auntie Lil shrugged. "I don't know. But whoever called
me up had to have known who Rosalie was."

Lieutenant Abromowitz stared hard at her. "Anything else?" he warned sternly.

"Well ..." She thought hard. "I really do think I hit someone when I struck out with those scissors. It may be a deep cut." She shivered, remembering the feel of the thick blade sliding into soft tissue.

"There wasn't much blood on the floor, probably just hers." Abromowitz nodded toward Casey. "But I'll be sure to strip-search any suspects anyway," he promised.

"I did stab someone," Auntie Lil insisted, offended by his attitude.

"No one is calling you a wimp," the lieutenant agreed. "I'm sure you tried."

T.S. was angered by his halfhearted sarcasm. After all, they were cooperating. He had no need to be a boor. "If my aunt says she stabbed someone, she did," he said stiffly.

"And what can you contribute to our group encounter?" Abromowitz asked T.S. He knew he was being more unpleasant than the situation called for, but it rankled him to learn that the feds had withheld information that could have been of help. This little old lady and her friends had known, while he had been kept in the dark.

"If you think this is just a big joke, I'll keep my information to myself," T.S. said.

"No. Go on. Maybe I'd better sit down." The lieutenant eased his bulk into one of T.S.'s sleek modern chairs and seemed surprised at its comfort. He sighed deeply and rubbed at one of his ankles. It had been aching all day. The others were silent, some of them feeling ashamed at their treatment of Abromowitz. He did look awfully tired.

"I learned some things that might help," T.S. told him. "Jake and Sabrina are leading an attempt to block the distribution of Max's estate. Also, everyone in the family knew that Jake was going to eventually head up Max Rose simply because there was no one else to succeed him."

"Unless the company was sold," Brody pointed out.

"True. But the family did not seem to know that was an option," T.S. said. "I also learned today, from Mr. Brody here, that the company itself stood to profit a great deal from Max's death. By three million dollars, to be exact."

"I know everything that Mr. Brody has to say," Abromowitz interrupted. "We don't need to get into that."

"I don't know everything he has to say," Auntie Lil pointed out.

The lieutenant looked grim. "I've talked to him and that's enough."

"No, it isn't," Auntie Lil insisted. "It's part my company now. I have a right to know."

"I think that she does have a right to know certain things, given that her life has been endangered by this whole situation," Brody told Abromowitz tactfully.

The lieutenant groaned and struggled to his feet. "I can't stop you from talking among yourselves. But I can't stay around and listen, either. I'm just plain too tired. I'll be in touch. Believe me, I'll be in touch."

He lumbered wearily out the door, wondering how in the world he would ever untangle this mess. He knew someone was guilty, but had no idea who. He sighed. The information on Galvano had been news to him. The feds had told him very little about that aspect of their investigation, claiming that it might compromise an ongoing case of theirs. Of course, he was expected to apprise them of every development in his case, no matter how small. He'd even phoned in news of Auntie Lil's attack tonight. But did they reciprocate? Of course not. Until Auntie Lil described her conversation with Galvano, Abromowitz had been largely guessing about the mobster's involvement with Max Rose

Fashions. How did the feds expect him to solve two murders with half the information? Thank God, he thought privately, for that old dame in there. I need her this time around. Not that I would ever tell her. No way. I'd rather give up doughnuts than let her know.

By the time Casey rejoined them in the living room, Lieutenant Abromowitz was well out the lobby door. To his chagrin, T.S. noticed that Casey had appropriated his terry-cloth bathrobe and had wound one of his favorite yellow towels around her head. If she leaked blood on it, he'd never get the stain out.

"I have my bandage on," Casey protested, reading his glare correctly.

T.S. sighed. He did not take to the female invasion of his abode very well.

"What other information have you given the lieutenant?" Auntie Lil asked Brody. She had moved beside him on the sofa and was giving him the full force of her attention, leaning forward and resting a hand on his knee. She crowded Brody so closely that it seemed to him to be physically impossible not to share his information with her.

"Max was with me right before he died," Brody explained. He shifted his body away and attempted to reclaim control of the conversation. "We'd been discussing the improving financials, but despite that good news, Max was not happy. Davy had apparently lost another bundle down in Atlantic City and wanted Max to bail him out for the umpteenth time. Max questioned the wisdom of keeping Davy around the firm's money. He already knew he'd had something to do with the V.J. Productions fraud, but at the time no one was quite sure what. They had a fight about it, but Davy was admitting nothing. I suspected it all led back to Davy and counseled Max to cut Davy off from access to funds immediately. He couldn't bring himself to agree. To top it off, Max's wife had wrecked her car the day before and was driving his. Max loved his old Audi. He was afraid that Sabrina would wreck it, too, and a little put out that he was having to take the train back and forth from the city until her car was fixed. Max wasn't into the trappings of wealth. He thought limousines were ostentatious. Jake rushed in with some damn-fool little question toward the end of our conversation and Max waved him away. After Jake left, Max just seemed to snap. 'I'm not changing my mind,' he told me, and I had absolutely no idea what Max was talking about. Then he returned to his office, and the next thing I know, there was an explosion half a block away. And it was Max. He died instantly."

"When did the employees learn of his death?" Auntie Lil asked.

"Almost at once. One of our salesmen had seen Max go into the garage and ran back to check with the attendant. After that, the rumor just swept through the floors. Next day, of course, a memo went around in the afternoon confirming that Max had died and letting employees know about the funeral arrangements."

"Did it say where he was being buried?" Auntie Lil asked.

Brody nodded. "Sure. A lot of the employees had worked for him for decades. They would want to pay their respects. We even closed down the shop the day of the service. Quite a few attended. I, uh, saw you there." He tactfully did not mention Auntie Lil's discovery of Davy's body or the rabbi and widow's slide down into the open grave.

"When did you notice that Davy was missing?" T.S. asked.

"We didn't," Brody explained. "None of the family came in the day after Max died. I assumed they were making funeral arrangements and dealing with their grief. Besides, it was not your typical workday. The police were in asking questions of everyone. After Davy was found dead, that got even worse. We were shut down, in effect, for days."

Under Auntie Lil's questioning, Brody turned his attention to the management of Max Rose Fashions. He recapped some of what he'd told T.S. earlier in that long day, including the fact that Karen had worked at Max Rose but left abruptly a few months after he got there. He was surprised to hear Seth's contention that someone had been framing Karen by creating problems with her accounts but promised to look into it.

"I wouldn't have recommended Jake as a successor to Max," Brody said in response to a question by Auntie Lil. "And Max would have asked my opinion. We got along well. Despite what the family thought, I think Jake suspected that Max would not name him president once he retired. Jake seemed almost desperate around his uncle, desperate to convince him that he was competent. It was pathetic and it bothered Max greatly."

Brody stared down at the area rug. "I knew how Max felt," he said. "The disappointment at not having anyone to leave his company to. Every man wants an heir to carry on the dream. I see that a lot when I go into companies that need help and it always gets to me. Men spend their lives turning their dreams into reality. Then they look around and there's no one to share the dream." He smiled bitterly. "I know how he felt. My own son is . . ." He paused. "Difficult. Unemployable. Schizophrenic, actually. Hospitalized much of the time."

So much for the theory about Brody wanting to build his own family dynasty, T.S. thought.

Brody stood up. "You people are tired. I know I am. And I'd better be at my desk bright and early tomorrow. Some Rosenbloom is bound to have turned up by then, and they'll be screaming about the mess on the cutting-room floor." Brody smiled, but the creases around his bright eyes hung heavily and his face shone with a gray pallor. He said his good-byes and abruptly left.

"When he runs out of steam, he really runs out of steam," T.S. remarked.

"That's what happens when people go through life full speed ahead," Auntie Lil said. "But I think he's a good man. Don't you?"

T.S. hoped that she was right. He led Auntie Lil to the spare bedroom and gave Casey the pillow and blankets she'd need for a night on the couch.

He was looking forward to a hot shower before bed and approached the mess in his bathroom stoically. Panty hose and underwear hung to dry on his towel rods; assorted tubes of cosmetics marched across his bathroom countertop. How did women fit so much makeup on so little skin? No matter, he'd be alone in the shower at least.

Even meeting Casey's newly washed dress hanging in the center of his shower stall did not deter him. He merely pushed it to one side and let the scalding jets of water wash the smell of Scotch and weariness from his skin. Someone had tried to hurt Auntie Lil tonight, he reminded himself. And he was going to find out who.

CHAPTER FIFTEEN

1. T.S. rose early, hoping to grab a few minutes of blessed quiet before Auntie Lil and Casey woke up. He was an orderly man and his morning routine was sacred: wake up, cuddle with the cats, shave in his bathrobe, brush his teeth, make coffee from freshly ground beans, prepare half of a toasted onion bagel with a tablespoon of cream cheese, squeeze eight ounces of fresh orange juice, and then sit down to a leisurely breakfast-and-newspaper session. He became grumpy whenever his regimen was interrupted. Consequently, he was extraordinarily grumpy that morning. For starters, Brenda and Eddie had deserted him for someone else's bed, and he had missed their morning purring acutely. Secondly, he stumbled into Casey's rear end when he entered his bathroom and nearly knocked his head on a towel rack. She was on her hands and knees—in his good bathrobe—examining two small swinging doors inset in his bathroom closet door.

"What are these?" she asked through a mouthful of food. T.S. realized with horror that she had set her morning bagel down on his gleaming countertop. What looked to be half a pack of cream cheese was smeared over his Italian marble. She had not even bothered with a plate. There was even a smidgen of cream cheese dangling from her head bandage. A trail of light brown drops across his clean tile floor led to an overflowing mug of coffee by her side.

How was it possible to be so disheveled that early in the morning? He shuddered and clenched his teeth. "Those are cat doors," he replied stiffly.

"Cat doors?" She poked one open with her finger. "I'll be damned. This leads to a special kitty-litter compartment? Talk about clean." Casey opened the larger closet door and peered inside. "Sticks of air freshener on special shelves surrounding the pan?" She turned and stared at T.S. "You make that guy in *The Odd Couple* look like a slob."

"Could I have my bathroom back?" T.S. demanded.

"Sorry." She collected her breakfast and marched dramatically from the room, leaving a trail of crumbs and coffee droplets behind her.

Women. They frightened him, with the exception of Lilah. When was she coming home anyway and when would this infernal disruption of his life come to an end?

At least Casey made decent coffee. T.S. sat with her at his dining room table, staring out at the winding line of cars that marked York Avenue during morning rush hour. He loved to watch the world hurrying to work while he sat at home, retired. He was grateful that Casey seemed more interested in eating his entire week's worth of groceries than she was in conversation.

The doorbell jolted him from his reverie. It could only be Herbert—Mahmoud would have called up to clear anyone else. But it was barely nine o'clock and Herbert knew quite well that only an earthquake was likely to raise Auntie Lil before the ten o'clock hour.

Herbert was toting a large laundry bag of Auntie Lil's neatly folded clothes. "It is impossible to anticipate her mood," he explained. "Thus I have brought everything that I could find. I will let her choose." He dropped the bag in the middle of T.S.'s spartan living room, where it loomed up like a small mountain amid the clean, uncluttered lines of his modern decor.

"What brings you out so early?" T.S. asked glumly. He was being invaded, piece by persistent piece. Soon all of New York would move in.

"I could not wait any longer. I wanted to see for myself that Lillian was well." Herbert sat at the dining room table and nodded at Casey. "I also wanted to discuss the case. I was pondering its mysteries early this morning while performing my mental exercises. There is much that disturbs me."

"Murder is always disturbing," T.S. said.

"No. It is more than that. The universe assigns a balance to all things. Even to murder. Sometimes we cannot see that balance until a long time after the fact. But if you look at these two murders together, there is no balance. One was quite efficient—a bomb in the car. Over in seconds. The other was messy and surely a difficult task: dragging a man into an open grave on a rainy night. They do not fit. I cannot make them fit. I believe that we may be looking at two separate events entirely—and if we continue to consider them together, we may be doomed to fail."

"What do you mean?" T.S. asked, his curiosity aroused.

"I mean that we must take a new look at each murder, separately, as well as the events before and after the killings. Let us see what we can deduce from each small event. It may be possible to then eliminate suspects from each murder. If we end up with people in common for both deaths, then perhaps we have our murderer. If not, let us consider two separate killers. If we combine them from the beginning, however, we will surely muddy the stew."

Muddy the stew? T.S. let it pass. Herbert's metaphors were off, but his deductive reasoning was sound.

A commotion in the hallway distracted them. Auntie Lil had been lured out of bed by the sounds of their voices and was busy scuffling with the cats for hall space. "Theodore, get these things off me," she demanded sleepily. "It's too early for one to be expected to show affection for another living creature." At nine o'clock in the morning, Auntie Lil believed it too early for anything, except downing as many cups of coffee as she could.

T.S. retrieved Brenda and Eddie and shooed them into the dining room, where they promptly curled up around Casey's ankles and fell asleep. He knew then where the two furry little traitors had spent the night.

"What am I missing?" Auntie Lil asked, heading for the coffee machine. T.S. watched her closely, disturbed by her pale coloring. She also moved slowly, as if her back hurt. He was used to pink apple cheeks and a robust bearing. It frightened him. Eighty-four was really quite old.

Herbert explained his theory to Auntie Lil and she became instantly alert. "Of course," she said. "You are absolutely right. This is what we must do today." She began to outline her ideas for a new plan until T.S. broke in.

"You're not going anywhere today," he said firmly. "Except to the doctor's."

Auntie Lil glared. Theodore rarely told her what to do, but when he did take a stand, it was near impossible to budge him.

"Don't even try to argue," he said calmly. "Your health is my responsibility. I want you checked thoroughly after last night."

"I am perfectly fine. I did not get clobbered over the head. Casey did."

T.S. glanced at Casey. "Good point. She can drive you to the doctor and get checked herself while she's at it."

"Is this doctor cute?" Casey interrupted.

"I find him very handsome," Auntie Lil replied absently.

Casey was convinced. "Count me in. I need some Tylenol three anyway." She touched a bruise cheerfully. "My head should explode any minute now."

"Good. It's settled." T.S. added milk to his coffee and avoided his aunt's eyes.

"Theodore." The one word was an eloquent study in frustration. Auntie Lil sipped her coffee and moped.

"You are going," T.S. told her. "Herbert and I will take care of questioning the security guard and the other errands."

"I must talk to Seth Rosenbloom myself," Auntie Lil insisted. "Soon. I promised his father I would get him to visit and he looks quite ill. We had better hurry."

"Okay," T.S. conceded. "I'll try to set up a meeting at the Swan Dive early this evening. But only if you get a clean bill of health. Let's say six o'clock."

Auntie Lil nodded and contented herself with sulking over coffee while T.S. made his phone calls. Seth was willing to meet them again, especially when he heard that Auntie Lil would be along this time.

Casey took the news that she would be seeing a handsome doctor with enthusiasm. She fled to the bathroom and shut the door, leaving the others to speculate what the clatter and groans were about. When she emerged, she was dressed again in her yellow sheath and had successfully covered some of the bruises on her face. But a purplish goose egg remained. It protruded prominently from the curve of her brow and no amount of makeup could disguise its size.

"Perhaps he'll admire your bravery in the face of adversity," Auntie Lil told her. "I know that I do."

2. When they reached Max Rose Fashions, T.S. and Herbert quickly ran out of luck. The old guard who had been on duty the night before was not due in for another four hours. His name was Hiram Tate and he had called his coworkers to warn that he might be sick.

"He said he was having heart palpitations or something," the chubby guard on duty explained with a yawn. "The old guy ought to retire."

With a promise to stop by later, T.S. and Herbert left the lobby. They planned to head for Sterling & Sterling to question the head of the firm's trust subsidiary.

Their disappointment at not finding Hiram Tate was assuaged by the sight of the limousine waiting for them outside Max Rose Fashions. Grady had buffed it to shining perfection. It stood out against the graffiti-scarred trucks of the busy garment district like a shark in a school of fat groupers.

"I could get used to this," T.S. admitted, sliding along the luxurious cushions.

Herbert did not answer. He was staring at a truck parked across the street that was in the process of being loaded. Racks of swinging dresses stood at the curb while a relay team of men passed handfuls of hanging plastic-wrapped garments up into the truck. A burly man stood guard, arms folded over his well-defined chest as he supervised the loading and ensured that no merchandise was lost to a snatch-and-run thief.

"What is it?" T.S. said.

"That's the truck that Lillian claims tried to hit her. I'm sure of it." Herbert pointed out a splash of graffiti near the cab: KID BLUE & POPPY. There was a large blue moon painted above the colorful lettering.

"You're sure?" T.S. asked.

"Yes. I recognize the blue moon." Herbert stared at the truck. "Seeing this truck so close to the factory is no coincidence. It confirms what Lillian told us. And we did not believe her. Someone did try to run over her deliberately."

"Wait here," T.S. said. "I'll see who it belongs to."

The street was crowded. He elbowed past a group of Scandinavian tourists, nearly got run over by a bicycle messenger, and bumped his shin on the fender of a station wagon backing up. T.S. was thankful to reach the other side of the street in one piece. He approached the man supervising the loading of the truck, noting uneasily that his face was as placid and immovable as a plastic Buddha's.

"Who owns this truck?" T.S. asked.

"What's it to you?" came the universal reply.

A lie leaped to his lips, evidence that he and Auntie Lil shared the same gene pool. "I'm a buyer for a large Midwestern retail chain. I've been looking for a source of affordable ladies' wear."

"Sorry, we don't carry your size," the guard told him.

T.S. slipped a twenty from his wallet and dangled it in the air.

"Belongs to Max Rose Fashions," the guard said, spitting the words out of the side of his mouth like a gangster in a forties movie. "Across the street. Top four floors." His hammy hand plucked the twenty delicately from the air. It disappeared instantly inside his shirt pocket.

T.S. hurried back to the limo, his mind considering the possibilities. Who had been driving the truck? Why hadn't he paid more attention to Auntie Lil's description?

He nodded at Herbert, who did not need a further explanation. They headed back inside Max Rose Fashions with a different destination in mind—the offices of Thomas Brody.

3.   "We have eight drivers on the payroll alone," Brody explained. "And maybe ten more on call if we need them."

"But how many of them are of slight build with dark coloring and a small mustache?" Herbert asked. He remembered most of Auntie Lil's description.

"How should I know?" Brody straightened his tie and scowled. "I can't be expected to recognize every employee on sight. For God's sakes, this is a temporary assignment."

"Thinning hairline but with long hair," Herbert insisted. "Pulled back in a ponytail. Big ears. Maybe Pakistani, Lillian said. He was wearing a plaid woodsman shirt."

Brody shook his head wearily. "I appreciate your efforts, but I really can't—" He stopped suddenly.

"What is it?" T.S. demanded.

Brody looked up at them. "That sounds a lot like the clerk I fired for signing off on those phony deliveries from the shell company Davy set up."

"Could we see his file?" T.S. asked. "Let Herbert get a look at his photo?"

"I'll see what I can find. It may be at the lawyers'. Tricky business firing someone these days, you know?" Brody left the office in search of the clerk's personnel file. Herbert and T.S. looked at each other.

"Maybe we should not attempt this by ourselves," Herbert suggested. "Perhaps Lieutenant Abromowitz is better suited to such things."

"What harm could it do?" T.S. asked. His adrenaline was pumping. He had stumbled on an important clue. He wanted to run it down, wring it out for all it was worth. Present Auntie Lil with new information for a change. Besides, how dangerous could one clerk be? When he wasn't behind the wheel of a truck, of course.

Herbert did not have time to answer. Jake Rosenbloom

loomed suddenly in Brody's doorway, his pudgy frame nearly filling the opening. He wore an expensive suit that had been tailored to fit perfectly about twenty pounds ago. It now strained at the chest and the shirt beneath gaped open, revealing a white T-shirt between the buttons. His belt was cinched too tightly and his stomach sagged over his pants like escaping pizza dough.

"Who do you think you are, coming here at a time like this?" he demanded. Jake's eyes burned out at T.S. like twin laser beams. But they were red and swollen from lack of sleep. He did not look well.

"I am a part owner of this company," T.S. reminded him. "And I have as much right as you to be here."

"We'll see about that." Jake turned abruptly and hurried down the hall.

"I don't know about you," T.S. told Herbert, "but I'm going to be looking over my shoulder until we get away from this place."

Brody returned with what little they had on the discharged shipping clerk. Most of the space in the folder was taken up by legal opinions and memos on the V.J. Productions mess. The single photo was grainy and blurred. It showed the young man posed against a white wall somewhere in the factory. The unflattering lighting bestowed him with a permanently guilty look.

"I don't even know why they bother to take anyone's photo," Brody admitted. "Everyone comes out looking like a convicted felon."

"This guy might end up being one," T.S. pointed out.

Herbert examined the photograph carefully. "Can't be sure," he finally said.

"We'll go see him," T.S. decided. "You can get a better look in person."

Brody shook his head skeptically as he scrawled the

clerk's address on a piece of paper. He snapped the file shut with a crack. "Hope you men know what you're doing," he said grimly. "And if you'll excuse me, I have to get back to work." He reached for the telephone.

The clerk lived in upper Manhattan, in a neighborhood called Washington Heights. Once a spacious haven for families, it was fast becoming one of the most troubled precincts in all of New York City. Drug dealers had moved in; families had moved out. The streets were littered with empty fast-food wrappers and tiny vials made to hold crack cocaine. The area was on its way down. Until the survivors could pull together in a cohesive front, it would not begin its way back up soon.

Grady double-parked the limousine in a narrow side street, directly in front of the address they'd been given. No other cars would be able to get by.

"You're blocking traffic," T.S. said.

"That so?" Grady emerged from the front seat and perched on the hood of the car, looking around like the driver of a stagecoach who was anticipating an Indian raid. He folded his long legs to fit on top of the bumper and settled back, scanning the apartments around him. T.S. had never noticed just how massive the man was until then. With Lilah gone, Grady had gradually permitted himself the luxury of more casual clothes. Today he wore a pair of neatly pressed blue jeans and a long-sleeved rugby shirt. His muscles flexed beneath the cotton.

"Don't like this street much," he told T.S. "Can't think why. Could be it reminds me of Belfast in the early seventies. You go in while I watch the car."

Grady was right. The street hummed with unspoken malevolence. Herbert could feel the implicit threat in the air. "Let's hurry," he said. "Take the clerk somewhere else to talk."

T.S. nodded. "Grady can convince him if he's reluctant."

They would never know if the shipping clerk was reluctant to talk or not. And they'd never get a chance to confirm whether he had been the driver of the truck. The beautiful young woman who opened the door made it quite clear: her brother had returned to his homeland. He was not coming back. Ever. If they wanted to question him, they would have to track him down in the wilds of Sri Lanka. She wrapped her ruby-and-gold sari closely around her, obscuring the bottom half of her face, then shut the door firmly on them. Only the pungent odor of curry remained.

"Made his money and went home," Herbert said glumly.

T.S. agreed. "Someone made it worth his while to go home," he added.

Grady recognized their disappointment. "Come on, lads," he told them, opening the limo door with a flourish. "Cheer up. I know a great place to have lunch. We'll have bangers and mash. And then we'll be hot on the trail again."

4. Auntie Lil snagged the sofa by cleverly distracting Casey with a request for a glass of water. She was not supposed to be home in her own apartment but did not care. Casey was with her and she'd be protected. She wanted to sit in peace and think.

The visit to the doctor had taken hours. Auntie Lil had hated the fuss. Dr. Osle was a lovely man but always clucked over her like she was a freak in a sideshow, murmuring about her extraordinary health and "enduring strength" as if it were a miracle instead of the result of her own good sense and hard work. It made her want to slug him so he could experience her enduring strength for himself.

"You didn't tell me he was married." Casey pouted. She

plopped down on the sofa beside Auntie Lil and touched her new head bandage gingerly.

"Sorry, dear. If he was a little bit older, perhaps I'd have noticed."

"Still, it's good to know that we're as healthy as horses."

"I could have told him that," Auntie Lil said. "And saved several hundred dollars in doctor's fees."

The phone rang shrilly and they jumped. "Who could that be?" Casey asked, settling back against a pillow and closing her eyes. "If it's good old Rosalie again, hang up."

Auntie Lil abhorred idle speculation, preferring elaborate speculation herself. She answered quickly and was rewarded by the disgruntled voice of Lieutenant Abromowitz.

"You're not supposed to be there," he barked without bothering to say hello. "I thought we agreed you'd stay put at your nephew's."

"I just dropped by to pick up a few things," Auntie Lil lied. "Why are you checking up on me?"

"Stand by," he said. "A call's coming through for you." She heard the click of his receiver. He was certainly in a fine temper that afternoon.

The phone rang again within minutes, cutting off their conjecture about who it might be. Auntie Lil made a great show of answering. "Lillian Hubbert speaking," she said in crisp tones.

"Frank O'Conner," a faint voice answered. Static and the babble of other conversations interfered with the transmission. "I'm calling from my car."

"I can hardly hear you," Auntie Lil shouted.

The connection cleared. "Well, I can hear you fine and I think you just blew out my eardrum," the special agent said. "I need you to meet me at Bellevue Hospital, third floor, as soon as possible. Intensive care. Bring that private detective. She was with you last night, right?"

"Yes. Why?" Auntie Lil asked.

"I think we've got one of the guys who attacked you. I want you to take a look and tell me what you think."

As soon as she agreed, O'Conner hung up, leaving no time for more questions. Speculation about how the feds had nabbed the man was useless. There was no time to waste.

CHAPTER SIXTEEN

1. Bangers and mash turned out to be giant sausages and a plate of dense mashed potatoes. By the time T.S. had plowed through half of his, Grady's plate was clean. Herbert had sidestepped the issue by ordering a small chop and a large green salad. He was as prudent in his diet as he was in life.

"I can't move," T.S. declared, sitting back with a sigh. He patted his belly. "There's no way I can muster the energy for Sterling and Sterling. The very sight of all that hushed elegance would send me into a stupor."

Herbert held out a quarter. "You are a rich man now. People must take your calls." He nodded toward a row of old-fashioned red British phone booths against one wall of the downtown pub.

Herbert was proved right. T.S. had Bob Adams, head of Sterling's trust subsidiary, on the line within a minute.

"T.S.," he boomed heartily. "Decided what to do with all that money?"

"Not quite," he said feebly, hating the reminder that there was still sixty-six million between him and Auntie Lil to contend with. "I just have a few technical questions for you. I realize they may sound a bit unorthodox, but with this lawsuit about the estate and all . . . we need your help."

Bob Adams had no problem answering any questions

that T.S. had: he was now a client. If T.S. had asked Bob to cut off his own arm, the man would have replied, "Below or above the elbow?"

By the time he hung up the phone, T.S. had his information. When Davy died, one half of Max's fortune had passed on to T.S. as the alternate beneficiary. This was a standard clause used in estate planning to avoid confusion and court fights in the event of a common accident. But if Max had not been prudent enough to insert such a clause in his trust provisions—and no one in the family knew that he had—then Davy's inheritance would have passed on to his own beneficiaries. Since Davy lacked a will, his beneficiaries would most likely have been his parents and, possibly, his siblings. The courts would have decided the issue.

What had been in Max's prior will, the one the family knew about? Instructions to divide half his cash estate among all the nieces and nephews plus Sabrina, with the other half going to Abe and Rebecca. Of course, the trust would still have taken effect and Auntie Lil would still have inherited half of the assets placed in it, but the family had not known that. In their minds, the entire pie had been divided among them. It was a motive for murder.

The rest of Bob's information was equally illuminating. Had Max moved to divorce Sabrina, the proof of her infidelity would likely have caused the courts to uphold the prenuptial agreement. She would have had to settle for relatively little. But since Max had died before he filed for divorce, there was no way to prove his intentions. This cast his will concerning Sabrina into a gray area of law. The courts did not look kindly on bequests that came with behavioral requirements attached, even standards set forth in a prenuptial agreement. Should Max's will go to court, Sabrina Rosenbloom had a very good chance of inheriting much more than she had been left.

Was Sabrina sophisticated enough to have figured this out? T.S. returned to his table, thinking it over. He was doubtful she could have analyzed her options so accurately on her own. But perhaps she had enlisted legal advice. Across a pillow, no doubt.

2. It was not hard to find the right room. Unlike the rest of the bustling hospital—which overflowed with the injured and anxious—the third-floor intensive-care unit was hushed and nearly deserted. A policeman sat on a plastic chair tipped against the wall, leafing through a magazine on muscle building. He looked bored, but he was still on duty: despite their innocuous appearance, he would not let Auntie Lil and Casey into the room until he had entered first and checked with Frank O'Conner.

The special agent hurried out to greet them. He took them down the hall to an empty waiting room where they could talk privately. The room was meant to be cheery, but like all hospital rooms, it was too sterile to lift the spirits. Small couches were clustered around barren coffee tables, and cold modern prints dotted the walls.

"This is the story," O'Conner said, not bothering to sit. Casey and Auntie Lil huddled around him like football players focused on their quarterback. "We were watching some of Galvano's men last night out on Staten Island. We had a tip from someone and we're trying to nail him on anything we can get. About three A.M., one of the agents involved reported muffled gunfire inside the apartment, but no one believed her because we didn't hear return fire and we could see people moving around inside like nothing had happened. But we started to believe her when a couple of guys came out of the apartment carrying what looked like a body wrapped in a blanket. We followed them out to the landfill where the goons proceeded to unload the trunk and dump their package on the water's edge. They're about to roll the guy into the water when we stop them. What did we find inside the package? Quite a present. He's lying in that hospital room. He works for Galvano. His name is Frankie Shanahan, also known as Frankie Five Alarm. I'm ashamed to admit that he's Irish." O'Conner shook his head. "He's tough. Smart enough to play dead. This is where you come in. Shanahan did something to piss Galvano off. Something big enough to merit three bullets. If we believe Galvano when he says he had nothing to do with Max's death, then maybe Shanahan was freelancing and Galvano found out. This guy could be involved in the attempt on your life last night."

"Lives," Casey interrupted.

"Lives. The timing is right. You get attacked, and a couple of hours later Galvano orders this guy punished." O'Conner produced a fuzzy reproduction of four color mug shots from his coat pocket. "See what you think." The photographs showed various views of Frankie Five Alarm Shanahan, including his left and right profiles and two head-on shots. He was tall with a prominent Adam's apple and huge ears shaped like emerging butterflies. His hair was the color of rusty carrots and stuck out wildly from his head like renegade clumps of sea grass.

"Good Lord. Talk about conspicuous." Casey took the photograph and stared at it curiously, holding it closer and then farther away.

"Look familiar?" O'Conner asked.

"I don't know," Casey said.

"I can't tell from a photograph," Auntie Lil interrupted. "Could we see him now? If you could get him to grunt or breathe heavily, maybe I could tell."

O'Conner stared at Auntie Lil. "I can't even get him to

say his name, so I doubt he'll grunt on command. But I'll take you in for a few minutes. Let me know what you think, even if you're not sure. He's put on weight since he had those photos taken. Abromowitz said your attackers were heavy."

"I thought they were," Auntie Lil corrected him. "I'm not completely sure."

O'Conner nodded. "Good enough. Just take your time, get a good look at him. Don't let the bandages bother you. Even if you just *think* it might be him, let me know. I'm not looking for evidence in a court of law. I'm looking for leverage. I need something I can threaten to charge him with to get him to talk."

A nurse approached them. "Agent O'Conner?" she said, her voice infused with unmistakable authority.

She was beautiful, but O'Conner did not notice. The man lived, slept, and breathed his job. "Yeah?" he asked, annoyed at the interruption.

"The doctor is in with your patient right now. I'm afraid you're going to have to wait until he's done before you disturb him any further."

O'Conner groaned in frustration and glumly plopped down on one of the couches. His scowl could have peeled the soft yellow paint from the waiting-room walls.

Even Casey could read his mood. She sat down with a silent Auntie Lil and quietly stared at the photo of Frankie Five Alarm in her hands.

3.   They still had a number of hours before their second meeting with Seth Rosenbloom. T.S. was not eager to return home, where he would be forced to endure pointed remarks by Auntie Lil about her excellent health. Herbert suggested they swing by Max Rose Fashions to see if the old guard, Hiram Tate, had come in yet.

"He's on his way," the chubby lobby guard told them. "Says he feels better. Guy is terrified of losing his job. Go figure. This is not what I would call a fulfilling career." He yawned. "Should be here in half an hour. I hope." He yawned again.

They spent the time waiting in the backseat of Lilah's limousine. The tinted windows afforded them privacy and made it easy to keep an eye on who went in and out of Max Rose Fashions. Very few people did. Nor did the suspect truck reappear. For all they knew, it was on its way to Kalamazoo.

The garment district was winding down. The dense human traffic thinned and the street noise abated to a more normal level. Inside the profusion of delis, waitresses wiped down counters and waited to close. Another busy day was nearly over.

Hiram Tate emerged from the nearby subway exit slowly, using the railing to pull his frail body up the steep stairs.

"That has to be him," T.S. said. "He's old and he's shaking. Just like Auntie Lil said."

More to the point, he was also wearing a guard uniform topped only by a windbreaker despite the chilly late-afternoon air. T.S. and Herbert stopped him before he reached the Max Rose Fashions building. They wanted to question him alone.

The man reacted to their sudden presence with the resigned air of one who is used to being kicked around. T.S. introduced himself as one of the new owners of the company. That, at least, seemed to galvanize the old guard.

"I'm being fired, aren't I?" he asked, his voice trembling. His lower lip quivered.

"Of course you're not. My God, man, absolutely not."

T.S. was horrified. He had not intended to terrify the man, only persuade him to answer a few questions.

"Doesn't matter," the old guy mumbled. "I will be. Just you wait. Jake Rosenbloom is going to can me real soon."

"That's what I wanted to talk to you about," T.S. explained. "My aunt told me about your concerns last night. She was one of the women that was attacked."

"Bad business." Hiram took off his cap and scratched at his thinning strands of white hair. "Didn't see a thing. Can't think how they unlocked the back entrance. Must have had keys."

T.S. nodded. "Looks like it." He shivered. "It's a little cold. Could we get into my car and talk?"

Hiram was about to balk, but the sight of the stretch limo convinced him that it was better to cooperate with the new owner. The guy was rich enough. Maybe he could help.

"Never saw anything like this," the old man marveled, running his hands over the leather upholstery. He perched on the edge of the seat like a child awaiting his turn in a spelling bee.

"This is my associate, Mr. Wong." T.S. introduced Herbert, who bobbed his head. "Could I get you a drink?"

"A drink?" Hiram's eyes narrowed. "This is a test, isn't it? You think I was drinking last night and missed something."

"Heavens, no." T.S. would have to be more careful. Here was a man intent on fulfilling his own premonitions of failure. "In fact, I'm not interested in last night at all."

"Then what are you interested in?" Hiram asked. He slid a few inches away from T.S. as if suspecting that he was up to some particularly sneaky trick.

"I want to know why you're so sure that Jake Rosenbloom is going to fire you."

The old man's face went pale. "I can't say nothing. I'd lose my job."

"He can't fire you. Not without the consent of the other owners. Not anymore."

"He can and he will," the old man said sharply. "He said as much to my face."

"He told you that you would be fired if you said anything about what you saw," Herbert broke in suddenly. His voice was calm and reassuring. "Is that right?"

Hiram nodded.

"But he wasn't talking about last night, was he?" Herbert prompted.

Hiram shook his head vigorously.

"Because he was talking about the day that Max Rosenbloom died." It was an astute and well-aimed guess.

The old man stared at Herbert. "You know about it, then?"

"Yes," Herbert lied. "There was someone else who observed you."

"Must have been behind the potted plants, then. I didn't see anyone else. Until the blast. Just him—meaning Jake—waiting down that little hallway that leads to the newspaper stand. He was pretending to smoke a cigarette." The old man rubbed his chin. "I thought it was a little peculiar. Man like that can smoke in his office if he wants to. But I didn't say anything. I thought maybe he'd had another one of his fights with his brother. Those two could go at it sometimes."

"Jake Rosenbloom was hanging around in the lobby of the building the day that Max got killed by the bomb?" T.S. asked.

"Yeah. Just sort of standing in the shadows, like." Hiram twisted his hat anxiously in his hands. "I saw Mr. Rosenbloom come down in the elevators, meaning Max. He'll always be the *real* Mr. Rosenbloom." The man's eyes filled unexpectedly with tears. "I might have been just about the last person he ever spoke to. He tipped his hat to me and said good night. He always wore this kind of English driving hat, with a bill on the front of it, you know? Then he noticed his nephew, and Jake sort of puffed up and said something to him. Sucking up to him, like. That boy wanted to take over the business bad. The older Mr. Rosenbloom was asking him a few questions, looked like business stuff, and Jake was nodding his head." The old guard paused and wiped some fine beads of sweat from his brow. "Hot in here."

"They were friendly?" T.S. asked.

"Oh, sure. Boy was falling all over himself to be friendly. Walked him to the door of the lobby. Heard him ask his uncle where he was going and Mr. Rosenbloom mumbled something. I couldn't hear, but I don't think that Jake could either. He just sort of turned away and went back to waiting in the hall."

"Why would he want to fire you over that?" Herbert asked.

"Don't know," the old man told him. "Maybe it was what happened next."

"The bomb went off?" T.S. asked.

Hiram nodded. "Maybe five or ten minutes later, it went off. I heard it from a block away. People were screaming and running down the sidewalk to see. I stuck my head out the door. Well, maybe I went out for a second or two. But I didn't leave my post. No, not me." He shook his head vigorously. "I was just coming back inside when Mr. Rosenbloom, I mean *Jake*, came up to me. He looked all pale and was sweating. 'What was that?' he says, grabbing my uniform and like to lifting me off my feet. I pried his fingers off and said, 'Well, sir. It sounded like a bomb.' I was in the big war, you know."

"What did Jake do then?" T.S. said.

"He turned on his tail and ran."

"Out the door?" Herbert asked.

Hiram shook his head. "No. Opposite direction. Toward the stairway. He opened up the metal doors and they banged against the wall something fierce. Then he started tearing up those stairs like he was going to run up all seven flights without stopping."

Herbert and T.S. exchanged a glance. Had Jake known what the bomb blast meant?

The old man was relieved to be unburdening his secrets. He could not shut up now. "A couple minutes later," he continued, "Gerry, one of the salesmen, comes flying in the front door and yelling something about Max, and he's gone up in the elevators before I can make sense of what he's saying. And then all hell breaks loose and people are pouring out of the elevators and the ladies are crying and the other nephew, Davy, comes flying *down* the steps. Booms out of those doors and liked to flatten two men who were standing nearby. He's running as fast as he can, just tears out through the front and hightails it down the sidewalk, following everyone else toward the blast. A couple minutes later I see Jake leaving the building. But he's holding a briefcase and wearing his jacket like it's just another regular night. He walks out in the crowd, and a few minutes later a lady comes in and tells me that it was *Max* who got blown up in the bomb. I couldn't hardly believe it. He was the one who gave me a job in the first place. My wife used to work for him until she got sick, and he knew that we needed the money."

Hiram paused and wiped his eyes again. "I should've told the police everything. But Jake came down a few days later and starting dropping these hints about how I'd never seen him and it was just between us and how if I liked my job, it was good for me to continue to be his friend because he was going to be the new owner. The funny thing is, I never would have remembered seeing him if he hadn't made such a big deal about it." Hiram's shoulders slumped. "It wasn't the honorable thing to keep the information back, I know. I should have gone to the police. My wife would be ashamed if she knew."

T.S. patted the old guy's knee. "We won't tell her," he promised.

4. Half an hour later the nurse awakened an exhausted Agent O'Conner. They could see the patient now. O'Conner was instantly alert.

As they entered the room the cop guarding the door looked up from his magazine just long enough to check out Casey's rear end. He yawned and returned to his article.

There was only one bed in the room and it was surrounded by a screen on all four sides. A small opening led them to the foot of the bed, where they could look down on the heavily swathed patient. Frankie Five Alarm did not look happy. Every inch of his exposed torso was covered in bandages. The left side of his head was wrapped firmly in padded gauze, including his left eye. A cross bandage extended over the bridge of his nose, masking the center of his face. The untouched quarters of his head stood out in startling contrast. One ear protruded like a flower, and a shock of bright orange hair sprouted wildly from between anchoring bandages. A single exposed eye stared out at them malevolently. It was bright blue, sharp, and alert.

"Frankie's refusing painkillers," O'Conner explained. "Just say no, right, Frankie?"

The man was silent.

Casey inched closer and bent over to stare him in his good eye. Shanahan did not flinch. He opened his eye wider and glared back. Casey backed away and looked thoughtful. Auntie Lil took her turn. She crept up to his side and peered down, then fumbled in her pocketbook for her reading glasses. She hated to wear them in front of other people but had no choice. She examined Shanahan carefully, dragging her gaze from his head down to his torso and even lifting the covers to peek inside.

"Hey!" came a grunt from the patient.

"He talks," O'Conner pointed out. "That's progress."

"See anything you like?" Shanahan mumbled, glaring at Auntie Lil with one bright blue eye.

"He's not bulky enough," Auntie Lil announced. "And he's too tall. I don't really think it could have been him."

The federal agent's shoulders slumped. He nodded and led them out into the hall. For a moment he said nothing. He just leaned against the wall and ran his fingers through his thick brown hair. "I'm trying too hard," he finally admitted.

"I've seen him before," Casey said.

O'Conner's head jerked up. "He was one of them?" he asked.

"No. Auntie Lil is right. The two that attacked us were bigger. Shorter and plumper. But I have seen this guy before. I mean, it's kind of hard to forget hair that color and his ears . . . well, those ears. But you know how it is when you sort of recognize someone, but on the other hand, maybe you saw them in a dream or saw their photograph in the newspaper or maybe just sat next to them at some diner last week?"

O'Conner fidgeted impatiently. "So you're telling me

that you dreamed about this guy?" he asked. The cop reading the magazine snorted. Women. What did they know?

Casey sensed their mood and it angered her. "Okay, smart guys. God forbid a female help you out." She glared at O'Conner. She was definitely over her crush. "Maybe I do remember where I've seen him before. And maybe I'm just not sure. And maybe if I did see him, he was with one of the Rosenblooms." She smiled sweetly and shut her mouth.

"You've seen that guy with a Rosenbloom?" O'Conner asked.

"Maybe." Casey examined her fingernails. "I'll tell you if you beg."

"Want him to roll over, too?" the uniformed officer asked. He guffawed and flipped to a new page in his magazine.

Auntie Lil intervened. "Casey, dear, you're a wonderful detective but really quite immature. Tell this nice special agent what you've seen, and tell him right now, or I'll repeat everything you said about him the first time you met." It was Auntie Lil's turn to smile sweetly.

"That's blackmail," Casey said. "And it's a deal." She took a deep breath. "Maybe I just might have possibly seen him, if I'm right, meeting with Davy Rosenbloom a couple of weeks before Max's death."

"Where?" O'Conner demanded.

Casey sighed. "The Hide-Away Tide-Away Motel in Long Beach."

"What were you doing following Davy Rosenbloom?"

"I was following Sabrina Rosenbloom," Casey explained. "At the request of her husband. She and Davy went into a room, not for very long. Then Davy came out and met someone in the coffee shop of the place. I think it might have been the guy in there. The guy had red hair, I remember that. And he was really tall."

"That's good enough," O'Conner said. "Wait here." He disappeared inside the room.

Auntie Lil and Casey looked at each other. They were near the door of the room but not close enough to hear what O'Conner was saying. Casey looked down at the preoccupied uniformed cop, then back up at Auntie Lil. Auntie Lil nodded.

"You lift?" Casey asked the guard, moving closer so that her thigh brushed against his arm. She bent over to examine the color photograph that he was scrutinizing. It featured a well-oiled weight lifter, bronzed and rippled. "He's a little much for me."

The cop grunted. "Guys like that don't have jobs. They can stay in the gym all day if they want."

"How many times a week do you work out?" Casey asked. She knelt beside him to get a better look. Her hand rested lightly on his chair, just brushing his leg.

"Me?" The policeman chuckled modestly. "I don't lift. Anymore."

"Sure you do." Casey squeezed his right biceps. "Tell the truth. You still lift, you're just embarrassed to admit it because the other guys would kid you. I think you look better than the guy in that photograph. He looks like a side of beef."

The cop laughed and admitted that, sure, maybe he did stop by the gym a couple of times a month, but he hadn't realized that it still showed. He began to describe his lifting routine with enthusiasm, flipping to certain pages and pointing out models to Casey.

Behind them, Auntie Lil slipped quietly into the hospital room. O'Conner was out of sight, the outline of his back visible inside the protective screen that shielded Frankie Five Alarm. She tiptoed to the far side of the screen and listened.

"You want a deal?" O'Conner was saying. "Okay, here's a deal: in a week, I release you with no protection. And we leak to the press that you're cooperating with a federal investigation into the activities of Joseph Galvano."

The muffled reply was part roar and part indignant squeal.

"I wouldn't take it either," O'Conner admitted. "You'll be dead in twenty-four hours. You ran out of luck on this one, Frankie. You guys aren't usually so sloppy."

Auntie Lil could not understand the muffled reply.

"I can't buy that," O'Conner said flatly. "I have a witness who saw you meeting with Davy Rosenbloom, so we know you're involved. It's a good witness, too. A professional. So don't tell me you don't know any Rosenblooms. If you keep saying you don't know any Rosenblooms, then I'm going to personally sign your release papers myself."

There was a long silence. O'Conner's shadow shifted: he was looking up at the ceiling, whistling a tuneless funeral march. Waiting for Frankie to make up his mind. Auntie Lil inched closer and her pocketbook grazed an extra IV stand. It clanged softly, but she was saved from detection when the patient began talking at the same time.

"I didn't take out the old man," Frankie Five Alarm said in a raspy voice. "It was an accident."

"What was an accident?" O'Conner asked calmly.

"The old man dying. The bomb was meant for the nephew."

"Why?" O'Conner asked.

"It's a long story," Shanahan mumbled.

"Then start at the beginning," O'Conner said. "I've got the time."

"Galvano had cut Davy off. From his money, you know?"

"Davy had already borrowed too much money from Galvano and had gambled it away?" O'Conner asked.

"Yeah. At first, he was paying him back. Some kind of scam at the company. But then he got found out by some new financial guy. He couldn't come up with the rest. So Galvano cut him off. And Joey wasn't too happy about eating the loss either. He'd rather have whacked the kid, believe me. But he needed Davy there in the company. Alive. He had these big plans for taking the company public and grabbing a piece of the profits. Davy was going to be his guy on the inside."

"But Davy kept gambling," O'Conner stated.

"Yeah. They always do. So the kid came to me. He'd heard that sometimes I do a little work on the side. You know, under the table. Lend a little here. Lend a little there. Nothing big. Joey probably knew about it."

"Sure," O'Conner said.

"He was a bad risk, maybe, but the kid said he was getting ready to come into some money," Shanahan explained.

"By killing his uncle?" O'Conner asked.

"No. I told you. That was an accident. The kid said he was cutting a deal with his brother. The kid was going to inherit big one day and everyone in the family knew it, so he was trading off a lot of money then for some money now. From the brother. It sounded good to me."

"Especially when he agreed to pay your vig," O'Conner commented.

"Yeah, well, he don't like my interest rates he can take his business to the bank." Shanahan coughed and continued. "I lent him what he needed. But he didn't come through with the payback on time. I called to remind him, just friendly like, of course."

"Of course," O'Conner said.

"He still didn't come through." There was a silence before Shanahan continued. "I was forced to take matters into my own hands, you understand."

"I do," O'Conner said solemnly.

"I called the kid again. He said he was going to get the money from someplace else. I believed him. I guess I'm just a trusting sort of guy. I met him in some motel out on Long Island where he was supposed to hand over the bucks. Except he's broke and we're back to where we started. Whoever was going to give him the money didn't come through."

"What did you do then?" O'Conner asked.

"I called the brother. You know—the fat one. Worked with Davy. The one that was supposed to advance some of his inheritance."

"Jake."

"Yeah, Jake. Told him that if he and his brother didn't come up with the money, I'd have to do something drastic."

"Like?"

"Something drastic. Let's just leave it at that."

"Okay. What did the brother say?"

"To go ahead and off the kid! Can you believe it?" Frankie sounded indignant. "His own brother and this guy is telling me to off him. 'If this gets around, your reputation's shot,' he says to me. I could hardly believe his nerve. Here's some fat suit telling me how to run my business. 'Everyone will know they don't have to pay you back,' he says. 'But that's your business. I just want to make it clear that I am not bailing my brother out.' Hey, with a brother like that, who needs enemies?"

"What happened then?" O'Conner asked.

"I tried to figure out what the hell was going on. I didn't want to walk into a trap, you know. I don't often get people practically asking me to off their relatives. But the guy was right. I had to do something."

"Before other people that owed you money found out," O'Conner stated. "Not to mention Galvano."

"Okay, yeah. I didn't want Davy going to Joey and begging him to save his ass. Maybe I was trespassing on Joey's territory a bit, but there's plenty to go around, you know? Galvano don't have to be the only game in town."

"Tell that to Joey."

Frankie paused. "I didn't kill the old man," he said.

"But you put the bomb underneath Davy's car."

"No. Not me. Another guy did it."

"Well, of course," O'Conner said. "Another guy always does it."

"The kid deserved it. He was disrespecting me. He was abusing his family. He was out of control." Frankie coughed. "I thought about letting it slide. I know you don't believe me, but I did think about it. But then the brother—Jake— calls me back, you know? He asks for a meeting and we meet in some dive, because he don't want to be seen with me, and he friggin' offers to help. Says he don't want anyone else to get hurt, so he'll let me know when the kid is going to be driving alone. I believe him. What's not to believe?"

"Honor among thieves," O'Conner said.

"Are you being smart with me? Because if you're being smart with me, I'm feeling kind of sleepy."

"Go on," O'Conner said wearily. "What happened then?"

"What do you mean what happened? Jake calls and says today's the day. But the wrong guy got in the car. How was I supposed to know that the old man was going to borrow his car? It was a good job, too. Clean. Time trigger. Should have been a piece of cake. Would have made a statement, you know. Frankie Five Alarm don't mess around. It would have been perfect, the underground garage and all. No one else would have been hurt but the kid."

"Pretty warmhearted of you," O'Conner said.

"I like to cover all the bases," Frankie said. "I consider myself a professional."

"What about Davy?" O'Conner interrupted sharply. "Who shot him?"

"Why are you asking me? I don't know. Wasn't me." There was a silence and Frankie broke it. "Don't look at me that way. Am I going to lie here and tell you about one murder but not another? That don't make sense. I don't know who killed the kid. It wasn't me. I backed off. You know, that old guy Max was all right. I saw him stand up to Joey once, threw him right out of his office. I kind of admired him. I thought it was a waste, you know. He deserved to go in his sleep."

"Not to mention that you knew the heat was on," O'Conner pointed out. "You couldn't go near a Rosenbloom after Max was killed."

"That, too. No one ever said I was stupid."

"You were stupid enough to let Joey find out it was you that killed Max."

"The guy who planted the bomb ratted on me," Shanahan whined. "Some people just can't keep their mouths shut."

"Fortunately for me," O'Conner said. "Who tried to hit the old lady last night?"

"What old lady? You got me on that one." Shanahan coughed. "Give me some water."

"In a minute. Let's talk about where the bodies are buried."

"What bodies? There ain't no bodies to bury. One guy got blown to smithereens. The other's in the morgue, I heard."

"Not those bodies," O'Conner explained patiently. "Let's go back a couple months, shall we?"

Auntie Lil could not bear to listen to any more. Tears sprang to her eyes. Max had been killed by accident, over nothing more important than money. It had been nothing but coincidence that had stopped him before she could see him again, stopped him just when he . . . She forced herself to avoid thinking about it. It was a waste, such a waste, that it just did not seem possible. Her job now was to restore his reputation. She waited for a moment, regaining her composure. Finally, she took a deep breath and tiptoed back toward the door before O'Conner discovered her.

Just as she reached the door she heard the cop on the other side ask, "Hey? Where'd the old lady go?"

"My aunt?" Casey answered. "Ladies' room."

"Where's O'Conner?" the cop demanded next.

"O'Conner?" Casey said. "Oh. The guy inside had to use the bedpan. O'Conner said he'd help him."

"No kidding?" the cop said. "It's tough being a fed." He laughed. "So, what do you think? Feel like working out together sometime?" He stared down at a photo of a woman in a string bikini. Her muscles would have intimidated Arnold Schwarzenegger.

Auntie Lil crept back out into the hall without being seen and tapped Casey on the arm. "Ready, dear?" she asked sweetly.

"Thought you'd fallen in," the policeman joked, looking up.

"I'm not feeling well," Auntie Lil explained. "I think we'd better go now." She grabbed Casey's arm and pulled the younger woman down the hall.

"What about working out?" the policeman called after them.

"I'll give you a call," Casey lied. They turned a corner and Auntie Lil began to race to the elevators.

"What gives?" Casey asked.

"Plenty. But let's get out of here before O'Conner finds us."

CHAPTER SEVENTEEN

1. "Where are we going?" Auntie Lil asked as she thumbed through Casey's folder on the Rosenbloom case.

"Long Beach. I'm going to nail that widow. I know she's wrapped up in this somehow. Here." Casey removed a photograph from the front pocket of her dress. "File this, will you? We're going to need it." She sped around a delivery truck and cut across two lanes of traffic. Cars honked angrily behind them.

Auntie Lil stared down at the set of mug shots. "Stealing from a special agent? Oh, dear. Won't you lose your license?"

"Don't have one," Casey explained. She winked at Auntie Lil. "O'Conner won't remember. He's flipped his man. We're history. He doesn't need us anymore."

Auntie Lil tucked the photo inside a manila folder. "Why do you carry all this around with you?" she asked, only partly referring to the file. The inside of Casey's car was like a portable apartment. She had a pillow and blankets heaped on the backseat, along with a cooler, a curling iron, several changes of clothing, a pair of bedroom slippers, and a six-pack of orange soda.

"Until this is over and we know who is killing who, I'm not letting the file out of my sight and I'm not keeping a routine. This is my portable office and home."

They rode in silence, Auntie Lil lost in thought. Had Jake Rosenbloom acted alone? Or was he in it with somebody else?

After they had pulled into the parking lot of the Hide-Away Tide-Away Motel, Casey applied fresh lipstick and fluffed her hair. "Never know when you're gonna need a little sex appeal," she explained. "That last guy boosted my confidence."

"Sex appeal?" Auntie Lil asked. "If he's over sixty, better leave him to me."

There were two men in the reception area this time. The lanky redhead with the bad skin stood at the check-in counter. Behind him, wedged into a cubbyhole office, a fat man with a dense head of gray hair was sitting at a cluttered desk reading the mail. He wore a maroon blazer with a yellow tie and had a name tag clipped to his pocket.

"Remember me?" Casey asked the redhead. "You handsome thing, you."

The young clerk looked at her. "You told me you were a cop." He pouted.

"I said no such thing. I merely pulled out two twenties and handed them over." She smiled knowingly at the kid and he shifted uneasily, glancing at the office behind him.

The fat man looked up, gave Auntie Lil a thorough once-over, shrugged, and returned to his mail.

"What do you want?" the kid whispered. "I don't want to lose my job."

"More information. I still have a little credit left, don't I?" Casey took the photograph of the Rosenbloom clan out of its envelope and slid it across the counter. "Remember this?"

"Sure," the kid mumbled miserably. "I already told you. I saw that lady *there* come in with that guy *there*." He pointed out Sabrina and Davy Rosenbloom.

"I asked you this before, but it's really important, so *think*. Do you remember how long they stayed?" Casey asked. "Was it just a short time?" She was trying to figure out if it was the same time as when she'd seen them together, or if they had returned again.

"Lady, I don't keep a timer going for every room in this place." The kid sneered, his confidence restored. He stroked a particularly bad patch of pimples on his right cheek.

"Young man, if you kept your hands off your face, it would clear up immediately," Auntie Lil informed him.

The kid stared at her but did not reply.

"Okay, now I want to know if you saw this man here at the motel," Casey asked. "The same time you saw the other two." She held up the composite photos of Frankie Five Alarm for the kid to examine. The boy took his time, secretly thrilled at the sight of actual mug shots. His concentration was intense.

The fat man in the office looked up and noticed that photographs were involved. He waddled, unseen by the kid, to the counter. Up close, Auntie Lil could read his name tag clearly. He was the manager. He stood just behind the boy, looking over his shoulder, gazing first at the mug shots and then at the color photograph of the Rosenbloom family.

"I might have seen him," the kid admitted. "Can't be sure."

"Can't be sure?" Casey asked incredulously. "Look at the guy. He's got ears the size of bats and his hair is oranger than Ronald McDonald's. You get many people that look like that in here?"

"I mostly look at the ladies," the boy mumbled.

"Okay. Well, did you ever see this guy"—Casey stabbed Frankie Five Alarm with one well-chewed fingernail—"with this woman?" She rested her finger on Sabrina Rosenbloom's face.

The boy shook his head emphatically. "No way. I know that lady. I keep track. She never came here with a man with red hair." The boy gulped apologetically and ran his hands through his own rusty strands. "Guess she don't like redheads."

Casey sighed. "What about you?" she asked the fat manager. "Seen him around?"

"What's this about?" the manager demanded. The kid at the counter jumped and turned near purple. The manager elbowed the kid aside and grabbed the Rosenbloom photograph.

Casey flashed her phony badge. It winked once under the fluorescent lights and was gone. "No big deal. Just trying to determine whether this woman was seen with this man." She nodded toward Frankie Five Alarm. "The boy here tells me she came in once with the man on the far end, but he can't help any more than that."

The manager stared down at the photographs, then smirked at the kid. "You screw up everything," he told the boy.

The young man became indignant. "I did see her with him. They came here about two weeks ago. I'm sure of it. The guy was driving a Porsche."

"It wasn't him," the manager said pompously. "It's that guy. The fat one." He covered Jake Rosenbloom's face with a plump forefinger. "They come in for a quickie a couple times a week, usually around about six." He patted the kid on the back paternally. "Not your shift, kid. Didn't mean to be so harsh. But you're looking for the wrong guy, Officer, if you think that lady's been hanging around with the skinny one." He slid the photographs back across the counter and leered at Casey's bosom.

"Thanks for your help," Casey told him, smiling sweetly instead of busting him in the chops like she wanted to. She could feel Auntie Lil trembling next to her and had to get her out of there before she said too much.

"Always happy to help out the law." The manager spoke directly to Casey's chest, as if she had a microphone buried there.

Neither Casey nor the kid corrected his mistake. If he thought Casey was a cop, then let him. "It's great to have the cooperation of businessmen like you," Casey told him. "Pills of the community and all that."

"That's pillars, dear," Auntie Lil said.

"Whatever."

The manager's eyes never left the front of Casey's yellow dress. "If you ever want a discount on a room . . ." he began.

"Thanks, but I have a home," Casey told him quickly. "I prefer to bunk there." She took Auntie Lil by the elbow and steered her firmly out of the motel. "Too bad that guy wasn't over sixty," she muttered.

"Put the pedal to the metal," Auntie Lil instructed firmly. "We have twenty minutes to make our meeting with Seth Rosenbloom and I intend to be on time."

2. The Swan Dive hummed thanks to a merry early-evening crowd. Auntie Lil led the way to an empty booth by the windows and they all packed in to wait for Seth.

"I feel like like an idiot," T.S. said. "People walking past are doing double takes. We look like a bunch of very lost tourists."

Auntie Lil waved cheerfully at one such passerby. "Perhaps if you and Herbert held hands, you'd feel more comfortable," she suggested.

Herbert's bubbling laughter filled the air, but T.S. wasn't so sure she was kidding. He dropped the subject.

They were waiting for Seth Rosenbloom and he was already nearly thirty minutes late. The delay had given them ample opportunity to exchange information. They were ready to move ahead with what they knew.

"He is coming, isn't he?" Auntie Lil asked for the fifth time.

"*He said he was,*" T.S. answered yet again. "Casey, why are you ogling the bartender? Surely even you must know that it's hopeless."

"I was not *ogling*," Casey informed him with attempted dignity.

"Lillian?" Herbert asked. "Are you all right?"

Auntie Lil was staring toward the doorway, her expression combining disbelief with lingering regret.

"What is it?" T.S. asked.

Seth Rosenbloom was walking across the room toward their table. He wore a suit and tie. His normally impeccable hair had been rumpled by the wind and it tumbled over his forehead. He looked very tired around his eyes.

"Well, here I am," he announced, placing his briefcase on the table. "What else do we have to discuss? I thought we covered pretty much everything last night. I should never have told you all those things about my family. I don't know what got into me. Too much to drink, I guess."

Auntie Lil was still staring at him. "You look just like him," she said, her voice full of wonderment.

Seth noticed her for the first time. "You have to be Miss Hubbert," he said. "Uncle Max talked a lot about you last time we met. You must have been on his mind." As if knowing that Auntie Lil would want to look at him, Seth slid into the booth across from her and smiled.

Casey introduced herself, explaining her role in Max's life over the months before he died. Seth nodded politely but did not comment. He looked around the table and noticed Herbert sitting in the corner. They shared a small, secret smile.

"When did you last talk to Max?" Auntie Lil asked. "You said he mentioned me."

"Yes, he did. He was in the mood to reminisce. It was a few weeks before he died. We had dinner together to celebrate my getting a job. It's not so easy for a lawyer these days. He was very proud of me." Seth ran a hand through his hair. "He was in a funny mood. Different. Defeated in some way. He looked so lonely and he looked so old. He had never looked old to me before." The young man sighed. "I think that he had realized just what a mess the family was in."

"It's worse than you think," T.S. said quietly. "It's much worse than you think." As T.S. told him about Jake's involvement in his uncle's death, Seth listened without expression. It was impossible to tell what emotions he felt inside.

"It *was* a mistake," Seth said after they had finished. "I don't think that even Jake would have killed Uncle Max intentionally."

"Not even to take over the company?" Auntie Lil asked. "Do you know your brother well enough to be sure?"

Seth shrugged. "Do I know my brother? No, not really. Jake and Davy came from another world so far as I was concerned. But I do know Jake well enough to guess that what he meant to do was kill Davy all along. They hated each other." Tears welled up in his eyes. He waited a moment before he went on. "God, Davy was impossible. Always borrowing money, getting in trouble, and charming his way out of it again. But he loved all of us and he had his ways of letting us know it. He was never like Jake, plotting for more power, more attention, whatever. I miss my brother. And now I feel like I've lost both of my brothers. Forever." He wiped his eyes and breathed deeply.

"Do you want to find out who killed Davy?" Auntie Lil asked quietly. "If it was Jake, and I'm not convinced that it was, I don't think he could have done it alone."

"Why do you say that?" Seth asked.

"As soon as that bomb went off, I think Davy would have known that it was meant for him," Auntie Lil explained. "He would have suspected your brother of setting him up if what you say about their relationship is true. I don't think he would have agreed to meet Jake alone after what happened to Max. Someone else must have been involved, someone that Davy trusted more than Jake."

"You mean someone else in the family," Seth said flatly.

"Maybe," Auntie Lil said. She paused. "Maybe not. We need your help to find out."

"How can I help?" Seth asked. "I've spent the last seven years of my life running away from my family just as fast as I could."

"I want you to come with me to visit your father," Auntie Lil explained. "I think he knows some things that he's not telling me."

"My father won't let me in the door of his house," Seth said.

"That's not true," Auntie Lil told him. "I visited him. He asked to see you. I promised I would try to convince you to come. He said to tell you that all the things he used to get angry about don't matter to him anymore. All that matters to him is that he gets to see his son. He misses you very much." Auntie Lil paused and took a deep breath. "Seth, I think your father is dying."

"My mother won't let him see me," he said quietly.

"She won't be there if we go tonight," Casey broke in. "She plays cards every Thursday night two blocks away."

Seth nodded. "I know. With the Friedmans. That's Abby for you. Routine counts."

"Seth," Auntie Lil said, "I loved your uncle very much. I can never begin to tell you what Max meant to me. I think he would want me to find out what happened. But I can't do it without your help. Your father has said all that he is going to say to me. But I think he would talk more freely to you."

"How sick is he?" Seth asked.

"He wasn't on the respirator when I was there," Auntie Lil told him. "But he seemed so tired." She paused. "I'm sorry, but he seemed ready to go."

Seth stared at the scarred wooden tabletop. His eyes followed the many carved lines of its surface, as if seeking a clear path in its pattern. He sighed. "What exactly do you want me to do?" he asked.

Auntie Lil told him.

3. Once Casey realized that only Auntie Lil would be accompanying Seth to see his father, she opted for an evening at home instead. "I need to fumigate this dress," she explained. "I've worn it three days in a row. And I also need to take about thirty-five more Tylenols."

The lack of Casey's car would not hurt them. Grady and his limousine could easily accommodate four in the backseat. The evening rush hour was over and the car sped smoothly along the Long Island Expressway. They were silent until they passed the Garden City exit.

"Poor Uncle Max," Seth said, breaking the silence. "He would be so ashamed if he knew. He always gave us anything we wanted. Boarding schools, college tuition, hot cars. You name it. Davy went through six Porsches by the time he was twenty-five. Yet all those things didn't matter to Uncle Max. I don't think money meant very much to him. He drove his old Audi for years."

Auntie Lil nodded. "It's true. Money never mattered to Max. It was the idea, the dream, that was important." She fell silent, watching the distant lights of the nearby towns as they sped by. Underneath, in her subconscious, something that Seth had said percolated. By the time they reached the exit for Abe and Abby's home, it burst into her consciousness with sudden clarity.

"The *car*," Auntie Lil cried as they swung onto the exit ramp.

"What car?" T.S. asked drowsily. The smooth ride had lulled him to sleep.

"The Audi," Auntie Lil said.

"What about it?" Herbert asked.

"His wife was driving it the day that Max died," Auntie Lil explained.

"So what?" T.S. asked. "Her own car was in the shop."

"But when we were searching her house, she drove up in her own car," Auntie Lil said. "It was a red sports car. I don't know what kind."

"Simple. Her car had been repaired by then," T.S. said. "That's all."

"I understand that," Auntie Lil conceded. "But where was Max's car?"

"In the garage," T.S. said.

"No," Herbert told him. "The garage was empty. I checked it on the way in."

Auntie Lil shook her head, mystified. "Where is Max's car? And why is it missing?"

4. The expensive suburb was silent in the heart of the evening. Every now and then they passed a window that flickered with reflected television light. Parents were home from work, dinners had been served. Some families, at least, were at peace.

Grady pulled to the curb a quarter of a block from the Rosenblooms'. Even at that distance, the strangely shaped shadows of the figurines dotting the lawn were visible.

"I can't believe that the neighbors haven't made them take those things down," Seth said. "It used to be a beautiful lawn, with shrubs and flowers and fruit trees. It started to die one year. No one could figure out why. And my mother started putting up those stupid ceramic gnomes. Every time one of us left the house for college, she would buy another." He shook his head.

After that, they waited in weary silence, watching for Abby to leave.

"There she goes," Grady finally said from his vantage point in the driver's seat. "She's getting in her car and pulling out of the driveway."

"Trust Mom not to walk two blocks," Seth observed. "She might get mugged."

Instinctively, all five of them ducked in their seats as Abby drove past.

"The coast is clear," Grady announced. He had yet to complain about the long hours, but he wasn't about to sit there all night.

Auntie Lil and Seth hurried to the front door. Herbert and T.S. stayed behind in the limousine. If Abby came home early, Auntie Lil had assured them, they were not to worry. She and Seth could handle Abby. But if Jake or Sabrina or any other unknown person appeared, they were to enter the house immediately.

As Abe had promised, the door was unlocked. The house was quiet. Seth shook his head at the plastic runner that covered the rug, then led Auntie Lil silently upstairs.

There was a light on in one of the spare bedrooms. Auntie Lil stopped to peek inside. Rebecca Rosenbloom lay sleeping on top of the covers, an open book propped upside down on her chest. She was dressed in a rose bathrobe. Her breathing was even, the hooded eye closed to the light. She looked deceptively peaceful in slumber.

Seth returned to see what was detaining Auntie Lil. "She's a piece of work," he whispered when he saw his aunt Rebecca. "But I'm worried that she's here. I hope Dad hasn't gotten worse."

Abe Rosenbloom lay in bed, pale and still. His eyes were closed but his hands fluttered slowly in time to the muted sounds of a classical symphony. A small radio was propped on the bedside table. His breathing sounded more labored than Auntie Lil remembered, but at least the respirator still stood against the wall, silent and unused.

"Dad?" Seth said softly.

Abe opened his eyes instantly. His eyes filled with tears. He nodded his head and Seth crept closer.

"It's Seth. Miss Hubbert said that you wanted to see me." He stood by his father's bed, looking down uncertainly, startled by Abe's fragility. Had it really been that long since they had seen one another?

"I'm sorry, Dad," he said. "I really should have come sooner. I wanted to. I thought that Mom wouldn't let me in."

Abe nodded once. His emotions required all of his remaining energy and there was little left for physical movement. He reached out, groping for his son. Seth stilled his trembling hand and enfolded it in his own. "I'm right here," Seth said.

"It's all my fault," Abe whispered. "I blame it all on myself."

"Don't say that," Seth said. "Things just turn out the way they turn out."

Abe managed a small headshake. It was brief but emphatic. "No. I blame it on myself." He coughed but recovered. He was determined to have his say. "I grew up hating my brother and look what happened—I taught my own children to hate."

"I don't hate you," Seth said loudly. "I don't hate anyone."

"No, I know you don't. You and your sister are different. But my poison spread. Look at your mother and all she has. But she always wants more. Look at your brothers and how they hate one another." He stopped. "*Hated* one another. Davy's dead."

"I know, Pop." Seth patted his hand. "I'm sorry. I should have come to see you. I should have known how bad you were feeling."

Abe sighed. "I don't know what to do anymore. I want to die, but I can't."

"If you're tired, Dad, don't hold on." Seth's voice quavered.

"I can't. I have to be here. It may come down to me, you see."

"What do you mean?" Seth asked, stroking his father's hand.

"I'm afraid for the family," Abe told Seth in a whisper. "I know that someone in the family must have killed Max and I think I know who killed Davy. There's nothing I can do about it now. But I don't want this to destroy the whole family, Seth. Promise me that you won't let it destroy the family."

"I promise, Pop. But what can I do?"

"I'm going to leave it up to you," his father told him in

a fading voice. "I'll tell you what I know and you decide what the family should do."

"Me?" Seth asked. "Why me? Being a lawyer doesn't mean I have any answers."

"I'm choosing you because you're my only remaining son," Abe told him. "Not because you're a lawyer."

"You have Jake," Seth said, the name bitter in his mouth.

"No. He's not my son anymore. I know he killed Davy."

"How do you know that?" Seth asked, interpreting Auntie Lil's frantic hand movements correctly.

"I heard them talking the night Max died. They were downstairs shouting. No one thinks I can hear anymore. They think because I can't breathe, that I can't hear either." He smiled thinly, but the smile faded quickly.

"Tell me what you heard," Seth asked softly. "Who was arguing? Who was downstairs?"

"Your mother," he began. "She answered the door. At first I couldn't tell if it was Davy or Jake. But I figured out it was Davy, later, when Jake arrived. When they're together, I can tell their voices apart."

"What were they shouting about?" Seth asked. "How much could you hear?"

Abe suffered a coughing fit and they waited quietly until he had regained his breath. "Davy was shouting at Jake, saying that he had killed 'him.' Later, I knew he meant Max. Jake shouted back, saying that he'd had nothing to do with it. That Davy knew damn well that the bomb had been intended for him. That it was all Davy's fault for having borrowed money from the wrong people."

"But why do you think it was Jake that killed Davy?" Seth asked.

"Davy was shouting that Jake would never get a penny of Max's money. That he would make sure Jake never saw a dime. It went on, it got uglier, my wife began shouting. She could not make either one of them stop."

Seth looked up, appealing to Auntie Lil for help. She stepped to the side of the bed. "It's me," she told Abe softly. "Lillian Hubbert."

"I know," he said. "I felt you standing over there by the door."

"You don't mind that I'm here?" she asked.

"No, not anymore. I want you to help my son decide what to do. I know you'll do the right thing. You always had more common sense than the rest of us put together."

"Don't talk so much," she said. She plumped the pillow behind his head and helped him sip from a glass of water. "I know this is hard on you."

Abe nodded. "I deserve it. My hate was contagious, you know."

"I know." Auntie Lil stood looking down at his frail body. "Why do you really think that Jake killed Davy? It must be more than the fight."

Abe sighed and gripped his son's hand tightly. "I heard Davy walking toward the door. Jake tried to stop him from leaving and they had a fistfight in the lower hallway. I could hear the thumping. I think a vase fell over and broke. Abby was screaming. Then the front door slammed and Davy drove away fast. It wasn't his usual car. I know the sound of his car. But it wasn't Jake's either. Jake drives a slower sedan."

"And then Jake followed him," Auntie Lil said. "And no one ever saw Davy alive again?"

Abe nodded. "The front door slammed again when Jake ran after Davy. My wife was crying. Jake's car drove away. He was in a hurry."

"Where was Davy going?" Auntie Lil asked. "To the police?"

"I don't know," Abe admitted.

Auntie Lil thought she knew where Davy had gone, but she kept her suspicions to herself. "And because Davy ran off, you knew that he was innocent in Max's death?" she prompted.

Abe nodded. "Yes. He'd never have threatened to tell about the bomb unless he was innocent."

"But what makes you so sure that it was Jake who killed Davy?" she asked.

"Because he's my son and I know him," came Abe's reply.

"He's not your son," an angry voice shouted. "Not anymore. You've betrayed him." Abby stood in the doorway, outlined in the light from the hall. Her hair frizzed out from her head in a wild golden nimbus that framed a face contorted in anger. "He's *my* son. I gave birth to him, I raised him, I loved him. You never even looked at him. You were too busy running after those cheap tramps you worked with. We should have had it all—the houses, the cars, the company. But you didn't want it bad enough. You kept everything from me, everything that I deserved. But you're not taking my son. Jake is my son and no one is taking him away." She glared at them, her eyes flickering over Seth as if she didn't know him. Her fists trembled at her sides.

"You can't do anything about it, Mother," Seth said. "Too many people know."

"Don't you call me mother," she ordered, moving into the room with surprising speed. "Jake is the only son I have left, and no one is taking him away from me. I'll kill all of you myself if I have to." She glared with hatred at Auntie Lil, then pushed her away from the bed as she reached toward the bedside table. Abby yanked the drawer open, hands groping inside, searching for the gun that Abe kept hidden there.

"Stop her," Abe croaked, and Auntie Lil threw herself against Abby, pinning her to the corner of the bedside table. Abby screamed and clutched at her side with both hands.

"You won't find the gun there," a commanding voice said from the doorway. Rebecca Rosenbloom stepped into the room. Her head was held high and her hands were firmly wrapped around the handle of an old brown revolver. "You really must think me quite stupid, Abby. Do you think that I would sleep in your home without protection? After what's happened to my brother and my nephew?"

Abby stood staring at her sister-in-law, breathing heavily. Inexplicably, blood was seeping through her blouse where she clutched at her side. "You wouldn't use that thing," she said. "You haven't got the nerve."

Rebecca looked down at the gun with a thoughtful expression on her face. Then she turned her gaze on the tableau before her. "You make me sick," she told Abby. "You knew who killed my brother and you never did a thing about it. Then you let your own son be killed." Rebecca shook her head in disgust and looked at the gun again. She seemed fascinated by its shape and weight. The others stared at her, mute.

"I'm not afraid of you," Abby said, eyes blazing with contempt.

"That could be a mistake," Rebecca said calmly. She pointed the gun carefully at Abby, then moved the barrel upward, squeezing the trigger at the same time.

The explosion was heart stopping. Auntie Lil threw herself down on the rug and covered her head with her hands. Seth shielded his father's body with his own. Only Abby still stood, eyes wide in disbelief, as dust showered from the ceiling onto her hair.

"What were you saying about me not using this gun?"

Rebecca asked. "Because I think I have four more bullets left."

Abby opened her mouth, considered, then closed it without speaking. She darted her tongue along her dry lips and looked around at the others. Auntie Lil sat up and struggled back to her feet. Seth unfolded his body from his father's and looked silently at his mother. He stared, head cocked to one side, as if trying to decipher a curious stranger.

"Well, Abby," Rebecca demanded. "Don't you have anything more to say?"

"I'm not saying anything until I get a lawyer."

"May not need one after all." Rebecca raised the pistol and aimed again.

"Don't," Auntie Lil commanded. "There's been enough killing." She stared at Abby. Blood had gathered at the hem of her blouse and was dripping to the rug at her feet. "Lift up your shirt," Auntie Lil told her.

"What?" Abby asked.

"Lift up your blouse," Auntie Lil said, louder. She took a step toward Abby.

"Do what she says," Rebecca commanded, steadying her aim.

"What?" Seth asked, bewildered.

"I know it was you," Auntie Lil said as she stepped closer. Abby did not move.

"Put your hands up," Auntie Lil ordered. Abby raised both hands slowly in the air.

Auntie Lil hooked the hem of Abby's blouse with a finger, then carefully peeled it upward to reveal an expanse of bloody skin. A jagged scar marred the left side of Abby's stomach. It was six inches long and ineffectually bandaged with a mound of gauze anchored by Band-Aids beginning to peel away from the flesh. Dried blood had formed a crust around the outer edges of the gauze and fresh blood seeped from under the border.

"You tried to kill me," Auntie Lil said quietly.

"Just scare you," Abby whispered back. "I had to protect my son."

"Oh, Abby," Abe moaned from the bed.

Abby began to cry. She folded her hands over her stomach and sank to the rug, her sobs rising in the silence. Her cries grew in volume and she struggled for breath, the rasping wails growing louder until they turned into a terrifying keening. The others stared, horrified, as her anguish grew in intensity. Blood ran from between her fingers and pooled on the pale blue carpet beneath her.

"Oh, Abby," Abe whispered again as he shut his eyes. Seth grabbed his hand and held on tight.

"Shut up, Abby," Rebecca commanded. "It's too late for tears." But her heart was not in her harsh words. The gun began to tremble in her hands.

Downstairs, a horrible pounding ensued. The thumps echoed through the house.

"Let them in," Auntie Lil ordered Seth. He let go of his father's hand and inched his way along the bedroom wall, keeping as far away from his mother and aunt as he could. He reached the safety of the doorway and dashed down the steps. Within seconds, Grady burst into the bedroom, T.S. and Herbert right behind.

"Was that a gunshot?" Grady asked. The big Irishman took one look at the scene and stopped. He held out a huge hand. "It would take more than one bullet to stop me," he told Rebecca calmly. "I'd have you before you got me."

"I have no intention of harming you," Rebecca said with great dignity. "I am simply protecting my remaining brother's life." She handed the gun over to Grady, who held it as if he had not expected such an easy victory and did not quite know what to do with the spoils. Rebecca suffered no such paralysis. She serenely stepped around Abby to reach her brother's side. She patted Abe's free hand reassuringly. "Are you okay?" she asked.

"Yes," came the faint reply. "Is Abby going to die?"

"No," Rebecca said. "The dying is over. I'm going to take care of you from now on."

"What should we do?" T.S. asked, staring at the disarray of the crowded bedroom.

"Call Lieutenant Abromowitz," Auntie Lil decided. "This time he's earned the glory."

CHAPTER EIGHTEEN

1. Two days later Auntie Lil sat with T.S. at his dining room table eating fresh bagels slathered with more cream cheese than was healthy for either one of them. The cats milled about their feet, mewing and hoping to nab any stray bits that fell their way.

Mahmoud had delivered the morning papers, folded, for their perusal. The doorman's dark eyes burned with unsatisfied curiosity, betraying his conviction that T.S. and his aunt were a permanent cabal as far as he was concerned.

Neither one of them planned to look at the headlines until they had their breakfast laid out before them. They wanted to make a ceremony out of reading about their triumph and intended to savor every word and photograph.

"I'll take *Newsday*," Auntie Lil said, holding out a hand.

"That's not fair. You know the *Times* will bury it somewhere in Metro." T.S. held the newspapers out of her reach.

"For heaven's sake, Theodore. Don't be a prig." Auntie Lil snatched the newspaper from him.

By regular standards, the solving of Max Rosenbloom's murder would have been front-page news. There was money involved, plus a cast of greedy family members to feed to the media for weeks.

But there was no mention of Max's murder anywhere in the newspapers. And it was all Auntie Lil's fault.

"Theodore," she said. "Are you reading what I'm reading?"

"I am," came the incredulous reply.

There it was, emblazoned across the top of even the staid *New York Times*: Joseph Galvano had been indicted by a federal grand jury on forty-one felony counts, the most serious being the murder of "Boom Boom" Fernando Galvez, whose mutilated body had been found crushed inside the wreck of an old auto at a Jersey City junkyard belonging to one of Galvano's known associates, Edward "Fat Eddie" Santucci. According to an unnamed source, it had taken authorities a week to locate the body using the highest-tech equipment available. But they had done it. Habeas corpus. Joey "the Snake" Galvano was going down.

"Listen to this," T.S. said. "It mentions *you*." He read an obscure paragraph toward the end of the story: " 'Authorities allegedly received their first big break in the case when an unnamed, wired informant elicited information from Joseph Galvano that led federal investigators to believe that the body had been hidden in Santucci's junkyard. This information was used to leverage more complete information from a highly placed second informant, who eventually led authorities to the body in exchange for immunity. As a security measure, the identity of this informant is being withheld by court order until the trial.' "

"Frankie Five Alarm," Auntie Lil said. "The man in the hospital. He's telling O'Conner everything he knows."

"Aunt Lil, do you know what you've done?" T.S. asked. "You've helped bring down a man who single-handedly added hundreds of dollars to what we pay to live in New York each year. All those bribes and kickbacks and extortion and labor manipulation. I'll probably pay five hundred a year less in taxes, thanks to you." He smiled fondly and refilled her coffee cup.

"My, but that big old hat came in handy," she mused, then stopped with a sudden thought. "Oh, dear, Theodore. We won't be paying less in taxes. All that money. I'd completely forgotten about all that money."

The money. T.S. had tried hard to ignore it. The written recommendations from Sterling & Sterling had arrived yesterday. The document was more than fifty pages long. His head swam with qualifiers and technical clauses. He yearned for the days of a good piggy bank.

"I was happy before I got that money," T.S. said. "And I'll be happy long after it's gone. I really don't deserve it. I didn't do a damn thing to earn it. And"—he took a deep breath—"I can't say that I really want it."

Auntie Lil examined him shrewdly. "Are you just saying that because you know I feel the same way?"

"No." He was emphatic. "I hate it. I hate all the phony smiles I get from my old friends at Sterling and Sterling. I hate the greedy glint I saw in all those Rosenbloom eyes. What if we turn out like that? Jealously guarding our dollars and always wanting more. I don't want it. You can have mine." He set his coffee cup down with a clink. Already he felt freer. "Besides, I can always sponge off Lilah," he joked.

"I don't want it either," Auntie Lil said. "That was never why I loved Max." She was silent for a moment, thinking of what Max might want. "We'll keep it in trust," she said. "Make it the Max Rosenbloom Foundation. We'll fund lots of projects that his relatives would really hate. Unwed mothers. Ghetto children going to camp. Fashion-design scholarships for the inner-city poor."

"New Porsches for the auto-impaired?" T.S. suggested.

She ignored him. "Ballet scholarships for people with two left feet."

"But first, we take out a little for your retirement fund,"

T.S. insisted. "Just to be safe. I know what you have. It can't hurt to have a little bit more. You and Herbert can go see Singapore together with the extra money. All that talk of his youth must have him pining to see the old home shores."

"Who says I'm ever going to retire?" Auntie Lil replied, a twinkle in her eye.

It reminded T.S. of an important problem. "There is one thing I'd like to do with some of the money before we tie it up in a foundation. It has to do with that old guard at Max Rose Fashions." Auntie Lil nodded. She knew what was coming next. "He has no pension, his wife is sick, and he's about to drop dead from the strain of working," T.S. explained.

"Okay," she agreed. "We'll shower him with bucks. Anything else?"

T.S. thought hard. "We could always hire you a maid," he suggested.

"Never, Theodore," she said firmly.

He shrugged. "Let's give ourselves a few days to think it over. We ought to pay Casey a whopping bonus for helping out. And Grady deserves a hell of a tip."

"Enjoy it while it lasts, Mr. Rockefeller," Auntie Lil warned, reaching for the second half of her bagel. She smiled. "Now that we're soon to be poor again, I feel my appetite returning. But I do think I'll be head of the foundation. I need a title. You can assist."

"Who better?" T.S. agreed. He looked down at the newspapers. "Are you disappointed that this news overshadowed ours?" He pointed toward a photo of Joseph Galvano in handcuffs, his coat hunched up over his face. "Look at him. He's hiding his face like the cheap hoodlum that he is."

Auntie Lil sighed. "It's not so much the publicity I

wanted. It was the missing pieces. You'd think Lieutenant Abromowitz would have called us by now."

His phone call came a few hours later, after T.S. and Auntie Lil had settled in chairs in front of the picture window to speculate about the case.

"It's for you," T.S. said, handing his aunt the telephone. "I think you deserve to hear it first."

"You aren't going to like what I have to say," the lieutenant warned.

"What's to like in this whole mess?" she replied.

"It's taken a few days to sort it out, pick up the nephew, and bring in the widow. We had to question the mother and find other witnesses."

"Well?" Auntie Lil asked. "Are you locking her up?"

Abromowitz knew whom she meant. "I told you that you weren't going to like it," he reminded her. "She's testifying in exchange for immunity."

"She lured that young man to his death," came Auntie Lil's sharp rebuke. "Davy would never have gotten in Max's car with his brother. Sabrina was involved."

There was a long sigh at the other end of the line. "I know that, Miss Hubbert. But without her, we have nothing to make it stick. Jake would walk free without her testimony. Besides, no jury would convict her. She's a great cryer. Had half the precinct on her side before she was done."

"Tell me the whole story," Auntie Lil demanded. "I want to know who in that family was involved."

"As near as we can tell, Jake did help kill Max accidentally," Lieutenant Abromowitz explained. "The bomb in the car was meant for Davy. When the plan backfired, Jake realized that Davy would have to be killed another way. Why? For one thing, Davy was threatening to go to the police and expose Jake's role in the bomb. For another, Jake

had been downstairs the time Max visited his father to tell
him about the will. He overheard Max tell Abe about
changing his will, especially the part about Davy getting
half. He didn't realize Max was talking about a trust. Jake
thought Davy was going to walk away from Max's death
with at least thirty-three million in cash and he knew that
if Davy died, his parents would get the bucks. He figured
that was as good as having the money in his own pocket.
His father was dying and he had his mother pretty much
under his control."

"Did Abby help kill Davy?" Auntie Lil asked.

"No. But when Davy's body turned up in the bottom of
the grave, she had a pretty good idea of who had done it.
And she kept quiet. She was determined to protect Jake.
She considered him her only remaining son."

"And what is Seth?" Auntie Lil asked. "Chopped liver?"

"Lucky, if you ask me," Abromowitz answered. "Any
decent person would be proud to be kicked out of that family. Anyway, after Davy and Jake argued at their parents'
house the night Max died, Davy apparently called Sabrina.
He said he had urgent news about Max's death and that
he'd be right over as soon as he took care of some business."

"He was still trying to keep Frankie Five Alarm off his
back?"

"Yes. He knew the bomb had been meant for him, and
he wanted to let Frankie know that he'd be coming into
some big money soon. He'd be able to pay him back from
what he inherited from Max."

Auntie Lil sighed. "So even Max's favorite nephew had
a streak of selfishness."

"As wide as the Mississippi," Abromowitz agreed. "By
the time Davy got around to calling Sabrina back, Jake had
been to see her first. The two of them had been playing

around, it appears—with each other, I mean—but for different reasons. I think Jake really thought he was in love with that black widow spider. He seems a bit incredulous that she's yapping about him to anyone who will listen."

"While Sabrina was just hedging her bets in case Max left her widowed one day without enough money to live in the style to which she had become accustomed?"

"I guess you know her pretty well." Abromowitz stopped for a second and Auntie Lil could hear the rattle of papers over the wire. "Here things get hazy. Someone—and Sabrina isn't saying who, but it's a pretty safe bet that it was her—agreed to pick up Davy in Manhattan. He'd borrowed the bookkeeper's car to go see his parents, since his had been blown to bits in the blast. He was returning it that night to Joyce Carruthers. She confirms he was there. Says she cooperated with Davy in his frauds over the past year because she thought that Thomas Brody didn't like her. She was afraid of losing her job, and Davy said he'd protect her and take care of her financially in return."

"How involved was she?" Auntie Lil asked.

"She was reporting on both Davy and Max to Galvano. At first, because she was trying to protect Max, believe it or not. Galvano promised to quit putting pressure on him if she would keep him informed. Later she developed a thing for Galvano. Helped Davy engineer the fake V.J. Productions account on his instructions as a way of repaying Davy's gambling debts. It worked for a while. Until Brody caught on. Joyce was also the one who arranged for your name to be put on the faked corporate papers. Galvano's idea. Someone in Sam Ascher's office tipped him early that you were inheriting. It was a perfect solution—he could explain away the payments to V.J. Productions by shifting the blame to you and possibly screw up your inheritance at the same time. You were an unknown quantity, and he wanted you out of the picture. Fast."

"What about Rebecca giving me the keys? Was that his idea, too?"

"No. She really did want you to investigate and tip her off first if a family member was involved." Abromowitz paused. "I think her feelings were hurt when her brother's will came out and it was obvious how much you had meant to Max. A lot more than she had, it seemed. She didn't have much of a life of her own, I understand. Accusing you was an act of anger. There's nothing we can do to prosecute her for it, if that's what you're thinking."

"No. I have no desire to punish Rebecca," Auntie Lil said. "Abe is going to need her in the months ahead. But what about the hundred thousand Davy borrowed from Galvano for the fake investment-bank study? What was that all about?"

Abromowitz laughed. "Sorry, I know it's not funny. But Davy conned Galvano into lending him the money so he could pay Frankie Five Alarm back the first time he borrowed from him. Galvano was pretty livid about it when he found out, according to O'Conner's informant. It's one reason he tried to ice Frankie."

"Davy could have been in the clear after that, but he couldn't stop gambling, could he?" Auntie Lil said.

"Not in a million years," Abromowitz replied. "He kept borrowing more from Frankie and losing it all."

"Karen Rosenbloom claimed that someone was manipulating her client accounts," Auntie Lil remembered. "Money was missing. Who was it?"

"You got me," Abromowitz admitted. "Take your pick. Either Jake was trying to squeeze her out of the company in a power play or Davy was trying to cover some debts. Does it matter?"

"Probably not to Karen," Auntie Lil admitted. "Either way, she was betrayed by her own brother."

"Don't worry too much about her," Abromowitz said. "Brody's hired her a lawyer and is making a lot of noise about protecting her. She's not going to be either poor or lonely in the years ahead."

"Good," said Auntie Lil. "There's enough loneliness coming out of this mess." She still didn't know how Davy had died, however, and returned to the subject. "What happened after Sabrina—I mean the unknown person—went to pick up Davy from Joyce Carruthers's house the night Max was murdered?" she asked. "Let me guess. This unnamed person picked Davy up in Max's own car. I wondered what had happened to it."

"Wonder no more. We found the burned-out shell of an old Audi in a deserted parking lot out at Jones Beach. We figure it got dumped there the night before the funeral."

"So Davy was killed in the car?" Auntie Lil said. "And stored there until they figured out what to do with him?"

"Probably. He took three bullets to the back of his head. Sabrina swears she wasn't there when it happened and claims Jake only told her about it later. But the lady is lying through her expensively capped teeth. All that business at the grave—her falling in and being distraught with grief over Davy's death? Think about it—this is one smart cookie. She already knew Davy was dead, but came up with a perfect way to distract people from suspecting her. By acting like she'd been having an affair with Davy and was in love with him, she threw people off the track. Who'd suspect her of having helped to kill him after that display? God, if she had harnessed all that acting ability twenty years ago, she'd have a closetful of Oscars by now."

"Was she having an affair with Davy?" Auntie Lil wanted to know.

"Nope. Davy wouldn't take the bait."

"So why were they meeting in a motel on Long Island?" Auntie Lil said.

"Just one of life's little ironies," Abromowitz explained. "The widow seems more upset over that little incident than anything else. It seems that Davy acted like he was ready to take the step, to, uh—"

"Sleep with her," Auntie Lil suggested grimly.

"Exactly. But once he got her alone, he made a pitch for money instead. The lovely Mrs. Rosenbloom was incensed and threw him out of the room. Leaving Davy hanging out to dry with the loan sharks."

"You think Sabrina actually helped kill Davy?" Auntie Lil asked. "You're positive?"

"Yeah," Abromowitz said. "Much as I hate to admit that we're going to let a murderer walk. The way I figure it is that Sabrina picked up Davy from the bookkeeper's house in Max's Audi. Jake was hiding in the backseat, listening to Davy tell Sabrina what a slimeball he was and how Jake had killed her husband. Once they were on a quiet road—or hell, maybe even the middle of the Long Island Expressway—Jake popped up and shot Davy in the back of the head. Knowing the widow, I doubt she even swerved when it happened."

The thought made Auntie Lil queasy. "Cain and Abel," she said.

"Pretty able, all right," Abromowitz agreed. "Sabrina claims Jake did it all, but two people had to be involved. The body was stored in the Audi for twenty-four hours, then dumped in the bottom of Max's waiting grave. It would have been the perfect hiding place if rain hadn't turned the dirt into a mud slide."

"And the Audi was set on fire later that night?" Auntie Lil said. "To destroy any evidence?"

"You got it. Which is why I think both Sabrina and Jake were in on it. Someone had to drive the Audi and someone had to drive the pickup car that would get them back from Jones Beach. The Audi was driven to Jones Beach, abandoned, and torched. But the heavy rain started soon after and slowed the fire. It was a half-assed fire to begin with. Car gas tanks don't really explode like in the movies. At least not usually. We're going over the Audi now, and I think we'll find what we need."

"What gun did Jake use to shoot Davy?" Auntie Lil asked.

"Sabrina claims Jake stole Max's gun from her house. I figure she gave it to him, but I can't prove it without making my only witness into a liar, so I'm swallowing her story. We haven't found the gun. We probably never will. I suspect it went over the side of one of the bridges out at Jones Beach. The widow's word will have to do."

"I found the empty storage pouch," Auntie Lil remembered. "In a drawer the night we searched Max's house."

"I didn't hear that," Abromowitz said.

"Who else in the family knew what had happened to Davy?" Auntie Lil asked.

"Well, Jake's wife knew something was wrong," Abromowitz said. "Because Jake asked her to lie about his whereabouts the night Davy died. She agreed to say that she had been with him and Sabrina, but as soon as we told her that the two of them were playing footsies, she changed her story. She'll testify. I guess she figures her husband is going down and now's the time to take his money and run."

"And when did Abby figure it all out?" Auntie Lil asked.

"I don't know if Jake ever actually told his mother or if she just put two and two together. But she knew enough to want to protect Jake from punishment from the start. When you started nosing around asking the family questions, visiting their houses, she got frightened. That's why she pretended to be the Benpensata woman. Her idea. And that's why she accompanied Jake to the factory the night they attacked you. She knew what had happened with Benpensata all those years ago. She kept a close eye on her husband's actual and attempted indiscretions," Abromowitz said. "Had a whole laundry list of transgressions. Who knows which ones were real. She's not in good shape right now."

"Are you charging her with attempted murder?" Auntie Lil asked. "It seemed to me that they meant business."

"That's up to you." Abromowitz paused. "We could. We could maybe even make it stick. You could testify, get your private eye friend to chime in. She'd do some time. But first we'd have to prove she was capable of standing trial. She's under psychiatric care right now. Like I said, she's not in good shape. What do you want to do?"

Auntie Lil was quiet while she thought it over. If only Max were alive to tell her what he wanted. No matter. She knew what he would want her to do.

"Let it go," Auntie Lil said. "She's been punished enough. She has no one left."

"That's mostly her fault," Abromowitz pointed out. "She has a perfectly good son and daughter she's choosing to ignore. I got kids myself and I could never do what she's done to hers."

"I know. But still—let it go."

"All right," Abromowitz agreed. "Your call. Makes it easier for me."

"You've done a good job of piecing everything together," Auntie Lil said.

Abromowitz sighed. "Thanks to you. Getting that family to talk was like trying to get a convention of clams to open up. I owe you thanks for all of your help."

"They're not going to win in estate court," Auntie Lil told him. "I'll fight them every step of the way."

"You won't have to," Abromowitz promised. "The murders happened in New York State. You can't profit from your crimes here. That's because we're supposed to be civilized. Jake won't be able to inherit a dime from your friend Max, ever, and this also gives you damn good ammunition to keep the widow at bay. Without those two, the family will let it drop. We aren't charging the widow, but that doesn't mean we can't give evidence in a civil trial. If you need it, you've got it. I owe you big time."

"Whatever for?" Auntie Lil asked.

Abromowitz hesitated. "Because I put you in danger," he finally said.

"The day the truck tried to run me over," Auntie Lil guessed.

"Yeah. It was stupid of me. I was keeping the family informed. Jake was the point man. I called him to calm them down, you know, to let the family know that I was bringing you in for questioning and that we were on top of the case. Rebecca was making a lot of noise about it with the higher-ups within the department. As soon as I told Jake you were coming in the next morning, he went to the fired shipping clerk who had helped Davy with the V.J. Productions fraud and offered him a lot of money to try to run you down. I'm sorry. I put your life in direct danger."

"You've already paid me back," Auntie Lil said. "I notice there's no mention of Max's murder in the papers today."

"That's right," Abromowitz said. "I'm holding it back for a couple of days. I'm saying I still have to tie up some loose ends to be sure."

"You're waiting for a slower news day," Auntie Lil guessed. "It's very kind of you."

"Well, Miss Hubbert, Max seems like he was a pretty good guy. And his name has been dragged through the mud. You were right. He had nothing to do with organized crime or any of this mess. I feel like he deserves a couple of headlines making that fact very clear to the public. So I'm going to wait as long as I can to make sure he gets better media play. Call it modern police management."

There was a sudden lump in Auntie Lil's throat and she had to swallow hard before she could speak. "Thank you," she whispered to the lieutenant.

"No—*thank you*," Abromowitz said. "I couldn't get through the family wall of silence. You did. I misjudged you. I apologize most sincerely for all of the trouble that we have had in the past."

She stared at the receiver. "Is this Lieutenant Manny Abromowitz or an impostor?"

His deep laughter boomed over the line, startling her. She had never heard him laugh before. "I misjudged you, too," Auntie Lil admitted. "Here's to the future as friends."

Abromowitz groaned. "Please. Having you around is like having a magnet for dead bodies dropped in your lap. Do me a favor. Take up knitting. Leave the investigating to us. And next time you feel like badmouthing the NYPD, remember who called to tell you thanks. I mean, have you heard anything from the feds?"

Auntie Lil was silent.

"I didn't think so," came the reply. "And that guy owes you a lot more than thanks. Good-bye, Miss Hubbert, and good luck."

"Good-bye and good luck to you." She replaced the phone in its cradle and looked at T.S. "She's going to go free," she said. "Sabrina will walk away unscathed."

"No, she won't," T.S. promised. "We've got plenty of

money for lawyers. We'll see she doesn't get a dime from the estate. And for her, that's a fate worse than death."

2. The afternoon light was fading. They had reached Casey and told her the details. She had been surprisingly philosophical about Sabrina's immunity. At heart, Casey was a realist. She agreed with T.S. that poverty was the perfect punishment for Max's widow.

With a promise to call them soon, she had rung off rather cheerfully. It appeared that Dr. Osle was not married after all. He was divorced and wore a ring to fend off amorous patients. It had been quite romantic, Casey explained to Auntie Lil. As he was unwinding her head bandage earlier that morning, he had asked her to dinner that night. Her headache had cleared miraculously.

"She's a piece of work," T.S. said when he heard the news.

"I'm sure Dr. Osle takes vitamins," Auntie Lil answered enigmatically.

Unable to reach Herbert, they spent much of the afternoon dealing with the question of Max Rose Fashions. If their math was right, and neither Jake nor Sabrina could inherit any shares, Auntie Lil now had enough equity between herself and a cooperative Seth to control the future of the company. She would suggest bringing back Karen Rosenbloom, she decided, and let Karen and Thomas Brody decide what to do next.

"That's the spirit. Delegate!" T.S. agreed with enthusiastic conviction. "By God, it's a great solution."

By late afternoon, they were sitting in front of his picture window watching the growing shadows of the nearby skyscrapers creep across York Avenue. They had cheated the cocktail hour by a good thirty minutes. Both sat holding glasses of Auntie Lil's famous Bloody Marys.

Auntie Lil's mind wandered far from questions of business and money. She had finally been set free. Knowing how Max had died and why he had died had loosened the stalled memories. All afternoon long they had bubbled to the surface, as vivid as a movie before her. She had shared many of them with her nephew, and T.S. had listened quietly, understanding her need to talk.

"But why did you leave him," he finally asked, "if you loved him so much?"

He finally got his answer. "It was so perfect, Theodore. So very, very perfect. I knew it could never last." She stared out into the gathering twilight. "By the time I met Max, I was already independent. I had seen the world and I wanted to see more. I wanted to be able to go where my feet and my heart led me. I wanted to be me."

"And if you'd stayed with him, you couldn't have done that?"

She shook her head. "Max cast a long shadow. I would always have been in that shadow. And as much as I loved him, it wouldn't have been enough." She sighed. "I think it would have killed the very thing that was so fine between us if I had stayed."

"You left while the going was good."

"That's putting it rather crudely, Theodore, but yes. I left while I still had something to hold on to forever. I knew that I would always love him—*always* love him. When it happens to you, you will know. You can never know until then." Her eyes roamed over distant York Avenue. "I left when I did because then I could have our love and myself, too. Staying would have killed one or the other. I wasn't willing to pay that price."

"I should have thought that awful family was reason enough to run," T.S. said.

"They weren't so awful back then. Not really. I don't know what happened to them. Was it the money? Too much time? Not enough work? Getting old? Jealousy? I just don't know." Auntie Lil shook her head sadly. "You should have known them when they were young. Abby was always a silly girl, but plump and pretty and full of fun. The last person dancing at every party. And Abe competed with Max, but the hate wasn't there yet. The adoration was. Rebecca was always sharp-tongued, but what strength of character she had. She cared for their parents, you know, until the day they died. She had no life so that the others could live." Auntie Lil sighed. "The older I get, Theodore, the less I understand this world. I should have thought it would be the other way around."

3. Her apartment seemed oddly cold. She had abandoned it for several days while she stayed at Theodore's, not wanting to be alone. But now, dear Theodore was making plans to pick up Lilah from the airport and practicing his crème brûlée recipe. Auntie Lil did not want to interfere. Let him enjoy the anticipation. Theodore and Lilah were just beginning their time together. They had a future shining before them.

And she was alone.

But no matter. She had the past.

Auntie Lil opened the photo album and ran her fingers over the black-and-white images contained inside. Max at the nightclub. Max at Coney Island. Max in the desert.

Max in the desert. The memory stabbed through her heart like a spear. What she would give to see his face again, to hear his voice, to hold his hand. If only she had been given the chance to sit down across from him one more time before he died, to feel the force that had been Max.

The phone rang. She resented the modern intrusion on her faraway thoughts. Still, it could be Herbert. He deserved to know what had happened.

"Yes?" she said quietly, one hand still turning the pages of the photo album.

"Miss Hubbert?" a voice said through static din. "I've been trying to call you all day."

"Who is this?" she demanded. "I can hardly hear you."

The connection cleared. "It's Frank O'Conner."

"And you're calling from your car phone."

"You got it. Will you be home for an hour or so? I have something to give you."

He arrived a half hour later with nothing in his hands.

"It must be mighty small," Auntie Lil said, ushering him into the living room.

"Well, I suppose I ought to first give you my thanks," he said. "And that's pretty big. You don't know what a good thing you've done. I think your friend Max would have been pretty proud."

"He never had much use for people like Joseph Galvano," Auntie Lil agreed. "I'm happy to have helped you out, but it is you who have done a good thing."

He ducked his head shyly and, despite his ruddy beard, suddenly looked very much like a boy. He thrust his hands in his pockets.

"What is it?" she asked. "Do you want me or Herbert to testify?"

"No. We're keeping you out of it. There's no need. Frankie Five Alarm will bury them all. You won't have to worry about Galvano anymore."

"Then why are you really here?" she asked.

"This," he said suddenly, thrusting a small microcassette tape toward her. "I thought that you might like to have it."

"I don't care about Joseph Galvano," she said. "I never did."

"It isn't the tape of your lunch with Galvano."

"Oh." She knew then what the tape contained.

"We had the office phones tapped."

"I see."

"We were trying to get Galvano with whatever we could. He'd been calling Max Rose Fashions. So we monitored their outgoing lines, too. We were hoping to catch him for extortion, racketeering, whatever we could."

"So you tapped hundreds of personal phone conversations?" Auntie Lil asked. "Without the people involved knowing at all?"

He sighed. "We do what we have to do, Miss Hubbert, to do what is right. The good guys don't have a lot of options open to them anymore. I'm sorry if it offends you."

She was silent.

"If it helps, I'm the only one who ever listened to it," Agent O'Conner explained. "Me and another guy, that is. I made you a copy. The original was destroyed."

She nodded and took the tape. It nestled in the palm of her hand.

"I have to go now. That's the only copy left, I promise." The special agent smiled. "You are an amazing woman, Miss Lillian Hubbert. It has been my great pleasure to know you."

He left quickly. Her heart was still thumping. She sat down on the couch and waited a moment. Then she rose and retrieved her microcassette recorder from a drawer in the dining room. She clicked the small tape in place and set it down on her coffee table. She perched on the edge of an overstuffed chair nearby and stared at the tiny machine.

Three times her hand reached out and stopped. The fourth time Auntie Lil pressed the play button. She closed her eyes and listened as the emotions of fifty years filled the room, as overwhelming as the day she first met him.

Suddenly there it was in the room—the force that had been Max. It filled her apartment and swelled in her heart, as real and as palpable as if Max were sitting there beside her at that moment. Was he? She reached out to touch the empty cushion beside her as the tape started to play.

"Lillian?" His voice was deep and strong, enriched with confidence. He did not sound a day older than when she had last heard from him over twenty years before.

"Max." It was a statement. She'd know his voice forever.

"You must be pretty surprised to hear from me."

"No. I'm not surprised at all."

He laughed low in his throat. "You always were one step ahead of me."

"How are you, Max?" Her voice sounded suddenly younger, almost girlish in its affection and concern.

"How am I, Lillian? Still half a man without you."

"Which leaves you twice the man of anyone else I've ever known."

"Flatterer. I see you still like to have the last word." There was a silence, and in the stillness, she felt his sorrow. "I've made some big mistakes in my life, Lillian. One of them was letting you go."

"There was nothing we could have done, Max, except what we did."

He sighed. "I've made other mistakes. I'm trying to correct them now. I want to make everything right before I die."

"Don't say that," she told him fondly. "You're never going to die. And just to be stubborn, I'm staying right here with you."

"It's a deal." He hesitated and his voice grew stronger. "Can I come over to see you? Right now?"

"It's that important?"

"Yes. It is," he said. "I've made up my mind about some things. I want to make them right. I want you by my side."

"Max."

"No, don't argue. I mean it, Lillian. With all my heart. We were meant to be together and we should be together. I want to start, today, to make it so."

She was silent. Time had erased her yearning to wander, while the memories of Max had only grown stronger with each passing day. She would at least talk.

"Together?" she teased him. "Forever?"

"Together forever. For as long as we both shall live."